4/1/29

'A ...... made me cry, made me laugh and
made ...... a gorgeous green-eyed Irishman!'
Lori (Goodreads)

'A sweet and funny Christmas tale'
For the Love of Books

'Enjoyable and heartwarming. It's just right for a cosy
night in, curled up with a vanilla coffee and candlelight.'
Jane (Netgalley)

'This book is packed full of giggles and tears. A fantastic
festive winter warmer.'
Natasha (Netgalley)

'A delightful wintery tale full to the brim with drama,
passion and heartwarming cheer.'
Gem~Bee

Maxine Morrey has wanted to be a writer for as long as she can remember and wrote her first (very short) book for school when she was ten. Coming in first, she won a handful of book tokens – best prize ever at the time!

As time went by, she continued to write, but 'normal' work often got in the way. Finally, she decided to go for it, and wrote. Really wrote. And after a while she had a bunch of articles, and a non-fiction book to her name.

But her first love is novels, and, in August 2015, Maxine got the call to say that she had won Carina UK's 'Write Christmas' competition, with her romantic comedy, 'Winter's Fairytale'.

Maxine lives on the south coast of England, and when not wrangling with words, can be found tackling her To Be Read pile, sewing, listening to podcasts, and walking.

www.scribblermaxi.co.uk

Twitter: @Scribbler_Maxi
Facebook: www.facebook.com/MaxineMorreyAuthor
Instagram: @Scribbler_Maxi
Pinterest: @ScribblerMaxi

The Christmas Project

Maxine Morrey

ONE PLACE. MANY STORIES

HarperCollins
PUBLISHERS
Since 1817

This novel is entirely a work of fiction. The names, characters
and incidents portrayed in it are the work of the author's
imagination. Any resemblance to actual persons, living or
dead, events or localities is entirely coincidental.

HQ
An imprint of HarperCollins*Publishers* Ltd
1 London Bridge Street
London SE1 9GF

This paperback edition 2017

1

First published in Great Britain by
HQ, an imprint of HarperCollins*Publishers* Ltd 2016

ISBN: 978-1-84845-725-6

MIX
Paper from
responsible sources
FSC
www.fsc.org
FSC™ C007454

This book is produced from independently certified FSC™ paper
to ensure responsible forest management.

For more information visit: www.harpercollins.co.uk/green

Printed and bound in Great Britain by
CPI Group, Croydon CR0 4YY

Also by Maxine Morrey

Winter's Fairytale

Coming Soon:

The Christmas Holiday
The Best Little Christmas Shop

To Mum and Dad

Thank you for introducing me to the joy of words and reading from such a young age. Even thought I know now how precious little time you had to call your own as you both worked so very hard, library trips and encouragement in my reading were never in short supply. Thank you.

Chapter One

I peered down at my feet and wondered exactly how many toes I'd have left when I finally got home this evening. It was totally possible to get frostbite in North London, right? The snow that had been threatening all afternoon had finally begun to fall about half an hour ago, right around the same time I'd lost all feeling in every single one of my extremities. It had already started settling and the heavy flakes now falling looked set to continue all night. And yet, here I was, huddled under an umbrella that was doing very little for the bottom half of my body, still waiting.

Had I known I was going to be stood outside, freezing my backside off whilst waiting for a client who was, at this point – I checked my watch – exactly fifty-seven minutes late, I would have worn my fur-lined boots rather than the gorgeous four-inch heeled Mary Janes that currently adorned my feet. Still, on the upside, I was at least fully colour-coordinated: my nose now matched my scarlet shoes and lipstick, and my hands and feet were likely a fetching shade of blue to tone perfectly with my tailored navy wool coat. Pulling my phone from my pocket, I checked the screen again - no new messages or missed calls. I'd give it precisely three more minutes and then I was off.

I gave another glance up to the house. In contrast to many others I'd passed down this avenue, there was no clue here that we were in the midst of the countdown to Christmas. No tree twinkled with fairy lights in the beautiful bay window, no decorations or cards lined the windowsill. Outside, in the tiny bit of garden that was left from making it into a parking space, instead of illuminated reindeer and snowmen, the border was filled with blackened, soggy annuals left over from the summer. The other houses looked warm and welcoming. This one appeared cold and impersonal.

I stamped my feet, trying to kick-start the circulation, all the while hoping not to break off any icicled digits. Next door, a late model 4X4 pulled up and two designer-clad children tumbled out the back doors, laughing as they charged up the path. From the driver's seat emerged one of the yummy mummies the area was well known for. I surreptitiously admired her crocheted beanie as she busied herself unloading the car. She wore it with the assured style of Kate Moss, and looked fabulous. I knew from experience the moment I put one on my head it magically transformed into a tea cosy. Bit unfair.

The deep, throaty rumble of a powerful motorbike caught my attention. As I looked up, the cyclops-like headlight flashed across me as it turned into the driveway on which I was standing, coming to a stop almost beside me. With a final throttle blip, the engine fell silent. The rider kicked out its stand and then swung a long leg over to dismount before turning to me. A hand lifted and flicked the visor up. Vivid green eyes looked out as the figure towered above me.

'Can I help you?' The tone was deep, Irish-accented, and less than friendly.

'Are you Mr O'Farrell?'

'That would depend on who's asking.'

'Hello, Michael,' Yummy Mummy called, several designer shopping bags looped over each arm. She flashed Motorbike Boy a stunning smile that showed impossibly white, perfectly straight teeth.

'Evening, Tamara.'

It was impossible to tell if he was smiling as he hadn't yet removed his crash helmet. But I took a wild guess at no, judging by those eyes.

'Good day?' she pursued. Her gaze flicked briefly over me before returning to focus on her neighbour.

He gave a non-committal shrug that made his leathers creak. 'You know how it is.'

She tilted her head and pulled a sympathetic face, oozing empathy and understanding.

Yeah, right, I thought, doubting very much that she had a clue what it was 'like', at all.

'Well, if you ever need anything, you know where I am.'

Mentally, I raised my eyebrows so high they barely connected with my face. Physically I kept my face impassive. I saw the man glance at me, briefly, before he replied. I studied my feet for a moment as I considered the possibility that my 'impassive' face may need some work.

'I do, thanks.'

She gave him another full-wattage smile before moving gracefully up the steps and in through the large black-painted front door.

The man turned his attention back to me and tilted his head in question, apparently still awaiting a reply to his enquiry.

3

'My name is Kate Stone.' The name didn't seem to spark any recognition. 'You had an appointment with me for six o'clock this evening.'

He lifted his arm and wiggled his wrist a little until a watch face peeked out enough from his sleeve to see the time.

'It's gone seven.'

'Yes. It is.'

'So why are you still here?'

This is exactly why I hate doing favours for friends. My business was in demand and had a waiting list. Without trying to sound smug, I didn't need this. Ordinarily there was no way I would have waited so long for a client to show. Add that to the fact that there was no explanation or even attempt at apology for his lateness, and my patience was being severely tested. But Janey had begged me to come and help her brother, even paying for the initial consultation herself. I'd rearranged other clients and missed my yoga class tonight because, according to him, six o'clock was the only time he could possibly make it this week. Or not, apparently.

'I suppose you'd better come in before you freeze to death.'

'Thanks. I'd hate to inconvenience you by croaking on your doorstep,' I mumbled.

'Sorry?' He spun round, the bottom of his boot grating on the step.

Whoops.

I shook my head innocently, grateful for the muffling properties of the crash helmet he still wore.

Mr O'Farrell made his way around the junk that consumed his porch, opened the door and strode in, leaving it to me to see myself in and close the door

4

behind me. As I did, he pulled off the crash helmet and sat it on a cluttered phone table that stood in the hallway. He was, of course, ridiculously good-looking once the protective head gear was removed. Perhaps that went some way to explaining the high opinion he clearly had of himself. Mind you, his hair, black as coal, definitely needed a good cut, and the stubble on his face was way beyond 'designer' but not a beard either. Maybe he felt he didn't need to bother with attention to personal grooming when women like his neighbour were already throwing suggestive invitations his way. Well, Yummy Mummy next door might find 'mean and moody' attractive, but to me, Michael O'Farrell was merely abrasive and rude, no matter how tall, dark and gorgeous the wrapping was.

Sitting heavily on a bench seat in the hall, my new client yanked off his boots. My gaze, however, was roaming around the areas of the house that I could see from the hallway. This was most definitely not going to be a five-minute job. Unfortunately. Because if first impressions were anything to go by, I was keen to spend the least amount of time possible with my new client.

'You didn't answer me earlier.' The soft Irish accent did nothing to hide the abruptness of his manner.

I frowned.

'Why you're actually here? I left Janey a message to tell you that I was running late and wouldn't be able to make it. I assumed she'd pass it on to you.'

'When did you call her?'

'About an hour ago.'

'She would already have been in yoga class by then. It has a strict policy of requiring all mobiles to be switched off.'

This time it was his turn to frown.

'I thought she said something about knowing you from that class. Don't you two go to yoga together?'

'Yes, we do. Ordinarily.'

I saw the penny drop.

'Right.' He stood.

Great. No apology for making me miss my class either. If this all proceeded, I was seriously tempted to shift him to my assistant. I'd dealt with enough 'challenging' clients in my time, and it would be good practice for her to take O'Farrell on. Mind you, Bernice was adorably cute and an absolute sweetie so in all probability would have him eating out of her hand within ten minutes. And that was fine too. Just so long as I didn't have to deal with him.

He unzipped the top of his leathers and began wrestling the upper half off his shoulders.

'Just so you know, Miss Stone, none of this was my idea. I have absolutely no wish for you to come into my home and start poking about, faffing and cleaning up. I'm more than happy with things just the way they are.'

Sorry Janey, but enough's enough. I wasn't prepared to waste my or my assistant's time with someone who clearly wasn't going to even try.

'Mr O'Farrell. I do not specialise in "faffing" or "poking about". Neither am I a cleaner. But I suspect you're already aware of all that. Clearly you have no interest in my services and, as such, I think it's probably best if we discontinue now in order to prevent either of us wasting any more time. If you could call your sister and explain the situation that would be most helpful. Goodnight.'

I turned and took the few steps back to the door, my hand upon the catch.

'Wait,' he called as a phone began to ring, its tone muffled. Digging into the rucksack he'd been wearing on the bike, he yanked a mobile out and looked at the screen.

'Shit.' Michael took a deep breath and answered. 'Hi, Janey.' His eyes focused on his socked feet as he listened, his gaze raising only briefly to glance over at me. 'Yes, she's still here...No, I...Of course I do...Fine, hang on a minute.' He looked back at me and held out the phone. 'My sister would like to talk to you.'

I hesitated. What was the most polite way of telling my best friend that her brother was a rude and arrogant dick who has no appreciation or respect for what I do, and no inclination to be helped anyway?

I took the phone. 'Hi, Janey. How – '

'I am sooooo sorry!' Janey interrupted. 'I just got the message on my phone that he was going to be late. I can't believe it! He promised me and I know you went out of your way to be there tonight. I love him and everything, of course, but Jesus, he really can come across as an arrogant shit sometimes. I know he's just trying to get out of doing it all.'

'It's fine. Don't worry. We've consensually decided that perhaps this isn't the right thing for – '

'No! No, no no! You have to stay! Please!'

'Janey. It really only works if the person involved wants it to. Otherwise everything will go back to how it was within weeks, which is just a waste of time for everyone involved. Not to mention a waste of money.'

'Wait. Don't leave yet. OK? Promise?'

I paused.

'Please, Kate. It's really important. He needs this.' Her voice was softer now.

7

'OK. Fine. As it's you.'

'Thank you, thank you, thank you. Right. Now, can you pass the phone back to my dick of a brother?' Her voice was louder again now and from the look on his face, Michael heard the comment. Which was good news for me as it meant I didn't have to find a way to tell Janey any of that stuff after all. She was clearly already aware. He held out one large hand which I put the phone in. He lifted the mobile back to his ear.

'Yes. No. I know. Yes. Yes, I promise. OK. What? No, you don't need…fine. Here…' He stabbed at his phone and Janey's voice came out on speaker.

'Is it on speaker?'

'Yes.'

I felt bad that I was perversely enjoying seeing this rude, arrogant man getting bossed about by his little sister. But then I looked down and saw my soaked, numb feet, and remembered how cold I was, and miraculously, all traces of guilt disappeared instantaneously.

'Kate, can you hear me?'

'Yes, Janey.'

'Right. Good. Now, Michael, we discussed all this. Your house is a bloody tip and your life's not much better.'

'My life is just fine.'

'No, it's not. And don't interrupt. You agreed to host Christmas this year – '

'Actually, I was just outvoted, if you remember.'

'Because we've all taken plenty of turns in doing it and you never have!'

'That's because I wasn't in the country most of the time.'

'Yes. Well. Nobody forced you to jet off every year instead of spending time with the family.'

'Janey. You know that it wasn't as simple as that. And could we please not discuss family matters in front of strangers?'

'Oh shush. Katie's not a stranger. She's a very good friend.'

'To you.'

'Yes. To me. And because she is such a very good friend to me, she's agreed to help you, you great lummox. So wind your neck in and start taking this seriously. You need to start getting your life back in order and find your way back to being the happy bloke you used to be. And believe me, Kate is your best chance at doing that.'

'Really.' He was clearly still unconvinced. It was the one thing we appeared to agree on.

'Yes, really. We're fed up of watching you work yourself into the ground, surrounded by all that crap. You've got a lovely house there but you wouldn't know it because of the state it's in! How on earth are you ever going to meet anyone else if you can't bring them home?'

'I'm not particularly interested in meeting anyone else. And when I do bring a woman home, it's not exactly to give them a tour of a house.' He looked over at me, as if awaiting a reaction.

If he was trying to shock me, he was way off the mark. I'd had him pegged as the 'wham, bam, thank you ma'am' type within about two minutes. Except minus the 'thank you'.

'Well, it's about time that changed. We all know you've been through the wringer, Mikey, but it's time to start moving on.'

'I have moved on. Weren't you listening to the last bit?'

'Having sex with strangers and moving on are two very different things. Now, your family's been behind you throughout all of this, despite how difficult it was at times, but it's time to get on with your life. And Katie's going to help you make that start.'

'Right.'

'She's your chance at finding a way to be happy again, Mikey.'

'Oh. Great. No pressure,' I mumbled.

For a split second I thought I saw the corner of his mouth twitch into the hint of a smile but when I looked again it was set back in a grim line as he stared at his feet.

'Tonnes of pressure, Katie. Sorry darling!' Janey's voice came from the speaker. 'But he really does need to get his arse in gear and I know you won't take any shit off him, so it's perfect.'

'Perfect,' Michael repeated, flatly. He lifted his gaze. 'Don't worry about it, my sister's just being dramatic. It's a habit.'

'Knock it off, Mikey,' Janey snapped. 'You need to start taking this seriously. Your life is a mess since Angeline left and you're a grouchy workaholic. It's about time you got your shit together and found happiness again, and Katie there's your best chance. So stop being an arse, listen to what she says, and do what she tells you because if you don't, so help me God – '

'Fine! Yes. All right,' he cut across her.

'I love you, you know. We all do,' Janey's voice was softer now and it was clear to hear the love contained within her words, 'that's why we're doing this.'

'Yep. I know. I love you too.'

I looked away and found an intense interest in the junk mail teetering on the phone table.

'Better not get all soppy. It looks like you're embarrassing your friend.' Michael's deep voice held a hint of amusement.

'Oh, Katie's all right, aren't you?' Janey's voice assured.

'Umm, yes. Fine.'

My client's vivid gaze fixed on me and he shook his head, that hint of smile back flickering around the full mouth.

'I'll behave for Kate, Janey. I promise.'

'Good. Because she has my full permission to kick you in the nuts if you don't.'

Michael burst out laughing and his whole face changed. The spiky demeanour transformed into something much closer to the warm, welcoming air that Janey always gave off. For the first time since I'd met him, I could finally see him as being related to my friend.

'I'm countering that permission and as they're my nuts, I have final say.'

'Just be good,' Janey said.

'I've said I will. So I will. Now, can I go?'

'Yes, all right. Bye, Kate. Thanks so much for this. Talk to you tomorrow.'

'Bye, Janey,' I called.

'Bye sis,' Michael added, before pressing 'End' on the screen.

Silence fell over us.

'So. I guess it looks like you're stuck with me then.'

'Yes, it does rather.'

More silence.

'When she said about you being my chance at...You know...She didn't mean...'

'No. I know.'

'OK. Good.'

'It's a bit of a cliché but I don't believe in mixing business with pleasure anyway.'

'Fair enough.'

'And I'm already seeing someone. Janey knows that.'

Why on earth was I going into all of this?

'Right.'

'And you're definitely not my type anyway. Janey knows that too.'

Michael rubbed the back of his neck and looked down at his feet. 'I'm beginning to wish I'd never opened my mouth.'

'Not at all. It's always good to be absolutely clear on things.' *For the love of God, Kate. Shut up!*

After a beat, Michael spoke. 'So, what happens now?'

I mentally squared my shoulders and shook my uncharacteristic babbling moment off. Focusing on what I knew best, I was back on firm ground.

'Generally, I assess the project, then I look at my schedule and you look at yours and we see when we can fit in some sessions that work for both of us.'

'Right.' He moved away from me, his back turned.

'But as I said earlier, I can only help someone if they want to be helped and are prepared to put in effort themselves. I realise that Janey is keen for you to do this, and that you clearly wish to please her, but if you're really not invested in this, then it's just a waste of time for both of us. It's a very busy time, and as such, I have plenty of other people who would benefit from my services far more.'

As Janey had warned, I didn't pull punches. I wanted her brother to know exactly what I expected from him.

'Oh, well, I wouldn't want to keep Little Miss Popular from doling out her beneficial services.'

I rolled my tense neck, sore from huddling against the cold earlier, and counted to ten. Ten wasn't nearly enough.

'Are you always this much of an arsehole?'

Michael didn't say anything but I was almost sure I saw his lips quirk briefly in amusement at my outburst.

I took a deep breath. 'I apologise. I shouldn't have spoken like that. It's been a very long day. Perhaps it's best if I leave and you take the night to decide as to whether you wish to proceed.'

'It's fine. I probably deserved it.'

Probably?!

'And in answer to your question, depending on who you ask, yes, I am always this much of an arsehole. And I don't need the night to think about, it. If I don't do this then I'm in the shit with my family, which I know you probably couldn't give a toss about, but I do. They've done a lot for me and I need to do this for them. Unfortunately, I can't do it without you.'

I raised an eyebrow.

'I promise I will take it seriously and do what I need to do to make them happy.'

'It's supposed to be about making you happier too.'

He shrugged. 'If that happens too, then it's a bonus, but don't get your hopes up.'

'Oh, don't worry. I won't.'

Chapter Two

Michael gave me an even look, assessing. We were sat in his kitchen. It was light, modern, spacious and absolutely crammed full of stuff, just like the rest of the place. It didn't look like he'd put anything away for years.

'So, explain again what it is that you do, as it's obviously not "faffing" or "poking about".' The even look remained. I knew he was testing me, seeing if I'd crack again. And although I was desperate to tell him exactly what I thought of him – again – I refrained. Not because of anything I felt for him but because of something I'd heard in Janey's voice on the phone. Getting this arrogant man's home, and life, better organised clearly meant a lot to her. That was the only reason I was still here.

'I run an organisation consultancy. I help people to declutter and organise their living spaces which in turn makes their home a nicer, more inspiring and serene place to be. And that in turn, is good for everyone who lives there. Being surrounded by clutter can be stressful for the mind, not just because it's hard to find things, but because it doesn't instil the peace and calm we crave as human beings in the sanctuary of our home. When a person's house is in order, it generally has positive benefits on other aspects of their life.'

Michael took a sip of the coffee he'd made. 'Right.'

The word 'sceptical' sprang to mind.

'But as I said, I can't do this alone, I need – '

'Me to get on board. Blah blah. I know. I get it. I just don't really buy it.'

I shifted in my seat.

'Don't worry. I've done plenty in my life that I didn't really buy into either and I got by. Just ask my ex-wife. So we'll get it done. You do your thing, I'll make the effort and then it's done.'

'Great,' I said, feeling pretty unconvinced myself now, which was the complete opposite to how I normally felt at this stage in the process. Not a great sign.

I pushed my coffee mug to the side and pulled out a folder from my bag, clearing a little space on the breakfast bar to lay it on. Michael took the mugs off the counter, rinsed them and then came and stood behind me, peering over my shoulder at the forms I had just begun filling in. As he did so, I got a subtle waft of aftershave. It was light and citrusy and, oddly, not what I would have expected from him.

'What's this then? Do you give out grades for first impressions?'

I shoved my stool backwards, causing him to move, as I then dismounted. Tilting my head back to meet the intense green gaze, I answered him.

'Perhaps it's just as well that I don't, Mr O'Farrell.'

'Oh. I guess, in the interest of fairness then, I should take that Yelp review down that I did when I nipped up to change my clothes?'

I turned quickly. 'What did you say on it?'

He shrugged. 'Just that I thought it was a novel approach for a business owner who comes into people's houses to call her client an arsehole within minutes of meeting him.'

My mouth dropped open and I felt my face drain of colour.

'That was entirely unfair of you! I apologised immediately! I know that's no excuse, but you were late, rude and disrespectful of what I've been hired to do!' A stray tendril of hair had come loose from my bun and I pushed it back from my face distractedly. 'This is my livelihood! How could you – '

He snagged his phone from the shelf and shoved it in the back pocket of his jeans as he threw me an amused look.

'Calm down. I didn't do anything of the sort.'

I felt the colour return to my cheeks.

'Oh. Right. Well, good. Thank you. And just so you know, I've never, ever done that before and have no intention of doing it again.'

He shook his head. 'Forget it. Believe me, if I Yelped everyone who thought I was an arsehole I'd be on the site all day.'

I didn't say a word but his mouth did that quirk thing again.

'It's all right, you can say it.'

'I don't know what you mean.'

'You can say you aren't in the least bit surprised.'

'I wouldn't dream of saying that.'

'Nothing to stop you thinking it though, eh?'

'Shall we make a start?' I said, uncomfortable at being quite so transparent.

His lips gave a little tug to the side. 'Absolutely. Tell me what you need me to do.'

'So, is there anything you're specifically hoping for with this process?' I asked, glancing at my notes.

When he didn't answer, I looked up to find him studying me.

'What?'

'Nothing. Just seems an odd question, bearing in mind you already know the only reason you're even here is because my sister cajoled you and my family forced me. If I wasn't looking for the process to happen in the first place, I can't see how I could be hoping for anything from it.'

I took a deep breath. 'It's fair to say that my clients are normally a little more pleased to see me than you are.'

'I can see that,' he said, leaning against the door jamb and crossing his ankles.

'But that doesn't mean, now that you're committed to the process, that you won't gain anything from it just because you came to it from a more unconventional angle.'

A grin flickered on his face, as fleeting as a guttering candle. 'Unconventional. That's one way of putting it.'

'So, having heard what I do, is there anything you can think of that you would specifically want to gain from all this?'

He straightened from the doorway and looked at me. I tilted my head back to meet his eyes. Now I'd taken my sodden shoes off, I had to look up even further.

'I'm not exactly sure what you want me to say, Kate, but if you're hoping for some sort of emotional blather about me wanting to find myself amongst all the clutter, then I'm sadly going to have to disappoint you. The only thing I'm looking for with this process is to turn my house into a place that's fit for a family Christmas.

At the moment, with all this stuff everywhere, it's not. I'm just wanting a tidy house, Kate. Not therapy.'

'Fair enough.' I scribbled a note and made to move on. 'It would seem your clientele are generally a lot deeper than I am.'

'Not at all. Everyone's different. I just want to make sure that I do the best job I can for each client, and that means finding out what it is they really want.'

'Don't they all just want less crap kicking around? Isn't that the whole point of your business?'

'Yes and no. That's usually what it starts off as them thinking they want, but quite often there's a deeper issue that they don't even realise is driving them until part way through the process.'

He gave a quick raise of his eyebrows. 'Right. Well, as you heard, the only thing driving me is a sister half my size.'

I felt the smile slide onto my face and for a moment he returned it.

'So, let's just accept that I'm shallow and move on. Where do you want to see first?'

He leant on the newel post and I watched the corded muscles on his forearm flex as his hand rested on the banister.

Was that true? Was he really that shallow, or was he, in fact, one of my most complicated clients? Usually about this time, I had a pretty good idea of who my client was, but with Michael O'Farrell, I still didn't have a clue.

'Shall we do bottom to top?'

He gave me a quick nod and led the way down the stairs to the basement level of the four-storey Georgian. Here the space had been given over to a large open-plan living area that had bi-folding doors leading out onto a garden. There was a small counter/kitchen area for preparing snacks and cups of tea, to save having to traipse up and down the stairs when time was being spent in here. A flat-screen TV collected dust against the wall and a couple of couches and beanbags sat unused underneath some appliance boxes and other discarded items. Looking out onto the garden, it could be a great space for entertaining, or just relaxing, but right now it was uninviting and cold. From my time studying the outside, and now here, there already seemed to be a theme emerging.

Next I followed my client back up the stairs to the ground floor where he stopped outside a room opposite the kitchen we'd sat in earlier. As I caught up to him, he opened the door. Inside was an architect's easel, a work station with a large flat-screen computer on it and a bookcase stuffed with books, papers and all sorts of other random items. Under another pile of papers a small two-seater sofa lounged against the wall. Michael walked over and flicked on the lamp over the easel. There was no window dressing of any kind and streetlight shadows from the trees outside danced on the stripped wooden floor. At least, what you could see of it.

'My office.'

'You work from home?'

'I do.'

I glanced around. 'And do you always know where everything is in here?'

He followed my gaze and I saw something cross his face. I wasn't sure if he thought I was being sarcastic so I clarified my question.

'It's just that sometimes, especially in work areas, what looks like a mess to an outsider is actually a very specific way of working for the person whose space it is. People find their own way of working and obviously I don't want to do anything to upset your working methods.'

He picked up a mechanical pencil from the desk and fiddled with it.

'As much as it pains me to tell you this, I can't actually find a bloody thing most of the time.'

'OK. We can fix that and find a much better system for you, which will make for a more pleasant and efficient working environment.'

'Just because it looks a tip doesn't mean I'm not "efficient" at my job. People might think I'm an arsehole but they still know I'm a damn good architect.'

I tried not to look surprised at his defensiveness. Time to employ some professional soothing. 'I never meant to suggest that you weren't. I'm sorry if it came across that way.'

He fiddled with the pencil a little more, then nodded, seemingly accepting my apology. 'But you are saying my office isn't pleasant?'

'I'm just saying that we can make it more pleasant.'

He gave a little shake of his head, that almost-smile flashing briefly. 'Very tactful.'

I looked up from my notes. 'So, what's next?'

Staying on the same level, he pointed to a door behind which was apparently a downstairs loo, before moving on to show me the living and dining rooms. Both were gorgeous spaces, not that it was easy to see that at the moment. But they could be.

'You play the piano?' I asked, seeing an upright groaning under another pile of magazines and general 'stuff'.

He shrugged. 'Used to. Haven't played for ages.'

'Why not?'

He gave the shrug again and then set off for the next floor. Here there were four spare bedrooms, two with small en suites, and one main bathroom. One of the bedrooms had been converted into a mini home gym which, unlike many I'd seen in my time, was clearly being put to good use. I made a note to suggest moving this equipment down to the basement level. There was plenty of space down there and it could always be screened off with a room divider. That would free up the bedroom, which, from what Janey had told me about the size of their family, could be useful. Plus it might be more inspiring for my client to work out looking onto the garden rather than staring at a blank wall as he clearly was at the moment. I snuck a glance at him. Admittedly, from what I could see under the slightly misshapen clothes, he didn't seem to be lacking in motivation to work out.

As we moved around, it seemed that most of the rooms had generally turned into a dumping ground for random items, boxes for appliances, motorbike parts and goodness knows what else.

'The master bedroom is on the top floor but you've pretty much got the idea as to what it's like from these.' He waved a hand at the rooms we'd already seen.

'It would still be very helpful for me to see it, if possible. So that I have all the information as to what we're dealing with. It's especially helpful in this case as we're on quite a short deadline.'

After his comment about one-night stands earlier, I was a little surprised that Michael had suddenly seemed to have turned a little shy. Frankly, I'd half expected it to be the first room he'd show me, maybe hoping for another reaction. But the truth was, I'd seen all sorts in my time and there was little that could surprise me now. I opened my mouth to reassure him but he took off up the stairs before I could say anything. Quickly, I followed. He opened the door and stepped in.

'Master bedroom, en suite, dressing room.' His voice was uncharacteristically flat.

I looked around the room before turning back to Michael. Unexpectedly, not to mention, annoyingly, he had indeed surprised me. Whilst everywhere else in the house was full of stuff, his bedroom – the one place where it should feel the most personal – felt the least. It was almost like a hotel room but with less soul. The room itself, like the others, was beautiful. In fact, it was even more so with its double-aspect windows, high ceilings and finished wood floor. It could be the perfect bedroom. My new client might be annoying, bristly, arrogant and rude but there was one thing he clearly wasn't short of, and that was personality – however desirable or undesirable its aspects. And yet this room had none. There was no sense of him at all. Of anything really. It was sparsely furnished and had none of the junk that the other rooms had acquired.

Evidently the surprise showed on my face.

'It seems unlike you to have nothing to say, Kate.'

I turned quickly, trying to regain my mental footing.

'I was…it's just that…'

Michael raised an eyebrow at me but remained silent, making no attempt to help me out.

I cleared my throat and smoothed my hair unnecessarily. 'Do you actually use this room?' I asked, making a couple of notes.

'I do.'

That wasn't the answer I was expecting. I just couldn't picture this man in such a bland space. Everywhere else in this house showed aspects of who he was: his work, his motorbike, the food he liked – mostly because it was all on display. But here there was nothing. Not an inkling of the person who spent his nights there. And then it dawned on me. Maybe that was precisely the aim.

'OK. You seem to have managed to maintain this one a little better, so that's helpful.'

'I'm glad you approve.'

I crossed the room and opened the door to the walk-in wardrobe, peering in. Much of it was empty and I had to fight the urge to fling myself down and weep for the space he had for clothes – a space that was only a little smaller than my entire flat.

'Are you all right?' The deep voice almost sounded concerned.

'Hmm? Oh, yes! Absolutely. This really is a beautiful room.'

'Thank you.' He turned to leave, clearly feeling that I'd got all I needed. As I followed, I gave it another look. It could be so much more for him. I wasn't a professional decorator but I loved the subject as a hobby and so it was easy for me to see how this could be transformed into a real oasis of calm for him. Somewhere he could escape the day, the stresses of work – assuming that all electronic devices were banned from the bedroom, as they should be.

'You know, you could really make that into a gorgeous space for you to – '

'I wasn't aware you were here to comment on my decoration tastes,' he snapped, pulling the bedroom door closed behind me.

'No, of course not. I just…' I met his eyes and saw there was no argument to be made. 'I'm sorry,' I said, attempting pacification with a smile. 'It's just that it's an interest of mine and it's hard not to get carried away in a beautiful house like this.'

'Perhaps you could try a little harder.'

I swallowed and gave him a tighter smile. 'Of course.'

He nodded sharply. 'Thank you,' he said, before standing aside and motioning for me to precede him down the stairs, apparently ensuring that I couldn't scoot off and peek at his bedroom again. A desire I currently neither had, nor ever planned to have.

'So, what's the verdict?' He indicated the notes I'd made as he'd shown me around the house and the few answers to questions regarding the process that I'd managed to pry out of him.

'All fine. I'll make up a plan of attack and email you a copy so that you know exactly what we're trying to achieve.'

'You reckon you can transform this place into an oasis of serenity then?' He raised an eyebrow.

I ignored the sarcasm. 'Of course. Janey's been a very good friend to me and I want to help her. If doing this with you makes her happy, then as you said earlier, we'll get it done.'

'Right.'

'The process always works best when several hours can be allocated to it together, rather than little bits here and there. So I would need to try and schedule some blocks of time that work for both of us. Perhaps tomorrow you could look at your diary and see what you have available and let me know? Once I know that, I'll do my best to work around it for you.'

'How long does the whole process generally take?'

'That really depends on the size of the place, how invested the owner is, what time they can give over to it, etc. Some people have a lot more stuff than others, some struggle more on what to discard, and so on. There's no set time. Every house is different because every client is different. Obviously we have a tighter timescale than I usually work to, bearing in mind you want this done for Christmas.

'But can you do it?'

'I'm fairly confident of it, yes. Of course, it depends on how much time you can put aside and how well things work. I will do my absolute best but I don't want to mislead you. You have to realise that trying to organise a house of this size with this amount of – '

'Crap?'

'I was going to say "accumulated items"– ready for guests in just over a month will be quite a challenging target.' I dropped my file back into my bag.

'I'll pay you double.'

I looked up, surprised.

'I don't work like that, Mr O'Farrell. That would be unfair and, to me at least, incredibly unethical. I don't categorise my clients by who can pay me the most!'

'I didn't mean to suggest that you did. I apologise.'

Oh. So he did actually understand the concept of apologising then? That was a start.

'I just…look, I really need you to help me with this, in that timescale. I realise it's difficult and I will do my utmost to obey whatever you say and get it done.'

'It's not about obeying me – '

'That's a shame.' He cut in, his lips hinting at a smile.

I pointedly ignored the remark.

25

'It's about putting in the effort and believing in what you're doing.'

'OK. Look. I get it. I can see the point of all this.' He waved his hand, encompassing me in the gesture. 'I have a cleaner in once a week but I'm fully aware I'm not that great at housekeeping, so to speak. I sort of lost my way a bit when...'

I waited. The hardness in his face faded. It was still all sharp planes and glass-cutting cheekbones but as his expression softened, he suddenly seemed more approachable, and less ...well, less of an arse. He looked back from where he'd been staring at the darkened kitchen window and saw me watching him. Immediately the hardness in his face returned.

'Carry on,' I prompted softly, trying to rescue the moment. If I could understand him a little more, it would help my job enormously. Organising a home was incredibly personal, which is why the owner had to be involved. But if I could understand that owner, what was important to them, what had happened to them in their lives, it made the whole process so much easier.

'Nothing. I just need to get this done for Christmas. It's my turn to host the family and if someone else gets stuck doing it because I didn't pull my finger out, then that's not fair and I wouldn't feel right even attending. But I've already missed far too many. So it's not an option. I do understand that you have plenty of clients vying for your time, so if you can't do it then I'll just get someone else in. I'm sure there are plenty of people who do this kind of thing.'

On second thoughts, I wasn't sure anything could make Michael O'Farrell less of an arse. It was clear that it was just his demeanour's natural setting.

26

'Yes. There are. I am, however, one of the best. I did you a favour coming tonight, and waiting until you eventually turned up. I've spent my entire evening here and am now aware of exactly what needs doing, all of which time will have been entirely wasted should you turn to someone else. And that, frankly, would be incredibly frustrating. I am prepared to take you on as a client of Stone Organisation, and reschedule others whose needs aren't quite so pressing in order to accommodate you, in order to please Janey. However, it is of course your prerogative to employ whomever you wish. In the circumstances, I would ask that you let me know by ten o'clock tomorrow morning so that we both know where we stand.'

I finished my spiel and turned away, quickly retrieving my coat from one of the overstuffed hooks that lined the wall of the hall.

'I want you.'

I turned, pausing in the belting of my coat.

'Pardon?' I squeaked.

'I want you.' He'd descended the stairs too and was now leaning against the banister, his green eyes fixed on me. 'I don't want to employ anyone else to do this. Janey recommends Stone Organisation, so that's who I want. I know that I'm difficult and impatient and impossible to deal with – God knows I've been told it enough times over the past few years. I'm also aware that I've given you a hard time this evening and you've taken it all in your stride and pushed back when you needed to. I need someone prepared to do that. Otherwise I'll take the piss and never get anything done and it really will be a waste of time.'

I looked away and concentrated on wrapping my scarf around my neck, taking a moment to gather myself. Even though he was far too annoying to fancy, Michael's soft Irish, deep gravelly tones saying 'I want you', completely out of the blue, was enough to throw any girl off her stride for a moment or two. No matter the context. Recovered, I turned back to face him.

'All right. Good. Here's my card.' He closed the distance between us and I handed him a pale Tiffany blue business card. 'Work out when you can set aside some time and email me. I'll look at my diary and then give you a call to plan the first session.'

'I'm assuming you don't work weekends?' he said, studying the card.

'I try not to, but obviously it's very difficult with the type of work I do, so it's all dependent on the client.'

'Right. Guess I blew that already then.'

'Yes, you did rather. But lucky for you, I adore Janey so, if weekends are all you can do, then that's what will happen.'

He gave a small smile. 'Thanks. I'll do my best to clear some space in the week so that I don't take up too many of your weekends. I'm sure your boyfriend probably likes to see you as much as possible.'

I retrieved the leather gloves from my pocket and started pulling them on. 'He's aware my work hours can be a little erratic. Besides, he travels a lot and is often away over weekends too so it's not such a big deal.'

Michael looked at me again, studying me, his eyes almost hypnotic in their concentration.

'What is it?'

He shook his head. 'Nothing.' He flicked the card. 'I'll email you tomorrow.'

I nodded. 'Great. Goodnight then.'

'Night.'

He leant over to open the door and glanced up and down the street. The snow was still falling but a little less heavily than it had been earlier.

'Where did you park?'

'I didn't. I got the Tube. Speak to you tomorrow then.'

'Wait. I'll walk you to the station.'

'No. It's not far. But thank you.'

'Janey would want me to.'

I gave him a patient look.

'Look, just wait while I find my shoes. I know the other one is here somewhere...' He began hunting around the 'accumulated items' in the hall for his other trainer.

I shook my head. 'Looks like you could do with a bit of organisation,' I quipped. Stepping past him, I opened my umbrella, heading off quickly before he could get himself organised enough to come with me. The Tube station was only a few minutes of quick walking away and the area was well-to-do and well lit. It wasn't anything I hadn't done a hundred times before and I certainly didn't need chaperoning by Michael O'Farrell just because his sister would have wanted him to. I soon reached the bright, fluorescent lights of the Tube station and headed into its underworld to catch my train.

Chapter Three

The following morning when I opened my emails, I was a little surprised to find one from my newest client, detailing a whole bunch of times he could free up in order to get his home organised. The brief, impersonal note advised that if I was able to work something out within my schedule for those times, he would appreciate it. If not, then could I let him know and he would take another look at his own diary and see what he could do. Perhaps he did actually mean to take this seriously after all, now that Janey had applied the thumbscrews.

I opened my calendar and took a look. I could probably manage it, but it was going to mean some serious juggling. The fact that I wished to spend as little time as possible with him wasn't helping matters.

'How did your appointment go with your friend's brother last night?' Bernice trotted in, her face all smiley and open. It was kind of infectious. I'd hired her as an assistant two years ago but she'd been keen to get into the actual business of organisation, so I'd agreed to train her. She'd now been a fully-fledged organiser for the past year and was loving it.

'Ah. Yes. That.' I pulled a face. 'Oh thanks! Perfect!' I said, taking the huge mug of hot chocolate she'd just made.

Bernice took a sip of her own from a similarly enormous mug and I waited until her face came back into view before continuing.

'Let's just say he and his sister are quite different.'

'But you're still planning to take him on?'

'Of course. I promised I would. But I think it's safe to say it's not going to be one of my most fun assignments.'

'Difficult?'

'The house isn't anything worse than I've seen before. But Mr O'Farrell himself is...quite something.'

'Sleaze?'

'No! Not at all. Nothing like that. Well, he made no secret of the fact he's a one-night stand kind of guy, but that's up to him. But no, he didn't make me feel uncomfortable like that.'

'So, what is it? Normally you're fizzing with excitement when you're about to start with a new client. And today you're definitely more flat than fizz.'

'He's just...'

'Oooh, is he gorgeous and you don't want to get caught in an awkward situation? I know you have this big thing about not mixing business with pleasure.' Bernice's big brown eyes widened as her mind went off into areas unknown.

'No. It's not that either. Although he is gorgeous, which he clearly knows. The only thing I'm worried about is that I might actually kill him and have him buried under the patio of his newly organised home.'

'Oh wow. That bad?'

'That bad. Think big Irish Grinch on a motorbike and you're pretty much there.'

'Actually sounds kind of yummy. Apart from the Grinch bit, obviously. So when do you start?' Bernice asked, getting up and wandering over to gaze out of the window at the rain that was now slamming against it.

I let out a sigh and peered again at my calendar, comparing it to the dates that Michael had sent over early this morning.

'I'm not sure. Trying to find a time when we're both free is beginning to look like more of an issue than I thought it was going to be. I think I'm going to end up having to see if he can do weekends by the looks of things.'

'Does he specifically want to work with you?' Bernice asked, coming away from the window to perch on my desk.

'No, he just said that he wanted Stone Organisation rather than anyone else as his sister had recommended us.' I distractedly flicked over the days of my calendar again, blindly hoping that when I looked at it this time there would magically be some space. I really didn't want to have to go back to Michael and ask for different dates. I just wanted to get this all done and over with.

'Bring my calendar up.'

'What?'

'Get mine up.' Bernice leaned over and took the mouse from me, making a couple of clicks until her own schedule displayed on my screen in another window. 'Now, when's he free?'

I pulled the email I'd printed off towards me and glanced between the two. Bernice had a space tomorrow that would fit in with Michael.

'There you go. Problem solved.'

I hesitated.

'What is it?'

I looked up at her. 'I feel like I'm fobbing him off on you! I've just told you he's a right royal pain and now I'm dumping him on you.' For all my thoughts last night about pushing O'Farrell to Bernice, I'd never really intended to lumber her.

'Do you really want to deal with him?'

'Oh God, no!'

Bernice laughed.

'Sorry. That was a bit too emphatic, wasn't it?'

'That's all right. I don't mind dealing with him. It's only a short-term thing anyway, isn't it?'

'Yes. It needs to be done by Christmas so we'll be shot of him then.'

'It's settled then. Do you want me to contact him?'

'No. I told him I'd call. I'll give him a ring now and advise him he's booked in for twelve tomorrow.'

'I can hardly wait,' Bernice teased. 'I'm totally intrigued now.'

'I still feel bad.'

'Don't. I volunteered and you can't change your morning appointment tomorrow. That's your final one with Mrs Clarke. She'd be devastated to not finish up with you.'

Bernice was right. This particular client had come a long way, physically and emotionally during the process, and the truth was I'd be upset to have to miss it too.

'Thanks Bernice. You're a lifesaver. It may be for the best anyway. You'll probably be able to bring out his better side. I'm pretty sure he has one. There was a tiny glimpse of it when he was on the phone to his sister, but it only appears for a few seconds at a time. With me, anyway. But you have that cutesy persona thing going on. It'll be perfect.'

'I can certainly try.'

'And bonus points if you can avoid calling him an arsehole within a few minutes of meeting him.'

Bernice was looking at me, her carefully painted Cupid's bow mouth forming a perfect 'O'.

'You did not.'

I cleared my throat. 'Yep, I kind of did.'

Bernice continued staring.

'Could you please stop looking at me like that. I feel bad enough already. I just thought I should fill you in because I wouldn't put it past Mr O'Farrell to bring it up and I didn't want you blindsided.'

'But you're always so…controlled with clients.'

'As I say. Probably for the best that you're doing it.'

'Wow. I really can't wait to meet him now. If he rattled your cage, he must be something.'

'Oh, he's something all right. And just so you have all the background info, he'd kept me waiting in the snow for nearly an hour before finally showing up, made absolutely no apology and just proceeded to tell me how much he didn't want our services. My patience was worn pretty thin by then.'

'Understandably. It's no problem. I can handle him.'

'Thanks Bernice. I really appreciate this. I really didn't want my falling out with him to affect my friendship with Janey. So this is the best of both worlds – he gets help and I don't upset my friend because I beat her brother to death with an egg whisk.'

'Is it actually possible beat someone to death with an egg whisk?'

'You haven't met him. It'd certainly be worth a try.'

Bernice grinned.

'I'll call him now and put it in your diary for tomorrow. The ones after that, perhaps you can discuss with him, once you see how you've progressed after the first session? I've typed up the notes I took last night, so I'll email them over to you.'

'Great, thanks.'

I quickly sent her the email before I forgot, then dialled Michael's number. After three rings it went to voicemail and his lilting voice told me he was unable to come to the phone and asked for a message to be left. So polite. So attractive. So unlike the owner of the voice.

'Mr O'Farrell, it's Kate Stone from Stone Organisation. Thank you for your email. Having looked at our schedule, there is a space tomorrow at twelve, which coincides with one of the times you sent me. In the circumstances, I've blocked that out and unless I hear differently, your first session will be at noon tomorrow. Thank you.'

I hung up and then quickly fired off a text to Janey telling her that we'd be starting on her brother's house properly tomorrow so she could relax and that it was all in hand.

A moment later a reply pinged back.

Brilliant! Thanks so much for letting me know. Can't thank you enough for fitting him in. I know you're rammed. Big kiss xx

I smiled and texted back.

No problem. Happy to be able to help xx

I checked the clock and scooped up some files from my desk.

'Right. Better scoot. You OK for this afternoon?'

Bernice looked up from her screen. 'Yep. Kenny Jakes has emailed to see if we can fit in another session as his mother is coming down for the holidays and he wants it perfect. I had a spare couple of hours so I'm going to go to him before Mrs Calder.'

'OK. Great. Call me if you need anything.'

'Will do. Have fun!'

I waved and snagged my umbrella from the hook before stepping out onto the rainy London street.

* * *

I'd just got back from my last appointment with Mrs Clarke in Wimbledon and had my head down answering emails when Bernice came into the tiny office.

'Hi,' I said, distractedly. Then pulled my head up again. 'Wait a minute. What are you doing here? Aren't you supposed to be at Michael O'Farrell's?'

'I am. And I was. But he doesn't want me there.'

'What do you mean?'

'Well, I got there and he opened the door. I get what you mean about the whole gorgeous thing now, by the way. Big, masculine, kind of rough around the edges, and, wow, those eyes – '

'Bernice?'

'Oh. Yes. Sorry. Well, I said who I was, and what I was there for. He asked where you were, so I told him you had an appointment elsewhere this morning. Then he thanked me for coming, apologised that my time had been wasted and offered to pay for a cab to take me wherever I wanted to go. All terribly polite.'

'That was it?'

'Yep. Bit odd I have to say. He definitely knew I was coming. I heard you leave the message.'

I was doing my best to stay calm but after everything I'd said to him, after everything Janey had said to him, he was still pulling the same stunt! I searched for his details and stabbed the number into my phone. He answered on the second ring.

'Michael O'Farrell.' The languid, gravelly voice floated down the line and if I hadn't been so mad at him, I might have considered again just how attractive it was. But I was. So I didn't.

'Mr O'Farrell, it's Kate Stone.'

'Hello, Kate.'

I waited for an explanation but the line stayed silent.

'I wonder if you would be so good as to explain why, when I go to the effort of reorganising our schedule to accommodate you, during a period which I have already told you is busy, you then choose to turn my colleague away from your door?' I carried on, not actually giving him a chance to explain because, whatever lame excuse he had, I was no longer interested.

'I have gone out of my way to help you, Mr O'Farrell, and you've done nothing but be difficult. I really don't appreciate you wasting my company's time and, in the circumstances, as it is clear that you have no wish to be helped, I would appreciate it if you could explain the situation to your sister. Goodbye.'

I hung up and realised I'd barely taken a breath. I sucked in some air and made an effort to bring my heart rate down out of the danger range. God, he was infuriating. It was just as well I wasn't working with him. If my dealings so far were any indication, I wasn't sure I'd get even halfway through the process before keeling over from a blood clot.

'You know you didn't actually give him a chance to speak, don't you?'

I looked at Bernice. She was chewing the inside of her lip. 'Maybe he had a good reason?'

'I'm not really one for excuses, Bernice. You know that.'

'I know, but – '

She was interrupted by my phone ringing. I looked at the number on the display and my gaze drifted up to the computer screen where Michael O'Farrell's details were still displayed.

'Oh crap.'

'Is that him?'

I nodded.

'You could just ignore it.'

'I can't. He'd keep ringing until the end of days just to annoy me.'

'Stone Organisation,' I answered, pretending I had absolutely no idea who was on the other end of the line.

'Hello, Kate. Michael O'Farrell here. But I'm pretty sure you knew that. It's just that you called me to ask a question, but then ranted without giving me an opportunity to answer it. So I'm wondering if I might be able to do that now? Only if you have a moment, of course? I know what a busy time this is for you and how in demand you are.'

Sarcastic git.

'I wasn't ranting. And, of course, please say whatever it is you would like to say to explain why you've wasted everyone's time.'

Bernice gave me a look. I pulled a face. Normally I was so good at being diplomatic but this man had an infuriating ability to push buttons I didn't even know I had!

'Are you done?'

'Yes. Go ahead.'

'Thank you. The reason I turned Bernice away this morning, perfectly lovely and efficient as I am sure she is, is that I made a deal with you. Not your colleague.'

'You made a deal for my company to help you organise your home.'

'No. My understanding was that you would be the one coming back in to my home. And not once did you ever suggest that it would be someone else. And the fact that you still didn't tell me you would be sending someone else when you called me, alerts me to the fact that you were, in fact, fobbing me off on someone else because you didn't want to deal with me.'

'Of course I wasn't fobbing you off!'

Across the desk, Bernice did a Pinocchio impression. I turned my chair so that my back was facing her.

'Or maybe you didn't think you were capable of dealing with me, for whatever reason.'

'I am perfectly capable of dealing with you, Mr O'Farrell. I just prefer not...'

Oh. Shit.

I could practically hear him smiling down the line as I dropped myself in it. I mentally added 'smug' to the list of his unattractive qualities.

'That's what I thought. There's still four hours of the session left, Kate. I'd appreciate being able to use that time if you're available. However, if not, I'm happy to reschedule to a time when you, personally, are able to attend.'

I gritted my teeth and pulled up my calendar. 'I'm sorry that there seems to have been some misunderstanding, Mr O'Farrell. I was under the impression that you were hiring my company and had no preference as to which organiser attended.'

'I wasn't aware there was anyone other than you.'

'Then I apologise for not making that clear, but I can assure you that Bernice is a very competent organiser and I've had nothing but positive feedback from all of her clients. I'm very aware of the time frame with you, and as Bernice was free earlier than I today, at a time that fitted in with you, it seemed ideal that she should come over, rather than having to put you off longer.'

'I'm sure that she is excellent at her job. However, when I said I wanted you last night, that's exactly what I meant.'

Oh God. I do wish he'd stop saying that.

Across the desk, Bernice tilted her head and raised an eyebrow as colour whooshed up my face.

'I understand. We've obviously already lost some time but I can do the rest of today's session. If that's what you wish.'

'I do.'

'Then I'll be there as soon as I can.'

'I look forward to it.'

Liar.

He hung up before I could say anything else. Snatching my coat from the hook, I rammed my arms into the sleeves, fuming at his laid-back self-assurance. And the fact that he'd tripped me up into pretty much admitting that I had been more than happy to bump him onto Bernice.

40

'You're going then?' Bernice asked, watching me savagely trying wrap a scarf around my neck as if wrestling a particularly venomous python.

'I don't think I have much choice now. Best just to get it all over and done with as soon as possible. Although, if I don't turn up tomorrow, it's because I've succumbed to my current desire to smack Michael O'Farrell right between the eyes with a snow shovel.'

'Be a shame to ruin a pretty face like that.'

'Fair point. I'll smack him in the back of the head instead.'

With that, I yanked my bag onto my shoulder and headed out the door.

Chapter Four

I rang the bell and heard the hurried thud of feet running down the stairs. A moment later I heard another thud, shortly followed by a few choice words before the door was pulled open. Michael O'Farrell stood there in a white T-shirt, faded jeans and bare feet, the right one of which he was holding up and rubbing.

'Are you all right?' I asked, as he mutely indicated me to step inside. 'I thought I heard…something.'

'Fine,' he replied. He waited whilst I took off my coat and heels and then began heading towards the kitchen. I followed. 'Would you like a drink? I'm making one anyway.'

My plan was to say no so that I could just get on with the task in hand but as he pressed the button on the coffee maker, buried amongst the junk on one of the work surfaces, the most delectable smell of coffee drifted out, melting my resolve in one tempting moment.

'That would be very nice, thank you.'

He nodded and pulled another mug from a cupboard.

'I saw that,' he said, without turning.

'Saw what?'

'You raised your eyebrows in surprise that I actually got something out of a cupboard instead of just off the worktop.'

I really needed to work on my poker face.

'You had your back to me. You have no idea what I did or didn't do.'

'I've eight nieces and nephews and spent a year teaching English in India. I've learned to have eyes in the back of my head.'

I rolled my eyes.

'I saw that too.'

'Oh, you did not.'

'Boy. You're bad at this game.'

I sucked in my cheeks and kept my mouth closed, as my eyes darted to the snow shovel leaning against the wall outside, next to the back door.

'I'd get to it before you.'

'Oh bloody hell!' I burst out.

Michael's face creased into a brief grin that faded as quickly as it had shown. 'I can see why Janey likes you.'

I didn't know what to say to that so I said nothing. But as the silence grew longer, my client seemed disinclined to fill it, happy, it seemed, just to lounge against the counter and drink his coffee. His gaze fell on me and the intensity of his eyes gave off the feeling that he could see much deeper than I was comfortable with. Which, of course, was ridiculous. I knew that. But still. I could also see why he was apparently never short of women to take up to his soulless bedroom. It wasn't just the good looks. It was easy to see how those eyes and that gaze could be used to make you feel like you were the only person around, even in a room full of people. Or a bar full of alcohol.

'What are you thinking?'

'What?' I asked, my voice coming out a little more squeaky than usual and colour flushing up my neck.

'You had a very...interesting...expression on your face.'

I wasn't sure what that meant but I did know I had absolutely no intention of telling my client that I'd been thinking about how easy it must be for him to pick up women in bars. I knew he'd just take it as a compliment. I'd hit myself in the back of the head with that snow shovel before I admitted to that.

'I was just thinking about the best place to start.'

Michael drained his coffee mug, watching me over the rim. 'Right,' he said, giving me the distinct impression that he didn't believe a word I'd just said.

'And what did you decide?'

Thankfully I had actually been planning the best way to go about this particular case on the Tube on the way over so I had a quick answer ready.

'I think the best thing to do is to start with your office. It's obviously where you spend most of your time when you're at home, and you told me yourself you find it difficult to locate anything quickly. Getting that into a better state will make it a better place to work and eliminate the stress of not being able to find things when you're working to deadlines. If there's anything work-related in any of the other rooms, they need to come into your office now so that we can see exactly what we have.'

He gave me another of those assessing looks.

'Who says it's where I spend most of my time? You're making me sound like some sort of workaholic.'

'Which, according to Janey, is exactly what you are. And, whilst I can't help with that, I can at least help you be one in a nicer space.'

44

'I didn't realise you and my sister had been discussing me quite so much.'

I pulled my notes out of bag and gave a little laugh. 'Don't worry. It was a very brief conversation when she asked me to do this with you. And she mentioned it again yesterday evening when you put her on speakerphone.'

'So she did. And what else did she tell you?'

I headed out into the hallway and stepped over what looked like a piece of bike engine and hung my bag from one of the coat hooks on the wall.

'Is that what you tripped over earlier?' I asked, stepping back over the item again.

Michael, having followed me, looked down at it and frowned.

'Probably. Stop changing the subject.'

I shook my head. *Add tenacious to the list.*

'For goodness' sake, what are you worried about? Janey told me you were planning to host Christmas this year, that you got divorced two years ago and since then the house has got into a bit of a state as you're a total workaholic and – I quote – "a bit of an untidy bugger". That's all, I promise. And as you've given me little else, that's pretty much still all I know. Oh, apart from the fact that your one-night stands don't get given a house tour. There. That is the total sum of my knowledge about you. Happy?'

'Ecstatic.' The flat voice was back. 'Shall we head to the office then?'

'Absolutely.'

Seriously. The quicker I got this over with the better.

***

45

Janey was waiting at a table when I pushed my way through the Friday night crowd at the pub.

'Sorry I'm late. Have you been here long?' I asked as I leaned over and gave her a big hug, discarding layers of outerwear as I did so.

'No, not long. Someone was just leaving their table as I got here so I jumped at it.'

'Well done. Shall we order? I'm starving. My appointments ended up changing today and the last thing I ate was a fun-size Mars Bar about half past ten this morning.'

'You must be starving! I'd be chewing on my own arm by now.'

'Hence the long sleeves,' I winked.

Janey grinned and waved at a waiter. She had the most beautiful smile and, as usual, it did the trick.

'What can I get you, ladies?'

We quickly ordered, barely looking at the menu we knew so well. The waiter stepped away and was immediately swallowed up by the crowd.

'So, how's your week been?' I asked Janey as another waiter appeared and placed our drinks on the table.

'Oh, not bad. The kids were both down with this fever thing that's going around, so that was fun.'

'Oh no! Are they better now?'

'Yeah,' Janey said, taking a sip of her orange juice. 'Thank goodness. It only lasted a few days but it was pretty miserable for them.'

'And how are you?'

Janey smiled. 'Tired, feeling enormous and gasping for a drink. Aside from that...'

'You are not enormous! You're like the poster girl for pregnancy – all glowy and blooming.'

46

'Blooming uncomfortable, right now. Honestly, I'm sure he's just doing the bladder bounce for amusement. The men in our family have a mischievous streak. Excuse me. I need the visit the ladies. Again.'

'Do you want me to come with you?'

She smiled and I briefly recognised the family likeness. Unfortunately, I'd only seen a glimpse of that same smile from her brother, unlike Janey who smiled easily and often.

'No darling, I'm fine. Honestly.'

She patted my shoulder as she headed off. I watched, trying to resist the urge to jump up and scoot round my friend, insisting everyone clear a path. And then I laughed when a group of lads, a little worse for wear, did the job for me. Janey flashed them that winning smile and giggled when one of them blushed.

'Told you I was fine,' she laughed as she retook her seat.

'I forgot about your magical powers. I don't know why I worry.'

'Because you're a sweetheart. And don't think I don't appreciate it.'

'No, I don't think that.'

'And talking of being appreciated, where is the man of the moment tonight?'

'Calum?'

'Unless there is someone else I should know about?' She sounded almost hopeful.

'No, of course not. He's fine.'

'Not around again tonight though.'

'No. He's working on some big project at the moment so he's tied up quite a lot.'

'Right.'

'Right, what?'

Janey gave me a blank look. 'Nothing. Just "right".'

'I know you better than that by now. Come on, spit it out.'

'Sure you want to hear?'

No.

'Yes.'

'All right. I think you're wasting your time on Calum.'

'Wow.'

'I asked you if you wanted to hear.'

'You did. And I did. Do you have a specific reason or did you just not take to him?'

'I take to most people, Katie. You know that. And he's charming and good-looking and all the rest but...'

'But what?'

'Where is he?'

'I just told you, he's working.'

'He's always working. He's always busy until he's not and then he expects you to come running. And you do. And honestly? It's not on.'

'Everyone's busy these days, Janey. It's competitive and people have to fight for their jobs.'

'Has he ever taken you away for a long weekend? Or even a short weekend, come to think of it?'

'Well, no, but – '

'He couldn't find one weekend in – how long is it now? Six months to take you away for a couple of days.'

'We've had the odd night away.'

'As part of one of his many business trips! That's hardly the same thing.'

'I don't mind. I'm busy with work a lot of the time too. It's good to have someone who understands that.'

'I'm just saying you deserve better. You deserve to be treated better.'

'He treats me fine, Janey. Really.'

'Oh, Katie. You've too much to offer to accept "fine".'

I ran a hand back over my hair, smoothing in some escapees from my French plait, before taking a sip of my drink. Janey laid her hand on mine as it rested on the table.

'It's only because I love you. I want you to be happy.'

'I am happy, I promise.'

Janey gave me one of those looks that her brother was so good at. I tried to hold it.

'OK. If he's making you happy, then that's all I can ask.'

'He is.'

'Good. So, change of subject?'

'Please,' I grinned and squeezed her hand.

'How're things going with our Mikey?'

'Oh! Yes. Fine, I think. Well, we've really only had one session...half a session really. There was a bit of a misunderstanding.'

'Misunderstanding?'

'Yes. He assumed that I would be the one coming back after the assessment meeting to do the job.'

'Oh. So did I.'

'And I had every intention of doing so. But I know he's on a deadline and the first space he had worked better for Bernice than me, and she said she was happy to do it, if I didn't think he'd mind. Which I genuinely didn't.'

'But he did?'

'Yes. Apparently he understood that when he said he wanted my company to do the job, that also meant me doing the job. It didn't really come up that I had someone else working for me. We didn't exactly get chatty.'

'No. He said it was a little tense.'

Tense was an understatement. At least he'd had the grace not to tell my friend that I'd called her brother an arsehole.

'Does you sending Bernice along instead have anything to do with the fact you called my brother an arsehole within five minutes of meeting him?'

Oh crap. Yet another reason why I don't like doing favours for friends.

'He told you that then.'

'He did.'

I covered my face with my hands. 'Janey, I'm so sorry. If I could take it back, I would. I don't know what came over me. I'm not like that normally, you know that! It had been a really long day and I was soaked and freezing. I know that's no excuse and I'm so sorry. Really.'

Janey wrapped her hands gently around my wrists and moved my hands away from my face.

'I'll tell you what came over you – Mikey O'Farrell. He has a knack for getting under people's skin. Normally it's in a good way. Or at least it always used to be. But since the divorce, he's been known to…let's say, ruffle a few feathers.'

I'd felt less like I'd had my feathers ruffled and more like I'd been entirely plucked.

'Are you upset with me?' I asked.

'Me?' Janey replied, laughing. 'God, no. I grew up with him! I know exactly how bloody annoying my big brother can be, believe me. He's had plenty of kicks in the shin, and anywhere else I could reach, over the years.'

'Yes, but you're family. I'm supposed to be a professional.'

'Ah, don't worry. It's a good thing. You showed him you're not a pushover. It's set some boundaries.'

'I couldn't believe I'd said it.'

'Well, between you and me, he found it funny so don't go worrying yourself over it any more.'

'He did?'

'Incredibly. It tickled him that this super-professional, conservative-looking woman suddenly just lost it at him.'

'Well, I'm glad it amused him, at least.' I rolled my eyes and sat back as the waiter brought our food and placed it front of us, his appearance thankfully distracting us both from the subject of Michael.

After we'd finished dinner, Janey sat back, her hands resting on her bump.

'I feel as stuffed as a Christmas turkey.'

'Full to the brim,' I agreed.

'I'm sorry I questioned you about Calum earlier. I didn't mean to upset you.'

'You didn't upset me. I know you're just looking out for me. And I really appreciate that. It's…nice.' And I meant it. Having someone looking out for me was a relatively new experience in my life and it had taken a little getting used to initially, but Janey's care meant so much to me. More than I could ever put into words.

'OK good. Then it's probably all right for me to tell you I'm not really sorry. And I still don't think he's good enough for you.'

I shook my head, laughing. 'You are just as impossible as your brother sometimes.'

'You wouldn't be taking my name in vain there, would you, Kate?'

I jumped as Michael appeared beside me, his voice close to my ear in order to be heard over the din of the crowd.

'Mikey! I didn't know you were coming out tonight.' His sister smiled up at him.

'Neither did I. I was just on my way home from a meeting down on the coast. Thought I'd stop in.'

That explained the slightly more formal appearance. Although he still looked to be favouring the rumpled look.

'Didn't fancy ironing those clothes then?' Janey said, running her eyes over him.

'Lovely to see you too, sis,' he said, ignoring the jibe. 'How are you both?' he asked, his eyes taking in the bump as he bent and kissed her on the cheek before balancing himself on the edge of the bench seat I was on. I shuffled along a little so that he had more room and he did the same. As he did so, the fresh citrusy smell of his aftershave tingled my senses.

'We're fine, thanks.'

'Good. And you?' he asked, turning to me as he took a swig from his beer bottle. 'Had a good week?'

'Yes, thanks. Busy.'

'No difficult clients, I hope?' His eyes danced with laughter as his smile disguised itself around the top of the bottle.

'Only one. Thankfully. Huge pain in the backside.'

Janey laughed. 'I knew you wouldn't be able to get one over on this one, Mikey. She's got your number.'

'Oh, I'm always happy for a pretty girl to have my number,' he countered, grinning.

I made an 'ugh' noise which caused Janey to laugh even more.

'Oh God. Stop it. I need the bloody loo again now.' And with that she stood and made her way through the crowd once more.

Mikey stretched out his long legs in front of him, giving a glance around as he did so.

'No boyfriend tonight?'

'No, not tonight. He's working.'

'Tomorrow?'

I turned towards him. 'I don't know. Probably not. He's very busy at the moment.'

'Too busy to take his girl out on a Friday night?'

I squared myself against him. 'I'm not "his girl" and yes, he's busy on a Friday night. It's not the end of the world. And, as it is, I've had a very nice evening. So, it's absolutely fine.'

Mikey tilted his head. 'Have you been drinking?'

'No.'

Yes.

'I've had one glass of wine.'

One very large glass of wine.

'Glad to hear it. It clearly loosens you up.'

I made the 'ugh' noise again, mostly because I couldn't think of anything else to say. Annoyingly, I knew I'd have a humdinger of a witty retort ready in about an hour's time. He gave a chuckle and leaned in.

'I meant it as a compliment.'

'Then you need to work on your compliments.'

He nodded. 'You're probably right.'

I looked up at him. There was something in the tone of his voice when he said it, and his eyes had taken on a faraway look.

'Are you all right?' I asked, unsure why I was bothered as to whether he was all right or not. But I was.

He pulled his gaze from the middle distance and focused the full force of it on me. I really wanted to look away but right now that was proving harder than it should be.

'Of course. I'm sat next to a pretty girl who's nicer to me the more alcohol she has inside her. So how about I buy you another drink?'

I sat up straighter. 'Really? You really think that's going to happen?'

He shrugged and took another swig from his bottle, clearly not bothered as to whether it happened or not.

'Well, it's not.'

He turned his gaze back on me. 'I didn't think for one minute that it would.'

My mouth dropped open.

'So why even say it?'

'Because you're incredibly sexy when you're all worked up.'

'And you're…'

He quirked an eyebrow, waiting to hear exactly what I thought he was. The problem was I wasn't exactly sure what I'd been going to say.

'I'm what?' he prompted me.

'I don't know,' I said, admitting defeat. 'But it definitely wasn't anything good!'

He grinned and I took a vicious swig of my drink, just as Janey returned to the table. She looked from one of us to the other.

'Oh, for the love of God, Mikey! What did you do now?'

Chapter Five

I waited at the door, huddled against the biting wind that was barrelling along the avenue and insinuating itself into every fibre of my body, despite all the layers I'd equipped myself with. A few moments later, Michael opened the door, dressed as usual in his beaten-up jeans and a T-shirt that looked like it had never been introduced to an iron in its entire lifetime.

'Jesus, you look frozen to the bone. Get in here.' He reached an arm out and took the bag I was carrying, hurrying me through the door at the same time.

'It's so cold out there today!' I said conversationally as I shed my coat and almost immediately started shivering. I put my coat back on. 'Actually I think I might keep this on for a bit longer.'

'I'll get us some hot drinks. Don't worry, the bedroom is nice and warm.'

I looked up in surprise. And for once, Michael O'Farrell wasn't wearing that self-assured, confident look. His face showed almost as much surprise as mine.

'That sounded a lot different from how it was supposed to.'

'Right.'

'I just meant that the bedroom – the guest room – you wanted to make a start on today is warm. For us to work in. Work on. Oh, for Christ's sake. Put me out of my misery, will you?' His face was equal parts pain and amusement.

I laughed and saw his face relax entirely. It was something that had been happening a little more in the last couple of visits and I was glad of it. I'd hated the tense atmosphere of the first session. It wasn't only uncomfortable, but it stirred up memories I wanted to keep buried. This slight relaxation in the mood worked much better for me. And I couldn't help but think it better for Michael too. Don't get me wrong, we were hardly friends, but for the most part he wasn't glaring at me and I wasn't calling him names, so we had definitely moved on a little.

I pulled a couple of items out from under the spare bed. In one hand I held a copy of *The Hungry Caterpillar*, in the other the tiniest thong I had ever seen.

'Interesting combination.' I held them up to Michael.

'Oh! That's where it went. My nephew was looking for that.'

'Not to be judgemental, but I really hope you're talking about the book.'

He smiled at me. 'I am.'

I looked at the pants dangling in my other hand, barely held by the minimum portion of fingertip and thumb required.

'I think the hungry caterpillar may have been at these. They can't possibly have been that tiny to start with.' I shifted my eyes to him. 'I take it these aren't yours?'

'No. Not really my colour.'

'Any idea whose they are? Is she likely to want them back?'

He wrinkled his brow, then tilted his head at them, thinking. I gave an eye roll and shook my head.

'What?'

'The fact that you have to think that hard about it!'

'Oh, don't be such a prude.'

'I am not a prude! But neither have I ever left anywhere "sans knickers". Although frankly they're so small as to be practically pointless anyway.'

'I think they were more for effect.'

'Clearly they had the desired one.'

He tilted his head at me and grinned. 'Are you jealous?'

'What? Of course I'm not jealous. Don't be ridiculous.'

He gave me a look. 'If you say so.'

'I most certainly do say so. Now, what do you want to do with these? Will you be seeing her again and able to return them?'

He scrunched his face. 'Doubt it.'

'Oh. So you do at least remember who they belong to now? That's something I suppose.'

'I thought you said you weren't going to be judgemental.'

'I said that about your nephew. Not you.'

'OK. Then for your records – as you seem to make them for everything – her name was Eva. She's a Russian model, incredibly beautiful. I had an appointment first thing and she was very snappy that she had to leave early, from what I remember. Apparently not a morning person.'

'Whereas I'm sure you're absolutely delightful.' My tone implied I believed he was probably anything but.

'I am the epitome of cheer.'

I threw a disbelieving glance.

'Just bin them. She won't be calling.'

'Sure?'

'Positive. I got the impression she didn't get turfed out of a man's bed at 6 a.m. very often.'

'I imagine not.'

'In my defence, I had told her about the appointment and that I needed to leave early the following morning.'

'I guess she didn't think that applied to her too.'

'I was hardly going to leave her alone in my house all day. I'd only met her that evening.'

'And yet deemed that long enough to take her to bed.'

'It wasn't like I dragged her here. She came of her own free will.' His eyes danced with mirth at the double entendre. I flung the pants at him and walked out of the room.

'Can I ask you something?' I said, as I hauled some more 'accumulated items' out from the wardrobe.

'I should think so. Can't guarantee I'll answer but you can give it a go.'

I shot him a look that told him what I thought of that reply.

He shrugged. 'Honest answer,' he said, disappearing under the bed to unearth whatever treasures lay under there. After the pants incident, we'd decided to swap places.

'Evasive answer,' I said, stretching on my tiptoes to reach the higher items. My fingertips brushed them and I took a step back, looking to see if there was a chair I could use. I giggled as my gaze fell on Michael. He was wriggling about under the bed, pulling things out, interspersed with the occasional sneeze. What particularly caught my eye was how nice his bum looked in those jeans. I hadn't actually noticed before, but it really was –

'You've gone quiet. That makes me suspicious.' His statement interrupted my thoughts.

'What?' I said, blushing and supremely glad he was still wedged under the bed so he couldn't see.

'You said you were going to ask a question and then just went silent. Should I be worried?'

'No. I was just concentrating on…something.'

Which most definitely wasn't how nice your bum is.

'Right.'

I removed a pile of jackets from a chair tucked in the corner of the room and placed it in front of the wardrobe. Stepping up, I pulled out the pile of boxes from the top shelf. Turning, I jumped and wobbled as I found Michael stood in front of me.

Automatically, his hands shot out and rested on my waist. 'Steady on.'

'Do you have a stealth mode or something? Two seconds ago you were under that bed.'

'You learn to be quiet in a big family if you want to sneak out when you're supposed to be grounded.'

'And I imagine that was probably quite often.'

'I'm sure I don't know what you're implying.'

'I'm sure you do. Now take these for me, would you?'

He took the pile of items off me and put them down on the floor, along with all the other items we'd so far emptied from storage. I turned back to grab a few more items. Balancing on one leg, I reached up and stretched my fingers to pull the last items towards me. The chair gave a little wobble and I gripped the shelf to steady myself. I heard Michael mutter something under his breath and a moment later, two large hands were on my waist lifting me off the chair. He plonked me down on the floor and waited until I was entirely stable before removing them.

'Excuse me! I haven't quite finished!'

'You've definitely finished balancing precariously on chairs in my home. And anywhere else, I hope. You're going to damn well break something if you keep that up!'

I stood straighter, going into defence mode.

'In the nearly seven years I've been doing this, I have never once broken any possession of any client. So your items are entirely safe, I assure you.'

He screwed up his face for a moment. 'I'm not talking about possessions. I'm talking about you! I'd really prefer it if you didn't fall off and break your neck, if it's all the same to you.'

'That wasn't my plan. Besides, I've done it hundreds of times. I was perfectly all right.'

He looked down at me, still close from when he'd lifted me off the chair.

'I don't care if you've done it millions of times. I'd rather you didn't do it any more.'

'Some of us aren't blessed with your height. I need to be able to get to places.'

'Then use a stepladder! Something made for the purpose that you can hold on to. And don't overstretch yourself like you were just doing. It's going to end badly one day if you keep on like that. I'm amazed it hasn't already.'

I gave a huff. 'I still need those last few bits out of that wardrobe.' I pointed to where I'd been a few minutes before. Michael reached up to get the bits I couldn't, his T-shirt rising up as he did so, exposing the muscles of his lower back, twisting and taut as he felt around for anything left. I really ought to be looking away. Ideally.

Shortly after Janey had sat back down the other night, Michael had wandered off and, moments later, was leaning against a wall, chatting to a blonde who had been eyeing him up since the moment he'd walked in. From the way she'd been leaning into him and touching his arm every few seconds, it was apparent that his pastime of trying to get a reaction out of me had been transferred to his current company – although, admittedly, the reaction he was aiming for, and clearly getting, in that situation was entirely different to the one he aimed for, and annoyingly usually got, from me. Absent-mindedly, I wondered if his current practice of 'not giving anyone a tour of the house' might change once it was in a better state. Somehow, I doubted it. The fact that he kept his bedroom so impersonal hinted to me that he had no inclination of showing who he really was. And it didn't look like he was going to give me the chance to suggest how he could make his bedroom more welcoming either, judging by the fact he'd bitten my head off the last time I mentioned it. From what Janey had said, Michael hadn't always been like this. I guessed that the split with his ex-wife had really made an impact on him – and not for the better.

'Where are you?'

'Huh?' I jumped as Michael's deep voice drifted into my thoughts.

'You were miles away.'

'Umm...'

No, actually I was just at the top of this house, in your bedroom. Yeah, that definitely wasn't going to be the best answer.

'And now you're blushing.' His face took on a look of mild amusement.

'I am not blushing! How ridiculous. Why on earth would I be blushing?'

'I don't know. But I'm intrigued to find out.'

I shook my head. 'You're imagining things. Now come on. There's work to do.'

Michael gave me a look that suggested he wasn't even remotely convinced before looking down at the pile of stuff that covered his floor.

'I don't even know what half this stuff is! How can I have accumulated this much crap?'

I crouched and then sat on the floor. 'This is nothing. At least you can move in your house. You wouldn't believe some of the places I've been in.' I glanced up. Michael was looking around. His gaze travelled to the open door where another room's door stood open awaiting a similar fate. I reached up and tugged on his arm. 'What is it?'

'Nothing.' The shutters closed on his expression but I pressed on.

'Tell me what you're thinking.'

He ran a hand through his too-long hair. 'Nothing. I wasn't thinking anything.'

'I see. You know you can't lie for toffee, don't you?'

His gaze flicked to me and I held it.

'Fine. I was thinking that there is no way this house is going to be ready for visitors to stay in at Christmas.' He transferred his hand to the back of his neck and rubbed it a couple of times. 'You know what, Kate? This is just a waste of time. Yours and mine. And I really don't have it to waste. There are plenty of things I could be doing instead of faffing around here.'

I pushed myself up from the floor and faced him.

'What are you talking about? We've really only just started.'

'Exactly! We've only just started and in a few weeks' time I'm supposed to have a house that's fit for everyone to stay in and produce an outstanding Christmas dinner. It's all just bloody farcical!' His chest was heaving and his jaw was tight.

'What's so farcical about spending Christmas with your family?'

He looked down at me. 'That's not what I meant.'

'It's how it sounded. And it's how it'll sound to Janey and the rest of them.'

He gave me a look. 'Whilst I appreciate that you and my sister are good friends, I'd also appreciate you understanding that I know my family better than you do. Your family might be overly sensitive about petty things, but mine aren't.'

I turned for a moment, watching little flurries of snow tumble past the window as I ordered my thoughts, pushing the unnecessary ones away.

'I see. So, what is it that you're saying, exactly?'

'I'm saying that I think both of us can spend our time more productively. So, it's probably best if you left and attended to those other clients you mentioned before, all vying for your attention.' Michael caught my eye and for once, couldn't hold my gaze. If I didn't know better, I'd almost think there was a flash of remorse there. 'I'm sorry for wasting your time,' he mumbled.

I smoothed my skirt down. 'No problem. I have to say though, I never had you down as a quitter. Plenty of other things, definitely. But a quitter wasn't one of them.'

Michael turned and glared at me. 'I am not a quitter. I'm a realist.'

'Is that so?'

'Yes. It's so. And the realistic assessment of this… situation,' he flapped his arm to encompass the mess that currently surrounded us, 'is that however good you think you are, there is no way this place is going to be ready for Christmas. It's a joke to even think that I was ever going to be able to have my family here.'

I watched him for a moment, his fists clenched, the muscles in his forearm taut as steel cables, a flicker at his jaw as he tried to contain whatever it was that had kicked off inside him. And I recognised it. The anger that hid something far more vulnerable. I'd also had a lot of practice at dealing with it.

'Michael, I'm sorry if you thought that I presumed to know more about your family than you. Obviously that's not the case and it wasn't what I meant. What I do know is that it's important to them for all this to happen.' I repeated his action of encompassing the mess around us, albeit in a calmer manner. 'Not because they don't want to host Christmas this year but because they care about you and this is the best way of getting it done. Being given a deadline is something you're familiar with in your work. It's how you work best. You even said something similar yourself the first time we met. I know it looks bad now, but it always does at this stage. And believe

me, this really is nothing compared to some places.'
I leant and touched his knotted forearm and he
turned, his green eyes cool and shuttered. 'Michael,
I know you want to be able to have your family here
this Christmas – '

'Seems like you know an awful lot.'

I took a breath and ignored the jibe. Again, something
else I'd had experience of.

'I'm really good at my job and I have faith in you.
Both of which mean that I'm confident we can achieve
what we need to.'

He gave me a look under his lashes that hinted he still
wasn't entirely convinced.

OK, one more push.

'Assuming, of course, you really aren't a quitter.'

His head snapped up and I got a glare for my trouble.
Which was fine. Because I knew I had him. I plopped
back down on the floor.

'Right. Now that's sorted, you can get your backside
down here and help me see what we've got.'

***

'Morning, Kate! Cold enough to freeze the brass ones
off a monkey out there today!' Head vet, Mark held the
door for me as I attempted to struggle in with my load.

'It certainly is. The snow's just started again too.'

'What have you got there? More goodies?'

'Yes. Couple more blankets that I thought might be of
use.'

'Great! Another client or have you been treating these
pooches out of your own pocket again?'

I grinned. 'No. These were surplus to requirements at a client's so I asked if I could take them to donate myself.'

We'd found piles of blankets in a cupboard at Michael's house. Even with all those bedrooms, it was unlikely he'd ever need so many. Apparently the ex had really liked to shop.

'The tags are still on these blankets! And they're not cheap ones.'

'I know. I suggested selling them but the client wasn't interested. He just said to make sure they went to a good home, whatever I wanted. I couldn't think of anywhere better than here.'

'They're much appreciated, as always. Thanks, Kate.'

Mark took the items off me and headed off to put them in the supply store. I, meanwhile, set off to the kennels, grabbing a cleaning trolley on the way.

'Hi, Kate!' Sara, another volunteer, smiled as I approached the kennel block. 'How are you?'

'Good thanks. Busy week?'

Sara was a day trader in the city and in her working life wore designer suits and traded in numbers with so many zeros it made my head spin. Not that you'd know it looking at her now. But the smile she wore said it all. She volunteered here to escape the stress and even though that included undesirable jobs like washing out kennels and other chores that few people would put high on their list of 'things I like to do in my free time', it was all part of it.

The other part of it was the animals. The centre mostly catered for dogs but they also took in the odd cat to help out other local shelters and had recently acquired two horses, a donkey and a Vietnamese

Pot-bellied pig. These latest additions had been found in a barn after the owners moved, leaving no forwarding address. When John, the owner of the rescue centre, heard that there was the possibility of the horses being put down due to a lack of someone prepared to take them, he'd cleared an outbuilding and two days later had a comfy stable suitable for the animals to stay in. The pig also lived in there at the moment as it had delusions of grandeur and hadn't quite yet figured out that it wasn't actually a horse. But we were working on that.

'How's Bruno today?' I came up to the kennel she was working on. It smelled clean and fresh from her efforts. A large Labrador was lounging on the dog bed with his head resting on the leg of her ripped jeans. His eyes were closing as she rhythmically stroked his ears.

'Much better, thank goodness. He really seems to be settling. He's eating quite well now too so John is hoping to be able to put him on the website in the next couple of days.'

'Oh that's great! It won't be long before he finds a good home. Look at that face. How could anyone resist?' Bruno was now making satisfied groany noises as Sara found a sweet spot under his chin.

'I wish I could take him.'

I smiled, sadly. 'That's the worst bit, isn't it? Falling in love.'

'Depends on the circumstances.' She looked up at me from under her lashes.

I raised an eyebrow. 'Is there something I should know?'

Sara's smile widened and she pulled her other hand out from under Bruno's head, an action which he made no effort to facilitate. One eye opened as she stopped caressing his ears to pull her glove off. On her third finger was a stunning, not to mention enormous, diamond.

I grabbed her hand. 'Oh my God! He asked? You said he'd never ask!'

'I know! Believe me, I didn't think he would. He always said he wouldn't get married again, but then...' She looked down at the ring, her face radiating happiness, contentment and perhaps a little lingering surprise. 'I still can't believe it!'

I leant over the dog and gave her a hug. 'Oh, Sara. I'm so pleased for you, I really am. It's wonderful news!'

'Thanks, Kate. I can't tell you how happy I am. I thought I'd come to terms with the fact that I wouldn't ever get married, because I knew I didn't want my life to not have Henry in it. So, I'd just accepted that's how it would be. And then, this! Completely out of the blue.'

'Did he say why he changed his mind?'

'He just said that he realised he was judging every marriage by his first one and that wasn't fair on me, or himself. Now I think he's even more excited than I am that we're actually getting married!'

I laughed. 'That's brilliant! Oh, Sara. I'm just thrilled for you!'

'Thank you,' she smiled, pulling the glove back on. 'And what about you? How's Calum?'

'Oh, he's fine. Busy.'

'As always.'

I did a quick eyebrow raise. 'I know. But I'm sure things will settle down soon and we can get to spend some more time together. Right, I'd better get a move on. Congratulations again.'

'Thanks. I'll see you later.'

'OK. Bye.'

I grabbed the handle of my trolley and pulled it around to the block I usually looked after, pondering on the fact that my reply to Sara about Calum had just trotted out like a well-rehearsed line. Which I suppose it was.

It was true what I'd said to Janey about it being good to have someone who understood that I got busy, and I accepted that Calum worked a lot. He'd told me that from the beginning. Although, admittedly, I had thought we'd see each other a little more than we actually did. And the longer it went on, the harder it sometimes was. I was getting fed up of explaining away his absence so often and trying not to notice the private looks people exchanged when I did so. I got the feeling that some people didn't even believe he existed. It was hard to blame them. There were weeks when he was so busy he barely called or texted at all. But I liked him and he'd promised me things would change soon. So until then, I'd just put up with the looks and comments. Things would change for the better soon. I was sure of it.

I got to the edge of the block and opened the first kennel.

'Hiya Kong,' I called as I entered.

A tiny patter of paws barely made a sound as the dog scuttled towards me. I scooped him up and gave him a cuddle. The teacup Yorkshire Terrier had come to the centre so thin it was hard to believe how he was still even alive. None of us had expected him to last another day. He was roughly the same size as one of the Kong toys we stuffed with cheese and treats for the bigger dogs, hence his name, and we all prepared for hearing the worst the next time we came in. But on my next shift, to my great surprise, not to mention delight, little Kong was still there and had even gained some weight. The vets had had to be careful about building him up gradually but he was now at a much healthier weight, and we were just awaiting some results from some tests on his kidneys. If those came back OK, which Mark was pretty confident would happen, Kong would soon be gracing the rehoming pages on the rescue centre's website. He wouldn't be up there long. His loving nature combined with perfect portability meant he'd be snapped up in hours, I suspected. I'd miss his little snuggles and really wished I could have him for myself, but it wasn't possible with my job. And it wasn't exactly the first time I'd been told I couldn't have a pet. Even though this time I was the one giving myself the order. But at least now, here, I got to have the interaction with the animals that I loved.

I tucked Kong in the front of my hoody where he liked to sit whilst I cleaned out his kennel. From there he watched everything that was going on, keeping nice and warm. I chatted away to him as I did my chores and he sat, listening contentedly. Today I told him about Sara's engagement, that I hadn't been seeing Calum as much as I'd hoped, and then I told him about my latest client, Michael O'Farrell, and the fact that I still couldn't even begin to make him out.

Several hours later, I'd cleaned all the kennels in my block, helped feed all the guests and played with a puppy for far too long before its new owner came to pick her up.

'You look like that Stay Puft guy from *Ghostbusters*,' Mark said, laughing as he wandered over.

I pulled the scarf down that was currently tucked up to my nose.

'You say the nicest things.'

'I try.'

'How many layers have you got on?'

I paused a moment. 'Four, I think.'

He grinned.

'Who you taking?'

'Pete and Bonio.'

'Good choice.'

I smiled back and grabbed a couple of leads from the line of hooks on the wall.

'See you later.'

'See ya. Have fun.'

I tucked a tennis ball in each pocket and snagged a ball flinger from the shelf. 'That's the plan.'

With that I walked back in the direction of the kennels, collected my charges for the afternoon and set off for the fields adjoining the centre, a dog on each side of me. The snow had stopped for now and a watery sun was making a half-hearted attempt to shine through, even though it wasn't that long until it was time for it to think about setting.

'Right, lads,' I said, closing the gate behind me and bending down to unclip each lead. Both dogs waited, eager. Clearly these two knew who was the leader of the pack in this instance. Or maybe they just knew that I had tasty sausage pieces in my pocket.

Pushing a tennis ball in the cup of the thrower, I flicked my arm back and then let the ball fly. Bonio and Pete took off immediately. I loaded another and let it go, the ball zooming over their heads and Pete peeled off to chase the second one. Their enthusiasm and sheer joy made me laugh as I watched them. Bending, I called to them, my voice full of encouragement as I clapped my gloved hands. They charged back towards me, each with a soggy tennis ball held proud. Wagging their tails, they plonked their bottoms down in the snow and waited for a treat and a cuddle. I dropped down and gave them both, revelling in the warmth they radiated. And, if I was honest, also in the sense of being wanted, of belonging, of the love that they filled me with. I knew exactly where I was with these animals. There were no games, no falsehoods, no pretending-everything-was-fine. It was one of the many reasons I loved the time I spent here. I knew exactly where I stood.

Chapter Six

I sat on the train and gazed out of the window, watching the lights of the city grow closer. We pulled into the terminus and I stepped into the noise of the London station. I'd changed before leaving the rescue centre and now headed towards the Underground, bound for Covent Garden. I'd already got presents for Bernice, Mark and Janey and her family. They were really the only people I had to buy for, but I'd decided that perhaps a few little bits from Neal's Yard might be nice to go with the experience vouchers I'd already got for the girls. And maybe something else, if it caught my eye.

Having spent over half an hour perusing all the goodies on offer, sniffing various pots and potions and making up two baskets worth of organic treats, I left the shop and wandered out into the alley that the company took its name from. I loved the colourfully painted walls and the bare brick facades with their bright window frames. Decorated for the season, it looked even more enticing and cosy than ever. White fairy lights were entwined around a pair of doorway olive trees and a softly twinkling Christmas tree cast a soft glow in a shopfront window. I smiled at a couple apparently exploring the area for the first time, and the delight on their faces as they shared the experience, taking selfies galore. Moving on, I headed to the main part of the old marketplace, now decked out in all its Christmas finery. The huge tree shone bright and a street entertainer was making the crowd laugh with corny jokes as he proceeded with some sleight of hand. I watched for a few moments before heading inside to the old Apple Market, now filled with little boutiques. This year's decoration theme was gold and silver and the decorations spanned the width of the roof. Giant bell-shaped lights ran down the centre with smaller versions fanning out to the edge.

Window shopping passed another half an hour until I found a little café and ensconced myself at a table. Nearby a string quartet were busking, the live music adding to the atmosphere as people stopped to watch and listen. My gaze drifted to the passing crowds and the others at the tables surrounding me; couples opening bags and pulling presents from them to show the other their purchase, families laughing and, occasionally, squabbling after a long day as everyone became tired. I loved this time of year – the lights, the decorations, the music. It made me happy. For the most part. Although my formative Christmas experiences could have put me off for life, I'd held on determinedly to the joy that the season was supposed to bring, and hoped that, one day, I'd find it.

I had to admit that it wasn't always the easiest of tasks and just occasionally I floundered. A couple of times had seen me grab a last-minute break abroad to some sun-soaked spot instead, where I'd do nothing but read and sip drinks from glasses decorated with so much fruit

I could get my five a day from one cocktail. The peace of the places I chose for those holidays helped shift the focus of the past, helped me not to think about the possibility that I might never actually get that perfect Christmas. That it was all just a mirage I'd created in my head. Perhaps nobody really got it. But that didn't stop me wanting it. Deep down in my soul, away from the rational, organised me, the dreamer that I kept locked away still wanted it.

And this year there was a glimmer of hope. My normal levels of enthusiasm for the season had been heightened by Calum almost promising that we would definitely spend a few days together over the break. It would be the first time since we'd started dating that we'd be together for more than a few hours or one night. For once, it would actually feel like we were a couple.

I pulled out my phone and selected him from my contacts. It rang a couple of times before he picked up.

'Hi.'

'Hi, babe. How are you?' he asked.

'OK thanks. I'm just at Covent Garden, having a mooch around. I was just wondering if you might want to come and join me? We could – '

'Babe, I'd love to.'

My smile widened. I told myself off for prejudging him, having expected him to almost certainly say no.

'But I'm kind of tied up with something at the moment. Maybe later?'

My hopes deflated. I'd discovered a while ago that when Calum said 'maybe later' it was generally code for 'not a chance'.

'OK,' I said, unwilling to get into an argument about it right now. And who knew? Maybe this time he would surprise me.

'How long will you be there?'

'I'm not sure. I hadn't really decided.'

'Well, tell you what. I'll send you a text when I'm on my way. In the meantime, you just get on and do what you need to.'

'Sure. Sounds like a plan.'

In all likelihood a plan for him not to turn up, but a plan all the same.

'OK, babe. Gotta go. I'll see you later, hopefully.'

'See you later.'

I placed the phone on the table so that I would hear it if and when Calum texted. As I did so the waiter approached, holding a menu. I'd originally only planned to have a hot chocolate and maybe a slice of cake, but suddenly I wanted to extend the warm feeling of being wrapped up in Christmas. I took the menu and chose a meal and a glass of wine. Eating alone had never bothered me - it certainly wasn't a new experience. The waiter returned a few minutes later with my drink. I sat watching the Christmas world go by and sipped my wine.

Over an hour later, having soaked up the atmosphere, eaten and paid, I gathered my bags and shopping and picked up my phone from the table. There was no text from Calum.

***

'Oh, she was so happy!' Bernice enthused as I put the drink down on her desk. 'She couldn't believe that just organising her home would make such an impact on her life. It's incredible the difference in her. She's so much more pulled together now and we rediscovered all these beautiful clothes that she hadn't worn for years and she's started wearing them again. There's just this air of confidence and happiness about her now. It's wonderful! So different from the woman I met at the first consultation. Aren't these just gorgeous?' Bernice finished arranging the blooms that her client had sent her back with and looked around for a suitable place to put the vase. Not the easiest of tasks. The office wasn't large and I had to admit I may have gone a tad overboard with the Christmas decorations, so that it now had the distinct appearance of an elves' grotto rather than an office. But hey, it was only once a year and it was my office, and Bernice was all for it. On top of that, it made us happy, which trumped everything. Bernice shuffled a stuffed snowman to the side to make room for the flowers and stood back to admire them.

'They're lovely, Bernice. I'm so glad she was happy. And you obviously did a stellar job, as usual. Well done.'

Bernice smiled. 'Thanks.'

The week had been pretty crammed for both of us and we were exhausted from running about, trying to make sure all of our clients were happy and on top of things. One had rung in a panic, advising they had had a 'relapse' so we'd juggled diaries and I fitted them in to mine, scooting over early this morning to see what calamity had occurred. In the end, it wasn't anywhere near as bad as I'd feared. The client had just had a bit of a wobble with the thought of various visitors coming to descend on her over the holidays, and had suddenly felt a little overwhelmed. But within a few hours, we'd tackled the problem and the client was back in control and ready for her seasonal visitors.

Michael O'Farrell was next on my list and I was a little surprised that I was almost looking forward to the appointment. I was pretty sure that this feeling was down to the fact that, as we cleared out the space, the real character and beauty of the house was becoming easier to see and appreciate. It really was the most beautiful house. I only hoped that he appreciated it as much I did. Indeed, more so, since he lived there. However, as he kept his thoughts about anything remotely personal to himself, he could be either completely oblivious or entirely ecstatic and I'd still be none the wiser. I finished my drink and hooked my bag over my shoulder.

'Off to see the delectable Mr O'Farrell?' Bernice asked, grinning.

'Does your fiancé know you're referring to clients as "delectable"?'

She laughed. 'I said he was delectable. But he's still not as delectable as my Rufus.'

'Glad to hear it.' I smiled. 'Have a good day and I'll see you tomorrow.'

'Have fun!' Bernice waved and I pulled the office door closed behind me.

***

Michael was on the phone when he answered the door to me. He gave a brief smile and gestured me inside as he continued the conversation. Work stuff, by the sound of it.

'Can you hang on a minute, Bob?' Michael pulled the phone away and pressed mute. 'I'm sorry, I don't know how long I'm going to be on here.'

'It's fine. We'd planned on tackling your books today. That's a favourite bit of mine anyway so I can just get going on that if you don't mind me starting without you.'

'Not at all. But I know the deal was for me to take part in the process. A fact that you were insistent on making crystal clear on your first visit.' His mouth was serious but there was a hint of mischief in his eyes.

'It was and you are. But there's got to be flexibility built in to the process. Carry on with your call. It sounds important. I'll see you when you're ready.'

'Thanks, Kate. I'll be as quick as I can.'

I nodded and turned to hang up my coat as Michael resumed his conversation, then headed across the hallway before casting a sneaky glance back. I saw him run a hand through his hair, still desperately in need of a tidy up. There were dark circles under his eyes and his skin had a pallor to it that didn't exactly scream healthy. I might just mention it, in passing, to Janey the next time I saw her, just so that she could check he was OK. I knew she'd want to know.

Turning away, I walked into the dining room where Michael had decided that he'd like to keep all his books. I stood for a few moments and couldn't help but smile at the beautiful, white-painted bookcases that now lined one wall of the room. Glancing back, I noticed Michael had now followed me into the room. He raised his eyebrows at me, almost in question, as he continued his phone call. In return, I made a circle with my thumb and forefinger, signalling that I thought the new addition to the room was absolutely perfect. He gave a rare, beautiful smile and the green eyes crinkled at the edges before he turned away and took the phone call out of my hearing.

It was over forty minutes later when Michael hurried back into the dining room and found me kneeling on the floor, surrounded by piles of books.

'I'm really sorry about that.' He looked around, his brow creasing. 'Maybe I should disappear more often. You seem to be even more speedy when I'm not here.'

I sat back on my heels. 'Don't even think about it.'

'Worth a try.'

'Are you finished or do you need to get on with some work stuff? It's OK. I can get these organised myself and we'll just schedule another appointment when it's more convenient to do the bits we need to do together. I think we're making good progress, so it would be fine to do that.'

'No, I'm done for today.' He flopped down onto the floor beside me. 'In more ways than one.'

I looked down at him sprawled on the carpet, his head to one side. He looked more than capable of going to sleep right there with very little encouragement. Perhaps a little break would be a good thing. In truth, I was actually a little worried about him. Just because we hadn't exactly started out the best of friends didn't mean that I was completely oblivious to his current state.

'Long morning?' I enquired.

He rolled his head onto his bicep so that he was looking at me. 'Long afternoon, evening, night and morning.'

I frowned. 'You worked all through the night?'

'Last-minute crisis. And then they wanted a meeting about it at 9 a.m. I've had a four-hour round trip this morning.'

'Why on earth didn't you tell me?'

He gave a gentle laugh as, with some effort, he pushed himself up into a sitting position. 'I thought about it. And then I thought how well me ringing you and saying, "Hi, Kate. Do you think we could we postpone our appointment today? I'm a little tired," would go down.'

'You make me sound horribly unreasonable.' I'd learned years ago not to care too much about what people thought of me. So why did it bother me what Michael O'Farrell thought now?

He gave me a look. 'I messed about with your schedule once before and it didn't go well.'

I sat straighter. 'That was completely different and you know it. For one thing, you've apologised this time.'

'I'm sure I apologised that first night too. Eventually.'

'No. You didn't.'

He shook his head. 'I must have. In a roundabout way. Maybe you missed it.'

I gave a prod to move him off a book his legs were lounging over. 'I didn't miss anything, thank you very much. You didn't apologise at all. In any form, roundabout or otherwise.'

'Really?'

'Really,' I confirmed.

Michael raised his eyebrows in thought. 'Right. Then I guess you were absolutely right to call me what you did.'

'You've only just realised that?'

He let out a laugh that for a moment disguised the weariness of his face. 'I guess I walked into that one.'

I smiled and continued working. Feeling Michael's eyes on me, I spoke without turning my head.

'Feel free to help.'

He knew by my tone I was joking. Mostly. I was acutely aware of the deadline on this job and although it had all been progressing fairly well in the last couple of weeks, I'd been caught out in the past by someone suddenly producing a hidden mountain of items from their loft/garage/Great Aunt Maude, with the casual declaration that they had 'just a few more things'. I was desperately hoping that wasn't going to be the case here and, when I'd enquired as to whether there was anything lurking elsewhere, Michael had confirmed that everything I'd seen was everything he owned. I didn't think he'd be purposely hiding anything but, as he had the occasional tendency to seem distracted, I wasn't ruling it out one hundred per cent.

'Right. Yes. Of course. So, what exactly are we doing here?'

Having explained how I was categorising his books by subject for non-fiction and by genre for fiction, I asked him to go through them, putting aside any that he no longer wanted. Those could then be donated to a library or charity shop, or if he preferred, he could sell them online. Michael had immediately opted for the charity shop, mentioning that he always took his stuff to one in particular.

'What?' he asked.

I looked up, confused. 'I didn't say anything.'

'You didn't have to.'

I sat back on my heels again. 'What are you on about?'

'When I said I always take my stuff to a particular charity shop you pulled a face.'

'I most certainly did not.'

'I hate to disagree – '

'I doubt that,' I mumbled.

He shook his head. 'Don't you approve of charity shops?'

'Of course I do!'

'So what's with the face?'

I blew out a sigh. 'I did not pull a face – '

'Yeah. You did.'

I fixed him with a look. 'If I did, then it was merely an expression of surprise.'

'Surprise that I would donate anything? Thanks. I know I'm not exactly your favourite person but that's a bit harsh, even from you.'

'Of course that's not what I meant. It's just that...'

'Go on.'

I really needed to look into courses that would teach me how not to show everything I was thinking. Although, oddly, Michael O'Farrell was the first person to have ever picked me up on this.

Glancing over, I saw that he was waiting for an answer, his intense green gaze unreadable. Unlike me, apparently.

'Fine. I was just a little surprised that you donated anything.'

He opened his mouth to speak but I got there before him.

'Not because I don't think you would, but it's just... well, it doesn't look like anything has left this house in quite some time, barring you.'

He watched me for a moment or two longer before turning away and beginning to methodically go through the books in the pile in front of him.

'I was referring to...before.' His voice was flat and I wasn't sure if I'd offended him. If I was honest, there was a lot about this client that I wasn't sure about, and right now it was why I was feeling so awful about the fact that I might have hurt his feelings. 'And you're right. I haven't taken anything there in ages. I really don't know how I let things go quite so much.' The last sentence was quieter, almost as if it were to himself. But I'd seen this so many times before. I wanted to let him know that it wasn't unusual. That it wasn't some sort of failure on his part.

'It's pretty common actually,' I began, 'when there's been some sort of major event, as there has been in your life. It's perfectly natural to – '

'Kate,' he turned to me, 'I appreciate what you're trying to do but I'd appreciate it even more if you didn't do the psychobabble thing on me.'

'I wasn't. All I'm trying to – '

The mobile on the floor next to Michael began to ring loudly, interrupting me.

'Michael O'Farrell,' he answered, looking away.

I took a deep breath and reminded myself it was just a few more weeks.

'I've already sent all those details.'

Sat close to me as he was, it was hard not to overhear the conversation. And hard to not notice that it was clearly not one Michael was enjoying. His jaw was so tense I was surprised he could even speak.

'No. That's not what they said, and not what they asked for…' He paused, listening. 'I realise that but… no, it's fine. I can do it now and email it over. OK. Yep. You'll have it shortly.'

He hung up and looked at me, running a hand across the back of his neck.

'It's OK,' I said, before he had a chance to say anything. 'Go and do what you need to do.'

'I'm beginning to think this client is more trouble than they're worth,' he said, as he stood. 'Ever have any like that?' He sounded shattered but I heard the attempt at a truce.

'Now and again,' I replied, not looking up.

'So, what do you do about them?'

'Oh, just try and get the job done as quickly as possible, generally.'

'Sounds like a sensible plan. Although it's unlikely to be anything else with you.'

I looked up but he already had his hands up. 'That came out like an insult when it was meant to be a compliment. I just meant that you have your head screwed on right.' He ran his hand over his face, the tiredness making deep shadows under his eyes. 'You're right. I really do need to work on my compliments.'

'I'm not here for compliments, Michael. Don't worry about it.'

He nodded. 'Fair enough. I shouldn't be long on this.'

'OK.'

He turned and left the room. Moments later I heard the slight squeak from the hinge of his office door as he pushed it to.

Two hours later and Michael still hadn't reappeared. I'd long since finished sorting his books and had given up waiting. Fetching the cleaning supplies, I'd made sure all the new shelving was free of dust, done the same with the books, then begun putting them on the shelves. The top shelf was higher than I could reach and I'd cast a glance at a dining-room chair before remembering the promise I'd made to my client about not climbing on such items. It'd be just my luck that if I was going to fall for the first time ever it would be here, immediately giving him the opportunity to say 'I told you so', which, frankly, would be unbearable. I recalled seeing a small stepladder in the utility room so, grabbing that, I began filling the shelves.

It was long since dark when I finished and the house was oddly silent. I packed the books Michael had pulled out for donation into a box and put it by the door. Glancing back, I smiled as I looked at the room. There was still a little bit of work to do in here but its transformation so far was amazing. From a bland, empty room, it was now showing its owner's personality, which is what a home should do. Although, admittedly, that was usually easier when you understood that personality in the first place.

And now what to do? Did I just leave? Did I call out to him? What if he was in the middle of something? I didn't want to interrupt. But if I did just leave, then would he feel that I was being rude? Ugh. I put a hand on the banister, enjoying the smooth feel of the oak under my hand as I pondered my decision. If I just peeked my head in to his office and waved on the way out I felt that covered me for not just leaving but wasn't a big disturbance either - a good compromise.

I reached the door to Michael's office, which was ajar, and tapped lightly on it. When no answer came, I tried again, but there was still nothing. I glanced around but no light filtered from any of the other rooms so I could only assume he was still in this one, especially as he'd said he'd return to help me once he finished.

Pushing the door open a little more, I peered around it. I was happy to see that the room was still as tidy as we had made it during the first session. I looked over to the desk. The lamp stood on it cast a pool of illumination and within that pool was Michael. His head rested on one arm with the other out to the side, his hand splayed across a laptop, his breathing steady.

86

I hesitated where I was for a moment. I should probably just leave now. He couldn't get snarky at me for leaving without saying goodbye if he was asleep. Perhaps I could leave a note? I looked around. A sticky notepad sat on the side of his easel so I scribbled a note and stuck it on the door.

Right. I should go then. Now, probably.

My gaze drifted back to the sleeping form. The lamplight cast long shadows from his eyelashes onto his cheek and the overlong designer stubble. His breathing was even and deep, the sleep obviously much needed after working thirty-six hours straight. I really should just leave. Why was I even still here? I made to turn and froze as Michael stirred. Cautiously I turned my head but he'd barely moved, clearly exhausted.

Oh for goodness' sake, Kate. Just do what you need to do so that you can get out of here.

I kicked myself into gear and moved quietly to the sofa in the corner. Lifting the cashmere blanket off of it, I popped it over my shoulder for a moment. I returned to the desk and, as gently as possible, lifted Michael's arm from where it was resting on his laptop. He didn't stir at all as I laid it back down and pushed his computer back on the desk so that he wouldn't knock it off if he woke suddenly. Draping the blanket over him, I then leaned across and switched off his lamp. Moonlight mixed with the streetlight filtering in allowed me to see my way.

Pulling the door closed quietly to keep the warmth in, I read the note I'd stuck on it over once more, just to check: *Have put the items you wanted donated in the box by the door. All others are currently on the shelves. They are in fairly obvious categories at the moment but these can always be changed, if required – Kate.*

Crossing the hall, I picked up my coat and accompanying items, bundling myself up, ready for the onslaught of bitter wind that had been hurtling around the city all day. Before leaving I switched on the table lamp that balanced amongst the junk on the hall table and turned off the main one, giving a little light to the area and making it seem less like the house was empty. Plus, even amongst the mess that we were yet to tackle, it made things seem a little more homely. With one last glance at the closed study door, I opened the front door and stepped out.

Chapter Seven

Accounting was the least favourite part of my job and I was currently wading through invoices, fortified by a huge cup of tea and far too many Bourbon biscuits when my phone rang.

'Stone Organisation,' I answered the phone on speaker, concentrating on the screen in front of me, rather than the one on the phone.

'You should have woken me.' The deep, melodic tones filled the quietness of the tiny office.

I immediately sat up straighter and switched the phone off speaker. Opposite me, Bernice's mouth dropped open and her eyes grew wide. I waved my hand frantically at her to signal that it wasn't anything like what she was clearly imagining. By the fact that she was now grinning inanely, I guessed my message wasn't getting through.

'Erm, hi!' I said, temporarily thrown off guard by the greeting, delivered in Michael's admittedly sexy voice. (I'd had to eventually concede to that point, no matter how annoying he could be.) Bernice's reaction wasn't helping.

Bernice grinned even wider. Ugh. I really wasn't helping my own case here.

'Hi.'

'How are you?'

'Good, thanks. If a little embarrassed.'

'Oh, don't be silly. There's nothing to be embarrassed about.'

Bernice now looked just about ready to implode with curiosity so I spun my chair away from her.

'I think it's fair to say that I've hardly made a good impression on you and then I leave you so I can go and take a nap?'

'You'd been awake for hours. And you didn't leave to take a nap, you left to do yet more work. Unless that whole phone call was a set-up?

'No,' he laughed, 'it wasn't. I promise.'

'There you are then.'

'The dining room looks amazing. Thank you. Your idea of having those bookshelves in there is brilliant. I love it.'

'You do?' I said, unable to stop a huge smile forming on my face.

'I really do,' he replied, his voice softer this time.

'Oh, I'm so pleased.'

'And thank you for the blanket...and stuff. That was very sweet of you.'

'You almost sound surprised,' I said, unable to stop myself, and wondering why I cared as to whether Michael O'Farrell thought I was a nice person or not.

'No! No, not at all. It's just that...Well, it's no secret that you and I don't always see eye to eye. And before you say anything, don't worry, I'm perfectly aware that a lot of that is down to me. I just... It was very thoughtful of you. Thank you.'

'You're welcome. I was glad to see the office still looked nice and tidy.'

He let out that tantalising laugh again. 'Yes. I don't think I could risk your wrath at letting it go back to how it was quite so soon.'

'Golly. You really do think I'm a dragon!'

'No, I don't. But tell me honestly, if you'd have come in there and it was a state, would you have been calm and collected or would you have just smothered me with that blanket instead?'

He had a point.

'Your silence says so much.'

I smiled, despite myself. 'Are you still happy to proceed with your next appointment?'

'Absolutely. And I'll even stay awake this time.'

'That would probably add to our productivity.'

He laughed and I couldn't help but smile at the sound. 'I'll see you soon.'

I hung up and made a point of not looking at Bernice, pretending to be immediately absorbed in my invoicing again.

'Oh, no no no!' she said, scooting her feet along the floor in order to propel her chair around the desk and park it next to me.

'No, what?' I asked, doing my best to feign innocence. It didn't work.

'You know exactly what. "You should have woken me?" Er, hello! You can't just put that out there and then not say anything about it!'

'I didn't put it out there and there is nothing to say about it.'

'So why's he embarrassed? Couldn't he…you know…'

I frowned, not understanding. Bernice huffed at me, then held her forefinger out straight before letting it slowly droop down. I watched her mime, confused. Then it dawned.

'No! I mean, I don't know! I mean…Oh God. He'd been working straight through the night and got a call to do something else so had to disappear off to his office shortly after I got there, and never came back. I didn't want to leave without saying goodbye, so I poked my head in and he was asleep with his head on the desk. I put a blanket over him and switched off the light. That's all!'

Bernice raised one expertly shaped and tinted eyebrow. 'That's all?'

'That's all.'

She sat back in her chair. 'You like him.'

'I do not like him. I mean…'

The other eyebrow came up.

'I don't entirely dislike him as much as I did initially. Most of the time. But I don't like him like you're suggesting I like him. Definitely not.'

'Definitely not?'

'Most definitely not. Besides, I'm already seeing Calum, who I do like in the way you're suggesting.'

Bernice made to start scooting her chair back, but I caught her expression as she did so.

'What was that look about?'

She turned back to me. 'Honestly?'

'Of course.'

'I think "seeing Calum" is a bit of an overstatement. You hardly ever see him!'

'He's – '

'Busy. I know.'

'Why does everyone have it in for him?'

'We don't. But the fact that several people have made the same observation should tell you something.'

I shuffled some papers and made a point of looking busy and efficient. Bernice got the hint.

'It's just because we care about you, Kate.'

I nodded, which was just about all I could do.

* * *

Janey was sat on her yoga mat next to me, eating a yoghurt whilst I looked at her upside down from my current full bridge position. The yoga teacher had been giving her various suitable exercises to do during her pregnancy but it seemed that tonight Janey was disinclined to do many of them.

'I'm going to be the size of a house,' she whispered, opening the lid of another yoghurt which squirted me right in the eye as the seal broke.

'Oh sorry!' Janey dabbed at my ever reddening face with a tissue.

The teacher released us from the position and I shuffled on my mat to get ready for the cool down exercises. Janey wiggled herself around and stretched her legs out in front of her. It seemed only the men had got the height in her family. She moved her toes back and forth in a half-hearted attempt at doing something resembling what we were there for.

'Jesus,' she whispered. 'Look at that woman's arse. How is that even possible? It makes Kylie's backside look...well, like mine!'

She had a point. The woman's backside was bloody perfect and the fact that I was stuck right behind her was doing absolutely nothing for my ego.

'You're not going to be the size of a house. You're pregnant, for goodness' sake. There's another human being inside you!'

Janey was still focusing on the woman in front of me. 'Do you think she spends all day doing squats or just won the arse lottery?'

Laughter burst from me in the middle of a deep breath in and we got a look from the instructor that told us we were heading for the naughty step.

'Stop it,' I whispered. 'You're getting me into trouble.'

'Ah, a bit of trouble can be good for you.'

I glanced over and Janey winked.

'I don't have time for trouble.'

'Is that so?'

'Absolutely so. Now shush and lie down for a few minutes. The rest will do you good.'

Janey pulled a face at me but did as she was told. I closed my eyes and let my thoughts drift. A hand touching mine pulled me back. I rolled my head to see Janey. She squeezed my fingers and smiled, her eyes remaining closed.

'You've a kind soul, Katie girl.'

I returned the finger squeeze and then resumed concentrating on my breathing, pushing out all the thoughts and memories that were threatening to invade.

***

As I stood on my client's driveway waiting, yet again, I was seriously reconsidering my declaration to Bernice the other day that I didn't entirely dislike Michael O'Farrell as much as I had done initially. I'd texted and got no answer and when I called a quarter of an hour later, his phone had gone straight to voicemail. I'd already waited over half an hour and had absolutely no inclination to waste any more time. I couldn't believe that he'd done it again!

Picking up my bag, I began marching back towards the pavement when the sound of a motorbike getting closer made me pause. But only for a moment. I didn't have time to be messed about. He'd have to reschedule this time. The bike swung onto the parking area and Michael was off it quicker than he had been before, pulling his helmet from his head as he walked towards me. I watched for a moment and frowned.

'Katie, I'm so sorry! I know you're probably mad as stink with me, but I swear to God, this time – '

I tilted my head, my frown deepening. 'Are you limping?'

'What? Oh, yes, maybe a bit.'

I peered around his bulk at the bike behind him. Half the fairing was cracked and the paintwork was all scarred down one side. I looked up at him, my annoyance replaced with concern, a silent question on my face.

'Some idiot opened his car door without looking.'

My eyes widened.

'Stupid bastard.' He looked down at me. 'I tried to call you, but I think I must have landed on my phone at one point, and it kind of ended badly for the phone.'

'At one point?'

'Yeah. There was some acrobatics involved. Quite impressive, if I do say so myself. At least a nine point seven.'

He grinned but as he began walking up the steps, I could see the pain behind it.

'You need to go to hospital.'

'No, I don't.'

'Michael, something might be broken!'

'They gave me a good check over at the scene. It's fine.'

'But there might be something internal! Really, you should go. Please!'

I heard the crack in my voice at the same time as Michael did. He stopped and looked down at me, the intense gaze full of question.

'What's going on, Katie?'

I took a breath. 'Nothing. I'm just saying. Some injuries aren't always obvious. It's best to be safe.'

'I'm going to have some bruises, that's for sure, but that's all it is. I promise.'

I nodded, and broke the gaze.

'Thank you for your concern though. I do appreciate it.'

'Janey would be devastated if something happened to you.'

Not looking at me, Michael hesitated with the key at the lock for a moment before plunging it in and turning. 'Of course.'

'You know, you probably ought to rest. It must be a shock, something like that, apart from all your bumps and bruises. I can sort another time for this session, even if it's the weekend, so that we don't get behind.'

'No plans for the weekend then?'

'No, not really,' I said, keeping my voice light. No need to tell Michael that all my recent suggestions for plans with Calum had come to nothing.

'The man's a fool.'

'So everyone keeps saying.'

'Maybe you should start listening to everyone then?'

I let out a sigh. 'Could we get back to you?'

'Sure.' He smiled.

I rolled my eyes. 'I should have known that would be a favourite topic.'

He really did have a nice laugh, I had to admit that, no matter how infuriating the rest of him could be at times.

'And what would you like to know about me?'

'I'd like to know when best to rearrange this appointment for because you're not doing anything this afternoon apart from putting that leg up and resting.'

'Is that so?'

'Yes, it is.'

'You're pretty confident of that considering you're half my size.'

'I am not half your size and besides, size isn't everything.' As soon as the words left my mouth, I knew it was the wrong thing to say.

'How refreshing that you think so.'

'That's not what I meant and you know it.'

'What exactly is it that you didn't mean?'

I glared at him which merely caused him to laugh again, briefly. The squint of pain gave him away.

'Michael, you might have cracked a rib. You really ought to go to hospital and get checked out.'

He'd unzipped his leathers now and was wriggling out of the top half, struggling more than he had the last time I'd seen him do it. Automatically, I reached up and pulled the shoulder of the suit past his own.

'Thanks. They've earned their keep today.' He pulled the sleeve around and inspected it for scuff marks, giving a sigh when he found plenty.

'They can be replaced. You can't.'

'Ah, Katie. Are you saying I'm irreplaceable?'

I levelled a look at him. 'I'm saying there is only one of you. Thank goodness.'

He smiled. 'Fair enough. Look, I'm going to go and change and then I'll be back and we can set to doing whatever it is that you had planned for today.'

I shook my head. 'Did you not listen to me?'

'I did. I just chose to take another option.'

'There is no other option. You resting is the only option.'

'So you're not staying.'

'No. I can come back in a couple of days and we can catch up then.'

'Right. But it was the living room you were planning on tackling today?'

'It was. But another couple of days won't hurt.'

'OK. I'll just go and change and then I can make a start without you.'

'What?'

'What?' he replied, his face the picture of altar boy innocence.

'You're not starting anything without me.'

'Why not? Afraid I'll muck it up?'

'I just told you why not!'

'And I told you I'm fine.'

'And clearly you're not. You're black and blue, you're limping heavily and it's obvious your ribs hurt.'

'Only when you make me laugh.'

I tipped my head back and closed my eyes. 'I knew it would be my fault.'

He laughed again. 'Ow.'

I gave a sigh of exasperation. 'How on earth do your family put up with you?'

'Practice.'

'Go and get changed. I'll make you a cup of tea.'

'You don't need to – '

'Go!' I said, pointing straight-armed at the stairs.

'I'm going, I'm going.' And he began climbing the stairs, unaware that the fact he was doing so slowly, one by one, unlike his normal jog of two at a time, told me everything I needed to know.

***

'Kate?' Michael called.

'In here,' I called back from the living room.

He appeared at the door wearing tracksuit bottoms that had seen better days, a T-shirt that didn't look too bad from what I could see and the zip-up hoody he'd thrown over the top and left unzipped also had some hope for it. We'd had a brief discussion about sorting his clothes at some point, but as these lived in the master bedroom and he'd already declared that as not needing attention, I was still unsure whether I was ever going to get my hands on his wardrobe. Michael glanced down at his clothing.

'I'm getting the impression my outfit doesn't meet with your approval.' His expression was hard to read.

'You look fine. Why would I mind what you wear? And they look...comfortable, which is the important thing.'

He gave me a look.

'What?'

'There's a "but" there.'

'There isn't a "but".' *How did he do that? I had to admit it was getting more than a little disconcerting.*

'Oh, there is definitely a "but".'

'Are you going to get your weight off that leg and sit down or not?'

'When you tell me the truth.'

'Fine,' I shrugged. 'It's your discomfort. Doesn't bother me.'

Michael tilted his head in acknowledgement. 'What are we doing?'

'Basically pulling out everything that's in this room and putting it into categories. I think half your jackets are down here so, for example, they can be taken and hung up in your wardrobe. Assuming you want to keep them.'

'Perhaps I'd better ask you if I should keep them as you seem to have an opinion on my clothing.'

I rolled my eyes and said nothing. He chuckled and then sucked in his breath as his ribs protested. I glanced round but he was carrying on with the task I'd detailed. Bending down, he scooped an armful of jackets up and straightened. He said nothing but the pain was so clear on his face it made me wince.

'Right. That's it. Put those down.'

'What? Why? I thought this was the plan.'

'It was the plan before you started auditioning for Cirque Du Soleil this afternoon.'

'I told you, I'm fine.'

'And I didn't tell you, but you should already know, that I'm not an idiot.'

'I never thought for one moment that you were.'

'Then stop trying to pretend you're not in pain. If you're not going to go to hospital, the least you should do is sit down and rest. Look, sit there.'

I steered him towards a space I'd already made on the sofa whilst he'd been upstairs changing.

'Sit.'

Michael looked down at me and I held his gaze firmly.

'I said, sit. Please.'

A flicker of a smile played on his lips and he obeyed.

'Tea.' I handed him the mug I'd made.

'You're kind of bossy sometimes. You know that, don't you?'

'It's not bossiness. It's called being sensible and organised.'

'Are you always sensible and organised?'

'Pretty much.'

'Let me guess. You were a wild child growing up but you've got all that out of your system now.'

Boy, he couldn't be any farther from the truth if he'd tried.

'Not at all. Now. If I pull stuff out, then you can tell me whether it's still wanted and we can start finding homes for it.'

Something caught my eye and I crossed the room to get it. Upending the pile of goodness knows what that had almost covered it, I found a beautiful footstool upholstered in pale blue and white Toile de Jouy. Bending to lift it, I was halted in my tracks.

'Don't you dare.'

'Excuse me?' I said, turning to find Michael approaching me. 'And I told you to sit down.'

'I'm not going to sit there and watch you heave furniture about. I know you consider me some misogynistic Neanderthal – '

'I never said that.'

'You never say a lot of things.'

I stuck my tongue out and he laughed, wincing again as he did so.

'It's a footstool. I'm not proposing I move a sofa on my own. Although, for your information, I'm quite capable of doing so and have done in the past, more than once.'

'Then your clients should be ashamed of themselves for letting you do so.'

'It wasn't a client and that's a very old-fashioned view.'

'One I make no apologies for. So who was it? Not the boyfriend?'

'No. And I'm surprised you're not more modern than that. I can't imagine Janey lets you get away with your dinosaur values.'

'Janey is a very intelligent woman. She has no qualms about getting any and all heavy lifting done by someone else if it's at all possible. You could learn a few things from her.'

'I've already learned a few things from her,' I said, raising an eyebrow.

Michael looked at me and tilted his head back a little more, bravado kicking in. 'Oh? And what things would those be?'

The truth was I hadn't learned anything about Michael from Janey that he hadn't confirmed himself but the tease seemed too good an opportunity to miss.

'Nothing you would be interested in. Just girl talk, you know,' I said, airily.

He narrowed his eyes at me.

'Now. Can you please go back and sit down so I can get on with things?'

'If by getting on with things you mean moving furniture, then no.'

I threw my hands up. 'You are entirely impossible.'

'I am. At last, we actually agree on something.'

'Fine,' I conceded, 'we'll do it together then.'

He smirked.

'Oh, grow up,' I said, which only proceeded to make him laugh and wince again.

'Right. Ready? Go.'

We moved the footstool, with me directing, to the sofa where he'd been sitting.

'Down.'

Michael glanced at me, but obeyed.

'I thought this was going to be for you to sit on.'

'It's for your foot. I think it's best elevated.'

'Kate. You're fussing way too much. It was just a bump.'

'So you didn't hit an open car door, get catapulted across a busy London street and narrowly avoid being squashed into the ground by passing traffic?'

The thought, now voiced, made my blood cold and I felt the colour drain from my face. I sat down quickly on the footstool, my head feeling suddenly light. I knew it was just because the thought of Janey losing someone she loved would be so awful. Obviously I wouldn't want anything to happen to Michael either, but I hardly knew him well enough for me to be as upset as I felt at this moment. I guessed it had to be some sort of 'referred' upset.

Large, warm hands on my shoulders brought me back into the moment.

'I'm fine, Kate. Honestly.'

I took a breath. 'Yes, all right. But you should still rest. It's common sense – something that was clearly knocked out of you during your exploits. Now please sit, before I have to ring your sister.'

Michael sat.

'Foot up,' I said, pointing at the footstool I'd now vacated.

He looked at me.

I raised an eyebrow.

'I'm fine.'

'You won't be if you don't do as you're told. You'll be nursing another broken rib. Now just put your damn foot up and stop being such a pain in the arse.'

Michael burst out laughing and immediately regretted it. Unable to stop, he countered the action by holding his chest tightly until he calmed.

'You really are something,' he wheezed.

'I dread to think what you believe that "something" to be so I'm going to suggest we move right along now. OK. Let's start with this pile.'

Chapter Eight

Four hours later and we'd made quite an impact. There were four boxes full of items for the charity shop and another full of recycling. I'd chucked the rubbish straight out. In between the organising, I'd made more tea and persuaded Michael to take some painkillers as it was obvious he was in more discomfort than he was letting on. As they began to kick in, his face relaxed and I felt a little more at ease with his decision not to be taken by the paramedics for a check-up.

'It really is a beautiful house,' I said, stretching my back and catching sight of the ornate plaster ceiling rose above me.

'Thanks. I know I'm lucky to be able to live here. I'm sure you think I don't appreciate it because of the state I've let it get into.'

'No, not at all.' And it was true. I knew it was all too easy to make sweeping judgements about a situation from the outside. And just how hurtful those judgements could be.

Michael studied me for a moment, assessing me with those incredible eyes and that look that felt like he could see further than I might want him to.

'My grandfather's a canny man when it comes to property. He started out with nothing and built up his business gradually, taking on places that needed work and selling them on for a profit. All this area used to be cheap flats run by shady landlords. Maintenance was practically unheard of. Grandad got a couple of places at auction. They were in such a state and in a bad bit of town so there wasn't a great deal of demand. But he felt that things were going to improve. Of course, everyone thought he was barmy when he said that, but he made similar investments in various parts of London and he got it right every time. There's no way I'd be able to live here if he hadn't had that insight all those years ago.'

'So you bought it off him? He must have still done you a heck of a deal!' I said, caught up in the story before realising that my comment was probably incredibly inappropriate. 'I'm sorry. I didn't mean to – '

'No, it's fine. I actually rent it. We talked about me buying it off him a few years ago but he wasn't ready to let it go. All the time that property values here are going up, it's the right thing for him to do.'

'You didn't mind that he wouldn't sell?'

He gave me a quick smile. 'Not at all. In fact, I was pretty damn grateful he didn't.'

I shook my head. 'I don't understand.'

'When I split up with my wife, she seemed to be under the impression that I owned this and wanted it sold and half the profits.'

'Oh. You never told her you rented?'

'I never told her I owned it. She assumed. And I assumed she knew it wasn't mine. It was all kind of a whirlwind thing, her and I getting together. And then I guess because I did all the maintenance and so on, she just thought I owned it.'

'She didn't get a clue from bills and stuff?'

'Angeline never bothered herself with little things like that. I paid all the bills, handled all the paperwork. Which I was happy to. It wasn't really her thing.'

'I'm not sure it's anyone's "thing". You just have to get on and do it.'

'Unless you have some mug to do it for you.'

I pulled a face, unsure what to say.

'If I'd have realised what she thought I would have told her, of course! It just never occurred to me that she thought I was wealthy enough to own a place like this.'

'She never asked to contribute to the mortgage when she moved in?'

Michael pulled a face. 'No. That's not really her style.'

'Oh.'

'Anyway, the look on her face was pretty priceless when we split up and she realised that nothing to do with the property is in my name. It's all in Grandad's. So she couldn't touch it.'

'I imagine she was a little put out.'

The lips quirked again. 'You could say that.'

'Grandad just smiled when I told him. He told me I'd worked hard in helping him on this house in holidays and stuff, so it would have been wrong to have to split it with someone who didn't love it like I did.'

'He didn't trust her.'

'No, I don't think he did. She wasn't exactly into family the same way I am. It was always a bone of contention between us.'

'I'm sorry.'

Michael flashed me a look. 'Thanks. All in the past now though.'

'So you helped work on this place?' I said, glancing around and sensing that moving the subject on might be for the best. 'That's great! I love Georgian architecture. They really had some wonderful ideas about light and space.'

'They certainly did. All us kids did bits on various houses when we could. Helping out, you know. But I guess I always felt a connection to this one. It was in a right state but when I saw it in the auction listings, I persuaded Grandad to get it anyway. It was a family decision in the end, as a lot of things are in my family – something you've probably already worked out.'

I smiled at him. 'Their support must have been very greatly appreciated.'

'Definitely. Quite literally in one instance when I walked into an upper room one day and nearly ended up in the kitchen.'

'Oh my goodness! Were you all right?' I leant forward, fascinated at hearing the history of the house.

'Yeah. My brother managed to grab my arm just as the joist gave way.'

'That must have been frightening for you both.'

He gave a quick eyebrow raise. 'More so for me. He was in no great hurry to pull me up and instead made me apologise for every mean thing I'd ever said or done to him.'

'Really? I imagine you were dangling there for quite some time then.'

He gave a little outward huff of air from his nose, a concession of amusement. 'Touché.'

***

Michael had been doing his best to help, determined not to give in but in the end I managed to persuade him to sit quietly and just close his eyes for ten minutes. A short while later, his voice cut into my concentration, making me jump.

'I really hate those curtains.'

'Oh my…' I gasped, my hand on my chest. 'You made me jump. I thought you were asleep.'

'No. You'd know if I was asleep. Snore like a train, apparently.'

I knew it wasn't true, but played along. 'Attractive.'

His lips hinted at a smile.

I glanced around at the curtains he was focused on. 'What don't you like about them?'

If I was honest, they weren't exactly to my taste either but it was obvious to anyone that they were expensive and my next move would depend on what Michael said.

'I don't think they suit the room. One of the things I love about this house is the sense of space, the proportions of it. Ideally I want that feel in the rooms too. It's my own fault though. I said I'd go and look at some with my wife, but kept putting it off when other things came up. She got fed up with waiting in the end and had these made. Cost a bloody fortune and I can't stand them.'

'So what would you prefer?'

'Something lighter in colour. Something that…I don't know…seems less funereal.'

'Then you should get rid of them.'

His sleepy eyes widened. 'I can't! The amount they cost, I should be using them for the next thirty years at least!'

'Michael,' I said, sitting back and scooting my legs out to the side a little as I started getting pins and needles. 'Everything we're doing here is about making your life better, making your home somewhere you enjoy being, whatever room you're in. Making you happier. This room is one of the main living spaces, so I hope you'll be using it more once we're finished, because it really is quite lovely. But if the first thing you're going to think every time you come in here is how much you hate those curtains, then they have to go. It's as simple as that. There are places that you can take designer curtains like these and they'll sell them on so you get some money back – a bit like second-hand designer clothes agencies – so it wouldn't be a total loss.'

He frowned. 'I'm not…I hope you don't think I'm being tight, or anything, when I say that.'

'Not at all. They were expensive and getting rid of them seems wasteful to you.'

'It does.'

'I've been doing this a long time. Don't worry. And I don't think you're being a scrooge, don't worry about it. Even if I did, that's your prerogative. It doesn't matter what I think.'

'It matters to me.'

I looked up, surprised.

With perfect timing, Michael's phone began to ring.

'Hi, sis,' he answered.

I finished off arranging the photo frames he'd wanted to keep out on a shelf on the dresser, having given it a good clean first. Although I'd told Michael in our first, rather heated discussion that I wasn't a cleaner, that wasn't entirely true. There was no point putting things back if the place they were going back to was dusty or dirty, so generally the houses I helped organise also got a damn good clean. Having said that, I wasn't about to clean anyone's toilet but my own. I often went above and beyond, but I had limits.

I tuned out of Michael's phone call and instead concentrated on the pictures I was putting on the shelf. There had been a couple of him with his wife that had obviously survived an initial onslaught of being got rid of and he had pulled those out of the frames and put them in a pile. Most of the ones left were of family. It was clear from spending time here just how important family was to this man. I turned my attention back to the photos – I recognised Janey's husband in one with Michael, their arms round each other's shoulders, both caked with mud and holding aloft some sort of trophy. There were a couple of rugby team ones, and another of him sat, his shirt open and catching the breeze as his legs dangled over the edge of a boat. My eyes kept drifting back to this one. It was tricky to ignore the fact that under the shapeless, worn clothes Michael now seemed to live in, there was an extremely hot body. It was kind of a shame he covered it up most of the time. Running my gaze over the rest of the photos, it was obvious that at one point, he'd taken more pride in his appearance. Not in a vain way, just that he'd perhaps taken a little more care and interest in it – his hair was shorter, his clothes tidier, his face more inclined to smile.

I'd been honest before when I'd said I didn't care what he wore. But I did want him to care a little more about what he wore because I knew from years of experience that feeling good in your clothes could make a real difference to one's mindset.

'Who's the dog?' I asked, as I sensed Michael approaching.

Reaching my side, he picked up one of the photos which featured him with a Heinz 57 type dog.

'Monty.'

'Whose is he?'

Michael took a breath and shifted his weight, the painkillers apparently beginning to wear off.

'He was mine. Daft dog. Passed away.'

'Oh no! Oh, I'm so sorry. I wouldn't have said anything – '

Michael shook his head and smiled, the sadness in it evident, no matter how he tried to disguise it.

'It's fine.'

'Have you never thought of getting another? I mean, you're at home most of the time? And there are doggy day-care places if you needed to go out for longer than you'd want to leave him.'

He peered down at me. 'Doggy day-care?'

'Yes.'

'Do I really look like someone who would use the phrase "doggy day-care"?'

I rolled my eyes at him. 'Call it what you like then, but I'm just saying maybe getting another dog would be something to think about.'

'I have thought about it, and I thought no.'

'Oh.'

Michael replaced the photograph. 'This looks really nice. Thank you,' he said, standing back from the dresser to study it better.

'I'm glad you're pleased. Lots more to do yet though.'

We stood in silence for a moment.

'But going back to the dog thing,' I said, immediately hearing Michael sigh, 'it would be great company for you. This is a big house and I think it could be nice for you to have another being here. I volunteer at a rescue centre just outside London. I could get them to keep an eye out for you, if you wanted?'

'Kate, it's very kind of you, but I am not interested in getting another dog, OK?'

'OK,' I said, chewing the inside of my mouth as my thoughts wandered off in another direction. 'I'd better be off then. You could take some more painkillers now if you wanted,' I told him, glancing at my watch, 'it's been over the time.'

'You're leaving?'

'Yes. Why?'

'Do you have another appointment?'

'No. Not this evening, thank goodness.'

'Meeting the boyfriend?' He raised an eyebrow.

I raised my own in reply.

A smile flickered. 'Point taken. It's just that Janey and the crew are coming over. I texted my brother-in-law about not going to rugby training. The daft sod told Janey I'd come off my bike so now she's insisting on coming over to make sure I'm still in one piece and it's turned into a family expedition.' The smile on his face when he said this showed just how much this meant to him. It was the same joyous smile they all wore in the photographs I'd been arranging so carefully earlier.

'Oh, that's lovely. It'll be nice for you to have them here, and there's even space of a sort now too.'

'I know. They won't believe it. They'll have you up on sorcery charges.'

'Hardly. Well, I'd better get going then. I don't want to interrupt your family time.'

I made to leave but Michael caught my arm.

'I…Janey and I thought you might be able to stay. They're bringing fish and chips, and I have to say, they're the best you'll ever have. I'd hate for you to miss out on such an amazing culinary experience.'

I smiled. 'That's quite a claim.'

'All true.'

I was tempted. I'd been so busy with everyone having last-minute panics before Christmas and arranging bookings for a raft of New Year resolution clients that Janey and I hadn't had a chance to catch up as much as we usually liked to. It would be lovely to see them all.

'Go on. You know you want to.'

I did want to. The thought of going back to my tiny flat and working late into the night, accompanied only by a microwave meal for one had so much less appeal than staying a little longer here in this beautiful house sharing a meal with people I cared about. And Michael, of course.

'Janey will be upset if she finds out you left just before they got here.'

'Emotional blackmail? That's a low blow.'

'Did it work?'

I fiddled with one of the photo frames, moving it a miniscule amount, then moving it the same amount back.

'Yes.'

'Then I'm unrepentant.'

I tilted my head back so that I could meet his gaze. 'Now, why doesn't that surprise me?'

The doorbell rang and Michael turned.

'Wait,' I said, putting a hand out to stop him, 'let me go. I can try to reassure Janey a little that I've been keeping an eye on you this afternoon and you're OK.'

Michael looked down. My hand was resting on his chest. Suddenly, my brain acknowledged the hard muscle, the warmth, the definition of his pecs through the fabric of his T-shirt. I snatched my hand back.

'Sorry.'

'No problem.'

The doorbell rang again and I scooted out the living room door to answer it.

'Katie! Is he all right? That bloody motorbike! If I've told him once, I've told him a thousand times. Honest to God, in this weather too. I – '

'Janey, he's fine,' I said, giving her a hug and taking her coat as they all piled through the door.

'Are you sure?' she asked quietly.

'Yes. I've been here for most of the afternoon and I kept an eye on him. He's pretty bruised and bumped but of course being stubborn about it. His ribs are sore, but hopefully they're just bruised rather than anything else. I gave him some painkillers earlier and eventually got him to rest most of the afternoon. He's due some more pain relief about now

115

if he wants it. They seem to have helped take the edge off things.'

'If you're finished discussing me out there, I'm starving!' Michael emerged from the living room and although he was smiling, I could see the tightness in his face from the pain.

'Stop whingeing, you big wuss,' Patrick, Janey's husband laughed. 'We're coming,' he said as he gave me a hug and unbundled the children from their coats, hats and mittens.

'Uncle Mikey!' they cheered as they careered across the hallway, making enough noise to rival a baby hippo.

'Hiya squirts!'

'Uncle Mikey, pick me up, pick me up!' the younger one chanted, bouncing up and down on the balls of her feet, her arms stretching up towards him.

Michael hesitated a moment, clearly unwilling to disappoint his niece, and then began to bend towards her.

'Michael Francis O'Farrell, don't you dare.' Janey was marching towards her brother.

He halted mid motion.

'Lily. Uncle Mikey fell off his motorbike today and hurt himself so he can't pick you up. Besides, you're getting too big to be picked up these days.'

'She's never too big,' Michael countered.

Janey ignored him, ushering the children into the dining room. 'Patrick, could you bring the food in please?'

'Coming.'

Chatting happily, Patrick and I diverted off into the kitchen.

'Shall I get some plates?' I asked.

'Let's be reckless and eat out of the paper, shall we?' Patrick grinned at me.

I returned it. 'Why not?'

We moved around the kitchen, hunting and gathering the rest of the supplies amongst the still-to-be-sorted chaos of the room. Soon we had everything we needed – Patrick brought the various packets of food and I carried the cutlery, tomato sauce, salt and vinegar. Following the sound of voices, we headed to the dining room. The door was ajar and, hands full, I pushed it open a little more with my hip. At which point I nearly dropped the whole lot. Opposite me, Michael stood shirtless, jogging bottoms riding low on his waist. Without doubt it was one of the most beautiful sights I'd seen in a long time. Maybe any time. The definition and muscle I'd got an idea of from distractedly putting my hand on his chest earlier was now displayed in its full glory. And glorious it most definitely was. In front of me stood a body that would make the Hemsworth boys feel like they'd been slacking at the gym.

'What about there?' Janey pressed on her brother's side gently and Michael shot away from her.

'Jesus Christ! For f...' He stopped himself as he caught sight of his niece and nephew watching the proceedings, wide-eyed. 'Yes. That bit is a little tender.'

'I can take that,' Patrick said, attempting to retrieve the vinegar bottle I was now gripping with enough force to make my knuckles go white.

'Huh?' I mumbled, pulling my gaze away from Michael's half-naked body – a feat that was far easier said than done. 'Oh. Yes. Yes, of course,' I said, relinquishing it as I surreptitiously checked that the only drooling I had been doing was of the mental kind.

'Janey, please can we just eat now?' Michael nodded his head at the food his brother-in-law had laid out on the table.

'In a moment. If you're going to ride that stupid machine, you're going to have to put up with being poked about when you come off.'

'I've no aversion to that if it's a pretty nurse doing the poking.' He winked at Patrick. Janey prodded her brother a little harder than was probably necessary and he grimaced.

'Point taken,' he conceded, his teeth gritted.

'Keep an eye on those ribs and don't ride that bike for a while.'

'Yes, Ma.'

Janey threw his T-shirt at him. 'Get dressed and eat something.'

'That's what I've been trying to do ever since you got here.'

'Oh? You were undressed before we got here?' Patrick commented, his expression innocent.

Michael pulled a 'smart arse' face at him.

'Why were you undressed before we got here, Uncle Mikey?' Joseph was currently at the age where he liked to question everything and everyone.

'I wasn't, Joey. Your dad is just trying to be a funny man. And failing miserably.'

I smiled at the good-natured teasing as I took a forkful of fish and chips. *Oh my God.*

'Didn't I tell you?' Michael looked over, smiling.

'That's soooo good!' I said, covering my mouth with my hand as I broke etiquette and spoke with my mouth full.

'You think I'd lie to you?'

I chewed and swallowed. 'No. I just...wouldn't put it past you to exaggerate occasionally.'

'Oh, he definitely does that,' Patrick grinned.

'You know we could get Janey to divorce you if we wanted.' Michael pointed his fork at him.

Patrick's eyes danced with laughter, his mouth full of chips.

'Mummy, are you getting divorced from Daddy?' Lily's voice was tiny and heartbreaking. We all looked over to where she was tucked in at the table, a couple of cushions piled on the chair to help her reach. The big green eyes, so like her mother's, were shimmering with unshed tears.

Janey reached out a hand to her daughter. 'No, sweetheart. Of course we're not! Uncle Mikey and Daddy were just being silly.'

I looked over at Michael. Already pale from the pain of the accident, he seemed to have greyed even more and was now resting his elbow on the table, his hand over his mouth as he realised what he'd done, his eyes focused intently on his little niece. The chair scraped and he limped quickly around the table towards her.

'Mikey,' Janey warned.

Ignoring her, Michael pulled the little girl's chair out and scooped her up into his arms, his jaw clenching against the pain the movement caused. Instinctively, Lily clasped her hands around his neck and burrowed her face into the curve of his shoulder.

'I'm sorry, sweetheart. It was just your Uncle Mikey being silly. Mummy and Daddy are very happy and love each other so, so much. You'll all be together for a long time yet, OK?'

A sniff came from his shoulder area.

'But you got divorced.'

Michael closed his eyes briefly. 'I did, Lily. But that was because I didn't marry the right girl. Your dad married exactly the right girl.'

His niece lifted her head and studied him for a moment. 'You promise?'

'I promise.'

She reached a hand out and played with his hair where it was curling onto his collar.

'Who should you have married instead, Uncle Mikey?'

'Ah, well that's the million dollar question, sweet pea.' He cuddled her for a few more minutes before lowering her back onto the chair. Tucking her back in, he crouched down beside her. I saw Janey tense as we all saw what the movements were costing him.

'You OK now?' he asked Lily.

She nodded.

'Your chips still hot?' He stole one to try and she giggled. 'How about I go warm them up for you?'

Lily nodded again.

Michael stood and leant to take the plate, his face pale behind the smile for his niece.

'I'll do it,' I said, pushing my chair out. 'I'm finished anyway. I can get you some more painkillers on the way.'

'I'm fine, Katie. Honestly.'

I met his eyes. Yep. Totally not fine. 'Go and sit down. I'm not getting lumbered finishing this house on my own just because you made yourself worse.'

Without waiting for an answer, I took Lily's plate, then swiped Michael's too and took them across to the kitchen to stick in the microwave for a couple of minutes. I got a glass of water, a couple of the painkillers from the box he'd used earlier and then put the packet back up on a high shelf just in case the children wandered in later. The microwave beeped and I unstacked the dishes and put them on a tray I'd managed to unearth.

Pausing at the kitchen door, I smiled at the laughter drifting from the adjacent room. The sound of it reminded me of what I'd always wanted. And what I'd never had. Pushing those thoughts from my mind, I nudged the dining-room door open and entered the room. It made me smile to take in the scene. The room being used for what it had been originally intended: people being together, enjoying the house, enjoying each other's company, enjoying good food.

Placing the tray on the table, I unloaded the plates and glass. Putting Michael's dinner in front of him, I handed him the tablets and the glass of water.

'Thank you.'

'Take them now so that they can get to work.'

'I seem to remember you saying something about this process not being about me obeying you.'

'I didn't think you could handle the truth at the time.'

The smile that appeared relaxed his face.

'So what is the truth?'

'That sometimes it will be about obeying me. Now take those tablets and finish your food whilst it's hot.'

His smile widened.

Janey clipped him around the top of his hair.

'What was that for?'

'For whatever you were thinking.'

'How do you know what I was thinking?'

Janey gave him a look.

121

I carried on round the table to Lily and left the siblings to it.

'Here you go. All nice and hot again.'

'Thank you, Katie.'

'You're welcome,' I smiled, running a hand over Lily's curls before returning to my seat.

'Uncle Mikey?'

'Mmmhmm?' Michael smiled at his niece in answer, his mouth full of battered fish.

'I wish you'd married Katie. She's nice.'

Michael continued chewing his food, his face giving nothing away.

'So what exactly happened this afternoon, then, with the bike, I mean?' Patrick asked, deftly changing the subject. I could have kissed him.

* * *

'This room is looking great,' Janey said to me as she took a walk around the room after dinner, stretching her back and rubbing her baby bump. She stopped at the dresser and looked at the photos I'd rearranged earlier.

'Was that the Iron Man challenge?' she asked, holding the photo up to Michael and Patrick.

'Yeah. God, that nearly killed me.' Patrick looked at his brother-in-law. 'Remind me never to listen to anything you say again if it starts with the words "I've got a great idea".'

'Oh, you loved it!' Janey said, laughing. 'Look at your little face in this.'

'Tears of a clown,' Patrick replied.

'Or maybe just a clown,' Michael added.

'Ah, look at that,' his sister picked up another frame. 'I love this one of you and little Monty.'

'He was hardly little.'

'No. But he thought he was. He loved sitting on your lap. It was adorable.'

'Some people found it less so.'

Janey sniffed. 'Yes, well. There's no accounting for taste. I don't know why you don't get another dog. You loved that mutt to bits. It'd be great company for you.'

I turned and met Michael's gaze with a triumphant look.

He just gave a little shake of his head, rolled his eyes and turned back to concentrate on Lily, who was now trying to crawl her way up onto his lap.

Chapter Nine

'Sorry about the awkward moment earlier,' Janey said, as I helped her back into her coat. Lily was now sleeping in her father's arms and they were about to head home.

'Oh, don't worry about it.'

'One of Lily's friend's has parents going through a divorce at the moment and let's just say, I don't think it's amicable. The poor little thing understands enough but not enough, if you know what I mean. And since her friend has been coming in upset, Lily has developed a fear that Patrick and I are going to split up.'

'I suppose that's understandable in a way.'

'Oh, totally. We're just trying to reassure her that it's all OK.'

'I think most children worry about their parents splitting up at some point.'

'Sadly, you're probably right.'

Michael and Patrick joined us, little Joey holding his uncle's hand. Michael leant over and kissed his niece's temple. She barely stirred.

'I'm so sorry about earlier. I didn't think.'

'It's all right. We know you're an idiot and that we have to make allowances for you at times.'

Michael pulled a face, kissed the top of his sister's head and touched her bump. 'Look after yourself.'

'I might say the same to you. I'll be asking Katie here to report back, you know.'

'A spy in the camp, eh?' Michael winked at me.

'Not a very good one, I'm afraid. I haven't another appointment with him for a few days now, which hopefully will give him time to rest a little at least.'

'Is that a hint or another order?'

'I don't mind how you take it so long as you do it.'

Janey grinned. 'See? I knew she was the one for you.' She looked up from pulling on her gloves to find us both looking at her.

'I meant for this!' she said, waving her hand around to indicate the house. 'For this job. She won't be putting up with any of your lip.'

'I never give anyone lip.'

I snorted. Michael ignored me.

'If you say so. Either way, it's incredible the difference she's making already.'

Patrick hoisted Lily a little higher, her arms dangling over his shoulders. 'Definitely. I love the dining room now. With those bookshelves in there and so much less clutter, it's really beginning to look like a home, Mikey. The woman is a miracle worker.'

I laughed. 'Hardly. But we're getting there.'

'Still got those ugly as sin curtains in the living room though, I see.' Janey wrinkled her nose.

Michael frowned. 'Since when don't you like them?'

'Since always! They're so wrong for that room. Don't tell me you like them?'

'No, I don't.'

His sister looked at him, questioning.

'I know! I know! They're coming down tomorrow.'

I put a hand on Michael's arm. 'Well, maybe not tomorrow but soon. I don't think stretching about lifting heavy curtains will do much for your injuries right now.'

'Listen to her.' Janey pointed at him.

He gave a little salute, but I could see the strain of the day beginning to show on his face.

'Now, are you lot ever leaving?' He clapped Patrick on the shoulder, thanking him for coming round and telling him he'd see him at the rugby club, even though he wouldn't be playing. Joey gave his uncle a hug around the waist and then transferred his hand to his mother's as they left the house. We stood and waved before Michael, having waited until they'd got to the car, closed the door against the freezing air that was making us both shiver.

'I'd better be going too,' I said. 'I'll just nip and get the bits from the dining room and put them in the kitchen for you.'

Michael caught my arm as I made to turn.

'Katie, I'm not an invalid and you're not my maid.'

I blinked. 'I know that. But it won't take a minute.'

He didn't let go.

'OK. This obey thing? Does it go both ways?'

'No.'

'Why did I have a feeling you were going to say that?'

I smiled.

'I'll clear the stuff in a minute. If I don't move around, I'll stiffen up and everything will feel twice as bad. Believe me, I know from experience.'

Reluctantly, I stepped back to get my coat. 'You should go and have a soak. That might help.'

'Sounds like a good idea.'

'Don't fall asleep in there though.'

Michael tilted his head and sighed. 'Do you ever stop worrying about other people?'

'I'm not worried. I'm just saying.'

'Right.' He took my coat from me and helped me put it on. As l looked up from belting it tightly, I shook my head.

'What?' he asked. 'Although from the look on your face, I'm not sure I really want to know.'

'No, it's nothing. I was just remembering our first encounter.'

'Not, perhaps, my finest moment.'

'Don't worry. You've improved a little.'

'You haven't. You still drive me nuts.'

'Good. It means the plan is working.'

'The plan?'

'Yes. Basically, I annoy you so much that you do what I tell you to, just to get all this over and done with as soon as possible.'

'I see. Just one thing.'

'What's that?' I asked, pulling my scarf back down from my face so that I could speak.

'You don't annoy me so much these days.'

'Huh. Guess I'll have to try harder then.'

He smiled and took the door from me as I opened it.

'And think some more about getting a dog,' I said, turning back to him from the top of the second step. 'It'd be good for you.'

'Kate?'

'Yes?'

'You're annoying me now.'

'Excellent. Goodnight, Michael.'

'Night, Katie. And thank you for today.'

'You're welcome,' I called, my voice getting lost in the wind whipping around the bare branches of the plane tree on the boundary of his property. I waved instead and made a shooing motion with my hand, indicating he should get back inside. He raised a hand and I did the same, before bending my head against the wind and battling down the road towards the Tube.

***

During the process of organising a house, there are occasionally times when people are unsure about getting rid of an item because of the memories attached to it. I'd seen people chuck out everything, declaring that it was an entirely fresh start, but then a few months later, regretting that they no longer had those love letters or that photo or that piece of jewellery because, although there'd been pain in those memories, there had also been joy. What I liked to advise in such circumstances was that I put the items in storage for a set amount of time, and then, having had that distance, and living 'without' those possessions for a while, the client could make a less emotional decision as to whether to keep or discard. Obviously, I only had a tiny office so storage space was limited but I did what I could, and explained this to every client during the process. And, in truth, it wasn't something that happened very often. Deep down, most people knew what the right decision was.

'But you said you could look after things that were sentimental, until I decided,' my client said, confusion on her face.

'Umm, yes. I did say that.'

She looked at me. I looked at the bag.

'It's just that it's usually items like photographs or an engagement ring. Items that spark memories…'

Not items that spark Richter scale orgasms!

'Oh, my dear. These do spark memories! Wonderful memories! There was one time I particularly remember when – '

'OK! No problem. Of course, I can take them,' I said, interrupting.

'Oh, you are a poppet, thank you! Gerald, God rest his soul, and I had such fun with these but, I have to say, Antonio is really quite resourceful, so I'm not sure I'm going to be needing them any more, but I'm not sure I can throw them away just yet. Do you know, the other night, he – '

'Oh, I'm sorry, that's my phone. Do you mind?'

Normally, during my time with clients, I just let my phone calls roll to voicemail but right now I needed an escape. Bernice had said she'd call after the meet with her new client and let me know how it had gone. Glancing at the clock, she was right on time, in more ways than one. I grabbed the phone out of my bag and answered it, stepping into the hallway as I did so.

'Perfect timing! I could kiss you!'

There was a moment of silence.

'Well, don't let me stop you.'

Oh! Bugger.

I pulled the phone away from my ear and checked the screen, something I clearly should have done before answering it. Michael O'Farrell.

'Sorry, I thought you were Bernice.'

'Oh really?' I could hear he was smiling.

'Not like that. It's just…never mind. How can I help you?'

'I just wondered if you had any spare time today?'

'Is everything all right?'

'Oh. Yeah. Fine, fine. I just wanted a bit of…umm… advice.'

'Michael?'

'Hmm?'

'What have you done?'

His laugh made me smile.

'It's worrying that you know me as well as you do.'

Who was I to tell him that most of the time I had no idea what was going on behind those hypnotic eyes? But if he was under the impression he couldn't get anything past me, then I wasn't about to shatter any illusions.

'So?'

'I thought I'd make a start on the kitchen.'

'And?'

'And I have no idea what I'm doing. You have to help me! I don't even know what half of this stuff is for, let alone whether I need it. And now the place is in even more of a state than it started in.'

'I find that hard to believe.'

'So cruel.'

I laughed. 'Look, I'm just finishing up with a client. I was going to catch up on some stuff in the office this afternoon but I can come round to you for a couple of hours if it's an emergency.'

There was a pause. 'Let's say I don't think it's good.'

'Right. Just step away from whatever it is you've done so far and we'll tackle it together. Give me an hour. Is that OK?'

'Perfect. Thanks, Katie.'

'You're welcome. I'll see you in a bit.'

'Bye.'

130

I hung up and returned to my client.

'Sorry about that, Mrs B.'

'Not to worry, dear. So you don't mind looking after these for me for a little while then?'

My gaze fell on the bag again. The old adage about always making sure you had clean underwear on just in case you got knocked down by a bus suddenly sprang into my head. My logical mind had always had a problem with that scenario as I was sure seeing a double decker hurtling towards you probably didn't do a lot for the state of your underwear anyway, whether it had started out clean or not. But right now, I was pondering a similar scenario. What if I got knocked down by a bus and this lot tumbled out of my bag? I'd be praying for the driver to back over me and end the mortification.

'Dear?'

'Sorry? Oh yes, yes, of course. No problem whatsoever. I can keep it until the New Year and then you can make a decision and let me know.'

'Perfect. Thank you so much.'

I took the bag and stuffed it in my oversized shoulder bag.

'I'm so happy with what you've helped me achieve here, Kate. I can't thank you enough.'

'You're very welcome, Mrs B. I'm so pleased you're happy.'

'You're a good girl, Kate. I don't know why you're not snapped up, pretty little thing like you. I don't know what these young men are about these days.'

'That's all right, Mrs B. I'm really in no hurry to settle down with anyone.'

She reached out and patted my hand. 'I expect you know what's best for you. I'm probably just a little old-fashioned.'

This coming from a woman who had just handed me a bag with two nine-inch vibrators, one of which claimed 'lifelike properties', a pair of handcuffs (and I'm not talking the gentle fluffy kind), a butt plug, a flogger and a spanking paddle (her favourite item, apparently). Honestly, I really could have done without the itemisation but my lovely, and now super-organised, client had insisted. I made a non-committal noise.

'I'm sure once you meet the right man, you'll feel differently.'

I smiled and changed the subject. 'I'd best be off then.'

Mrs B followed me to the door. 'Have a lovely Christmas, my dear. Are you spending it with family?'

'Oh, just having a quiet one this year.' I trotted out my usual response to this enquiry. 'I'll contact you in the first few weeks of January and you can decide about your...items.'

'Lovely. Thank you, dear. Bye bye now.'

'Bye, Mrs B.'

I set off towards the nearest station, acutely aware of my luggage. Who knew a shopping bag full of sex toys could weigh so much? As I approached the entrance to the station, my phone began to ring and I pulled it out of my bag, being careful not to dislodge anything else. This time I checked the screen before answering.

'Hi Bernice. How'd it go?'

'Brilliant! I'm so excited. And the client is so excited. Everyone's excited! I think it's going to be great. And she said if it goes well, she has a whole bunch of friends to recommend to us.'

'Excellent!'

'How was Mrs B?'

'Erm...OK. Apart from the fact that she gave me a big bag full of sex toys to keep for storage whilst she decides if she needs them any more.'

I thought for a moment my phone had lost signal and pulled it away to check. It was still showing connected. Then I heard Bernice taking short gasps as she tried to stop laughing.

'I don't believe you!' she said eventually.

'Oh, believe me.'

'But she looks like one of the nanas that knit Shredded Wheat! What would she know about sex toys?'

'Apparently she's quite the expert! And now I know way more than I ever wanted to as she insisted on telling me the pros and cons of every item in the bag.'

'Wow! I never would have thought it!'

'Me neither. I thought I was past being shocked and it's hardly the first time I've pulled a vibrator out of a drawer.' A man walking in front of me did a double take. 'It's just that when you look at her...'

'No, I know! I kind of fancied her as a surrogate gran but you've shattered all my illusions now.'

'Sorry about that.'

'Not your fault. Are you on your way back in now?'

'No, I'm heading over to Michael O'Farrell. He called and asked if I could come over to help him wrangle the kitchen. It sounds like he's started and got a bit overwhelmed.'

'Not unusual.'

'No.'

'OK. Give him a snog whilst you're at it.'

'So not going to happen.'

'Shame.'

'Hardly.'

'Talk to you later.'

'Bye!'

* * *

'Thanks for this. I know it wasn't one of the scheduled appointments but I wasn't quite sure what to do.' Michael took my coat and hung it on one of the hooks. I noticed several of his were alongside instead on being chucked on the console table or floor, as they usually were.

'It's all right. What's the problem?'

'Well, I've been watching you and you make it seem so easy, so I thought I'd have a go at the kitchen. You know, how hard could it be?' I tilted my head back to meet his eyes. 'Turns out it's harder than I thought.'

'I suppose I'd better take a look then.'

Michael stood aside and I walked into the kitchen. Or at least as far in as I could get, which wasn't very far at all.

'I see.'

'It's bad, isn't it?' His gravel-edged, melodic voice was close behind me.

'No. It's…I've definitely seen worse.'

He laughed. 'Things must be improving between us because you wouldn't have cared about being diplomatic before.'

I turned, finding him closer than I thought but unable to take a step back because of all the crap on the kitchen floor. He caught my arm as I wobbled momentarily.

'I…'

I swallowed as the scent of his aftershave mixed with soap teased my senses. He let his hand slide gently down my arm until it finally just lay wrapped loosely around my wrist. And, disturbingly, that felt insanely good.

'You all right? You look a bit flushed.'

Bloody Mrs B.

I nodded several times. 'Absolutely. Cold out there, hot in here.'

'It is pretty warm in here, no doubt about that.'

I kicked something out of the way and casually took a step back. Michael didn't move, but his hand dropped away from my wrist.

'I'm always diplomatic.'

'Calling me an arse was diplomatic? Remind me not to send you to the Middle East to negotiate peace talks any time soon.'

'Oh ha ha! Are you going to bring that up every time we disagree?'

'I haven't decided yet.'

I rolled my eyes at him. 'Fine. You want the truth?'

'Always,' he said, looking at me, that intense gaze doing its thing again.

'Right,' I said, turning back to the kitchen and away from his entrancing eyes. 'Congratulations, you have succeeded in making it twice as bad.'

'That sounds more like it.'

I looked back at him. 'I wouldn't say that to anyone but you, you know that, don't you? Tact is my middle name.'

'I'm honoured to be special then.'

I shook my head. 'Oh, you're special all right.'

'Aww, I'm so glad you think so.'

'Oh for goodness' sake! Stop arsing about and help me find the kettle. I need a cup of tea before tackling this.' I dropped my bag outside the door and began trying to pick my way though the detritus on the floor.

Chapter Ten

We were knee-deep in kitchen utensils and Michael's face had taken on a bewildered look.

'I don't even know what this is. It looks like something liberated from a medieval torture chamber.'

I glanced up. He was peering at a scissor-like contraption with a half dome on each end. His fingers worked the mechanism and the two halves came together to form a globe.

'I think it's a meat baller.'

He looked at me, blankly.

'You know. For making meatballs.'

'She never once made meatballs. She barely ever cooked at all, actually. I can't believe there's all this stuff in here.'

'Kitchen gadget catalogues can be very enticing.'

'Really?'

'Yes. They make things sound so good that you wonder how you've lived without these wonderful inventions for so long.'

'Oh.' He paused, looking back at the item hooked on his finger and thumb again. 'So do you have a meat baller?' He snapped the ends together a couple of times and I giggled.

'I do not.'

'Do you want one?'

'I don't. Thanks all the same.'

'Not much of a meatball maker then?' He pulled the gadget off his fingers and tossed it into a box for donation.

'I just use my hands.'

'Usually the best tools,' he said. 'Do you cook a lot?'

'When I get time. And have the inclination.'

He nodded acceptance. 'Did your mum teach you how to cook?'

I cleared my throat a little. 'No, not really. She wasn't really much of a cook. I taught myself really. It's not rocket science. If you can watch telly and you can read, then you can usually make something edible.'

'That's true.'

We continued in silence for a few more moments.

'You said "wasn't".'

'Huh?'

'You said "wasn't". Is your mum not around any more?'

'No, she died about ten years ago.'

'I'm sorry.'

'It's fine.'

'And your dad?'

'He lives abroad. I don't see him.'

Michael nodded, obviously getting the point that this wasn't a subject I wanted to talk about. For some reason, I wanted to tell him not to take it personally and that I didn't really talk about any of this stuff with anyone. Janey was an exception but I'd only told her everything accidentally thanks to a second bottle of wine and a particularly crappy day.

'Do you cook?' I asked, then glanced up at the state of the kitchen. 'When you can find the oven, of course?'

He gave me a tilted head, you're-being-a-smart-arse type of look and smiled.

'I'm not bad. Ma taught us all, wanting to make sure that we didn't starve when she sent us out into the world.'

'That's good.'

'Yeah, I don't mind it actually. Although I'm kind of rusty at the moment. I've not really done a lot for a while. I'm going to have to brush up if I'm to make anything decent for Christmas dinner.'

'I'm sure the others will help you out if you get stuck.'

'Probably. Or they may just sit and enjoy watching me struggle and squirm. You know, like brothers and sisters do.'

I smiled. I didn't know.

Michael picked up on my non-committal reply. 'No siblings?'

I shook my head.

'Did you not find that lonely growing up?'

'That's everything from those drawers,' I said, changing the subject. 'Do you want to start going through them and see what you think you might want to keep?'

Michael gave me a long look, aware that I had blatantly directed the conversation away from anything personal and back to work.

'OK,' he said, eventually. 'On the proviso that you're able to tell me what most of these things are so that I can make an informed decision.'

I smiled, trying to make up for having blanked his question about my childhood. 'I can certainly try.'

A short while later, Michael had just stepped out to take a call and was returning when my own phone, still tucked in my bag, began to ring. Engaged in trying to find all the parts of a cutlery set, I had my head down, knowing for sure that I'd seen a bunch of teaspoons around somewhere.

'Do you want me to grab that?' Michael called from the hallway.

'If you like,' I answered, distractedly. 'Aha! There you are!' I said, fishing out four teaspoons from under an upturned clay flowerpot.

'Holy shit!'

I looked up at his exclamation.

'Whatever's the...Oh no! No no no!' My horrified expression met his amused one as he entered the kitchen. In one hand he held my phone, which had by now stopped ringing, and in the other the bag I'd taken from Mrs B for safekeeping.

I snapped out of my shock and scrambled over, snatching the bag from his hand.

'It fell out when I grabbed the phone. Sorry.' He didn't sound sorry. At all. 'It's always the quiet ones, they say.'

'They're not mine.' I faced him and drew myself up. 'And even if they were, I'd have nothing to be ashamed about.'

'That's true. You're a modern, emancipated woman. Who looks ever so cute when she blushes.'

'Arrgh!' I gave him a shove to move him from the doorway and rammed the plastic bag down to the bottom of my tote. His laughter followed me out to the hallway and I couldn't help the smile that formed at the sound of it.

Returning to the kitchen, I went back to what I had been doing. Two minutes later, Michael spoke.

'Seriously?'

'Seriously, what?' I asked, looking up at him.

He gave a nod towards the hallway. 'You're not going to explain that?'

'Nope.'

'Oh, come on!'

'What?'

'Are they yours?'

'I already told you they weren't.'

'I know, but I thought you were maybe just being defensive, being caught on the hop, so to speak.'

'No, they're not. But even so, if I want to tote around a bag full of Ann Summers' best, then surely that's up to me?' I was doing my best to keep a straight face, but the odd thing was, contrary to what I had ever believed possible at our first meeting, I was enjoying the banter with him.

'Absolutely. And it certainly explains one thing?'

'What's that?'

'Why you're not so bothered about the fact you don't see your boyfriend all that much.'

I narrowed my eyes at him.

'Perhaps I could leave one of them here. You know, just in case? We wouldn't want any of your "visitors",' I made quotes in the air with my fingers, 'leaving disappointed.'

His mouth pulled to the side a little, amused. 'Oh, don't you be worrying about that.'

'Just trying to help.'

'Of course you are.'

I smiled and put my head down to get back to work.

Michael was emptying the taller cupboards, as instructed. His height meant he didn't have to use a stepladder like I did, so the process was much quicker. But two minutes later he broke the silence again.

'Oh come on, Katie! This is killing me!'

I turned from wiping out the now empty cutlery drawer to where Michael was now leaning on his worktop, piles of crockery surrounding him.

'What is?'

'Why you're carrying all that...stuff. Do you have another job I'm unaware of?'

I rolled my eyes. 'Why do you care?'

'Because I'm interested in you.'

The smile on my face faltered for a moment. 'Why?'

'What do you mean, why? It's not every day a woman walks into my house, secretly armed for combat.'

Why I thought he was being anything than intrigued at the situation, I don't know. Although the bigger question currently bouncing around my brain was about the weird feeling I'd got when he'd clarified his area of interest. If I didn't know better, I'd have called it disappointment, which was ridiculous. Of course, I wasn't disappointed that my client's interest in me didn't go any deeper. It was fine. More than fine. Ideal, in fact. And hardly surprising, anyway. All right, Michael O'Farrell and I were definitely in a better place than we had been, but we weren't exactly best buddies, and he certainly wouldn't be interested in me. It was clear that his interests, when it came to women, were of the knockout stunning kind and although I did OK, I definitely wasn't anywhere near that category. And I generally liked my relationships to last more than one night which was another thing we disagreed on, apparently. And he drove me nuts. And I drove him nuts. So...what was I even doing thinking about all this stuff?

'Katie?'

'Huh?'

'You were miles away.' He almost looked concerned.

'Oh...no. I was just thinking of...um...'

Michael raised an eyebrow and I could see the grin he was struggling to stifle.

'For goodness' sake. They are a client's, OK? Sometimes, when people can't quite decide as to whether there is something they should throw away, I'll keep it for a few weeks until their head is a little clearer on it and then they decide. Admittedly, it's usually something like a wedding album or a bunch of old love letters, but I am nothing if not adaptable.'

'So I see.'

'Do you think you can focus on something else now?'

'I don't know. I have to say it was all quite shocking for a man of my delicate disposition. I might need a lie down. If you could see yourself to placing a cool flannel on my head and saying "there, there" occasionally, I might just recover.'

'I can see myself saying a lot more than that if you don't get your backside in gear in the next thirty seconds.'

'A man's got to try,' he said, opening another cupboard and reaching in to begin emptying it. 'I wouldn't want you to say I wasn't trying.'

'Somehow, I highly doubt anyone would ever say that about you.'

***

'Is this him?' I asked Mark as we approached the kennel.

'It is. Meet Rooney. What do you think?'

My smile gave him the answer.

'He's had a behaviour test and come through with flying colours. He's just a big, soppy dope really but he

142

loves to play. Having said that, he's equally happy to just snooze or lounge on you, so he's pretty adaptable. He's really good on the lead and off it, and comes back when he's called.'

'Why on earth is he here?'

'Got too big, apparently. They didn't realise that a Labrador Rottweiler cross might get bigger than a miniature poodle.'

I gave a head shake.

'At least they've trained him well.'

'I think it's really just his nature. He's a pleaser.'

'Has anyone shown an interest in him yet?'

'I've not put him on the website yet because he sounded exactly what you were after. But I don't want to keep him in kennels too long if I can get him out to a good home.'

'Of course not. Can we take him out?'

'Sure.' Mark opened the kennel and the dog loped towards us, nuzzling his head into my hand where the treat hid.

'Ooh, smart boy,' I said, holding my hand flat so that he could take it, which he did with the gentlest of movements.

'So he's good with kids too?'

'His owners said that he was, and the two little kids that came with him were clinging to him like they never wanted to let him go. He didn't react to it at all and all the tests we've done would indicate he pretty much gets on with anything and anybody. Does the potential new owner have kids then?'

'No, but I'd guess he might in the future, I don't know. But he does have nieces and nephews he's very close to, so it's vital that the dog is kiddie-friendly.'

'This one is everything friendly.'

From the way the dog had curled up and put his head on my lap as we sat on the floor talking, he certainly seemed that way.

I left Mark and took Rooney on a long walk, meeting plenty of dogs, people and livestock, and he behaved beautifully throughout. My excitement was mounting at the prospect of finding him a forever home.

'How was he?' Mark asked as he saw us plodding back in through the gate, the mud halfway up my wellies as the wind blew Rooney's ear inside out. I bent over and folded it back.

'Brilliant. I love him. I want him!' I laughed, honestly wishing that I really could take the dog home.

'He's a great mutt.'

'He is.'

'Do you think your friend will like him?'

'Client more than a friend. But I hope so. Although he is adamant he doesn't want another dog.'

Mark looked at me.

'What?'

'You know people have to get a dog when it's right for them. If it's not the right time, it'll only end up bad for everyone involved. He's too good a dog to be messed about.'

'I know.'

Mark didn't seem convinced.

'I promise. He's not a man to do anything lightly so if he really doesn't want a dog, believe me, I'm the last person who'd be able to persuade him. I just want to, I don't know, remind him of what he's missing and how much happier he was when he had a pooch keeping him company.'

'OK. I'm not questioning your motives, you know that.'

'Of course I do. You want what's best for the animals. I do too. I promise.'

Mark flicked the bobble on my bobble hat. 'I know. So when can you get your guy down here?'

'Tomorrow? Can you hold him until then?'

'Sure. Let me know if anything changes.'

'Will do. Thanks again, Mark. I really appreciate it.'

'No problem.' He frowned up at a sky that was becoming increasingly leaden. 'I grew up with Bondi Beach and endless days of sunshine. What the hell am I doing?'

'Loving every bit of it.' I winked.

'You're smarter than you look, you know that?'

'You're not as funny as you think, you know that?'

He grinned and I did the same.

'OK. Better go and wash this boy off and get him looking super-duper for his visitor tomorrow.'

'Have fun. Give me a shout when you're ready to go and I'll whizz you to the station.'

'Oh, you don't need to do that.'

'You saw that, right?'

He turned me by the shoulders to face back out the way I'd come. The gentle, occasional flakes of snow that had tickled my eyelashes whilst out walking were now on the verge of a full-blown blizzard.

'Oh.'

'Yeah, "oh". Give me a shout. But make it quick. Even the Landy has her limits.'

'Will do. Thanks, Mark. Come, on Rooney. Let's get you spruced up.'

Chapter Eleven

Admittedly, Michael and I hadn't exactly hit it off the first time we met, but I had thought we'd got past that, especially as he'd been the one encouraging me to stay to have dinner with his family at the beginning of the week. Don't get me wrong, I was under no illusions that I was anything like his "type", and frankly, as his type nowadays seemed to be of the one-night stand variety, I had no wish to be. But I had thought we'd at least got to a point where, if I turned up outside an appointment time, I might be received with a teensy bit more enthusiasm than the blank look I was now getting.

'Hi,' I said, when it was clear he wasn't going to say anything.

Michael gave a start. 'Please don't tell me I forgot an appointment? Did we have something arranged for today? I could have sworn I'd put everything we had planned so far in my diary.' He pulled his phone out from his jeans pocket and began pulling up his calendar.

'No,' I said, reaching out to touch his arm and still the frantic searching. 'You didn't forget anything.'

Relief flooded his face. 'Thank goodness for that! I'm pretty sure even having Janey for a sister won't be enough to save me after another late show.'

'Let's not find out.'

'Sounds good to me. Anyway, come in.'

'Am I interrupting...anything?' His previous look had me suddenly debating how wise it had been to turn up unannounced on Michael's doorstep on a Sunday morning.

'Such as?' His expression was pure innocence. I didn't buy it for a moment.

I tilted my head. 'I didn't know if you had a...guest... or something.'

'Nope. I like to make sure they're out the door by seven-thirty at the latest, so you're fine.'

Wow. He had even bigger issues than I thought.

'Your face,' he said, shaking his head before turning towards the kitchen. 'Want a coffee?'

'Umm. OK, thanks. What's wrong with my face?' I said, struggling to unwrap my scarf and pull off my gloves as I followed him. Head down, I didn't realise he'd stopped and I bounced off him.

His arms quickly reached out, steadying me. He waited a beat and then let them drop. 'There's nothing wrong with it. But your expression when you thought I kick out any overnight guests early in the morning was pretty priceless.'

'Well, I'm just saying it wouldn't come as a big surprise if you did.'

He paused in his coffee-making endeavours. 'You don't have a very high opinion of me, do you?'

'No! I mean, yes. I mean...that's not what I meant.'

Michael resumed his task. 'So what did you mean?'

What exactly did I mean?

'I...err, I don't know. Nothing really.' I kept a lightness to my tone and hoped he'd let it pass.

'If you think I'm going to believe that Miss Organise And Consider Everything just made an off-the-cuff remark without it meaning something, you're sadly mistaken. So, come on, spit it out.'

Why had I ever opened my mouth?

He turned and handed over a mug, locking his gaze onto me as he did so.

'You know, I really didn't...' Michael raised an eyebrow and I crumbled. 'OK fine,' I sighed. 'It's just that, from what I saw, you keep your bedroom very impersonal, which seems a little unusual. But then I remembered something Janey had mentioned about your...penchant for one-night stands, and then you saying about the fact they don't exactly get a tour of the house...Well, I guess it just wouldn't surprise me if you were one of those guys who wants a girl to leave as soon as dawn breaks.'

He considered my answer for a moment and then took a sip of coffee, watching me over the rim of the mug.

'Like I say, you don't have a very high opinion of me.'

'That's not true. But you must admit, it's not unreasonable that I'd think that, bearing in mind you told me yourself you ushered the owner of that tiny thong out of your house at some ungodly hour the following morning.'

His jaw tightened for a moment. 'There were special circumstances that time. As I explained to you.'

'You did. But there are men who would always find a "special circumstance".'

148

'And you consider me to be such a man?'

'No. Not necessarily. I'm just trying to show you how it might be easy for someone to form that opinion of you, from the information at hand.'

Michael took a deep breath, his expression unreadable. 'So, if I haven't missed an appointment, to what do I owe the pleasure today?'

I was pretty sure 'pleasure' was an overstatement, considering how I'd just blurted out that I thought he was a cold-hearted shag monkey who kicked his choice of the night out at first light. Even though I wasn't entirely sure that's what I did think. To be honest, most of the time he still had me baffled.

'Well, first of all, I wanted to see how you were feeling, after the accident?'

'Much better, thanks. Ribs are still a little sore but the rest is pretty much back to normal.

I'd noticed he was barely limping at all and his movements seemed far less stiff than they had done at the beginning of the week.

'That's great.'

'And second of all?'

Hmm. What had initially seemed like a brilliant idea yesterday, and pretty much until I had stepped inside the house, now seemed a little...ambitious. Not to mention awkward.

'I...'

He fixed me with that look again but I could see the barest hint of a smile teasing his lips. I took a deep breath.

'I found you a dog.'

His face lost the smile.

'Kate, I told you I'm not interested.' He turned away.

'I know you did. I just think if you saw Rooney – '

'And I am definitely not taking on a dog called Rooney.'

'You could change his name. I'm sure he wouldn't mind.'

Michael turned back to face me. 'You don't think he'd mind?' he repeated, bemusement clear on his face this time.

'Please,' I said, putting my hand on his arm, 'please, just come and see him?'

'Katie, I appreciate everything you're doing. But I won't change my mind. I'm sorry you've had a wasted journey out here.'

I thought of Rooney's gorgeous face, the joy I'd felt fill my soul at his loping about in the fields as we played, the warmth of his body as he snuggled up to me when I brushed him after washing him off following our walk.

'OK,' I said, changing my tactic. 'Then how about Sunday lunch? I mean, only if you don't have plans or anything.'

'Sunday lunch? You and me?'

He sounded a little more incredulous than I might have hoped and I did my best not to take offence.

'Yes. To celebrate how much you've achieved so far with the house.'

He was still just studying me. I shifted under his gaze, forcing myself not to scoot out of there as fast as I could. I just hoped that Rooney appreciated all the embarrassment I was currently going through for his cause. A thought suddenly crept into my brain.

'It's nothing...weird. You know, I'm not hitting on you or anything.'

'I wouldn't think for a moment that you were. I've a far too untidy character to fit into that tidy,

150

compartmentalised way of living that you seem to favour.'

I didn't say anything. Basically because he was right – that was the way I lived and it worked for me. It clearly wasn't something that would work for him but, then again, he had his family around him. The circumstances were entirely different and I wasn't about to defend myself against him.

'You're probably right.' My hopes for Rooney were fading.

'I do, however, get the feeling you're up to something.' He was looking at me, his head tilted a little, signs of intrigue showing on his face. I could work with that.

I put my hand on my chest and widened my eyes in innocence, which at least brought a smile.

'So where exactly did you have in mind for this lunch?'

'There's a great pub I know. It's a little outside London, but they do the best Sunday roasts. I think you'll love it.'

'OK,' he said, slowly, apparently still unconvinced that my motives were pure. Although they really were. Kind of.

'So you'll come?' I couldn't help smiling. 'Great. We should get going then.' I made to move towards the door.

Leaning against the doorframe, Michael folded his arms, the action pulling the old T-shirt he wore tighter across his chest. My mind flew back to the other day when I'd seen exactly what was under that shirt. I swallowed and pushed the image away, moving towards the door. But Michael didn't move. I raised my eyes to find him watching me.

151

'What is it?'

'I've got a couple of questions before you drag me out of my nice warm house into the snow.'

'It's actually stopped now and they said the roads are clear.' I glanced towards the window. Admittedly the sky didn't look all that promising. 'For the moment, anyway.'

Michael didn't reply.

'OK, fine. What are the questions?' I asked.

'Are you getting tetchy?'

Yes.

'No. Is that one of the questions?'

Think of Rooney. It's all for a good cause. Even though this man drives you round the bend, you know he'd be a perfect match for that dog.

'Liar. And no. It's an extra one.'

I took a deep breath.

'What would you like to ask?'

'Firstly, it's Sunday morning.'

'It is.'

'So why aren't you lounging in bed with Conor or Colin or whatever his name is, reading the papers and eating bacon sarnies?'

'Isn't that a little personal?'

'I'm sorry? Didn't you just ask me if I was doing the same thing when I opened the door?'

'Not at all. I just wanted to make sure that I wasn't disturbing you.'

'Which you were.'

I dropped my head, feeling that I was on a losing battle here. I ran my hand over my eyes, suddenly feeling like a complete idiot.

'Look, I'm sorry, I – '

Michael's hand caught mine.

'That doesn't mean to say all disturbances are unwelcome. I'm sorry. I'm not the most sociable these days and I'm a little out of practice.'

'No, you're totally right. I really should have called first.'

'It's fine, and you're here now. Which is nice. Even though I'm still sure you're up to something.' He let go of my hand.

'His name is Calum. And he's out of the country at the moment, working. But to be honest, I'm not one for lounging in bed, reading the papers. They're too depressing most of the time.'

'So read something else then.'

'There's far too much to do to be lounging around.'

'Rubbish. It's what Sunday mornings were invented for. Just don't tell my grandma. She's under the impression we still all go to Mass first thing.'

'Really?'

'Pretty sure.'

'Wow.'

He smiled. 'What?'

'I just wondered how she's going to react when she finds out her grandson isn't a cassock-wearing altar boy but a boxer-wearing lothario who lounges around in bed on Sunday mornings, eating bacon sandwiches.'

'She'll get over it. More to the point, how do you know my preference for underwear?'

'I was guessing. You don't look like a Y-fronts kind of guy. Thank goodness.'

He grinned and I blushed.

'I mean. Not that it makes any difference to me. Although they do say that it's more healthy to wear boxers than other, more restrictive, styles of underwear.'

What the hell was I saying? More to the point, why the hell was I saying it? And to Michael O'Farrell of all people?

'Apparently,' I added, casually.

'I appreciate the information.'

Oh God. If a random sinkhole appeared beneath my feet right now, I wouldn't complain. I waited a moment but nothing happened. It looked like I was actually going to have to deal with the aftermath of my ramblings. Bugger.

'So, if that answers the first question, what's the second one?' I aimed for a nonchalant air, as if I hadn't just had a conversation with an incredibly gorgeous client about his underwear preferences.

He let out a breath of air in amusement, and shook his head, but did, thankfully, let the subject drop.

'This pub?'

'Yes?'

'It wouldn't be anywhere near an animal rescue centre, would it?'

Uh oh. Rumbled.

'That's what I thought,' he replied, even though I'd not said a word.

I looked up.

'Your face said it all.'

I let out a sigh. 'How come you can do that? I've always been pretty good at hiding what I'm thinking and then you come along and keep...outing me!'

He stared at me for a moment and then laughed a deep, rich rumble than spread up from his chest and filled the room.

'Outing you?'

'Yes! It's really annoying.'

'Why? Because you want to hide stuff from me?'

'Sometimes!'

'Too bad.' He scooped an arm around my shoulders and squeezed. 'Come on. Let's go and find this pub.'

'Really?' My hopes for Rooney suddenly reignited.

He looked down at me, his arm still slung around my shoulders. When he spoke, his voice was soft. 'Why not?'

'It's not too long on the train.'

'It's OK. I can drive us.'

I stepped back, forcing his arm to drop. 'Thank you, but no. I don't do motorbikes. Not to mention you might be feeling better, but if you think getting back on that thing right now is a good idea, then...' My eyes widened as Michael put two fingers on my lips.

'I've got a car. We'll take that.'

I nodded.

He dropped his hand, momentarily looking awkward. 'Sorry. You were kind of on a roll and I didn't know how to stop you. I thought about putting my hand across your mouth but figured that might result in me nursing some bruising lower on my body than my ribs.'

'You figured right. Do you mind driving?' I asked, changing the subject. I did my best to ignore the rush of warmth I'd felt as Michael placed his fingers on my lips, and that the feel of his touch still tingled on my mouth.

'Not at all. That way, if the weather turns we can head back immediately, rather than be at the mercy of the trains.'

'Good idea.'

'Give me a second to change. I had a clean T-shirt down here somewhere.' He started hunting around. My gaze landed on a pile of laundry sort of folded near the dryer.

'Here.' I picked one off the top and tossed it across to him. 'We really need to sort your clothes this week. Normally I'd have done that first.'

'So why didn't you?' Michael asked as he yanked his T-shirt off.

I thought it best to turn away this time. If I didn't know better, I'd call this feeling misplaced lust. Calum had been so busy lately and then with this trip abroad, we'd hardly had any time together. I'd never consider doing anything about it, of course. And I knew Michael certainly wouldn't. But it was pretty hard for anyone to miss that my client was classically, drop dead gorgeous, not to mention the owner of a body that, should he ever take up going to Mass again on a Sunday morning, may have a few nuns rethinking their career choice. I started folding the clothing piled above the dryer whilst I waited.

'Because,' I answered, distracting myself, 'when you first gave me the tour of the house, you clearly didn't want me anywhere near your bedroom.'

'You don't have to do that. You're off duty, remember?' I turned back to find Michael dressed in the clean T-shirt and pulling on a baseball cap. 'You should have told me you had a system.'

'I adapt things for each client anyway. And for you, I felt that getting your office in order was the best place to start. It would give you a better working environment, and hopefully, would show you what a difference doing the same in the rest of the house would make.'

'I see. Sneaky.'

'Call it what you like if it worked.'

He adjusted his hat. 'It did. Come on.'

Rummaging under a pile of stuff, he eventually located his keys. 'You know. All this never used to bother me. And now it does.'

'Good. That means you'll be even more keen to change it and then keep it that way.'

'But in the meantime, you're just adding more frustration to my life.' His voice had changed and I looked up, meeting his eyes.

'That isn't my intention, I promise. And soon it'll be done and I'll be out of your hair. I promise. We're on schedule and you've been brilliant, despite your initial misgivings. Honestly, there's no need to worry. Things will be perfect come Christmas.'

Michael gave a little frown. For a moment he looked like he was about to say something but instead he just nodded, before flashing a brief smile. One I noticed never reached those incredible eyes.

'Sure. Of course.'

He pulled the door shut behind us and we began walking towards the road.

'Just down here,' he said, pointing down the avenue towards a black pickup with the words M F O'FARRELL – ARCHITECT decaled on the side door. It didn't look like it had seen a bucket and sponge in a while. 'Sorry about the state of it,' Michael apologised. 'One of the jobs I'm working on is a bit out in the sticks.'

'It's fine. There aren't many clean cars around in this weather anyway, what with the snow and the salt. Besides, I'd rather you were driving a dirty pickup than a clean motorbike.'

'Aah, it's almost like you care.'

'Almost,' I replied, giving a tight smile, but I knew my eyes gave me away – at least with Michael.

157

He grinned and opened the door, waiting for me to settle myself before closing it and making his way around to the other side. Thankfully the truck's interior was fairly tidy. Which seemed odd.

'Uh oh,' Michael said, as he plugged in his seat belt and caught my glance.

'What?'

'Your brain is doing cartwheels.'

'Oh, sorry. Are you not used to women whose brains do that?'

He raised a dark brow. 'Ouch! Sharp as a knife, even on a Sunday. What I meant was you have something on your mind and I get the feeling it concerns me.'

'All right. I was just surprised that your car is quite tidy.'

'Does that mean it meets with your approval?'

I nodded. 'It does.'

'Do I get a gold star or something for that?' He turned the engine over and flicked on the heated seats, which began emitting their warmth almost immediately.

'No. You just get the relief of me not telling you to tidy your truck too.' I wriggled in the warm seat. 'Ooh lovely! Now that certainly isn't something the train offers.'

He gave me a little wink and pulled out onto the road, following the directions I gave him.

'Shall we eat first?' I suggested as we got closer.

'Sounds good. That way there's less chance of long, awkward silences because of the fact I haven't rehomed this dog.'

I rolled my eyes at him and he smiled.

Chapter Twelve

The warmth hit us as soon as we opened the door. Michael ducked the low beam and closed the heavy oak door behind him. To one side of the bar, a log fire burned brightly, the woody smell filling our nostrils. On the other side, a huge Christmas tree lavishly, if a little randomly, decorated touched the ceiling. Tinsel was pinned along the top of the bar and cards hung from string all around. It was busy, despite the weather, and we shuffled through the tables and people to get to the bar.

'Kate! What a lovely surprise! We haven't seen you in here for a few weeks now.' Linda, the landlady beamed. Her gaze locked behind me and I had a pretty good idea as to what, or rather who, had caught her eye. 'And now I can see exactly what's been keeping you busy. Good Lord, I don't blame you. You know darlin', our food is great here, but if it's a choice between that and staying in bed with him...' She'd dropped her voice to a whisper. Unfortunately, in order to allow for the general chatter of the pub, this was still pretty much normal volume for most people, which meant I was fairly sure Michael had heard every word. 'So, what I can get you?'

I looked round at Michael.

'Just a coke for me, thanks.'

'And a lime and soda for me, please. And do you have a table for two?'

'When for? Now?'

'If possible,' I smiled, hopeful. I didn't want to wait too long to get to the rescue centre so that we would still have plenty of time to take Rooney out before it got dark.

Linda patted my hand and gave me a wink. 'Leave it to me,' she said, giving Michael a broad smile which he returned before she disappeared off to the restaurant side of the pub.

'She seems nice.'

'Mmmhmm,' I agreed, hoping that he hadn't picked up on what Linda clearly thought was going on.

'You've been here a few times, then?'

'We come as a group sometimes, all the rescue centre workers and volunteers. Linda has had a couple of rescues from us and she's great at finding people who might be looking for a new pet too, so she's a good resource.'

'Looks like she's got us a table,' Michael said as Linda waved at us across the room.

'Great. I'm starving.'

'That's what happens when you don't have bacon sarnies in bed,' Michael whispered close to my ear as he bent to avoid another beam.

I looked round and his eyes were dancing with laughter. He wiggled his eyebrows and I couldn't help laughing.

'Harlot.'

'I try.'

I shook my head and scooched into the corner seat by the window that Linda had found us. Michael took the one opposite.

'Do you know what you want or do you want some time to look at the menu?' Linda asked.

'I'm going to have one of your Sunday roasts, but Michael might want a few minutes to look.'

'No, I'm fine. If she says the roasts are good, that's enough recommendation for me. I'll have the same.' He smiled and Linda nodded, a big grin on her face. Taking the menus off the table, she turned to me.

'I'll put a rush on them,' she said, then walked off, fanning herself with the menu.

I couldn't help but laugh.

'Sorry,' I said, not quite able to look at him.

'What for?'

'Linda's...misconceptions.'

'Why should you be sorry?'

I shrugged my shoulders. 'I don't know. Just seems a little awkward.'

The drinks arrived and I gratefully took advantage of the distraction.

'Don't worry about it. The fact that she thinks we're ordering quickly so that I can get you back to bed doesn't do my ego any harm.'

I felt my mouth drop open. Michael's lips teased a smile at my expression.

'I don't think your ego is ever in any danger.'

Michael did a maybe yes maybe no head wobble and took a sip of his drink.

'I'm sorry if it's made you feel uncomfortable though. I can put her right if it'll make you feel better.'

I lifted my eyes. His face was serious.

'Katie – '

'Two roast beef with all the trimmings,' the waitress announced before lowering the plates and catching sight of my lunch companion. At which point, his plate went down on the table and the contents of mine went on my lap. Stuck in the corner, I couldn't jump up quick enough and, shit, that gravy was hot!

'Oh my God!' the waitress shrieked as she realised what she'd done. 'I'm so sorry! Are you OK? Can I get you a cloth?'

'Take both of those back to the kitchen, Emily,' Linda said, bustling up. Like any good landlady, she had eyes everywhere and had obviously seen the mishap. I, meanwhile, had wiggled out of the window seat and was now frantically wiping at my jeans to remove food detritus. In my hurried attempts to get out of my seat, I'd also managed to knock over my drink, which although making the mess worse had at least stopped the burning sensation from the gravy, so silver linings and all that. Linda handed me more napkins and, after a few minutes, I had at least got the worst off. My jeans felt cold next to my skin, I felt a complete idiot and I was still starving. But apart from that, everything was just peachy.

'I'll go and get you both new meals. I'm so sorry, Kate. Of course, all of this is on the house.'

'No, Linda, please. It was an accident. I want to pay.'

'Too bad. I'm not taking your money. Now, I've found a table nearer the fire, it'll help dry you out.'

'No, really. We're fine here. Honestly.'

'This table is booked. Sorry, my mistake. That one by the fire is the only one free.'

I gave Linda a look as we changed tables and she smiled.

'I'm never coming here again, you know that?' I said.

'Sure, sure. Now, here you go. Isn't that better?'

It was, I had to admit.

'Now, I'll be right back with your food and another drink for you. Do you want anything else, sweetheart?' Linda directed her question to Michael.

'No, I'm good thanks.'

She smiled. 'I bet,' she winked at me and headed off to the kitchen.

'Are you OK?' Michael asked once she'd gone.

'Yes, yes,' I said, waving the enquiry away, trying to pretend I wasn't horribly embarrassed at the whole scenario.

'You really don't like people making a fuss of you, do you?'

'It's not that. I was just fine where we were.'

'Katie, jeans are bloody horrible when they get wet and your teeth were beginning to chatter.'

I conceded that he might have a point.

'Are you warming up?'

'Yes. Thank you.'

He shook his head.

'What?'

'When you realised I'd come off my bike the other day, you were fussing around me within moments – in a good way!' He held up his hand before I could say anything. 'And I know for a fact you are always checking on Janey and the kids, especially now with the baby coming. But the moment someone tries to do the same for you, you look like you just want to disappear.'

I pulled a napkin off the table and dabbed at my lap with it, more as something to do with my hands than for any effective purpose.

163

Because Michael was absolutely right. It wasn't that I didn't like people fussing over me. It was more that I just had no idea how to react to it. It had always been me taking care of others, a role I had grown up with and got used to. It was the way it had always been and one I knew I was good at.

I shook my head and tried to laugh it off. 'I just don't like a fuss.'

Michael looked like he was about to say something else but Linda's arrival with the dinners interrupted him.

'Right. Let's try again, shall we?' She placed the plates and my drink down safely. 'Are you warming up again now? Are you sure you don't need to check that gravy didn't burn you?'

'No, really, Linda, I'm OK. Honestly.'

'It's just – '

'I'll make sure she's all right,' Michael interrupted, a charming and disarming smile on his face.

Linda looked at him, then at me, smiled and nodded. 'OK. Well, so long as I know you're in good hands.' She winked at me again. '*Bon appetit.*' And she was off.

'Now she definitely thinks we're an item.'

Michael shrugged as he dug in.

'It did the trick, didn't it?' He took a forkful. 'Mmm, this is really good!'

He was right. It had done the trick. Of course it had.

I loaded up my own fork. 'Must be nice.'

'What's that?'

'Women bending to your every whim, taking your word as gospel.'

He pulled a face. 'It can be. But that's why I like spending time with you.'

'Oh, I can't wait to hear this.'

'You help keep me grounded.'

'God, you're arrogant.' I laughed, taking a mouthful of roast.

'Maybe you can work on that for me too, along with the house.'

'Sorry. Some things are beyond even my help.'

'Ouch. And after I'd rescued you from all the fussing too?'

'Rescued me? I hate to break it to you, but I don't think Prince Charming has got anything to worry about just yet.'

'Is that so?'

I shrugged. 'Sorry to be so blunt.'

'I'll get over it.'

'I'm sure you will.'

Michael lifted his gaze and met mine. Shaking his head, a resigned smile on his face, he set back to demolishing his dinner.

* * *

'God, you smell delicious!' Mark declared as he let us in and gave me a quick hug. Taking in the look of surprise on my face, and then the six foot four brick outhouse standing behind me, he seemed to suddenly feel the need to elaborate. 'I mean, literally delicious. Like food. Like...' He leant over and sniffed me again. I fixed him with a look and he backed off. 'You smell like roast beef.'

'Yes. Well, Emily had a moment and it ended with a roast dinner and all the trimmings in my lap.'

'Oh.'

'Anyway, Mark meet Michael, Michael, this is Mark. He's our head vet and pretty much runs this place.'

They shook hands and Mark threw me a private look which I made a point of ignoring.

'So, how's things?' I asked.

'Good. Timmy got picked up today and I swear to God he was smiling.'

'I told you he smiled.'

'Yeah. Well, I just thought you were a bit nuts.'

'Thanks. He just never smiled at you because you're a vet and do nasty things and I do all the nice things.'

'Rubbish. He just smiled at you because he's a tart and you're pretty.'

Michael chuckled and I rolled my eyes.

'And you heard about Sara's engagement?'

'Yes! Isn't it wonderful? I'm so happy for them.'

'Bit of a surprise, I have to say. Never thought old Henry would come round to the idea of marriage again. Sounds like his first one was a right disaster.'

I was madly making signals with my eyes, hoping that we could drop the subject of first marriages that hadn't gone particularly well, bearing in mind my present company. Unfortunately Mark wasn't picking up on any of them.

'But you can't assume just because one didn't go well, the next one won't. I mean, it's a whole different set of circumstances, isn't it? Thank God Jilly didn't give up on the concept after her first one ended.'

Forgetting the task of trying to avoid potential awkwardness for a moment, I smiled at his expression. 'You old romantic,' I said, nudging him with my arm.

He gave me a look that as much as said 'you caught me'.

'So, anyway. I imagine you want to know how your boy Rooney is today?'

'Rooney,' Michael said quietly, shaking his head.

'Bit of a crap name, isn't it?' Mark agreed. 'You could always change it. He won't mind.'

I stifled a smile. Mark had used practically the same phrase as me but Michael saw it anyway and shot me a look. Which made me smile even more.

We got to the kennel block and Mark turned to Michael. 'Look, I know this is all Kate's idea more than yours. I'm not doubting your ability to look after a dog, or anything, and I know you've had one before, but like I said to Katie, it's got to be the right time for you. Sadly there are always new ones coming in so if it's not the right time, then it wouldn't be fair on the animal if you took him now, only to bring him back a bit later. I'm sure you're a great guy and everything, or Kate wouldn't have even brought you here – she's kind of protective of our charges.' Michael and Mark both looked at me and I found a fascinating spot on the ground to study. 'But please think about this before you make a final decision. I'm sorry if that's blunt, but I have to put the animals first, even before people's feelings.'

Michael nodded. 'Not a problem. I totally agree.'

'OK then,' Mark said. 'Let's go and say g'day.'

Rooney's tail was wagging so hard he was practically bending himself in half when we got there.

'He heard your voice,' Mark said, smiling as he unlocked the door.

I snuck a glance at Michael laughing at the dog as he wiggled himself silly.

'I'll leave you to it.'

'OK. Thanks, Mark.'

I headed into the kennel and Michael followed, closing the door behind him. Rooney bumped against my legs, his bum still wiggling like mad. And then he

167

started licking my jeans, ramming his nose into my leg. I could hardly blame him. If Mark could smell it, then Rooney's sensitive nose must be driving him mad.

'He obviously thinks you smell delicious too,' Michael laughed as I pushed the dog off me. Crouching down next to me, he called Rooney who bounced over, shoving his head against Michael's thigh and making happy little groaning noises as Michael gave him a good scratch and rubbed his chin.

'Want to take him out for a walk with me? I mean, if you're feeling up to it and don't mind hanging about a bit longer...'

Michael looked up at me from where he was now sat on the floor with Rooney sprawled across one of his legs.

'Sounds great. If only to get the feeling back in my right leg.'

I giggled and pulled out a doggy treat from my pocket. With the uncanny ability that dogs have to sniff out a treat at a hundred paces, Rooney looked at Michael for a second and then, with a scrabble of toenails, scooted himself up to hurriedly pad over in my direction, whereupon he sat down a little sideways in front of me.

'Lie down.'

The dog did so.

'Good boy!' I ruffled his jowls and he bounced up, waiting for the next fun thing to happen.

'He's had training then?' Michael asked, pushing himself up and half-heartedly brushing at his jeans.

'Yes, he's good on the lead and off. Seems to have all the basics down. Isn't possessive about food or toys, and gets on well with other animals and children.'

'So what's the catch?'

'Huh?' I asked, looking up at him whilst clipping a lead to Rooney's collar.

'Why's he in here?'

'Oh.' I explained about the size issue. 'But he's fully grown now so he won't get any bigger. And there are plenty of people who will want him. Because you're a sweetheart, aren't you?' I said, nuzzling my face close to the dog's, which he reciprocated, speeding up his tail and giving Michael's leg a good thwack in the process.

I pulled my head up, just in time to catch him wince.

'Oh no, I'm sorry. Is it still bruised from the accident?'

'It's all right,' he brushed it off, watching me.

'What?'

'I'm thinking you should have Rooney.'

I handed him the lead. 'If I took every dog I've ever wanted out of here, I'd need a vastly bigger place than the broom cupboard I currently live in. Besides, I'm not home enough with my job and I can't take a dog into people's homes. Some would be fine, but some people don't like dogs or are allergic or whatever. It just isn't feasible unfortunately. Which is why I get my pooch fix like this.'

We walked out of the block and I opened the gate that led into the fields next to the centre. Michael pulled his baseball cap down a little more.

'You could do with a woolly hat to keep your ears warm. Let me see if there's – '

Michael caught my arm. 'My ears are just fine. Now just relax and walk with me and this damn dog you've dragged me down here to see.'

***

'I can't believe how anyone could give him up.'

'I don't think it was an easy decision. Mark said the kids practically had to be peeled off him when they left.'

Michael shook his head. 'Jesus. I don't envy the parents living with that for a while. Janey had to throw away one of Lily's dolls when its head broke off and you should have seen the drama! I can't imagine taking away a living, breathing friend like this.'

We had paused for a moment and were sat side by side on a fallen tree. The dog was lying in front of us, playing with the ball we'd brought along and which Michael had been throwing for him, wearing both of them out.

The light was fading a little now and the air becoming damp and heavy. They'd predicted snow for this afternoon which hadn't arrived but it was looking now like the forecast had just been a little off in its timing. But a part of me didn't want to move from here, even though my bum was getting cold and I was losing feeling in my fingertips. I wanted to stay, breathing in the clean air, feeling joy from watching the dog tap the ball away with his nose and then slap a paw on it to roll it back, and sensing the solid bulk of Michael sat next to me, his knee brushing against mine as he moved to lean and give the dog a pat.

'We'd better head back if we're going to beat that.' Michael's voice broke into my thoughts. I followed his gaze to the sky and nodded. He hadn't said anything about taking the dog home. But I'd had a feeling about Rooney and that had only been confirmed by how Michael's whole demeanour had changed the moment he'd crouched and called the dog in the kennel. The tenseness in his jaw, the way he held his shoulders – the

170

moment he connected with that dog, it all dissipated. And I knew he felt it too.

As we got back to the kennel block, Michael handed me the lead.

'Can I meet you in the car? I missed a call and I need to call them back.' He bent over Rooney and gave him a cuddle. 'See ya buddy.' And with that, he strode off back towards the entrance.

I watched him go, stunned. The longer we had spent with the dog, the more sure I was that Michael felt that same way as me – that he too knew this was the right thing for him. The dog loved him, he loved the dog and could provide a wonderful home for him. What more did he want? I looked down. Rooney was watching the retreating figure. When Michael turned the corner and disappeared from sight, the dog looked up at me and gave the smallest whine. At which point I, most unexpectedly, burst into tears.

'I'm so sorry, puppy,' I said, as I finished towelling off his fur and fluffing up his bed and blankets. 'But you know what? It's his loss and you're going to find a lovely home very, very soon.' I wrapped my arms around him and hugged him to me. He snuggled his head into my shoulder and I felt the tears start again. He was a great dog and I knew this was the last time I'd see him. By the time I was back in he'd have a new home. But I was also sad at the missed opportunity for Michael. I wanted to be angry at him but I couldn't. Like Mark said, and like I knew to be true, it had to be the right time. I'd thought it was the right time but maybe it wasn't only Michael who could be arrogant at times. Perhaps I'd assumed I'd known more than I had, even if it had been meant with the best of intentions.

'I can finish up here.' Mark's voice made me jump. 'I'm pretty much done.'

'OK. Your friend is out waiting for you. Probably best to go now, before the weather sets in.'

I nodded. 'Yes. Right. OK. Bye then, Rooney. You be a good boy now.' I bent and kissed the top of his head and then walked out of the kennel. As I turned to lock the door, he was looking up at me, his head resting on the edge of the bed.

'Shit,' I whispered, my voice cracking.

Chapter Thirteen

'It's all right.' Mark squeezed my shoulders as I did my best not to cry in front of him. 'He's going to be just fine, I promise.'

I nodded. 'Yep, I know. I was just...so sure.'

'I know. Now, go on before he leaves without you.'

'That's not beyond the realms of possibility, so I better had.'

'See you next week.'

I gave him a quick hug and did a fast walk to the car park, where the pickup's engine was now running. Pulling open the door, I jumped in and grabbed the seat belt, quickly plugging it in.

'Sorry. Had a couple of things to do.'

'No problem.' Michael put a hand on the gearstick and then shifted a little in his seat. 'You OK?'

'Mmmhmm.' I nodded, pasting a smile on. 'It's nice and warm in here.'

Michael's hand curved around the gearstick, then uncurled again. I looked up at him.

'He'll be OK, you know.'

'Huh? Oh yes! I know. Of course I know.' I made light of it. 'It was just a suggestion anyway. And it was

173

nice to get out of the city and have a walk anyway, wasn't it?'

'It was. And thanks for lunch.'

'I didn't pay.'

'You kind of did, in a way.'

I brushed my jeans, the stains obvious. It was a hell of a good job I wasn't trying to impress Michael O'Farrell because between the serving disaster, stained jeans, frozen nose and what I was pretty sure now were at least marginally puffy eyes, I would most definitely have failed.

'Worse things happen at sea and all that.'

'That is true.' Selecting reverse, he backed the truck out of the car park and headed back in the direction of London.

We'd only been going about five minutes when Michael started smiling. Obviously I was way more upset about leaving the dog behind than he was. But remembering that I was supposed to not be taking this to heart, I went along with it.

'What are you smiling at?' I asked.

'You.'

Now I frowned, suspicious. 'Me? Why?'

'You're making me hungry.'

'What?' I squeaked, scooching around in my seat to face him. My reply seemed to amuse him even more.

'Calm down. It's your jeans. The warmth from the car is bringing out the food smell in your clothing again. You smell edible.'

'Ha ha.'

We drove for a few more minutes in silence before Michael spoke.

'Katie, look, I really appreciate what you – '

My phone started ringing, cutting him off. 'I'm sorry,' I said, fishing it out of my jacket. I checked the screen: Calum.

'Hi!'

'Hi, babe. I'm so sorry I haven't called. Work's been so crazy.'

'That's OK. I've been pretty busy here too anyway. Are you back?'

'I am. I wondered if you wanted to get together? I thought as I've been so crap lately I'd splash out on a nice room somewhere.'

'Are the builders still working on your house?'

'Yeah. They've only gone and put down the wrong flooring whilst I was away. Can you believe it? So it's going to be even longer now before I get rid of them.'

'I don't mind the mess, really.'

'No, I know. But I don't want you to see it all like this. I want to show it to you all perfect and finished. Hopefully it won't be too much longer.'

'OK. But you don't need to get a room. You can just come to my flat.'

'Too late. It's all booked. And dinner. Can you meet me at the restaurant at seven? I'd come and pick you up but this way is much easier.'

For you.

'When?'

'Tomorrow, of course!' he laughed.

'Oh. I wasn't sure when you were back exactly. I have an appointment. I'll have to see what I can do.'

'But it's all booked, babe.'

'I know, Calum. I'm sorry. I will try but I can't arrange things around you if I don't know when you're going to be here.'

'We're not going to go over that again, are we? You know I'm swamped with work.'

'No,' I said, quietly, acutely aware that in the confines of the pickup's cab, Michael could likely hear every word. 'I'm just saying…look. I'll sort something out, OK? Which restaurant is it?'

'Marco's.'

'OK. I'll meet you there at seven tomorrow.'

'I'll make it up to you.' His voice dropped, 'I promise.' I heard something in the background. 'OK. Got to go. Looking forward to it, babe.'

'Yes. I –' But he was already gone.

Michael drove on and although neither of us said a word, I had a feeling we were both thinking a similar thing: the appointment I'd mentioned to Calum was with Michael and scheduled from three until seven. I calculated how long it would take me to get home, change, then get to the restaurant. Way too long. I could squash a dress in my bag, change in the loo at the station and then…I was still going to be late but…

'We can reschedule tomorrow, if you like.'

I turned my head.

Michael shrugged, his gaze flicking to me briefly. 'Sorry. Kind of hard not to hear.'

I shook my head. 'No. It's fine. And no, I'm not cancelling on you. Absolutely not. He has to realise that I'm not at his beck and call.'

'Right.'

'What's that supposed to mean?'

'What? All I said was "right".'

'It was the way you said it.'

'Jesus,' he sighed. 'Look, just finish a bit earlier with me. You can change at my place and then still get to the restaurant in time to meet him.'

I looked out of the window, but the darkness now fallen meant I saw little but my own face reflected back at me.

'At least he didn't just turn up tonight and see me looking like this.'

Michael pulled up at a red light and looked over, his brow furrowed. 'Like what?'

I waved my hands over my face and clothing. 'This.'

'You look perfectly...fine.' The light changed and he found first gear a little more forcefully than he had on previous times. 'If he can't see that then the man's an idiot. Oh, that's right. He is.'

I threw my hands up. 'How can you say that? You don't even know him!'

'I know all I need to know. He calls and you jump. And apparently expects you to be perfectly dressed and fully made-up whenever he does.'

'It's not like that,' I replied, although there was less conviction in my voice than I had intended.

'Right,' he said again.

From the corner of my eye I saw the streetlights flash across us, briefly illuminating Michael's face with each pass. His jaw was tight and his hands gripped the wheel more intently than they had on the way down. He rolled his neck and, as if sensing my thoughts, flexed his long fingers from the wheel. It was clear neither one of us was going to break the silence, so I rested my head on the window and stared out past my reflection, into the darkness beyond.

'I'm sorry to have wasted your time today,' I said, as Michael pulled up outside my flat. 'I got a little carried away.'

'You didn't waste my time. It was good to get out.' He stopped the engine.

I nodded and gave a tight smile. 'Right then. I'll see you tomorrow. Goodnight.'

'Katie, wait.' Michael's hand caught my arm as I reached for the door catch. He ran the other hand over his face and gave his overgrown stubble a scratch. 'I shouldn't have said anything about your boyfriend.'

I gave a small smile, preparing to accept the apology.

'How you let him treat you is none of my business.'

The smile left my face.

'Excuse me?'

'What?' he asked, looking at me.

'Is that your idea of an apology?'

Michael's face remained blank.

'You know what?' I said, grabbing for the catch. 'You're pretty unbelievable!'

'Now what I have done?' He sat back, apparently genuinely perplexed.

'The fact that you don't even know what you've done is just – '

'Don't give me that "if you don't know what you've done" shit. You're better than that and you're usually not afraid to tell me when I've fucked up. Which, by the way, is something you ought to try on your so-called boyfriend. Because from where I'm sitting, he's treating you like crap and yet you never pull him up on it!'

'So much for you feeling that you shouldn't be commenting on my love life! That didn't last very long, did it?'

178

'Maybe because I wasn't actually sorry in the first place, but felt I ought to say it because for some reason I felt bad for upsetting you!'

'Maybe because you thought I'd run and tell your sister on you? Well, don't worry. I had no plans to do that, so feel free to say what you think. I'm a big girl and I can take care of myself. This is between you and me, and whatever I think of you and your misplaced opinions, I would never tell tales to your family. But it's nice to know that you think I would!'

'That's not why I said it. I didn't think you'd be "telling tales" at all. Besides, it wouldn't really make any difference bearing in mind Janey has the same opinion of this Colin bloke as I do.'

'Calum! His name is Calum! And really? You're going to sit there and lecture about the right way to treat women?'

'What the hell is that supposed to mean?'

'You think he's using me?'

'I don't know what he thinks he's doing. But I think he's getting it easy, with you just being there when it suits him.' He held up a hand, as I made to protest. 'And yes, I know, I know, he's busy. Jesus, Katie, we're all busy but that doesn't mean you go weeks without seeing someone you care about if you can help it!'

'He can't help it. Don't you get it?'

'Kate. He's in feckin' sales, not a war zone! Believe me, he can help it.'

I felt my chest heaving and unwrapped my scarf, suddenly hot in the cab of the pickup. Michael turned his head towards the side window, away from me.

'What did you mean about me and the way I treat women?' He looked back at me. His jaw was set, the street lights casting deep shadows on his face, the only illumination now that the interior light had flicked off, its time up. 'You think I use women?'

'I should go.'

'I want to know.' His voice was soft, questioning. 'Is that really what you think of me?'

'Does it even matter what I think, Michael?' I was suddenly so tired, and the slight headache I'd had at the start of the journey was now building into something a lot more intense.

'Yes, in this case.'

'Why?'

'Because, although I don't give a shit about what a lot of people think about me, I do, for some reason, care if you think I'm some misogynistic user of women. Because I'm not.'

'OK.'

'OK? Is that it?'

'What do you want me to say?'

'I want you to say what you really think! I'm not Colin or Calum or whatever the hell he's called. You don't just have to agree with every word I say.'

'Good. Because, believe me, that is never going to happen!' I yanked on the door catch, ready to make my dramatic exit. Which would have been perfect except for the fact that I'd forgotten to undo my seat belt and instead ended up practically winding myself as the belt retracted against my exit force.'

'Shit!' I squeaked.

Michael pressed the seat belt button and it released itself, and me, from tension. I got out, slamming the door behind me and stalked around the vehicle towards the entrance to the flats. Unfortunately, Michael was also out of the car. And in my way.

'I'd like to go in. Excuse me.'

'You think because I don't have relationships that I don't value women?'

I looked up at him. 'Michael, you admit yourself that you don't see the same woman more than once. Twice if she's lucky. Your bedroom is completely devoid of anything that would tell said woman anything about you and you also admit that you don't show them the rest of the house. The whole point of you even going to speak to a woman is for you to have sex with her. That's it. You've absolutely no intention of showing any of them who you really are. It's about finding someone to fulfil a basic need. So if that constitutes me thinking you're using them, then yes, you're right. I do think that! Now, can I go please?'

'No.'

'What?'

'Did you ever stop to thing that the women I sleep with are using me for exactly the same purpose?'

'If you think you're going to turn this into a sympathy vote, then you've got another thing coming.'

'Believe me, I don't. And I don't want to. I'm just saying that, in every instance, it's two consenting adults. I'm absolutely always upfront about what I'm not looking for, i.e. something that goes beyond that night or maybe that weekend. The women I hook up with are looking for exactly the same thing I am. There's no way I'd hit on someone…someone like you for example.'

'Oh well! That is a relief.'

'What I mean is that you're after a hell of a lot more than a one-night stand.'

'You have no idea what I'm after!'

'I know you're after more than that loser is giving you! You want it all, Katie. And that's fine. Why shouldn't you? But you're not getting it and you're not even trying! Instead you just waste yourself on men like Calum and spend your time looking after friends – and even clients you don't like very much – in order to fill whatever void it is that you have in your life.'

'You have no right to judge me! And last time I checked, being kind wasn't a crime.'

'Of course it's not. And as for judging you, you seemed to think it was OK to judge me and my treatment of women, so I'm just returning the favour. The difference is, I'm comfortable with my relationships.'

I made a noise at his use of the word. He ignored it.

'Clearly you're not, which is why you run around trying to put everything and everyone into neat little boxes, trying to fix people's lives when, in truth, you need to take a good hard look at your own. And that would start with your so-called boyfriend. If you're happy to let him treat you like you're not the most important thing in the world to him, then that's fine. But you can't force people who care about you to think it's OK.'

My eyes blazed and I could feel the tears shining in them as I willed them not to fall in front of him.

Michael took off his cap, ran a hand through his hair and then replaced it. 'I know that you deserve more than he's giving you. And I think you know it too.' His voice was softer now. He took a step back and leant on the car. 'I'm sorry, Katie. I didn't mean to shout at you.' He looked across at me. 'You know, my sister would tell me about you sometimes, how frustrated she was over you seeing this guy. She loves you to bits, you know.'

I nodded and a tear dislodged and rolled down my face. I swiped at it with the back of my mitten.

'Anyway,' Michael continued, 'I'd just listen to her. You know, let her get it off her chest and then not think about it any more. But then I met you and now I can see why Janey is so upset about you wasting your life on him.'

I shook my head as he stepped towards me.

'Katie.' Michael's thumb touched my cheek, gently wiping away the tears. 'You're talented, gorgeous, funny, intelligent, kind. You've all the good stuff going on. You should be with someone that appreciates all that.'

'I'm sorry I upset Janey.'

'Ah, she's fine. And once you come to your senses about this guy, she'll be even better.'

I looked up and saw the conciliatory expression and the hesitant half-smile. But still...my mitten made a *thwump* sound as it hit the padding of his coat sleeve: I wasn't about to let him off entirely.

'It's really not as bad as it seems, you know. I'm busy too so quite often, it's...' I stopped as I saw the look on Michael's face. He was done exploding at me, but it was clear he wasn't going to change his view on my relationship with Calum any time soon.

'Come on, I'll walk you to your door.' He tilted his head at me. 'You could at least try not to look quite so surprised. I know you think I'm a complete Neanderthal, but I do have some manners.'

I was too tired to protest and actually it was kind of nice. Unless he was coming in, Calum usually dropped me at the kerb and left. It would have been nice occasionally for him to have walked me to the door, especially as it wasn't like you could see it from the pavement, thanks to the bushes and a large London plane tree that stood in front of the building.

I fished my key from my pocket. As I lifted it to the door and turned, Michael stepped back, allowing me room to go in.

'Night, Katie.'

'Night, Michael.'

***

Are you in? x

The text came back almost immediately.

Yes. Are you nearby? x

Got some time between appointments. Can I pop in? x

Kettle's on. Get your arse over here :D x

I giggled at the reply and shoved the phone back in my bag, picking up my pace as I turned towards Janey's house. The air was crisp in my lungs as the sun hung low in a cloudless blue sky. A jogger overtook me, which, bearing in mind she wore trainers and I wore four-inch platform court shoes, wasn't that much of a surprise. Although, having had to belt for a bus in the same shoes in the past, I did at least know I could probably still give her a run for her money if I had to. My gaze fell on the little dog that trotted alongside her, a pink fluorescent jacket wrapped around its fluffy white fur. I tried not to think about Rooney. My determination lasted until the end of the road when I pulled out my phone, scrolled to Mark's name and sent a text.

How's Rooney this morning?

As I approached Janey's house, my phone chirped and Mark's message flashed on the screen. I stopped as I read it.

Morning. How are you? I'm fine thanks, Katie.

A pokey tongue face served as punctuation, before he continued.

As for the boy in question, you'll be glad to know he has found a home. I think it's going to be great. As you said, we knew he wouldn't be here long.

Part of me was over the moon – I never wanted Rooney to be in kennels long – but, deep inside, I knew I'd hoped to have another go at changing Michael's mind, at convincing him he was ready for another dog, and that dog was Rooney. Or whatever he chose to call him. And now he'd been gazumped. But I knew Mark would only let animals go to people he knew were absolutely committed to giving that rescue dog the best life it could have, so whoever was lucky enough to be the new owners of that soppy date had really got a great deal.

Chapter Fourteen

'You look like your dog just died,' Janey said as she answered the door. Her hand flew to her mouth as she realised where I often spent my weekends. 'Oh shit!' she said from behind it. 'One of the dogs didn't die, did it?'

I leant in and gave her and the bump a hug. 'No, it's fine. One of them just got rehomed.'

She closed the door behind me and gave me a look as I took off my coat and hung it on the coat rack.

'So, isn't this the point, you go "yay, one of them got rehomed."' She did a sort of jazz hands thing to add illustration.

'Yes. No, I'm thrilled. Obviously.'

'Obviously.'

'It's just that...have you spoken to your brother today?'

'Michael?' she asked, turning away to rummage in the cupboard for teabags. 'Earlier, yes.'

'Did he say we went out yesterday?'

'You went out?' She spun round.

'Yes, to the rescue centre.'

'Oh. Oh yes. That. Sorry, I thought you meant...never mind. Tea?'

'Yes please. And the other? Definitely not going to happen.' I half laughed, remembering how yesterday he'd categorically stated he would never ask 'someone like me' out.

'Because of Calum?'

'Because of a lot of things.'

'He's not that bad, you know.' Janey's voice had a defensive note.

'Oh God, Janey, I know!' I leant over and caught her hand. 'I didn't mean it like that. Honestly I didn't. I know he's not. For goodness' sake, the waitress in the pub tipped my dinner over me yesterday because she was so busy gawking at your brother.'

'No!'

'Yes.'

'I do wish he'd tidy himself up a little.'

I took a sip of the tea she'd placed in front of me. 'He's fine. But him and I? Not happening. We'd drive each other bonkers in no time for a start.'

Janey shrugged her shoulders. 'So, what's with the look you had when I answered the door. Is it to do with yesterday?'

'Kind of. Remember we had suggested to him about getting another dog?'

'Mmmhmm,' she said, disappearing behind her mug of tea.

'Well, there was this dog at the centre and I knew he'd be perfect for Michael. I got him to go down there and we had a really lovely walk together.' Janey looked up. 'With the dog,' I added hastily. 'It all seemed to be going really well. It was clear he thought Rooney was great.'

'Rooney?'

'I know. But apart from the name he was perfect! And he just took to Michael like he'd known him for ever. I really thought he was going to take him. And then, when we got back, he just handed me the lead, gave him a hug and left, saying he had a phone call to return.'

'Oh.'

'And then Mark's just texted to say they've found him a new home.'

'But surely that's good?'

'It is. Of course. I know, I know! I sound mad. I just really wanted it to be with Michael. Oh Janey, you should have seen them together, it was so cute!'

She smiled. 'I can imagine.'

Pushing the biscuits towards me, Janey snagged one herself and took a bite. 'Things will work out for the best, Katie. Don't worry.'

'Yeah, I know.'

'Did I hear you have a date tonight?'

I stopped chewing.

'What's that look for?' she asked.

'Nothing.'

Janey raised a disbelieving eyebrow.

'Fair enough. Michael and I sort of had an argument yesterday, and he was worried about me running to you to tell tales on him, which I told him I would never do. But apparently it doesn't work the other way around.'

'Bollocks. He's not worried about you telling me anything. When you come from a family like ours, it's pretty much the rule that whatever you say will, sooner or later, be known by all the others. And Michael's not one to say things he doesn't stand behind, so he doesn't tend to mind who knows, and certainly not me.'

'But the only way you know I have a date with Calum tonight is because Michael told you.'

'That's true. And you know why he told me?'

'Do I want to know?'

'I don't know. But I'll tell you anyway. He said you got pinned down to a time that wasn't really convenient – '

'I wouldn't exactly say "pinned".'

Janey gave me that look that she and Michael did so well. The one that seemed to see right through me.

'OK.'

'So he offered for you to change at his place and go from there, right?'

'Yes. Although I wasn't entirely sure if that was still on since we sort of had that row last night.'

'He doesn't go back on his word, and I'm guessing it is because he mentioned it this morning.'

'He's of the same opinion as you about Calum.'

Janey pulled a face.

'I'm going to talk to Calum tonight about things.'

'I hate to doubt you, sweetie, but you've said that before and I've not seen a lot of change.'

'No, I know. I mean it though, I promise. And I think, once he knows that I'm not happy with how things are, that he will try and make some changes.'

'OK. Good.'

'How are the kids now?'

'Much better, thank goodness. Lily's upstairs having what's she's taken to calling a power nap, and Joey's school has an inset day today so I've just dropped him off at a friend's for the afternoon.'

'That's good. I think my previous client might be coming down with what they had. It really seems to be going around. She was looking pretty dreadful so in the end I just told her she ought to go to bed and give me a ring when she's feeling better.'

'Why didn't she cancel before now, instead of dragging you out and risk giving it to you?'

'Oh, she's been so excited about getting started. I can't blame her.'

'Of course you can't.' Janey rolled her eyes.

'What?' I laughed.

'You. You're impossible. You project this no nonsense, strict school mistress persona – always smartly dressed, hair up, make-up immaculate – '

'That makes me sound horribly dull, you know that don't you?'

'Don't knock it. Some men love that look.' She gave me a wink.

'I sense a but.'

'But it's all bunkum.'

'Excuse me?'

'Underneath it all you're as soppy as the rest of us.'

'Rubbish.'

'Don't worry. I won't tell anyone. Although, between you and me, anyone worth their salt already knows anyway.'

I got the distinct feeling that my friend didn't count my current boyfriend as being amongst this group.

'Right, I'd better be off.' I slid off my stool. 'Thanks for the tea and natter.'

'Any time. Are you off to Michael now?'

'No, I've got someone else in-between. Just a follow-up, so I'm hoping, unless something's gone horribly wrong, that it shouldn't take long.'

'Have fun. I hope things go OK tonight with Calum.'

I tilted my head. 'Do you?'

Janey gave me a squeeze and then held me by my upper arms. 'I'm afraid I'm too much like my big brother to pretend I like something when I don't. I am not Calum's biggest fan, that's for sure. I think you deserve someone who makes you a whole lot happier and pays you a hell of lot more attention than he does. But I'm not going to fall out with you over him. I've a feeling you'll see the light yourself eventually anyway.'

'I don't really know what to say to that. Thank you doesn't really seem applicable.'

Janey grinned. 'At least make sure you order the most expensive thing on the menu.'

I shook my head, slid my feet into my shoes and pulled my coat from the rack. Jancy tucked a hair behind my ear.

'We just want the best for you, you know. That's all.'

'I know you do, Janey.' I gave her a hug. 'I'm so grateful for your friendship, and everything you are. You know that. Even if I'm not always very good at showing it, I promise you, I am.'

'I know you are. Now, go on, be off with you and stop cluttering up my house. And text me later.'

'I will. I promise.'

Checking my watch, I calculated I had nine minutes to get to the next client. It should only take seven so I was pretty much on schedule.

***

I walked up the steps to Michael's house and rang the bell. The previous client's follow-up had taken even less time than I'd planned as they had had done so well and were still happy with the way things were going.

191

I'd texted Michael and explained the situation, suggesting that as I was cutting the appointment this evening shorter, I was happy to come a little earlier, but only if it suited him. He'd replied almost immediately saying to just come whenever I was ready.

To be honest, I was a little nervous after the row and the walking me to the door. I felt a bit odd and slightly awkward. We seemed more than just client and service provider, but were we actually friends? And why was he so bothered about who I dated? I squared my shoulders and reminded myself that this was the very last time I did a favour for a friend. If this was the level of complication it caused, I could most certainly live without it.

I pressed the doorbell and almost immediately Michael opened the door, making me jump.

'Gosh! Were you hiding behind the door!'

He smiled. 'No. But I saw you walking up the street from my office.'

'Oh.'

'Here.' He took my coat and hung it on a spare hook. I stared. For the first time, I could actually see most of the hall floor.

'When did this happen?'

He rubbed his hand over his stubble. 'Last night. I couldn't sleep so I thought I'd get up and do something useful. I mean, I know it's not perfect, but I tried to remember everything you said and put it into practice. And I took all those boxes to the charity shop and the dump this morning. That's made quite a lot of space.'

I couldn't help smiling. The house was really coming together. For the first time since we started, I was actually feeling sure that we could really make the Christmas deadline.

'I bet it has. Are you pleased?'

'Huh? Yes. Yes, of course.'

'Oh. Good.' I struggled to maintain my smile. Michael didn't look as pleased as I'd hoped he would, which made me worry about the longevity of the organisation. I'd never had anyone totally 'relapse' yet, but, then again, I'd never had a client come to me in quite the same set of circumstances as he had.

'Is everything all right?' I asked.

'Yes. I need to show you something.'

'All right.' I bent, took off my shoes and tucked them against the wall, then turned back to Michael.

'Lead the way.'

To my surprise, he merely took a few steps and then stopped outside of his office.

'Oh no!' I put my hands up to my mouth.

'What?' he asked, concern creasing his face.

'You messed it up?' I raised my eyes to his.

'You know, a lesser man might be hurt at your complete lack of faith.'

I rolled my lips together. 'Sorry.'

'I'll forgive you. This once.'

He put his hand on the door handle, and hesitated, looking down at me. 'About last night...'

'Let's just forget about it. Now, what's in here?'

'I never meant to upset you.'

'You didn't.'

'Katie. Even I can see when I've made a woman cry.'

'Look, I was tired, I was a bit upset about saying goodbye to the dog and I had a steaming headache. I know you meant well so let's just leave it at that, all right?'

He opened his mouth to say something, looked at me, then closed it again. 'Sure.'

'Now, please! What's this big surprise?'

Michael opened the door and I stood for a moment, shocked. I looked up at him and he couldn't keep the grin off his face as Rooney scooted towards us, tail wagging madly, toenails clicking on the floorboards. I dropped to my knees and he barrelled into me for a cuddle, rubbing his head on my shoulder and my cheek, making me laugh as he practically pushed me over in excitement.

'Steady on, mate.' Michael eased the dog back and helped me regain my balance. Standing, he held out a hand to help me up which I took. We walked further into his office and I noticed a dog bed now sat between the easel and the desk and there was a blanket on the sofa where I assumed the dog was now also allowed.

'I don't understand. Yesterday...'

'I had to be sure I could have him looked after when I have to go away, meetings I can't take him to, etc. And I had to be sure he was good with the kids. My neighbour used to look after Monty sometimes and she was chuffed to bits when I asked her last night about the possibility of some more dog-sitting.'

I cast my mind back to our first meeting and his neighbour flirting with him in front of me.

'The...yummy mummy dog-sits?'

He screwed his face up a moment. 'Tamara? God no! The other side. Retired couple.'

'Oh, that makes more sense.'

'Yeah. To be honest, I'd rather not be beholden to Tamara for anything, if you know what I mean.'

I could take a wild guess. Then I remembered my text from earlier.

'But Mark said this morning…'

'Yeah, I kind of spoke to Mark on my way out last night and explained the situation. Don't be mad at him,' he added, seeing my eyebrows shoot up. 'I asked him to keep it a secret. If I'd known you were going to be so upset about it all last night, though, I'd have told you. I thought you were just upset about me slating your boyfriend.'

'Let's not talk about that. And I promise I'm not mad at Mark. I just…Does Janey know?'

'Of course. She and the kids came with me this morning to meet him. He was brilliant with them. So that was that. With a stop for food, bedding and, by the time the kids had finished, pretty much every toy in the place, we were done.'

'Sneaky moo.'

'Excuse me?' he laughed.

'Your sister. I was round there earlier! I had a break between clients close to her house so I stopped in for a cuppa and she never mentioned a thing.'

'Yeah, that's kind of my fault too. I wanted to surprise you.'

I laughed. 'Well, you most certainly got your wish.'

We were sat side by side on the little sofa in the corner of the office, weakening rays of winter sunshine filtering through the window, the dog lying in the middle of them, watching us through sleepy eyes.

'We had a run in the park earlier, so he's a bit pooped.'

'He looks it.'

'There's one thing though.'

'What's that?'

'The name. I'm sorry. It has to go. I've been calling him "boy" all day. I can't stand bloody football at the

195

best of times, so his current name really isn't going to work.'

'He's your dog now, call him what you want. He'll soon get used to it.'

'That's the thing. I don't know what to call him. I thought you might have an idea.'

'Me? I can't name your dog.'

'Yes you can. You're the reason he's here. You have a vested interest. Come on, please?'

I sat back on the couch, tucked my feet up beside me, then peered around Michael to look at the dog.

'You know, one name does come to mind.'

'What's that?'

'Have you read *Jane Eyre*?'

Michael shook his head. 'No, sorry.'

Handy.

'One of the main characters, Mr Rochester, has a dog. He's called Pilot.'

Michael nodded. 'Pilot. I like that.'

'You do?'

He shifted to look at me. 'Yeah I do.'

The smile broke on my face. 'Oh my gosh! I can't believe you have him! I'm so happy you took him after all.' Without thinking I flung my arms around Michael's neck and hugged him. His arms wrapped around me and pulled me closer.

'I should be thanking you.' His voice was soft near my ear, and I was suddenly aware of the hardness of his chest against mine, the warmth of his hands through my dress and the way his arms held me tight. It felt... Oh my God. It felt good! Which was bad! So, so bad! That damn dog had my emotions all over the place. I was getting all sorts of confused! I pulled back.

'Right!' I said, over brightly, causing Michael to wrinkle his forehead.

'You...OK?'

'Uh huh! So! Let's crack on, shall we?'

'All right,' he said slowly, standing as he did so. 'You said before that you normally start with clothes and stuff. So I thought, especially after what you said last night, that maybe it was about time we got to work in the bedroom... on the bedroom. You know. And if you...erm...had any ideas about what you think I could do to make it a bit more...personal, then I'd be happy to hear them.'

I smoothed my dress, remembering what had happened the last time I tried to suggest something to that effect.

'I know I bit your head off last time you tried to help me. I guess I didn't see it then. But I do now. And you're right. You were right last night too, about some of it. But not all of it.'

'No, I know. I'm sorry,' I said.

'I just needed you to understand.'

'I do.'

'I didn't tell you everything though.'

I looked up and met his gaze.

'The reason I didn't exactly give anyone a tour of the house? Honestly? How could I? You saw the state it was in when you got here. It's all to your credit that you didn't turn tail and take off.'

'I've seen far worse than this.'

'Well, I haven't. And it kind of mortified me that I'd let it get to this state. I don't even know how it did. After Angeline left, I guess I didn't really want to face anything and then when I finally looked up again it was to see all this. And by then I didn't know where to start.'

'But look at it now. We're so far along.'

'I have something else to apologise for.'

'Crikey! You're on a roll.'

'I know. Take advantage because it might not happen again for a while.' He gave me a sideways look and I couldn't help but smile.

'I dismissed your notion before that all this, this thing you do, could have an effect on more than just my house. But you were right. I'm calmer with work now I can find everything and I'm much more productive. I'm in the running for a really big project, which may well not have happened if I hadn't been organised enough to pitch. And, of course, this one.' He bent down and rubbed Pilot's tummy, at which point the dog rolled completely onto his back with all four feet in the air.

'Oh, now that's just charming in front of guests, boy. Really classy.' His new owner laughed and stood. 'Come on, Pilot.'

The dog looked at him, cocking his head to the side.

'Yep. That's you now. Better get used to it. Come on.'

Scrabbling about for a moment, the dog righted himself and followed us up the stairs to the master bedroom.

Chapter Fifteen

Unlike many of my clients, Michael didn't actually have acres of clothing. Once he'd scooted around the house and gathered up various items that had never made it back to the wardrobe, there was certainly more than I'd seen on my first visit, but it still wasn't as intimidating a pile as many I'd seen. Going through everything, choosing what to keep, didn't take that long either. Michael was actually getting pretty good at this now. He'd even started tossing out the shapeless T-shirts he was invariably dressed in, as well as the worn out shirts. When he hesitated on one particular shirt, it was clear that there was something bothering him.

'What is it?' I asked, as I sat on the floor, folding T-shirts for the keep pile, Pilot's head resting on my thigh.

'Nothing.' He hung the shirt up but his hand hovered before moving on to the next.

'Come on. There's obviously something. You've been flying through the rest of the stuff.'

'Nothing. It's stupid. Really.'

'I'm sure it's not,' I replied. 'Tell me.' I tugged on his jeans leg for emphasis and he glanced down at me.

'Should you be sitting on the floor?'

'Pardon?'

'I just…you always look so nice when you come here and then you go scrambling up into cupboards or plop yourself down on the floor. Shouldn't you be in jeans or joggers or something?'

'I've never met a cupboard I couldn't tackle however I'm dressed and I prefer this for work. Now, stop changing the subject.'

He tipped his head. 'Huh. You caught that, then?'

'I did. And I'm still waiting. What's the story behind the shirt?'

Michael flipped the sleeve of the shirt. 'It's the one I wore on my wedding day.'

Oh.

'But I shouldn't throw out a perfectly good shirt just because of that, should I? I mean, I could wear it any time.'

'You could, you're right. The question is, will you and more to the point, do you want to?'

'I do like it.'

'Well, maybe you can give it a new association. Put it on when you're doing something nice, going somewhere special. But if you're always, in the back of your mind, going to associate it with something that no longer makes you happy, then it's like we talked about with the curtains – it's that first feeling you get when you see something. It has to be a good one, not ambiguous and certainly not bad.'

I tipped up onto my knees and Michael automatically put his hand down to help me up. Pilot whined.

'She can't act as your pillow all day, you lazy mutt.'

Pilot let out a resigned sigh and slid into a seated position by the door.

'I can see he's regretting moving out of the kennels. Poor, hard done by dog.'

200

I grinned, shaking my head.

'I can't tell you how happy I am you decided to take him.'

Looking down at me, Michael laughed. 'You don't need to. You're practically bouncing up and down. Are you always this happy when a dog gets rehomed?'

'No. I mean, yes! Yes, of course I'm thrilled! It's just that some dogs really get to you. The moment I saw him, I fell for him.'

'So basically you got me to take him just so you could come round and cuddle him?'

'No,' I laughed, batting his arm, 'he was perfect for you. And you know it. Otherwise you wouldn't have taken him, no matter what I thought.'

He gave me a look.

'It's all right. I'm not offended!'

'Really. A woman who doesn't go into a huff if I don't agree with her?'

'I can't promise that every time, but on this occasion...'

Michael nodded. 'Then I will take that.' He turned, took the shirt off the rail and put it on the donate pile.

'Sure?' I asked.

'Absolutely.' He bent and gave his new companion a tickle. 'New start for everyone.'

'OK, then let's get this stuff put away.'

Michael checked his watch. 'Don't you have to be getting ready?'

'Oh no, I've got ages...' He put his wrist in front of my face. 'What?' I said, grabbing his arm. 'How did that happen?'

'Time flies when you're having fun.'

'Oh gosh! Are you sure you don't mind me getting changed here? I can do it at the station, it's no problem.'

'I think that might cause a stir.'

'In the loos. Obviously.' I pulled a face at him.

He took my hand and led me out into the hall before bowing before a door, waving an arm. 'The guest bathroom awaits, m'lady.'

'You've gone from grumpy to bonkers.'

'Normally I'm a little of both.'

'Well, that's better than a lot of the former.'

'Point taken. Now go and do what you do or you'll be late for Colin.'

Opening my mouth to correct him, I caught the twinkle. I narrowed my eyes at him and he quirked an eyebrow at me, before I closed the door, trying to stop the smile that desperately wanted to play on my lips.

Smoothing down my dress, I gave a last check in the bathroom mirror. I couldn't get over the feeling that it would be odd to take a shower in Michael's house, despite the fact that he'd sweetly left everything I might need laid out, just in case, so I'd had a quick wash instead and then set about redoing my make-up and unpinned my hair. Brushing it out, I hooked one side behind my ear and told myself that would have to do. The shoes I'd worn over were a good match to the dress, which had saved me lugging another pair around after Calum's short notice arrangements.

I left the bathroom and headed to the stairs, stopping as the sound of music caught my attention. If my many hours of listening to Classic FM had taught me anything, it was Beethoven's *Moonlight Sonata*, one of my favourite pieces. Sliding my hand along the banister, I slowly descended the stairs, knowing by now which creaked and which didn't. The sound got louder as I moved towards the living room. Quietly I stepped through the half-open doorway.

Michael's hands moved assuredly over the keys, his long fingers covering the chords easily and naturally. There was no music in front of him and his head was bent in concentration, his brow slightly furrowed. The light from the lamp to his side cast a shadow over his face, accentuating the high cheekbones and strong jawline, now ragged with overgrown stubble. To the side of the piano stool, Pilot laid contentedly, head on his paws, eyelids drooping as his master soothed him to sleep.

I felt my breathing grow shallow, afraid to make the slightest noise and shatter the scene in front of me. The fact that Michael was playing after so long of not doing so made me feel joyous. It was moments like this that made me love my job even more. I was helping. But I felt instinctively, in this instance, there was something more. Something I couldn't name or even entirely recognise. But I knew it was different. And I wasn't sure what that meant. Or if it even meant anything at all.

'Oh no! Please don't stop,' I said, as Michael looked up, his hands stilling over the keys as he saw me in the doorway.

He shook his head, his half-smile almost bashful. 'Bit rusty.'

'No! No, really! It was wonderful. Honestly. That's one of my favourite pieces.'

'You play?' he asked, closing the lid on the instrument as he stood.

'Oh goodness, no. Sadly not.' No point telling him that more than anything I'd wanted lessons as a child but that wish, like a whole bunch of others, never came true. 'But I love to listen to it, especially "live" as it were.' I immediately felt silly for doing the bunny ears and shoved my hands behind my back.

'Well, Pilot's not howling the place down so that's something.'

'I think he found it relaxing.' I pointed to where the dog had now flopped onto his side and was gently snoring.

As we left the room the dog pulled himself up and padded sleepily behind us, just in case he missed something. As we got to the bottom of the stairs, I realised Michael was looking at me a little funny.

'Oh no. What? What is it?' I ran my hand over my hair and checked for runs in my stockings.

'Nothing! Nothing's wrong. You just look…wow… really nice. I don't think I've ever seen you with your hair down before.'

'No, it's not really practical for work but I can't bear to cut it.'

'You definitely shouldn't.'

I smiled. 'Thanks.' I slipped my arms into my coat as Michael held it out for me. 'Calum thinks it'd be less hassle if I cut it,' I said, lifting my hair from the collar so that it wasn't tucked in. 'But I refused.' I looked up through my lashes at Michael. 'So you see, I don't always just jump when he says so.'

'Like I said before, he's an idiot.' He handed me the wrap I'd been using as a scarf. 'Admittedly he's a lucky idiot but an idiot all the same.'

'Oh shush, you,' I said, not wanting to argue again tonight and accepting that, mixed in there among the boyfriend insults, was a compliment. 'I have to go.'

'We're walking you to the station.'

'No, it's freezing out there. Stay here in the warm.'

'Yes, because I can see that you're dressed for Arctic conditions in that dress.'

'I have a coat on!'

'You should have three more layers at least and a bobble hat,' Michael replied, pulling on his boots.

'Hat hair wasn't exactly the look I was going for.'

'It's a much underrated look, I've always thought. And you've no choice on the company. Come, Pilot.' Michael clipped the lead on the dog, shrugged into his own coat and opened the door for me.

As we walked along to the station, I secretly began to think that Michael might have been right about the extra layers. A harsh north wind had been building all day and the clear sky had turned into a clear night, which probably meant that somewhere through all the light pollution, millions of stars were glinting, hung in an inky sky. It also meant that I was freezing my butt off.

'Wishing you had those extra layers now, aren't you?' Michael read my thoughts.

'What makes you think that?'

'I can hear your teeth chattering.'

I bit down and locked my jaws together.

Michael put an arm out and squished me against him, protecting me from the wind and immediately making me feel more cosy.

'Better?'

'Yes. Thank you.'

'No problem.'

We arrived at the entrance where a small of group of carol singers had braved the weather and were cheerily belting out a chorus. Michael let his arm drop away and I immediately missed the warmth he'd provided. My teeth began chattering again almost instantly.

'Go on. Get down into the Tube and warm up. And try not to freeze the other end. Get a taxi if you need to.'

'And you say I fuss,' I teased.

He tilted his head, the fleecy beany he wore pulled down to his eyebrows.

'Can you begin to imagine the grief I would get from Janey if you turned up somewhere tomorrow morning frozen solid like an ice pop.'

I gave an eyebrow rise of acceptance.

'Bye, Pilot. See you in a couple of days.'

'Last big push, eh?' Michael said, his face showing a hint of concern.

'One of them. Not long to go now but I'm confident we'll get there in time for everything to be just perfect for you all.' I gave his forearm a gentle shake. 'Really, it's going to be finished in time. Stop worrying. Now, thanks for the company but you need to get that dog back into the warm.'

'All you care about is the dog. You're a hard woman, Katie Stone.'

I shrugged, half smiling.

He glanced at the entrance then back at me. 'I suppose it's pointless me asking you to stand him up.'

I shook my head a little sadly. 'Please let's not do this again tonight? We've managed to move past yesterday's...moment and had a really good day. I don't want to argue with you any more, Michael. Please?'

He nodded, his eyes still fixed on a point behind me. I waited for a moment and the intense green gaze moved and found my face.

'I'd better go.'

He nodded, then leaning forward, he kissed me on the cheek.

'You look really beautiful, Katie.'

A smile flickered on my lips as I tilted my face up and met his eyes. He held the look a moment then stepped back, calling the dog and set off at a jog back towards the house. I watched their retreating figures, the touch of Michael's lips on my cheek still clear in my memory and warm on my face. Giving myself a mental shake, I turned and began walking through the concourse, heading for the escalator down to the trains. Clearly I'd missed Calum's touch more than I thought if a simple, innocent kiss on the cheek from Michael O'Farrell could have me feeling like my insides were made of melting chocolate.

* * *

'So how was the trip? Did you get to see much outside the office?' I asked, as I finished the last mouthful of delicious cheesecake and laid the dessert spoon to the side of my dish.

Calum had been talking about work for most of the dinner and I was happy to listen. Although it might have been nice if he'd asked how things had been going for me once or twice.

'Oh. Yeah. Well, no, not much.'

'That's a shame. It looks like you got a bit of tan though, so you must have done a bit of bunking off,' I teased.

He chuckled. 'So long as you don't tell the boss. There was a pool at the hotel so I grabbed a couple of swims when I could.'

'Why not?'

'Exactly. That's what I thought.' His eyes drifted over my face and his hand, under the table, drifted over my thigh. 'God, I missed you.'

I dropped my gaze and smiled. It didn't matter what Janey or Michael or Bernice thought. He did care.

'I missed you too.' Which was true. In the times that I hadn't had back-to-back appointments or been up to my elbows in kennel detritus. 'In fact, I was thinking that maybe I could take a few extra days off at Christmas and we could go – '

'I can't, Kate. I'm sorry.'

I sat back, confused. 'You don't even know what I was going to say.'

He let out a sigh. 'You were going to ask to spend some more time together over Christmas.'

'It'd be nice if you didn't make that sound quite so distasteful to you! And frankly, I shouldn't have to be "asking"! Most normal couples would automatically assign some time together over Christmas because they actually want to be together.'

'Kate, don't do this. Not tonight.'

My anger began to bubble. 'Frankly I'd have liked to have said something before now but I've hardly bloody seen you and you're not exactly what anyone would call chatty on the phone.'

'I'm busy!'

'Everyone's busy!' I said, my teeth gritted in an attempt to keep my voice low. 'All I want is some time with my boyfriend! Is that really too much to ask?' Much to my disgust, my voice broke on the last words and Calum's face immediately softened. He reached for my hand.

'Kate, please don't be upset. I'm sorry. You're right. It's been crazy lately and I've neglected us far more than I should have. Look, I'll work something out and we'll definitely have a few days away together, like you said. OK?'

I nodded and took a deep breath. I hated rows like this. I'd witnessed too many and, although Janey was right in that I didn't take any crap from people in my work, I still always did my best to avoid confrontation when I could. Apart from with her brother, but he really was a case unto himself. And luckily, it seemed that we had managed to get past that stage now anyway. Mostly.

'So, what about you? Things going well at work? You said you had a new client who was proving a bit difficult. Did you move him to Bernice in the end?'

I took a sip of red wine and shook my head. 'No, I couldn't. He wanted to continue with me.'

'Did he now?' Calum said, leaning back and picking up his own glass.

'It's nothing like that. He's just quite...private and didn't want to go through everything again with someone else. Janey had recommended me to him so he just wanted to stick with me.'

'Ah, the delightful Janey.'

I gave him a look. 'Yes. She is delightful.' The tone in my voice warned him not to push that way.

'It'd be easier if she liked me a little more.'

'She does like you. She likes everyone.'

This time it was Calum that gave me the look and we both knew I was being diplomatic. Also known as fibbing a little.

'Once things settle a bit with your work and we get to see each other a little more, she'll come round. I promise.'

Calum said nothing.

The waiter drifted past, stopping momentarily to top up our glasses from the wine bottle sat on our table. He then left the bill on the side of the table and glided away. Beside us, a table of eight began singing happy birthday and I looked round to see several waiters accompanying

209

a large cake being wheeled on a dessert trolley. I smiled at the family gathering as photos began being taken, the flashes illuminating the area in bursts. Glancing back at Calum to share the enjoyment, his head was down, brow furrowed as he studied the bill. I was about to look away again when I noticed something.

'What the hell is that?' I asked, my voice raised to compete with the singing opposite. Which of course finished just as I spoke, resulting in my question being heard by far more people than just the one I'd directed it at.

Calum's face darkened.

'Keep your voice down, for God's sake!'

My eyes widened. 'I beg your pardon?'

'You heard me! What the hell's got into you, drawing attention to us like that?'

I felt the blood rise in my face. 'It wasn't intentional! And right now I don't actually care. I want an answer to my question?' I grabbed his left hand and pointed to the distinct tan line on his third finger. 'Why the hell does it look like you've been wearing a wedding ring?'

Calum pulled his hand out of mine, both of us aware that the birthday party was now far more interested in our discussion than in the cake in front of them.

'Because I have.'

'Oh God. I'm going to be sick.' I gripped the edge of the table.

'Wait.' He stopped me. 'It's not what you think.'

I held up my hands, palms upward, silently asking him what the hell else it could be.

'Come on. Let's go to the hotel and talk about it there.'

I shook my head. 'No. I want to talk about it now.'

'Kate, please. You're – '

'Now, Calum.' My voice was calm and back to its normal level. But even I could hear the steeliness in the tone.

'Fine. It's kind of silly really.' He gave a laugh. I didn't join him. He cleared his throat and continued. 'The company I was working with, they're really family-orientated and they like all the people they deal with to be "on the same page", as they say. I heard another company lost a contract with them because the guy mentioned something about him and his girlfriend living together. I didn't want to lose the contract so I bought a cheap ring just to wear whilst I was out there. Once things go through, it'll all pass to a different part of the company and I won't be dealing with it any more.' He looked at his hand, the telltale sign barely noticeable in the candlelight. 'I guess I must have forgotten to take it off on one of my swims.'

I sat watching him, wanting to believe him.

'Honestly, babe, that's all it is. You know. Playing the game. You know how traditional people can be out in places like Alabama.'

He reached for my hand and I pulled it back away from him.

'Babe, come on, I – '

'Alabama?'

'Yeah.'

'Not Arizona?'

'What?'

'You told me the firm you were visiting was in Arizona. Not Alabama.'

'I don't think I did. You must just be remembering wrong. Like you said, you've been crazy busy too lately.'

'I'm not remembering it wrong, Calum. I know what you told me.'

'Fine. Then I guess I said the wrong state. It's not a crime. You're making a big deal out of nothing.'

'Am I?'

'What's that supposed to mean?'

'Why don't we go to your house tonight, instead of the hotel?'

He picked up the napkin off his lap and put it on the table. 'I've told you that's not possible. It's still being worked on.'

'I don't mind. I'd like to see it.'

'I don't want to drive out there tonight, besides we've both been drinking.'

'I'll pay for a taxi.'

'Don't be ridiculous. It'd cost a fortune.'

'It'd be worth it to see this amazing house.'

'What's got into you?'

'Me?'

'Yes!

'Nothing. I think the fact that I'd actually like to see where my boyfriend lives after six months of dating is pretty damn normal! In fact, I'm wondering if me letting it go this long is something I'm going to regret.'

'Of course it's not. Kate, I told you. It'll be done soon and we – '

'Are you married?'

'What?' Calum asked. 'Of course not!'

But I saw it. That moment of hesitation. That flicker.

I dropped my head, my eyes focused on my hands as I held them on my lap, the knuckles white as I twisted the linen napkin between my fingers.

'How could you?' I whispered. 'After everything I told you about my parents?'

There was a pause. He knew he was caught. 'Kate. I'm sorry. I never meant...' He stopped as I lifted my head, my eyes dry, gaze boring into him.

'Where were you really? These past few weeks? On holiday with your wife?'

He nodded. 'Mexico.'

'Do you have children?'

The hesitation again.

'Shit,' I whispered, my throat feeling tight and raw as I swallowed.

Downing the rest of my wine in one go, I pushed my chair back. 'I need to go,' I said, throwing the twisted napkin on the table.

'Kate. Wait.'

I unhooked my bag from the back of the chair and stood. As I turned to grab my coat, the woman sat across from me caught my eye. A look passed between us and she momentarily dropped her gaze to a glass of wine on the table before catching mine again. *Abso-bloody-lutely.*

'Do you mind if I borrow this?' I asked her.

'Be my guest.'

'What the fuck?' Calum spluttered as red wine dripped down his face. 'Do you know how much this shirt cost?'

I leaned towards him. 'You know what? I don't give a shit because whatever the price, it's far less than your lying has cost me!'

'Oh come on, Kate! You can't tell me that you didn't have your suspicions? It's not my fault if you decided to blind yourself to them and just saw what you wanted!'

I stared at him, open-mouthed, my brain whirling.

'The fact that you even think that shows how little you really know me.'

He looked me up and down, his eyes lingering. 'I wouldn't say that.'

And with that I flung what was left of his own red wine on top of the already spreading stain on his previously pristine white shirt.

Turning my back on Calum, I faced the other table, just as a waiter hurried up beside us.

'Please could you replace this lady's drink,' I instructed him, opening my bag to reach for my purse. Her hand reached out and rested on my arm. I looked up.

'That one's on me, love.' She winked and patted my arm.

I have to say that, ordinarily, I'd have been mortified at someone overhearing such a personal conversation, but bearing in mind my mortification levels were already off the scale by this point, it didn't really seem to matter all that much right now.

I nodded and briefly laid my own hand on top of hers before stepping back and walking out of the restaurant, head held high with not one glance back.

Chapter Sixteen

Janey opened the door, took one look and pulled me inside without saying a word.

'I am such an idiot!' I declared as Janey handed me another mug of tea.

'No, you're not. Don't you dare start thinking that any of this is your fault!'

'But he was right, wasn't he? I should have had an inkling that something was amiss. A normal person wouldn't have just swallowed everything he told me about always working or travelling!'

Janey's expression changed, her face taking on a seriousness that I was used to seeing on her brother, but rarely on her. Leaning across, she grabbed my hands so that I was turned to face her on the sofa.

'Now you listen to me, Katie Stone. You're not an idiot and you're not abnormal. You trusted the man you were in a relationship with because you are a good, sweet, loving woman. And all that is good stuff! It's nothing to be ashamed of or sorry for. The villain here is that shit Calum who took complete advantage of all of that.'

'I should have sensed something, Janey,' I said sadly.

'Why would you? You're a lot of things, love, but you're not a mind reader.'

'I should have seen the signs. You know I should. God, I saw them enough at home! How could I have missed them here?'

'You can't compare all that to this,' she said, softly, gently rubbing my back as more tears trickled slowly down my face, plopping rhythmically onto the fabric of my dress.

'But I do. It's the same thing.'

'It's not. Not at all.'

'Perhaps it's something in the genes. Maybe I'm not meant to have a normal, happy relationship.'

'Well, that's the biggest load of bollocks I've ever heard come out of your mouth.'

'I hated my dad for what he did to Mum. Cheating on her, sending her further and further into depression. I wanted her to just leave him. I couldn't see why she wouldn't. And every time I begged her, tried to get her to see that we could start again, just me and her somewhere else, she just shook her head and told me that she loved him.'

Janey reached over and tucked my hair behind my ear.

'Not everyone's as strong as you, Katie.'

'It's not that, Janey. I think I've spent so long trying not to be Mum that I've turned into my father.'

'What? Don't be ridiculous.'

'I've been sleeping with a married man, for God's sake!' I said, leaping up from the sofa. 'Maybe I did know! How could I not have some sort of suspicion? Jesus! My mum was in a drunken stupor most of the time and even she knew my father was up to something. And here I am, an apparently intelligent, successful businesswoman who just accepts that her boyfriend can't see her very much, who has his phone switched off at the weekends most of the time to "destress", and who can never take me to his house because it is continually being worked on. Maybe I did know, or suspect, and I just buried it deep inside because I didn't want to admit that I'm just as bad as my father!'

Janey began pushing herself up a little awkwardly from the sofa and I automatically held out my hands to help pull her up.

'Thanks. Now, I'm going to ask you something and you have to give me the absolute honest truth.'

I pushed my hair back from my face.

'OK.'

She took my hands and met my eyes, her intense green gaze boring into mine. 'Look me in the eye and tell me if you ever had any, even the tiniest, thought that the man you were seeing was married.'

I looked back, the answer tumbling about in my head, frustrating me, yet freeing me at the same time.

'Oh God, Janey. I didn't have a bloody clue.' I felt the tears prick my eyes again.

My friend pulled me to her, the baby bump making me stick my bum out in an inelegant and slightly uncomfortable manner, but I didn't care. It was true. I hadn't known. It hadn't even crossed my mind. Calum must be a pretty good damn salesmen because he had sold me a scenario and I'd bought it without question.

Janey tipped me back. 'Right. Now. No more guilt. No more thinking you're like your dad. You're you, Katie. Underneath that efficient, organised, put together exterior is a fallible human being, just like the rest of us. You had no reason to doubt that what Calum said was true. And now you know, you can't go feeling guilty about it all.'

'But his wife…'

'Yes I know. It's shitty. But you have to remember it's not your fault. You didn't know. You had absolutely no way of knowing and if you'd known he was married when he first came onto you, you'd have told him to get on his bike! He's the one responsible for all the hurt here, Katie. Not you. And don't you ever think anything different.'

'I just feel so horrible.' I flopped back onto the sofa and Janey followed. And then a thought hit me.

'Janey, would you do me a favour?'

'Of course.'

'Please don't mention any of this to Michael, will you?'

She pulled a face. 'He won't – '

'Please! Just promise me. Until I get my head around it myself. I know you're right about it all. But let's face it, he's not going to be the most sympathetic – and please don't think I blame him. His wife cheated on him and completely broke his heart. If he finds out that I've been seeing a married man, I just…we've really been doing so well on the house and…everything. I don't want to spoil it now. Not now we're so close. Just let me finish the house with him so that it's all ready for your Christmas together and then I'll be gone and it won't matter what he thinks of me then.'

'I think you're giving him less credit than he deserves, Katie.'

'Please don't be angry with me. I know he's a good man. But I know he's been hurt and I don't want to do anything to…remind him of that hurt when he seems to really be moving on. You said just the other day that he finally seems to be getting back to his old self. And tonight, before I left, he was playing the piano.'

'He was?' Her surprise was evident.

'He was. And, oh Janey, it was so beautiful! He hardly ever bites my head off these days either...' I gave her a half-smile and she laughed. 'I just don't want to derail things by throwing something up that might remind him of more painful times.'

'And?'

'And what?'

'There's an "and", I know there is.' Her voice was soft.

I closed my eyes for a moment. 'And I don't want him thinking badly of me. At least not whilst I'm still there.'

When I looked up, Janey was smiling. 'Like I said, you should give him more credit. But!' She held up a finger, as I made to protest. 'I won't say anything, if that's what you want.'

'Thank you.' I hugged her. 'I know I'm putting you in a difficult position but it's not for much longer. And then I'll be out of his way and he can think what he likes about me.' I gave a shrug and wondered why that thought didn't give me as much comfort as it should have done.

***

I stopped at the boundary of the house and stared. The day had begun grey and had merely got darker and more gloomy as it went on, which only enhanced the effect of the transformation in front of me. White fairy lights were entwined in the bare branches of the plane tree in front of his house and more hung from the porch, each column decorated the same, the little twinkles wrapped in perfectly even spirals from top to bottom. On either side of the front door there now stood a lollipop-shaped box tree in a pale olive-coloured ceramic pot. These too had their trunks wrapped in white lights, daintier versions of those around the building. Despite everything that had happened last night, the sight in front of me tempted out a smile. I climbed the steps and rang the bell.

It was definitely a day for surprises. Getting rid of all Michael's baggy, long-past-their-best clothes had meant that the difference when he opened the door to me today was evident. He was still dressed casually, as seemed to be his preference, but he no longer looked as if he was spending every night camped out somewhere with Bear Grylls, which – and no offence to Bear – was a definite improvement.

'Hello.'

'Hi. Come in.'

'You've been busy.' I pointed to the tiny front garden as I stepped inside. In addition to the new plants and lighting, the front border had also received attention. Gone were the soggy, blackened summer plants that had greeted me on my first visit. The little bed had been dug over and covered with a layer of pale chippings and three illuminated reindeer now stood content behind the low wrought-iron edging of the border. The whole effect was stunning and made the house look, like Michael himself, a lot more cared for.

'I can't take all the credit,' he said, taking my coat from me.

'Oh?'

He nodded at Pilot, who was gently bouncing on all four paws in excitement as I bent to give him a cuddle.

'He definitely helped with some of the digging.'

I smiled and gave the dog an ear rub, which made him groan in happiness.

'It looks absolutely beautiful, Michael. You've clearly worked hard.'

'Thanks. I'm glad you like it. Kept me out of trouble this morning anyway. Tea?'

'Erm, no. I'm OK, thanks. Although just a glass of water might be good, if that's possible.'

Michael gave a little frown. 'Of course.' He paused. 'You all right?'

'Absolutely,' I lied. Try as I might to push the events of last night out of my head, I was, in truth, actually feeling a very long way from all right.

'OK.' Michael's tone suggested he wasn't convinced, but poured me water from a filter jug anyway. 'So, I pulled out all the photos, memorabilia and what you classed "sentimental stuff" like you asked.' He handed me the glass of water. 'I've made a bit of a start but I can see why you don't start with this. Even after getting into the swing of sorting and getting rid of a lot already, I still have to admit to feeling a bit overwhelmed right now.'

'That's perfectly normal. Most people do. But they all get there and you will too.'

'I feel like I could spend from now until Christmas just going through photos! You sure we can do this? It's not like there's that long to go now.'

'Absolutely.' I nodded. 'Don't worry. You're going to be ready and it's going to be a great family Christmas for you. I know Janey is very excited about it all.'

The smile on my face felt like someone else had stuck it there and hadn't quite put it in the right position.

Emphasising the final outcome of the process here with Michael seemed a good plan two minutes ago when it was clear he was feeling a little unsure about the timescale and needing reassurance. Unfortunately, what it had actually done was ram home to me the differences between our upcoming Christmas celebrations. His surrounded by loving family, and mine alone. Again.

His eyes studied me and I really wished that he wouldn't.

Turning away from his gaze, I passed in front of him and headed towards the stairs. 'Everything in the first spare room still?'

'Yep.'

I could feel him close behind me.

'Kate?'

'Yes?' I asked, not looking round and concentrating instead on finding a good place to sit amongst the many piles Michael had created. It was easy to see why he was feeling overwhelmed. Pilot, meanwhile, was clearly wondering the same thing. Giving up on the floor, he wandered over to the bed and hopped up on it.

'Pilot. Off.' Michael's voice was firm. The dog slunk down and came over to me, shoving his butt against my hip and sliding down onto the floor, whereupon he let out a big sigh.

'Looks like I'm out of favour.' I could hear the smile in Michael's voice.

'He'll get over it in about two minutes, I'm sure,' I said, keeping my head lowered. 'So, obviously I can't decide what you want to keep out of all this, so we'd better get on.'

I felt Michael's eyes on me. There was a pause before he answered. 'Sure.'

It was obvious to both of us that something was different today, no matter how I tried to hide or deny it. Being here just felt wrong today, even though I knew I wanted to be here – it was a good distraction. And so long as I didn't mention I'd helped destroy someone else's marriage vows, we'd be just fine.

Michael had clearly sensed that something was off and I could see it was killing him not to ask me. Like Janey, and as he'd proved the other night after we'd been to see the dog, Michael O'Farrell was not one to let things fester. But I needed him to hold on to the restraint he was evidently exerting for just a little bit longer.

Despite our bumpy start and our ups and downs throughout the past week, every instinct I had was telling me just to be honest with him. Honesty was his big thing. It was one of the many things I'd come to like about him. Things were what they were with him and they would be dealt with as needs be. Even with Pilot. When I thought back, not once did he ever actually say that he wasn't going to take the dog. I'd just assumed so from his actions. But he hadn't wanted to get my hopes up if he couldn't arrange dog-sitting, or if Pilot wasn't as good with kids as we'd originally thought. He'd never lied. Unlike Calum. But I couldn't tell him any of that.

'Katie, what's wrong?'

'Nothing.' I did the smile thing again and it felt even more unnatural than last time.

'So why don't I believe you?'

'I don't know.' I pushed myself off the floor, causing Pilot to look around dozily and then flop out and fill the space I'd been occupying. 'Are these all for dumping?'

I asked, pointing to a box he'd been steadily filling for the past couple of hours.

Michael nodded, watching me. As I bent to lift the box, he got up. 'I can do that in a minute. It's heavy.'

I gave a laugh that sounded a hollow imitation of my normal one. 'Michael, I'm quite capable of lifting a box.' I lifted it to demonstrate and staggered a step as it proved itself heavier than it had initially looked.

'Give it to me.'

'No.' I twisted away from him. 'I'm going to go and put these in the recycling. You get on with the rest.'

He moved to take the box again. 'You'll do yourself an injury. Give it here.'

'I'm more than capable of looking after myself, thank you. I don't need you – ' I stopped as I caught sight of his face. 'I'm sorry.' I swallowed. 'I didn't mean to snap at you. And I know you mean well, but the whole damsel in distress thing isn't really my scene.'

When he replied his jaw was tight and his voice measured. 'I wasn't implying you were incapable, Katie. I just didn't want you putting your back out, especially with Christmas coming.'

The fact that Christmas could now come and go in my world without me even noticing, let alone caring, gave his comment an ironic slant that he hadn't intended.

'I know, thanks.' And with that, I stepped past him and heaved the box to the top of the stairs. I put it down for a moment and my back practically groaned in relief. Pressing my hand to my head, I willed the headache that had been slowly building in my temple to go away. I closed my eyes for a moment as I did so.

When I opened them again, Michael was standing in front of me. He bent and swiped the box, the muscles in his back and arms tensing as he did so. I opened my mouth to protest.

'I can't afford a claim on the insurance on this place if you fall and break your neck.' He descended the stairs, opened the catch on the front door with his elbow and took the refuse outside. From the top of the stairs, Pilot and I just watched.

Twenty minutes later, Michael glanced over at me. I'd tried to clear the air a little after the box-dumping fiasco. Any other day I'd have seen he was just trying to be kind but today, with all my emotions having shot up significantly closer to the surface, I'd fallen back into a pattern I'd thought I'd managed to leave behind – that the only person I could really rely on was myself. I'd worked so hard to get through those issues. It had taken years, and Janey's friendship had helped enormously. But last night, Calum had smashed all the hard work to pieces. And now, today, Michael was getting the brunt of it.

'I'm sorry about the box thing. It was silly. I just don't like people thinking I can't take care of myself or that I expect a man to do things for me.'

'Don't worry. You definitely don't give off that impression.' His voice was flat.

Another few minutes went past before he spoke again. 'So. How was dinner?'

I kept my head down, intent on my task.

'Fine, thanks. The food was very nice,' I said, disregarding the fact that I'd thrown the whole lot up again about three minutes after Janey had opened the door to me. Putting that on TripAdvisor would be pretty cruel, bearing in mind I knew the sole reason for my nausea was the person I'd been having dinner with and not a dodgy scallop.

Silence descended again. Pilot lifted his head and looked at me, then at his master. He tilted his head and I leant down and kissed the top of it. The tension was palpable whether you had two legs or four.

'Did you have any luck in getting this guy to spend more time with you, like you said you wanted to?'

I sat up, exhausted from trying to keep myself together, from not blurting everything out when, deep down, I knew that was really all I wanted to do, whatever the consequences. But I knew I couldn't. Not with Michael.

'Michael. We're doing really well here but there is still a certain amount to do and I'd like to get it all done before Christmas, as I told you and Janey I would. Bearing in mind that's only two weeks away, whilst I appreciate you're trying to make conversation, I think it's probably better if we just focused on the task in hand today.' My voice had a tone of cool efficiency to it as I glanced up at him.

Michael's eyes blazed before his face took on the hardness I'd seen the first time I'd met him. The aloofness that surrounded him then suddenly wrapped itself around him again. As I watched, I saw him almost physically withdraw from me.

'Whatever you say.'

The next hour was unbearable. Even Pilot had taken himself off and now lay out in the hallway, his back against the banisters. Neither Michael nor I had spoken a word and I knew it was my fault. I also knew that the item I now had in front of me could push things either way.

'Michael, where do you want this?'

He looked over at what I was holding, rather than at me.

'Toss it,' he said, turning back to the pile he was working on.

'I...just wondered if you might want to...' I stopped as he lifted his head and looked directly at me, the cold, hard gaze so different from less than twenty-four hours ago when he and Pilot had walked me to the station. His eyes then had been so full of warmth. Now they were as cold as the ice shining on the frozen puddles outside.

He gave an impatient shake of his head. 'You wondered what?'

I took a deep breath. 'Well, it's just that sometimes people discard things like this, in the heat of the moment, and then, later, when they have a clearer perspective, they've regretted doing so. I just don't want you to do something you'll regret.'

'It's a bit late for that,' he mumbled, almost to himself. He turned to face me. 'Believe me, Kate, I'm not going to regret getting rid of that. I have absolutely no inclination to keep a reminder of the woman who vowed to love and be faithful to me, but instead decided to cheat on me with a man who had made the same promises to his own wife. Wedding vows clearly meant little to either of them so that album now means nothing to me.'

I bit my lip, all the fears of what he'd think of me, if he knew, were confirmed. The look on his face, the tone of his voice, the glittering hardness of his eyes – it was all there. He reached down and took the album.

'Don't you think that you ought to check and see if your wife – ex-wife – might want it before you consign it to the bin?'

I stood up, the tenseness in my back causing me to wince with cramp as I did so. Michael looked down at me. A muscle worked in his jaw as a half-smile slid onto his face. But, like the rest of his expression, it was cold.

'Let me get this right? This is the woman who made a complete fool out of me, out of our marriage, who let me almost entirely wreck my relationship with my family, causing me to miss out on things like births and first Christmases and all stuff that I can never, ever get back, and you think I should suddenly be all touchy-feely about hurting her feelings? Newsflash Kate: I don't give a flying shit about her feelings any more. If she'd have wanted it, she would have taken it when she left. She didn't want me or it, which is why she left in the first place.'

He tossed the album on the pile for discarding and ran his hands through his hair. Pilot had wandered back into the room at the sound of his master's raised voice and was now watching warily from just inside the doorway.

'I'm sorry,' I said, applying my professional placating voice to the situation. 'I never meant to bring up painful memories for you. I just need you to be sure that what you're doing is right, and that you're doing it for the right reasons.'

Michael shot me an incredulous look. 'Yeah, Kate. I know exactly what I'm doing. And, with respect, I think I probably know a hell of a lot more about these things than you do.'

'What's that supposed to mean?' So much for placation, but I couldn't help it.

'Nothing. Forget it.'

'No.' I stood facing him now, my back straight, chin tilted up, 'Clearly you have something to say and, as it's not like you to hold back, why don't you just say it?'

'Fine. I just think that maybe you should limit your advice to what you know about rather than things you have no experience of.'

'Meaning?'

He crossed his arms over his chest, the fitted T-shirt he wore moulding to the muscles that lay beneath it.

'Meaning that clearly you're very good at your job and at getting people's houses in order, but there are some things you need to let people figure out on their own.'

'I never tell people what they should and shouldn't keep! That's unfair.'

'You're telling me to keep a bloody wedding album that I don't want!'

'That's not what I was saying at all!'

'Look, Kate. Don't get me wrong, but just because you have this image in your head of perfect wedding days and marriage being all sunshine and roses, sometimes it's not. Sometimes it's bloody hard and heartbreaking and people get hurt! So, whilst I wish you all the best with this Calum bloke and hope that he does one day give you all the happiness you could wish for in that direction, I didn't get that and I don't need any reminders sitting around in this house of something that I'm finally moving on from.'

My mind was whirling and for a moment I couldn't find any words. And then I found some. In fact, I found a whole load of them.

Chapter Seventeen

'How dare you?' My voice was quiet but it was obvious that Michael sensed the anger within it. He opened his mouth but I cut him off before he could speak. 'You accuse me of talking about things of which I know nothing when you've just done exactly the same thing. You have no idea what I think about marriage or anything else, come to think of it! But just so you know, I actually do know a little about these things. I might not have been married myself but that doesn't mean I'm entirely ignorant about it all. And you couldn't be more wrong if you think I'm naive enough to think that marriage is some Disney-like state of affairs. I know it's not! Why the hell do you think I've steered clear of long-term relationships for so long?'

From not being able to find any words, it now seemed like I was unable to stop them.

'I'm sorry that your marriage broke down, I truly am. I know that she hurt you terribly and I'm sorry for that too. But don't act like it gives you the monopoly on the knowledge of painful situations Michael, because it doesn't. Not by a long shot!'

'Kate – '

'Do you want to know what my most vivid image of marriage actually is? It's of coming home from school to find my mother on the sofa, in her dressing gown, with an empty bottle of vodka on the floor beside her. It's of sitting beside her on the sofa at two o'clock in the morning as she waited for my father to come home, which he might or might not do. It's of cleaning the house and cooking the meals because she was rarely in a fit state to do it. It's of trying to remove the stain of a lipstick that isn't my mother's from my father's shirt and gagging at the smell of perfume from it that also isn't my mother's. It's of finding my mum at the bottom of the stairs and doctors telling me she has internal injuries. So, Michael, no, I don't have some sunshine and roses image of marriage and I know exactly how much hurt one person can cause another. So don't you dare accuse me of not caring or not understanding something just because I've never had a wedding band on my finger!'

Neither of us said anything for a moment. Our eyes were locked, mine blazing and his with the sort of shocked look to them that someone gets after they've just had the verbal equivalent of both barrels unloaded point-blank. The silence was heavy and suffocating. My chest heaved and I knew I had to get out of there.

'I think it's best if I left. You should do what you want with the album and the rest of the stuff. You know your own mind.'

I turned to go and Michael caught my hand.

'Kate.'

I shook my head and pulled away, half running down the stairs, thrusting my feet into my shoes when I got to the bottom. Grabbing my coat and scarf, I pulled open the door and stepped out into the lightly falling snow, shoving my arms into the sleeves as I ran along the road, needing to get away as fast as I could.

I'd never meant to unleash the torrent of words onto Michael. I knew his enquiries about my dinner with Calum had been made in the context of friendly conversation. And I certainly had never meant to tell him about my childhood with an alcoholic mother and a philandering father. I put my hand to my head, half in embarrassment at what I'd just revealed and half to try and still my now pounding head.

Hurrying along to the Tube station, I replayed my outburst, furious with myself for once again losing the professionalism of which I was so proud in front of Michael O'Farrell. Over six years and I'd never once lost it until I met him, on the first, and now what I imagined would probably be my last, appointment with him. Perfect bookends of embarrassment. He was well on the way to being done anyway and Bernice could deal with the last bits.

We'd spoken casually about me helping with some ideas on how to get the house properly finished from an interior design perspective a few sessions back, but I think it was safe to say that was now a non-starter. Apart from anything else, I wasn't sure I would ever be able to face him again. And certainly not any time soon. I pulled off my scarf, suddenly hot even though I hadn't yet descended into the warmth of the Tube tunnels. As I crammed myself in between the hordes of workers, tourists and Christmas shoppers all vying for a spot on the escalator, I heard my phone bleep with a message. I pulled it out and opened the text from Bernice.

Last-minute booking tomorrow. Tried to reschedule but client started crying so gave in! Full day now so won't see you until Monday. Just wanted to check all OK and to update you. Hope the session with the Gorgeous Grinch went OK today. Have a fab weekend and see you soon xx

Even though I'd explained that Michael was generally less Grinch-like now than at our first encounter, the nickname had stuck.

No problem. And you xx

I typed quickly and pressed send. Except actually, big problem. Because that meant I couldn't get Bernice to take over Michael's session tomorrow.

I got off the escalator and joined the throng of people turning right towards the platform I needed. It felt even warmer than usual down here this evening, probably in contrast to the cold weather playing out above our heads. I slipped off my coat and hung it over my shoulder bag. The train pulled in and we piled inside. All the seats were taken but I managed to wedge myself against the wall next to the doors and wrapped my hands around the yellow pole beside me, partly to steady myself against the couple of sharp curves I knew lay ahead on this line and partly because I had the odd feeling that if I didn't hold on to something I was going to end up on the floor.

* * *

'You should go home.' Michael's look brooked no argument when he opened the door to me the following day.

Great. I'd totally blown it.

I'd had a terrible night going over the argument with Michael in my head, and all the memories that it had dragged up, not to mention still trying to get my head around the whole Calum thing. I'd gone to bed, not being able to decide if I was hot or cold, and feeling like someone was using my cranium for cymbal practice and had woken up to find that the whole percussion section had now joined them. And just to add to the fun, talks to avoid a Tube strike had broken down meaning I'd had to hike along Hyde Park Lane, battling against forty-five degree rain and a headwind. And all for nothing as my client wasn't even going to let me in the door.

'Michael, please just let me explain. I totally understand that you probably don't want me anywhere near your house after my meltdown yesterday, and I was actually going to ask Bernice to cover these last sessions for me, knowing that you wouldn't want to continue with me – '

'That's not what I meant,' he said, scooping an arm around my shoulder and pulling me inside the house. 'I meant you look terrible and should be at home in bed.'

I looked at him properly for the first time since he'd opened the door and saw that his face was creased with concern, deep furrows on his forehead, and his mouth set in a grim line.

'You're soaked,' he said, helping me out of my coat. 'I know there's a Tube strike but please tell me you got a taxi.'

I raised an eyebrow. 'At this time in the morning, at Christmas, and when there's a strike on? It was quicker to walk. And I'm fine. It's just a little cold.'

He shook his head. 'What am I going to do with you?'

234

I looked up at him hesitantly. 'And what is the answer to that question?'

Michael tilted his head.

'I mean, am I fired?'

'Are you fired? For what? For finally telling me something about yourself? Of course you're not fired. Come on, let's get something hot inside you.'

I waved my hand and felt myself turn a little green.

'No, really I'm fine, thank you. I'm happy just to get this last – '

Michael's hand caught mine and pulled me back gently. His other hand went to my chin, tilting it up until my eyes met his.

'Kate. You're really not well. I'm not happy about you working like this. I already got loads done the other night after you left.'

'You did?'

He nodded. 'I needed something to focus on.'

I lowered my eyes, but my chin was still caught in his hand, the slight roughness of his fingers feeling disturbingly good against my skin.

'I really should have got Bernice on this job, I think. I've never once lost my cool with a client, and then you come along and ruin my perfect score.'

His mouth curved into a half-smile. 'Sorry about that.'

'Just so long as you don't put a bad review up online about me.'

'Definitely not going to happen.'

I smiled, still trying to ignore the clanging in my head. 'Thank you. And I really am sorry. I'm normally so much more professional than this.'

'There's nothing to be sorry for. Really. In my family, we say what we think. There are some arguments, sure, but then the air is clear. Everyone knows where they stand. And that's right behind one another. It's how things work. Doesn't do anyone any good to keep stuff bottled up inside. I just wish you'd said something earlier.'

His hands had moved to my shoulders now and I had the distinct feeling they were helping me stay upright, even if Michael didn't know it.

'I'm hardly going to go around telling clients something like that.'

'No. I just meant…'

I lifted my eyes to find him looking at me. I saw his Adam's apple bob as he swallowed. 'No, of course not. Come on, let's get you a hot drink at least. Do you have a jumper or something? You're shivering.'

'No, I'm all right,' I replied, feeling anything but and less so with every minute. But I was pretty sure I could work through it and distract myself by just getting on with the job as I usually did. 'And I don't feel cold at all.' This part, at least, was true. I actually felt pretty damn warm.

'Right.'

Five minutes later I was sat in the living room, where Michael already had the wood burner fired up. Pilot was lying in front of it, snoring. As we entered, he woke and lifted his head, his tail banging lazily on the floor as he decided whether he could muster the energy, or inclination, to relinquish his comfy spot.

'I went out for a run last night and first thing this morning. I don't think he's used to quite that much exercise.'

'I think you're right. He was a little overweight when he came to us. He did get walked, just perhaps not as much as he needed. Looks like that's changing.'

'I don't know if he's too impressed about that.'

I touched Michael's arm, still looking at the dog. 'He's loving it.' I broke away to lean over and give Pilot a stroke. 'I didn't know you were a runner.'

Michael lowered himself to the floor beside us, stretching his long legs out in front of him, one knee falling to the side a little.

'I'm not really. Too many years of rugby has knackered my knees a bit but I still do it sometimes. Good for clearing the head.'

I stored that nugget of information away. A bit of head clearing didn't sound like a bad idea to me at the moment. Although, let's face it, me and running equalled a very unlikely pairing. Especially today, when keeping upright was proving a tough enough challenge as it was.

'You know, you really don't look well. Why don't you let me take you home?'

I shook my head. 'It's nothing. I'm sure it'll go off.' I wished I was as confident of this as I made myself sound.

Michael watched me for a moment. 'And people call me stubborn.'

'It's not that at all. You of all people understand the kind of pressure running your own business puts on you. You can't just go taking sick days willy-nilly.'

'I get the feeling you don't do anything willy-nilly.'

'Great. Another statement that makes me sound incredibly boring.'

'That's not what I meant. So how many sick days have you taken since starting your company?'

The truth was I hadn't taken any. I'd rearranged a couple of appointments so that I didn't go taking germs to clients, but I'd never actually had a day in bed and not worked. My biggest concession was a couple of hours on the sofa on a particularly rough day. It was just what I did. What I'd always done.

When I was sick as a child, Mum generally wasn't in an appropriate enough state to snuggle me into the duvet and dose me up with Calpol. I didn't even know that was a 'thing' for ages. I never resented Mum for it, it was just how it was. I didn't really remember a time that it wasn't. So I just got on with it. On the times when she would sober up and hazily realise I was full of some bug or other, I'd see her overcome with a wash of guilt and she'd make an effort to try and do the traditional mum thing. Until she took another drink and her world became blurry again. In truth, it had actually been pretty good training for running my own business. Once again, it was just a case of getting on with it.

'I do understand. It's hard when everything's on you.'

I flicked my eyes up. 'I just hope I haven't brought any germs to you, though.'

He gave a half-smile. 'Don't worry about it. I'm pretty resilient. Even germs think I'm too much hassle to live with.'

I gave a weak smile, which exactly matched how the rest of me felt.

Half an hour later, I became aware of Michael studying me. I brought my head up, the effort of doing so seeming three times as hard as usual. He narrowed his eyes at me.

'OK. That's it. You're going home.'

'What? No, just let me finish – '

'The only thing that's going to be finished here is you if you carry on. You look bloody awful.'

I gave a watery smile. 'Thanks.'

'You've no colour at all and I can see a film of sweat on your forehead.'

The horrified look I gave him was swiftly followed by me scooting the back of my hand across my forehead, which did indeed feel damp. Lovely. Bearing in mind I felt about as warm as a bag of frozen peas right now, this seemed a little odd. Not to mention mortifyingly embarrassing.

'It's just a little warm in here. You're in a T-shirt! It's hardly the Arctic.'

'And you've shed three layers, put them back on, and then taken them off again since you got here and are now sitting in a sleeveless top shivering.' He leant over and put the back of his hand on my forehead. 'And you're burning up. You're done.'

I looked up at him, his hand still lingering on my forehead.

'Don't think I won't throw you out if you refuse to leave. You already know I can be an arrogant arse when I want to be.'

I tried to laugh and ended up coughing.

'Up you get.' He pushed himself up and reached a hand down to me.

Surreptitiously I wiped my own hand on my dress before taking his. As I raised my eyes, I saw the grin. Caught. It was testament to just how crap I was now feeling that I was almost beyond caring of this fact. Almost.

I stood, putting in what I felt was an Oscar-worthy performance of feeling better than I did. But apparently the Oscar this year was going to someone else because as I made to step towards the door, the world began turning a bit blurry. And then a lot blurry. And suddenly the floor looked a lot closer than I seemed to remember it looking a second before.

In the distance I heard someone calling my name. 'Kate? Katie?'

As my eyes regained their focus, I raised them and met Michael's. The normally faint lines on his brow were deeper as he looked at me, and my body was being held close to his. I could feel his heartbeat and the taut hardness of his chest against mine. And then his arms moved and I was scooped up.

'What are you doing?' I squeaked out, my throat now deciding to join in with all the other bits of my body that weren't functioning at optimum levels today.

'I'm putting you on the sofa and I'm phoning Janey.'

'No. Don't, please. She has more than enough on her plate right now. I don't need anyone.' I gave a push against his chest, which achieved absolutely nothing.

Michael bent his knees, two loud cracks emanating from them as he did so, and deposited me gently on the couch. I immediately tried to push myself up and felt the sweat break out on my forehead again. Michael gave me a look that as much as said 'I told you so'.

'Michael?' I said, my voice quiet.

He leant in, hand brushing my brow, his voice gentle. 'Yes?'

'I think I'm going to throw up.' At which point, I lost the ability to concentrate on the horrifying embarrassment of the situation and focused instead on trying not to heave over my client. As the world swam in front of my eyes again, I managed to focus on the bowl that Michael had produced within seconds – clearly his size belied his speed – and vomited. Excellent. My mortification was now entirely complete.

Michael ignored my request not to call Janey – big surprise – and the next thing I knew she was perched beside me on the sofa, stroking my forehead.

'Hello.'

'Hi. I told him not to call you. I'm fine. Really. Just ate something a bit dodgy probably.'

'Katie, love? Can I let you into a secret? And don't take this the wrong way.'

I raised an eyebrow in reply as it took less effort than speaking.

'You look like crap. And I mean that in the nicest way.'

'Of course.' I gave her a watery smile.

'It looks like you've caught that bug that the kids had the other week. It should only last a few days but I'm not letting you go home on your own like this. You're coming to our place where I can keep an eye on you.'

I mustered up all my strength, which admittedly right now wasn't a whole lot, but it was enough.

'No, Janey, I'm not. I'm going home. I promise I will go straight to bed, but I'm not imposing on you. You're pregnant, for goodness' sake, apart from anything else!'

'You're not imposing. And it's not optional.'

'You're overreacting,' I croaked out, and caught Michael in the glance. 'Both of you.' And then I threw up again. I sat back, vaguely aware that Michael was rubbing my back and holding my hair which, thanks to the wind and rain and everything else had now abandoned its foundations and given up on its updo status. I knew just how it felt.

Janey cast her eyes over me, down at the bowl, then back at me again. She didn't say anything but her look spoke volumes. Removing the bowl, she left the room and a few moments later the downstairs loo flushed.

'Mikey?' she called.

Calling Pilot, Michael leant over and scooped his arm under my legs.

'Hold on,' he instructed, and I did. All of a sudden I was exhausted, completely and utterly. Without thinking, I rested my head against his chest and felt his arms tighten around me. Janey laid my coat over me and all four of us, five if you counted the teddy Pilot now insisted on taking everywhere, left the house. Janey unlocked the car door with the remote and popped the boot as she got in.

Michael looked at the dog. 'Up.' Pilot obeyed, sitting down on one hip.

Michael tipped me towards his body, so that I was resting heavily on his chest for a moment as he quickly grabbed the boot lid and pushed it closed before wrapping his arm back around me. As he turned, I vaguely caught sight of the dog's face, replete with teddy dangling from his mouth by one arm, peering contentedly out of the back window.

Janey had already opened the back door for her brother and Michael now slid us both in the back seat. Adjusting our position, he reached over to fix the seat belt in place as my vague fumblings were having little effect. Plugging it into the holder, he gave Janey the OK and she pulled off out into the traffic.

Outside the window the sky was dark with cloud. It had barely lightened the entire day. Thankfully, Christmas lights threw their cheer from people's front windows, and strings of them stretched across the roads, their lights bright against the gloomy backdrop of sky. In fact, they seemed incredibly bright today. I closed my eyes against them momentarily.

'You OK?' Michael's soft accent drifted towards me.

I nodded, my hand immediately moving to the back of my neck as I did so, at the soreness the movement caused.

'I think we need to get you into bed.'

I bumped my head against his shoulder, in part because I seemed to have little control of it as we rounded a corner.

'I bet you say that to all the girls.'

His laugh was soft but I felt it rumble through his chest as he pulled me towards him. The kiss he dropped on the top of my head was even softer. In fact, it was so soft, and so…well, out of character for our relationship that I could only think that whatever delightful bug I was fighting was now causing me to hallucinate. But I'd had worse dreams than an undeniably gorgeous man holding me close, smoothing my hair back and resting a large, cool hand on my forehead so, right now, I was happy just to drift about in this one. And categorically ignore the bit of it where I'd thrown up in front of him. Twice.

Chapter Eighteen

The rest of the evening was all a bit blurry, which was just as well as I was pretty sure it had involved yet more hurling. As weak daylight pushed its way through the darkness, I lay in the bed and looked up at the ceiling, knowing I had to get back to my own flat. Although I was inordinately glad of the siblings' kindness yesterday, it wasn't fair for me to descend on Janey and her family. They had enough to cope with with two young children and a baby on the way, without me cluttering up the place.

I rolled my head – an action that took far more effort than it should have done – and looked at the clock, screwing my face up when I read the time. OK. So, maybe I'd just grab a couple of hours more sleep and then head off home.

When I woke, it was slightly later than I'd planned. As in, half a day later than I'd planned and Janey was sitting on the edge of the bed. On the other side, Lily was leaning on it, peering at me.

'Hi.'

'Hi,' I replied, in a raspy voice.

'How are you feeling?'

'Better.' Which was true. I still felt pretty damn dreadful but I did feel better than I had done yesterday. It was all relative.

'You're still looking pretty ropey,' Janey stated, before sticking a thermometer against my forehead. A second later it beeped. Janey looked at it and made a hmm noise before popping it on the bedside. 'Your temperature is still high and you'll be dehydrated after yesterday so we need to start getting some liquids into you.' Janey's nursing training kicked back in and I couldn't deny it was comforting to be here, but I knew I couldn't stay.

I took her hand. 'Janey. Thank you so much for taking care of me, but I really need to go home now.'

'Out of the question. I'm not having you at home on your own in that flat when it's far easier for me to keep an eye on you here.'

'You don't need to keep an eye on me. I really am feeling much better than I did. And I promise I'll drink, like you said.'

Janey tucked a strand of hair behind my ear. 'You can promise whatever you like, sweetie. You have a temperature of one hundred and two and you're not going anywhere.'

That at least explained why I currently felt like one of those cook-in-the-bag chickens.

'Don't you like our house, Katie?' Lily had been studying me and now her big green eyes were full of question.

'Oh no, Lily! It's not that at all.'

'What is it then?' she asked, her hand going to where mine lay on the outside of the duvet and her little fingers curling around mine.

'Well, your mum and dad are busy already and I don't want to take up any more of their time.'

Lily started playing with my fingers.

'When I was poorly Mummy looked after me.'

I smiled as did Janey.

'If you're not here, will your mummy look after you?' She lifted her innocent eyes to mine. I saw Janey's face tense. I shook my head, trying to ignore the swooshy feeling the movement caused.

'Why not? Is she far away?'

'Yes, she is, sweetheart.'

'Which is exactly why Katie is staying here until she gets better. Come on, Lily. Leave Katie in peace now. Did you finish your puzzle downstairs yet?'

Lily nodded. 'Uncle Michael and Pilot helped me.'

'Pilot's a smart dog.'

'I love him.' Lily beamed, making me smile too.

'He is rather wonderful,' Janey agreed, throwing a private glance my way. 'I'll be back in a bit.' She pointed a finger at me. 'Do not move!'

I gave a weak half salute and let my head flop back onto the pillow. Vaguely aware of the sound of rain beating against the window, I rolled my head a little to look out. Rain streaked down the glass, the droplets racing each other and melding together as more joined them. Looking past them, I watched the trees as they bent with the force of the wind.

'It's pretty vile out there.' The deep voice made me jump, mostly because it wasn't Janey's. 'Even Pilot gave me a filthy look when I took him out earlier.' Michael gave me one of those easy smiles, the one I'd seen him use with his family, but rarely outside that. His hair was damp and pushed back and he wore a semi-fitted black

T-shirt with khaki cargo pants. 'Can I come in? Janey's sent up some soup and a drink for you.'

'Of course,' I said, pulling the sheet up almost to my neck.

Michael waited whilst I settled myself. 'Comfy?'

I nodded.

He frowned, then put the tray down on the dressing table. Leaning over, he grabbed another pillow. 'Sit up a minute.' I did so and he squished another pillow behind me. 'Better?'

It was. Much. I nodded.

'Right. Here you go.'

It wasn't that it didn't look nice or smell good, I just wasn't sure I felt like eating anything right now. I lifted my gaze and found Michael watching me.

'Just so you know, if I go back with anything other than empty plates, it'll be my fault. That's already been made perfectly clear to me.' I pulled a face and he grinned. 'I'll leave you to it.'

'Thank you, Michael. For this and for yesterday.'

He shook his head and turned to go. I took a spoonful of the soup.

'I'm sorry about the whole boyfriend being married thing, by the way.'

I half swallowed and half choked on the food as the impact of his statement hit me. At the same time, my eyes took in the fact that Janey's guest bedding was pure white and the soup was tomato red. Michael was back across the room in two strides, removing the tray so that I could die choking in peace without ruining my host's bed linen. He handed me the glass of water and I managed to find a gap in the coughing to shove some down my throat, which thankfully began calming matters.

'OK?' he asked, bending to replace the tray in front of me, but staying poised to remove it should I try a repeat performance.

OK wasn't exactly the best description of how I was feeling so I didn't reply.

He put the tray down anyway, taking my silence as acceptance. I kept my eyes away from his and my mind focused on what had possessed his sister to tell him when she'd promised not to.

'Janey didn't mean to tell me.'

I remained silent, concentrating on spoonfuls of soup, my mind darting about, trying to get my groggy brain to find a way to leave without upsetting Janey. Or more likely finding a convenient drainpipe to shimmy down which was probably the only chance I had at leaving right now if my friend had anything to do with it. When I finished, Michael took the tray away and put it on the side. But he didn't leave. For a moment, neither of us said anything.

'Don't be angry at Janey for telling me.'

I shook my head. 'I'm not.' I knew telling him intentionally wouldn't have entered her mind once she'd promised me not to.

'I know you and I haven't always seen eye to eye about your boyfriend, but if you were mine...I mean...' He fiddled with the spoon in the soup bowl a moment. 'Well, although I agreed that Janey looking after you was the best thing, I thought that maybe we ought to let your boyfriend know. You know, in case he finally wanted to step up and do something for you.' I gave him a wary look under my lashes. 'Janey was busy mixing up paracetamol or whatever magic potion it was and was obviously distracted...'

Turning my head towards the window, I focused on the rain. 'What did she say?'

Michael hesitated. 'Something about his wife probably not being too keen on that idea.'

I closed my eyes and waited for him to leave.

His hand on mine made me start. My eyes flew open to find his intense gaze on me. Quickly, I looked down, focusing on the long, sturdy fingers resting on top of mine.

'I know that we started out a bit rocky and that I'm really just a client, so I know it shouldn't matter... It's just that I'd sort of thought we were becoming friends.'

I flicked my glance up to meet his for a moment.

'Admittedly friends that don't always agree but that's OK too.' He gave that twitch of a smile I'd seen the first day when I'd called him out for being an arse. 'But I'd hoped we'd got to a point where you could at least have told me you'd split up with your boyfriend. I would have made an effort to try and say the right thing. No guarantee I would have said it but I would have tried.'

'I couldn't,' I said, softly.

His brow creased. 'Am I really that bad?'

I shook my head and automatically moved my hand. He caught it and held it.

'What then?' his voice was soft, and when I looked up, his face was creased with concern, the green eyes that entranced me held my gaze, demanding an answer.

'Because I thought we...might be able to be friends too. But I knew that once you knew this about me... you wouldn't want anything to do with me.' I let my gaze drop. 'Even though you are the only client who has driven me to distraction, made me lose my temper, and self-control, for some reason, I didn't want you thinking badly of me.'

'And why would I be thinking badly of you?'

'You know why.'

'Because he was married?'

I closed my eyes and turned my head, bile rising again just at the thought of it all.

'A fact you had no idea of.'

I shook my head.

'So in what complicated little scenario would that make me think the worst of you?'

Calum's words bounced off the walls of my mind.

'He told me that I must have had some inkling, some idea that everything wasn't…as it should be.'

'Did you?' Michael's tone wasn't accusatory.

'No.' Finally I looked at him. 'I stupidly just swallowed every lie he told me.'

Michael studied me for a moment, before his fingers reached out to tuck a wayward piece of hair back behind my ear.

'Katie, just to be clear, I do not think badly of you. Him? Well, let's just say I was right when I said you deserved better.'

'I just felt the whole thing might be a little close to home for you, and I wouldn't have blamed you for feeling…something towards me.'

'I do feel something towards you, Katie…and don't look so worried.' His gentle laugh relaxed his face and body, and it was hard not to respond in kind. And I might have done, if I hadn't suddenly felt so tired. Knowing that Michael didn't hate me or think I was some sort of destroyer of families had released a knot of tension I'd been carrying since that night. Like I'd said, I hadn't even known why his opinion of me mattered so much. What other people thought of me wasn't usually high on my priority list. Unless I cared about them.

'You look exhausted.' Michael gently tipped me forward enough to whip out the extra pillow he'd used to prop me up to eat. 'Why don't you get some rest? We can talk some more later.'

I made a half-hearted effort to nod, my eyelids already closing.

'You're not alone any more, Katie.' The deep lilting voice drifted into my dream as I felt a large, gentle hand softly stroke the hair from my face.

Some time later, my eyes still closed, I became vaguely aware of the sound of snoring at exactly the same time as realising that there was someone else in the room. As, in theory, I was the only one asleep, it led me to conclude two things: that the noise was emanating from me and that I wasn't alone to hear it. These things all declared themselves in my brain at roughly the same time, culminating in me waking up, sitting bolt upright and announcing that 'I wasn't snoring'. Even though clearly I had been.

The figure in the room moved. Michael. He was folded into the nearby chair reading, one long leg dangling over the arm, a lamp beside him providing enough illumination without keeping me awake. Unfortunately. He leant forward, swinging his leg down and over Pilot who was sprawled out on the floor in front of the chair.

'You know, it's not a big deal. Women worry too much about that sort of thing.'

I must have looked even more horrified than I felt. Although, admittedly, that might have been hard.

Michael began laughing. 'Relax. It wasn't you.' I realised then that I could still hear the snoring.

Michael pointed at the dog. 'It's him. You and the rescue centre conveniently forgot to tell me he snores like a hippo with a head cold.'

Having flopped back down, I now rolled onto my side to look at the dog.

'I can't say I ever noticed it before. Maybe it's just when he goes into a deeper sleep, and he wasn't relaxed enough in the kennels to do that. It's not unusual.'

'The snoring?' Michael grinned. 'It might not be unusual, but it's loud.'

'It's not that bad. We can't all be perfect.' I reached down and stroked Pilot's ear.

'That's true. It did at least drown your snoring out, so there's that.'

My hand stilled and I shifted my eyes to him. He was rubbish at keeping a straight face and it was written all over his beautiful features.

'You're not supposed to be mean to the afflicted.'

'I know. I'm sorry. Couldn't resist.'

'But you could give it a try, Mikey,' Janey said, entering the room and flicking his ear as she passed him.

'Ow!' He frowned, but it did nothing to cover the laughter dancing in his eyes.

'How are you feeling, sweetheart? Apart from being irritated by this lummox.' She thumbed at Michael who mumbled something like 'charming' before bending down to stroke the dog. Pilot groaned, stretched, opened one eye briefly and then went back to snoring.

Janey placed the thermometer on me again.

'That's good. It's not back to normal yet but it is lower.'

'Does that mean I can go home?' I asked. The truth was, it wasn't the thought of sitting alone in my flat still feeling decidedly rough that held appeal for me, it was that I desperately wanted a shower. Having apparently sweated out most of the bug I'd picked up, I now felt decidedly icky.

'Nope. But you can have a shower or a bath if that's what you're thinking.'

Oh God. I ponged! I surreptitiously tried to give a sniff but Janey caught my eye. 'I just thought you might feel better for it. That's all. Don't go getting all wobbly in there though.'

'I promise.'

'I can give you a hand and make sure if you like. For safety reasons only. Obviously.' Michael winked at me as Janey turned to leave.

She rolled her eyes at me, ignoring him. 'You know where everything is. There's a towel, toothbrush and some clean jammies waiting in there for you.'

'Thanks, Janey.' I took her hand and reached up for a hug, my eyes unexpectedly, and inexplicably, filling with tears. Janey wiped a rogue one away as she stood.

'You're very welcome.' Her smile was soft and said so much more than her words. 'Right,' she said. 'We'll leave you to it.' She looked at Michael meaningfully. He got the hint and I could see he was about to wake the dog too.

'Pilot can stay. I mean, if you don't mind. It seems a shame to wake him. Unless you're leaving, of course.' I loved the feeling of having the dog lying there contentedly, keeping me company. And I knew it wasn't just the dog's company I would miss.

Michael gave a brief smile. 'No, we weren't planning on leaving just yet.'

I shifted in the bed, scooting myself up a little more, ready to get out. Janey prodded the back of her brother's leg with her knee.

'She doesn't need an audience.'

He tilted his head down at her. 'Jesus, you're bossy.' But there was nothing but adoration in his eyes. OK, there was a little mischief there too.

'See you later,' he smiled.

I gave a wave and they both left, leaving the snoozing dog and me to our thoughts and a much needed shower.

When I got back I could immediately see the sheets had been changed and a steaming cup of something sat on the bedside. Mentally I made a note to send Janey the biggest bouquet of flowers I could find when I got back home. The hot herbal tea instantly soothed as I snuggled into the freshly plumped pillows. I closed my eyes and sipped the tea.

Pilot had now moved his head and was now sounding less like a pneumatic drill. His steady, even breathing added to the calm I'd felt developing inside me ever since Michael and I had talked about the whole Calum thing. I'd hated hiding the truth from him, although how much I'd hated it still surprised me. Perhaps it was because I detested lying so much. And yet I'd found myself doing just that in order to prevent him putting an end to the organisation process – a process I knew was working for him, and making Janey happy. That had to be the reason. There wasn't really any other explanation.

They say that bacon sandwiches have been the downfall of many an ex-vegetarian. From the smell drifting up this morning, I totally got that. Not that I'd ever been a vegetarian. I freely admitted to loving bacon sandwiches far too much to ever give them up. Although I was feeling so much better than two days ago, even this morning's ablutions had made me feel like I'd just spent three hours prepping for the next Olympics. I sat on the bed, waiting for the burst of energy that I knew would come eventually if I concentrated hard enough on it. Or not.

A knock on the door made me look up.

'Come in.'

Michael's head peeked around the door.

'Are you decent?'

'It's a bit late if I'm not, isn't it?' I laughed as Pilot charged in through the door. He bounded up beside the bed and stood there, tail whacking the duvet, with a big, happy look on his face. This was what I loved about dogs. You could be gone for two minutes and they would greet you like it had been weeks. I rubbed his head and he did his little four paw bounce thing until Michael told him to sit, which he did, one side of his body pressed into the bed.

His master entered the room at a more sedate pace, carrying a tray. As I glanced up I felt a whoosh of heat hit my chest and zoom up my face.

'You all right?' he asked, concern in his voice. 'Still getting those hot and cold flashes? Hopefully it's on its way out now though.'

'Mmmhmm.' I smiled and dropped my gaze back to the dog for a moment, willing my colour back to normal. The truth was I was pretty sure the reason for my sudden temperature fluctuation was far more basic, and more to do with the fact that one of the most good-looking men I had ever met was now stood at my bedside, bearing a thick bacon sandwich that smelled divine. In fact, there was a split second when I wondered if the whole bug thing had actually been a little more serious than I thought and I'd passed on. There was a gorgeous man, a lovely dog, a comfy bed and bacon sarnies. If Heaven doesn't contain those things, then frankly I was far less keen to go. And then Pilot did something that confirmed I was still firmly earthbound.

'Holy shit, Pilot,' Michael cried, shoving the long sleeve of his T-shirt over his nose and hurriedly leading the dog out of the room. I meanwhile had slid back under the duvet which was now pressed against my face, just my eyes peeping over the top.

'Sorry.' Michael's voice was muffled by the fabric and his arm when he spoke. He pointed at the window. 'Just for a minute.'

I nodded vigorously.

Thankfully the air interchange was swift and effective, and, actually, it was pretty nice to breathe in the cool air after the last couple of days.

'I'm so sorry about that. I'd say I don't know what's got into him, but I think I do. Janey and Patrick were overjoyed that my nephew finally ate his Brussel sprouts for the first time at dinner last night. I didn't say anything, but I'm fairly confident Joey wasn't the one who ate them.' He pulled the window closed again, and I emerged from the duvet, whereupon Michael handed me the sandwich.

'Does Joey know you know?' I asked, taking a bite of the sandwich.

He screwed up his nose for a second. 'I've a horrible feeling I might have been the one to give him the idea.'

I tilted my head for an explanation as I chewed on the sandwich, which tasted even better than it had smelled.

'A while ago we were all talking about this old dog we used to have back home, when we were kids. None of us were fussy eaters but I did have a loathing for broad

256

beans. Still can't stand the things. When Mum mentioned that I was such a good lad because I ate them anyway, I had to admit then that I'd actually fed the beans to the dog under the table when no one was looking. I guess little Joey stored that away for future use.'

'Are you going to tell Janey?'

'Do I look like a snitch to you?' He grinned and I took an extra big bite to distract myself from how good that looked on him. 'Besides, I'm his favourite uncle and I'm not about to relinquish that title by dobbing him in on something I used to do myself.'

'That's fair.'

'You can't tell Janey either, though!' This time his face was serious.

I shook my head. He did the grin again but I'd run out of sandwich so I buried my face in the mug of tea instead.

'Is it snowing?' I asked, reappearing and squinting at the window.

'Started about half an hour ago. Fairly heavily too.' He slid a glance sideways at me. 'So if you're thinking you can just toddle on home, you can't. I've strict instructions to keep you exactly where you are.'

I smiled. 'Is that so?'

'It is. And as you know, not much scares me, apart from my baby sister, so please don't make me do something drastic like tie you to the bed.'

My eyebrows shot up involuntarily, immediately followed by Michael's.

'Admittedly that came out a little wrong.' He looked at me and I saw the twinkle. 'Although…'

The look I gave him caused his face to crease and a laugh rumble from his chest.

'Maybe when you're feeling a little better.'

I flopped my head against the pillow.

'I'm not sure which version of you I like better – the grouchy, moody one or the cheerier, but infinitely more perverse one.'

He wiggled his eyebrows and then flopped onto the end of the bed.

'I have to say thanks, Katie. I can't believe the difference you've made. Home actually feels like home now. I've always loved the house but now it feels…different somehow.'

'You sound surprised.'

He fiddled with the pintucks on the duvet cover, not looking at me. 'I am, if I'm honest. You know I only started all this because I had to. But it's really been good for me. In a lot of ways.'

'I'm glad to hear it, Michael. Really glad.'

He smiled back and, for a moment, I thought he was going to say something else. Downstairs the front door closed and we heard voices.

'Still alive up there?' Patrick called.

'No thanks to Pilot,' Michael quipped, shooting a look at the dog who had been lying at the doorway since his dismissal earlier. Pilot hid his nose under his paw.

Lily and Joey tore into the guest room. 'Katie! Uncle Mikey! It's really snowing! Like proper snow! Will you come out and play with us? Mum said we can go out after dinner.' Joey's face was shining with excitement.

'Did she now?' Michael bent his knees and scooped up his nephew. Lily, meanwhile, was clearly of the more sensible disposition and saw the snow for what it was – cold and wet but pretty to look at it from inside.

She had now climbed onto the bed and was sat beside me, playing with my hair.

'You have pretty hair. I wish mine was longer.'

'Well you'll have to make do playing with Katie's because I don't have to deal with tantrums washing hers,' Janey puffed out as she entered the room. I saw Michael's eyes scan her face.

'Everything all right? Why didn't you call up? I can get whatever it is you need.'

'Stop fretting, Mikey. It's good exercise. And I've done this twice before, don't forget.' When his face didn't clear, she reached round and gave him a squeeze. 'I won't overdo anything, I promise.'

He waited a beat and then squeezed her back with his free arm. 'You'd better not.'

'Is anyone else having any of this dinner or is it all for me?' Patrick called up the stairs.

'Me, me, me!' both the children cried.

Joey's legs were wiggling to get down. Michael cuddled him a moment longer, leaning conspiratorially towards him as Janey redid the clip in Lily's hair which was sliding downwards.

'And no feeding Pilot anything this time,' he whispered.

Joey looked at his uncle, their eyes level. He opened his mouth to say something and Michael did a tiny tilt of his head to stop him and shook his head, a smile on his face.

'I mean it. He nearly gassed us up here earlier.' His nephew giggled as Michael screwed up his face. 'What's on your plate goes in your tummy only, OK?'

'OK.'

Janey turned around from finishing with Lily. 'What are you two whispering about?'

Their innocent expressions matched perfectly as they both shrugged. Janey threw me a look.

'Like I believe that.'

Michael put Joey down and both children ran off downstairs.

'Hold the banister, please!' Janey called after them.

I'd politely refused any dinner, the sandwich from earlier still filling me, and Janey and Michael left me to get some more rest. The door closed and I rolled onto my side, better to see the snow falling outside the window.

Chapter Nineteen

I dozed on and off but couldn't sleep properly so after a while I got up and perched myself on the window ledge, surveying the neighbourhood as it turned white under the snow, and fairy lights began twinkling in the gloom of the afternoon. The door opened and Janey popped her head in.

'Oh, you're awake. I was just going to ask if you wanted anything.'

I opened my mouth.

'Apart from to go home. If you're all right tomorrow morning, Mikey's said he'll run you home. Until then, I'm keeping an eye on you.'

'Janey, I hope you don't think I don't appreciate everything because I really do.'

She came and sat next to me on the wide windowsill. 'I know you do. And you know, sometimes it's OK to actually let people take care of you.'

I must have looked a little unconvinced because Janey took my hand. 'It's not showing weakness, Katie. I know you didn't have the choice growing up and it was all up to you –'

'Mum tried her best.' Although I would get frustrated with Mum sometimes, my automatic reaction was still defence.

Janey didn't take offence. 'I'm sure she did. I'm just saying that, due to circumstances, things were different for you than they are for a lot of kids. You didn't have anyone to turn to. You were the support when, really, it should have been the other way around. But it doesn't have to be that way for ever.'

'I'm not sure about that.'

'Why do you say that?'

I leant my head against the window, watching the snow pile up in a drift against Janey's back fence.

'If I'm going to end up with people like Calum, then maybe I am just best on my own.'

'So you're going to write off all men as potential Calums?' She gave me the same look I'd seen her give Lily a few weeks ago when she'd claimed to have had no idea where Janey's new lipstick was. Unfortunately, the fact that, at that moment, Lily looked like a clown who'd put his make-up on whilst three sheets to the wind, and that the lipstick colour was remarkably similar to her mother's new 'Va-Va-Voom Red' rather gave her away. Janey's look categorically told Lily then, and me now, that what we were saying was rubbish.

'No. But even you have to admit I'm not so good at this whole picking the right man lark.'

'You have to let people in, Katie. Some of the others might have been OK if you'd not kept them at arm's length.'

'When I finally took that advice, it still turned into a disaster.'

Janey sighed. 'Admittedly, that wasn't ideal. But that doesn't mean the next man you open up to is going to be another Calum.'

'Bearing in mind the second man I told about everything was your brother, and I was yelling at him when I did, then whilst I agree he's definitely not another Calum, it wasn't exactly a warm and fuzzy moment either.'

'Yeah, he did call to see if you'd come to us that night. He mentioned that you'd had a bit of a heated moment. I told him not to worry. Obviously I knew you were on edge about the Calum thing but I couldn't tell Mikey that.'

I gave her a little smile.

'OK. I couldn't tell him about it at that point. It sort of slipped out later. I'm pregnant, you have to make allowances.'

I laughed. 'You're going to have to think of a new excuse once the baby comes, you know that, don't you?'

'Oh no, I've got a while with the "baby brain" excuse yet. Don't worry.' She grinned. 'I am sorry about letting that slip with Mikey though. I honestly didn't mean to. It just came out.'

'It's all right. I...sort of wanted him to know. We'd been getting on OK and then suddenly I was dodging questions. It felt like we'd taken a step backwards. But the circumstances...'

'He understands now. But you mustn't assume everyone will automatically think the worst of you.'

'No. I know that now...'

'It looks like there's a "but" coming.'

Janey knew me too well.

'But perhaps there's a reason. Perhaps I'm just not made for all this.' I waved my hand, encompassing Janey's life. 'Maybe the whole family home, husband, kids thing just isn't meant for – '

I stopped as my hand-waving reached the half-open door and I saw Michael, hand raised, about to knock. An expression I couldn't name fleeted across his face.

'Sorry. I didn't mean to interrupt. The kids want to go outside and Patrick sent me up for their snowsuits.'

Janey turned to me.

'What you just said? Total bloody rubbish. You witnessed a bad marriage and had a crappy childhood.'

'Janey.' I tried to stop her, flicking my eyes to Michael.

She waved her hand, dismissing my reservation. 'But we both know all that only makes you want to prove that's not always what it's all about. I also know you'll do just that.'

I screwed my face up a little, not wanting to disbelieve her, but not entirely able to swallow it all either. I knew she was right about the first part. Honestly? I did want it all. But whether I could actually achieve it, the thing she was so sure of, was another matter.

'Right,' she said, patting my hands and turning to her brother. 'I'll get the kids' suits, even though Lily will go out for less than five minutes probably. In the meantime, Katie's going to come downstairs. She's been cooped up here enough.'

I tightened the belt on my dressing gown but Janey was already pulling a white throw off the chair that Michael had been sat in earlier. She handed it to him.

'Here you go.'

Michael draped it around my shoulders.

'I'm OK. Really, I'm quite warm en…Argh! No, put me down. For goodness' sake, I can walk down the stairs! Michael, put me down. Please!'

He grinned down at me as he made his way towards the top of the stairs. Janey was following us, two small bright snowsuits over her arm.

'Janey, please tell him to put me down!' I said, pleading with her. 'He listens to you.'

Janey grinned in the same manner as her brother had. 'Off you go, Mikey.'

'Urgh!' I let my head fall to the side, bumping against his broad chest. I could feel the laughter in it. 'It's not funny,' I stated.

'Yeah, it is.'

'No, it's embarrassing. Look, we're at the bottom now. Please, I can walk fine. Please put me down.'

Michael, predictably, ignored me and entered the living room where the kids and Patrick looked up.

'Ooooh!' Lily's face was all excitement and giggles. 'Uncle Mikey, you look like when the Prince picks up his Princess after they've got married!'

I saw Janey and Patrick exchange a look and for a moment nobody said anything. Janey had mentioned before that marriage and Michael weren't generally topics that went well together as conversation starters, and even when brought up by the kids, it was evident the subject caused him tension. But pressed up against his chest, held in his arms, I had to admit, I didn't feel any tensing at all.

Michael looked down at me. The throw was wrapped around me but some of it trailed over his arm, looking to Lily at least, enough like a wedding dress train to prompt the comment.

'Ah, Lily, I think our Katie here is far too wise to marry me.'

Lily looked up at me as Michael, finally, let me down and held my arm gently as I got comfy on the sofa.

'Don't you like Uncle Mikey?' She blinked.

'Oh…I…yes, of course, Lily. He's very…nice.'

From the corner of my eye, I saw Michael smother a laugh. I gave a look around, pleading with my eyes for some help. All I got were grins in return. *Great.*

'Uncle Mikey picked me up from school once and I heard one of the other mummies saying that she thought he was sixty.'

Patrick gave a snort of laughter.

'Oh,' I said, floundering for a moment. There was no doubt in my mind that the mummy in question had actually described Lily's uncle as 'sexy', but if I said that, I knew the very next question would be, 'What does "sexy" mean?' I might be feeling better but I definitely wasn't up to that. Thankfully Michael stepped in.

'Must have been a rough night. Looking older than my years.' He winked at me. 'Right, who's up for snowman building!'

Janey and I sat quietly, watching through the glass doors as the men, Pilot and little Lily began on their quest. Lily lasted just over ten minutes before opting for the warmth of the house but the boys stayed out and the snowman building, inevitably, descended into a snowball fight. We watched for a while, laughing as Patrick and Joey ganged up on Mikey and then we left them to it. Janey lent me a book and quietly started reading another to Lily.

* * *

'Well, you look healthier than you did a few days ago,' Michael declared as he entered the room, rubbing his hair with a towel having now showered to warm up after tea. He disappeared for a moment to hang the towel up to dry in the utility and then flopped down on the sofa next to me. The citrusy scent of his shower gel drifted towards me.

'I feel miles better, thanks.'

He leaned in a little. 'You had me worried there for a moment.'

I looked round. His face was close and I could see he wasn't joking. His gaze held my eyes until it, momentarily, dropped to my mouth. I felt myself swallow and force a smile, sitting myself back a little. His eyes were back on mine. In fact, the glance he'd given to my lips was so brief... Was I imagining things? Let's face it. I'd been pretty out of it there for a while and although I felt much better, I knew I wasn't entirely back up to speed yet. And this weekend, being surrounded by so much care and, well, love, it was easy to get carried away. Luckily I hadn't got too carried away. Because if I had, I might have just made yet another faux pas with this particular client.

'Don't be silly. Just a little bug,' I replied lightly, trying to distract myself from the disturbing knowledge that Michael O'Farrell most definitely had the most tempting mouth I'd ever seen. I pulled myself back and caught sight of his face. Worried that I had sounded far more dismissive of his concern than I'd meant to, I added, 'But thank you. For everything you've done.'

'Apart from the carrying down the stairs.' That hint of smile played around the edges of his lips.

'Apart from that. Did you have fun out there?' I nodded towards the window.

He smiled widely. Relaxed. 'I did.'

'Good.'

I read another page of my book, or at least tried to, as Michael leant forward and grabbed his own from the coffee table.

'Do you often spend the weekends round here?'

He slid me a sideways glance and shook his head.

'Oh. Well, it's clearly something everyone loves when you do.'

'It's mutual.'

'Oh come on. Admit it,' Patrick laughed, taking a chair opposite and pulling Janey gently down onto his lap. 'You just didn't trust us to look after Katie well enough. He's got a little of the control freak about him, don't you, Mikey?'

'I've absolutely no idea what you're talking about.'

'It's all right,' I laughed. 'I'll be fine to finish the house off. Although there's really not much left to do. Which is just as well as it's only a week away now.'

'I hope you have a tree on order. The kids will refuse to come in if there's no tree for presents,' Janey added.

Michael shot me a panicked look that told me he'd completely forgotten about getting a tree.

'Don't worry,' I said, moving my hand and squeezing his gently, out of sight of the others. 'It's all in hand. I suggested to Michael that it was probably better to get the house finished before getting anything like that so that he could easily see the best place for it.'

'Great!' Janey smiled. 'I can't remember the last time that house saw a Christmas tree.'

'Don't worry. I know a great place,' I whispered as Janey and Patrick began talking between themselves.

'You're a lifesaver. I don't know how she does it, but my sister always manages to catch me on the hop.'

'Probably just because she knows you so well.'

He gave an eyebrow shrug of concession. 'Thanks for bailing me out.'

I smiled and went back to my book. But not for long.

'Although I do have one bone to pick with you.' His voice was still quiet, but now a little stern too.

I looked up to see him holding his book up for me to see the title.

'*Jane Eyre*? You're reading it?' This man continually surprised me.

'I am. I thought as you had named my dog referencing it that I'd better read it.'

I got the feeling I knew what the bone was he had to pick with me.

'So Pilot is Rochester's dog, right?'

'Mmmhmm.'

'And Rochester so far appears moody, short-tempered and frankly a bit of a cold fish. I'm beginning to wonder if there is more to the naming of that hound than your innocent claim of just liking the name?'

'I'm sure I don't know what you mean.' I tried not to smile and pretended to concentrate on my book, despite the fact I'd now been on the same page for the last ten minutes.

'I'm pretty sure you know exactly what I mean,' he replied, opening the book to where the bookmark lay.

I risked a glance. He caught me and held the gaze a moment, before shaking his head.

'But Rochester has his reasons and he does improve as the book goes along,' I started digging.

'So you're saying there's hope for me yet? Is that it?'

'No.'

His eyebrows shot up and that tempting mouth began to curve.

Oh.

'I mean...not that you couldn't improve...haven't improved...'

It curved a little more and I wondered if my fever might be making a resurgence because it was suddenly so much warmer in the room than it had been a few moments earlier.

'Or rather that...' I lifted my eyes and met his highly amused ones. 'It's just a name in a book,' I finished feebly.

Michael leaned in.

'You're such a bad liar. But I'm glad that there's hope for him at least.' He flicked through the book momentarily. 'I thought I heard somewhere that he ends up marrying his employee.' He flashed me a look.

'I'm not your employee!' The words were out before I had a chance to filter them.

He looked at me evenly, but I could see the merriment in those beautiful eyes. 'I was merely referring to the fact that the story has a happy ending for him.'

'I...of course. I knew that.'

'I know you did.' He shuffled himself down a little on the sofa and stretched his legs out in front of him, settling the book on the top of his thighs. Turning a page, he glanced up at me. 'But like I said, you're "sixty" when you get fired up. And when you blush.'

I gave him a look and then held my book up in front of my face, intent on concentrating. Unfortunately I could see his grin from the corner of my eye and with his shoulder resting against mine, could feel the laughter as they moved. I risked another look as he did the same.

'Go on now, Jane. Back to your book reading.'

'Hilarious,' I stated flatly.

He chuckled again and went back to his novel.

***

A couple of days later I was just heading out to Michael's after dropping in at the office to rendezvous with Bernice and do a bit of catching up, making sure she was happy with everything. Thankfully, as usual, Bernice had everything under control.

'Off to Mr O'Farrell again?'

'Yep,' I replied, buttoning my coat, before pulling on my hat and winding my scarf round my neck. I knew that soon I'd be doing the usual thing of taking it all off in order to prevent melting whilst on the train and then putting it all back on to stop myself freezing on the walk between the station and his house.

'You don't seem so reluctant to go there these days.'

I ignored the prompt.

'And you say he stayed at his sister's the whole weekend too?' Bernice tried again.

'There's nothing going on between us,' I stated. No need to add that I'd had a moment when I'd wanted nothing more than for him to kiss me.

'Right,' Bernice replied. 'But you don't want to hit him with a snow shovel any more either, do you?'

I turned, my hand on the door handle. 'Not most days, no.'

'That's what I thought.' Bernice waggled her eyebrows and I left the office to the refrains of *Love is in the Air*.

The trouble with someone who is completely and utterly loved up is that they then feel it is their mission to get you to the same place. Which is a sweet sentiment, but not necessarily achievable. And frankly, after the last debacle, perhaps just giving myself and everyone else some space, might be the best plan moving forward. Yes, Michael was gorgeous and yes, I'd had a moment or two of weakness when a random thought had popped into my brain reminding me of his tempting mouth, or the body that I knew lay beneath the clothes. Well, obviously I didn't know all of it. That was…

Crikey, I thought, *it's warmer out here than I thought*. I pulled at my scarf and flapped some cool air around my neck and face as I made my way towards the train that would take me to Michael's.

***

'I'll see you soon then.'

My step faltered as I turned onto the drive and looked up. Stepping out from Michael's front door was a tall, expensively dressed blonde. As I hesitated, her arms slid around his neck and he responded by hugging her close. As she stood back from him, she drifted her hand to his face and then leant and kissed him, somewhere between his mouth and cheek.

'It was good to see you, Michael.'

I saw him respond, but thanks to a passing ambulance and its wailing siren, what he actually said was lost to me. From their smiles though, I guessed whatever it was had been pleasing to them both.

Feeling horribly awkward, I slowed my pace even more, not wanting to interrupt. And mostly just wanting to find an accommodating hedge to hide behind for a few minutes, but that, apparently, wasn't to be.

'Hi, Kate,' Michael called as he finally saw me. I smiled and waved as I approached the doorway. My client turned to his companion. 'This is the woman I was telling you about.'

Oh?

'Ah! You are the miracle worker?' She laughed, her gorgeous French accent topping off her perfection. No wonder Michael was looking so pleased. 'Michael has told me what a difference you have made to his house. It is all so beautiful. I can hardly imagine it as he describes it before.'

Oh. Right. Of course. So, I guess that meant the house tours were back on now.

'It's what I do!' I sort of half laughed and turned my palms up, as I locked away everything that had begun revealing itself over the weekend spent at Janey's, realising now that any thoughts in that direction were completely misguided. *See? This is what happens when you start opening up to people.*

First the Calum disaster and now thinking that there was the distinct possibility I had feelings for Michael and the even more ridiculous notion that he might return them. What was I thinking? I glanced back at the woman, thought of the photos of his wife, and the woman I'd seen him chatting up in the pub that time. They had one thing in common: they were all outstandingly beautiful. I glanced back at Michael as he kissed his visitor on the cheek. As was he.

For God's sakes, Kate. Get a grip. You were never in with a shot here.

His visitor stepped elegantly down the steps and waved before sliding into a brand new sporty Mercedes. She started the engine, blew Michael a kiss through the window and pulled away.

'I…err, hope I didn't interrupt anything. It's always OK to reschedule if something…comes up.' That probably wasn't the ideal turn of phrase but I was already committed.

'Not at all. Selene was just leaving anyway.' His smile was open and friendly. I stepped inside and shed my outer layers, saying hello to Pilot and giving him a good ear rub at the same time.

'How are you feeling?' he asked, taking my coat off me to hang it up.

'Great, thanks. You?'

He smiled. 'I'm fine. But I wasn't the one who was sick.'

I waved my hand. 'I'm all done with that. No more time to dedicate to lounging around.'

Michael gave me a head shake.

'Your friend seemed to like the house. I'm really happy that you're feeling more comfortable about having people round now. That's really great progress, Michael. I'm so pleased.'

'Oh yeah. She was really impressed. Don't be surprised if you get some commissions from her. Would you consider travelling to Paris for the odd job?'

I laughed, and then realised he was serious.

'What?'

'Selene's family has a construction business that, although based here, does a lot of work in Europe, France especially. When I told her about what you'd done here, she mentioned that she thought some of her friends might benefit from your services.'

'Oh right. Well. Wow. I guess I'll just cross that bridge if and when I come to it. Thank you though, for whatever it is that you said.'

'You're your own recommendation, Katie.'

My mind was turning over his words. 'So, she's in construction?' I asked, attempting to put as much casualness into the conversation as humanly possible.

'Yeah.' He gave me a quizzical look. 'Why do you ask?'

'No reason. Just being conversational.' He was still giving me that look. 'Looking at her you'd think she was in fashion, rather than construction. She's gorgeous.'

He made a gesture of acceptance with his head. 'She is. And, of course, ordinarily she wears a hard hat all the time. I don't know why she didn't today. It normally finishes off her look beautifully, I think.'

I pulled a face. 'Funny.'

He gave me an amused look in return. His face looked so much more relaxed these days, and the hard planes of it now just added attraction rather than enhancing a spikiness of character.

'Anyway,' I said, 'I'm glad that we've made enough difference for you to feel happy enough to show your... friends around. That's obviously a big improvement on where we were a month ago.' I smiled and tried to push away the disappointment I felt, not to mention confusion at that disappointment even existing.

'I know. Who'd have thought, eh? And, more good news, there's this huge project I wanted in on and apparently it's now down to me and one other guy. They're going to make a decision later this week.'

'Oh, that's great! I'll keep my fingers crossed for you.'

'Thanks. I already have you to thank for getting me this far.'

I had a foot on the bottom step, and his words made me turn.

'Me?'

'You,' he said, coming up to me. Even one stair up, he was still taller than me. 'Without you coming here and doing this, and making the decision to sort out my office first, I never would have got it together enough to get my pitch in on time.'

It wasn't very cool or professional but I couldn't stop it – I beamed at him. 'Really?'

'Really.'

'I'm so pleased, Michael, I can't tell you how much. I could tell you loved this house and the history you have with it, with your family, but it was pretty obvious you weren't getting everything out of it that you could. Looking at you now, you just seem so much more relaxed, and well, happy to be here. And the fact that you're being more productive, it's just great because that's clearly making you happier too.'

'It is. But there's something else.'

'Please don't tell me you've found another ten boxes of stuff!'

He shook his head. 'No. I think it might be worse than that.'

'Oh no.' Just as I was convinced we had managed to hit the target Janey and Michael had set. What on earth could it be?

'Katie – '

His phone started bouncing on the table as it vibrated, trilling out its ringtone.

Michael's eyes closed briefly before he turned to grab it. He looked at the screen. 'I'm sorry. I really need to take this.'

'It's OK. I'll head up and just take a note as to what's left to do now. Just come up when you're done. No rush.'

He nodded and answered the call. 'Matt, hi. How are you?'

Chapter Twenty

Climbing the stairs, I racked my brains as to what the thing was that could possibly be worse than another pile of previously undiscovered boxes of stuff. Oh well, not much I could do about it until I found out more. Whatever it was, we would deal with it. In the meantime, I had work to do.

When Michael finally got off the call, I'd made up the beds in all the guest rooms and made a list of some items for him to either borrow or buy for them and the guest bathrooms. All of them were now looking decidedly more inviting and like somewhere he could be proud to have people to stay in.

'I'm in here!' I called as Michael shouted to find out where I was. I gave the throw I'd found in the linen cupboard, still in its packaging, a final adjustment as I lay it on the end of the bed. I was just smoothing it over with my hand when Michael entered the room. He didn't say anything and for a horrible moment I thought that maybe I'd made a mistake, that something I'd used in here was a glaring reminder of his ex.

'You can change whatever you want, obviously. I just thought I'd make them up whilst I waited for you, so that you can see how they'll look.'

He looked down at me, then back around the room. Admittedly, it did look different. No longer was it like a disused room in a wing of an old hotel. Now, it was welcoming, chic and cosy.

'It looks...amazing. I can't believe you did all this.' He glanced at the door and then his watch. 'How long was I gone?'

'Oh, I can work pretty quickly when I need to.'

'My sister-in-law said she'd give me a hand making the rest of the rooms up when they –'

'They're done.'

'All of them?'

'All of them. I assume the children will be sleeping in travel cots or on the floor or something. So they'll need sorting but the beds themselves and rooms are all ready. Well, guest bedrooms anyway. Yours still needs a bit of TLC, I expect.' I hadn't dared go in there and face the rumpled sheets that probably still existed from his evening with the Parisian bombshell I'd seen leaving.

Michael was just staring at me.

'Did I do something wrong?'

'What? No! No, not at all.'

'What then?'

'I'm just a little worried about you.'

'Me? Why?'

'Because less than a week ago you could barely stand up and had a temperature similar to that of the surface of Venus. And now you're running around like a whirling dervish doing things that are way beyond your remit anyway. I don't want to turn round and find you in a heap on the floor.'

'Because it'll make your now super-gorgeous house look untidy?'

He stepped closer and picked a pillow feather out of my hair. 'Because despite the fact I'm a grumpy sod who reminds you of Mr Rochester, I'm not entirely devoid of the caring gene.'

I looked up at him and laid my hand on his forearm, feeling the corded muscles and the tickle of hair against the softness of my palm. 'I know you're not. And like I said, Mr Rochester improves once Jane's there to show him what's what.'

Michael's eyes began to twinkle. I rolled my own.

'Men,' I said, walking away. 'Come on. Tell me where you've hidden the Christmas decorations and we can start getting some up.'

'Oh. Yes. Right. About that?'

I looked back over my shoulder. 'Oh dear. This doesn't sound good.'

'I don't exactly have a lot of decorations.'

I turned a little more. 'When you say that you don't have a lot, what exactly do you have?'

'Nothing.'

'Nothing?'

He pulled his mouth to the side. 'Nothing. I got the stuff for the outside when we got all the things for the dog as there was a garden centre next door to the pet shop. I found one ratty bit of tinsel in the attic, which I binned, but that's it.'

'Not to worry. Although, admittedly, it does make starting immediately a little more difficult.'

Michael sat on the end of the bed, and Pilot, who had now wandered in, came and flopped down on the floor beside him, his head resting on his master's foot.

'You're really wishing you'd never taken this job, aren't you?' He ran a hand through his hair, pushing it back.

I looked at him and my answer surprised me. 'Not for a moment.' Despite everything, even down to seeing a beautiful woman wrapping her arms around his neck first thing this morning, I knew this was the truth. I wouldn't have changed a thing.

From the look on his face, it seemed I wasn't the only one surprised.

'I know. Shocker, huh?' I walked back and sat next to him. 'And if you'd asked me when I started if I'd ever be saying that, I'd have thought you'd been hitting the eggnog. But I have to say, despite you being the most annoying client I've ever had,' he grinned at the tease, 'this has actually turned into one of my most favourite jobs.' I lifted my eyes and found Michael watching me.

'Only one of them?'

I dropped my glance, ostensibly to lean down and play with Pilot's velvety ears, but also because the impact of Michael's viridescent gaze still had the ability to disorientate me and my thoughts.

'Don't push it,' I replied.

His laugh surrounded me, the sound of it warming me from the inside. It made me happy to hear. Happy because I knew, just from our initial meeting, and from what Janey had told me over time, that laughing wasn't something he'd done a lot of in the past few years. Seeing any client happier made me happy. But with Michael, it had a bigger impact. It went deeper than I was used to. Of course, this was just because I knew that his happiness had a knock-on

281

effect of making my best friend happy, so it was bound to affect me more. Not to mention the fact that he had rescued Pilot and was giving him a wonderful life.

'You can't blame a guy for trying. So, what happens now? I guess I need to go shopping. Anywhere you recommend?'

'John Lewis is always pretty good for decorations or Marks at Marble Arch. Liberty obviously always has gorgeous stuff but as you'll be buying in bulk that might be pushing it a bit. Once you've got all the basics covered, you can always add to it if you see something special somewhere.'

'Right,' he said, pushing himself up off the bed. 'I guess I'd better get on with it then.'

'Would it be possible to put any less enthusiasm into that statement?'

Michael rubbed the back of his neck. 'That obvious, huh?'

I did a quick sideways tilt of my head. 'You might get away with it with some people but I'm an expert, remember?'

'How could I forget? Talking of which, I guess I've mucked up the plan for today by not having supplies ready. I'll pay you for your time, obviously. I've just had my head stuck in that pitch and then this thing with Selene came up that I'm really excited about. I guess I didn't really think.'

'Not a problem,' I said, pasting on a smile. So, Selene was more than just a one-night stand then? It would seem that Michael O'Farrell really was moving on – in all directions. 'I'm sure you can manage and if you can't, then just shout and I can always pop round one evening to help you finish off.'

'Yes, right. Sounds good.'

'You sound about as thrilled at that prospect as of shopping,' I said, looking up at him. 'Or perhaps Selene could help? She's clearly got great style.'

'Yeah.' He nodded distractedly. 'I've been thinking about what you said about my bedroom needing some attention.'

'Oh?'

'I mean, if I'm going out for this stuff, maybe I should just go the whole hog and get anything I need for that too. At least the whole place is finished then.'

'Sounds like a sensible plan. And it'll be good for you to have somewhere that looks less...blah.'

'"Blah"?' He quirked an eyebrow at me.

'Yes. Blah.'

'You're calling me "blah"?'

'No,' I said, standing and turning to smooth the edge of the bed where we'd been sitting. 'I'm saying your bedroom should reflect who you are a little more. And whilst you're a lot of things, Michael O'Farrell, "blah" is definitely not one of them.'

He frowned at me. 'I think, if I dig deep enough, there might be a compliment in there somewhere.'

I smiled and headed out of the room.

Michael followed me. Then he stopped. 'Wait a minute.'

I turned.

'Why on earth would I ask Selene to help me decorate my home? I mean, yes, you're right, she does have great style and she loved the house, but I think asking a prospective client to pop round and stick up some tinsel might not be the professional action I could take.'

I stared at him for a moment. 'She's a... Oh... I just thought that... And you said she... And you were both...'

'Are you actually going to finish any of those sentences?'

I thought for a moment. 'Probably not.'

He gave me a half-smile. 'So you thought me and Selene were a thing?'

'She's very beautiful. And she was leaving your house early and looking very friendly. It was hard not to assume...'

'She's flying to New York this morning but wanted to pitch something to me before she went. I've known her and her father – and her husband – for years now and have done some work for them before. They have a project they're proposing in Paris and I'm their first choice for architect. She wanted to talk to me about it before she jetted off, just to see if I was interested. It was just a business breakfast meeting, nothing more. She's effusive in her attentions to people she likes, male and female. It's just her way. But it wasn't anything more than that.'

'Oh. Well. That's great then. I mean, about the possible Paris job. Not about you and her not being an item. Which is fine too. Obviously. I mean, it'd be fine if you were, although, not technically, as she's married but you know what I mean.'

Michael was looking at me, bemused. 'Glad that's all cleared up then.'

I think I need a lie down.

'So, getting back to my bedroom and your accusations, what do I need to do to make it less... "blah"?'

I shrugged. 'It's your room. You know what you like. You're an architect and you said you've been doing up

284

houses with your family since you can remember. You must have an idea by now.'

'I'm a design guy – structural stuff. Colours and twiddly bits like cushions were always dealt with by the girls.'

'How very modern and enlightened of you.' I cocked an eyebrow at him.

He held his palms out. 'Hey, I didn't make the rules! Although it may have had something to do with me and my brothers thinking navy blue was a great idea for one of the bedrooms in a place once.'

'Navy can be nice.'

'True. But probably not for all the walls and ceiling.'

'Ah yes. Well, now I can see why the decision-making privileges on that aspect might have been withdrawn.' I slid him a look. 'You're not thinking of doing that in there, are you?' I nodded up the stairs and he laughed.

'No. I hasten to point out that we were teenagers at the time. I'd like to think my taste has improved a bit since then. Although I'm still a bit lost when it comes to twiddly bits.'

'I can give you a list, if you like?'

'Can it be an incredibly detailed one?' His tone was hopeful.

I sighed. Michael looked at his watch.

'It's nearly lunchtime, how about I take you to lunch and maybe you can just kind of give me a few pointers whilst we're out?'

I frowned and looked at my own watch. 'Michael. It's half past ten.'

'Even better,' he said, resting his hands on my upper arms. 'How do you feel about breakfast?'

'I'm not sure I have any specific feelings about it.' I couldn't help smiling.

'Great. I know just the place. Come on.' He turned to go, taking my hand as he did so.

'Michael, you don't have to buy me breakfast or lunch to get me to help you with this. I'm happy to do it.'

He took a couple of steps down the stairs, then looked back at me. 'And I'm happy to take you to breakfast.' He came back up a step, causing me to tilt my head to look at him. 'Hopefully it'll go some way to making you forget what a pain in the arse I was when you first started here.'

'I'm not sure I'll ever forget that. But,' I moved my head to keep his gaze as he began to look away, 'it doesn't mean I haven't forgiven you for it. You don't need to buy forgiveness from me.'

'I'd still like to take you to breakfast.'

'You mean you still want help with the shopping.'

'If I can only have one, it's breakfast.'

'Because that one features food?'

Michael laughed. 'Give me a break, woman. You're ruining all my romantic gestures here!'

Both of us stopped. I felt my jaw gaping and snapped it shut.

'I mean…that didn't exactly come out like I meant it to.'

'No.' I swallowed, feeling a stab of disappointment I couldn't explain, and tried to smile. 'I don't imagine it did.'

'Just as well, eh? You looked pretty horrified!'

I did?

'I really didn't mean to.'

Surprised? Yes. Horrified? Hello? Have you looked in a mirror lately?

Michael gave my fingers a gentle squeeze before letting go of my hand. 'It's OK. I could never accuse you of not being honest with me. I'm just going to pop the dog next door to my neighbours in case we're out longer than expected. I'll be back in two minutes.' He hesitated. 'Assuming you're still up for it?'

'Of course.'

'Good.' He smiled, but his enthusiasm was more tempered than it had been earlier. He jogged down the stairs, the dog at his heels and grabbed Pilot's 'go bag'. This made it easier for him to take the dog round to Janey's or next door or wherever quickly and only required him having to collect a couple of things.

'Find your Ted, boy.'

Pilot skidded on the wood for a second as he looked around for his teddy. Catching sight of it halfway down the stairs, he thundered up, clamped his jaws around it and then charged back down to Michael, his tail wagging at the prospect of whatever exciting thing was happening next. Michael grabbed his keys, ushered the dog out of the door and pulled it closed behind him. In the silence of the house, I sat down heavily on the stair and tried to untangle my thoughts.

I was well aware that my attitude to this job was different now. As Bernice had noticed, I was far less hesitant now. In fact, it was probably fair to say I eagerly anticipated my visits.

I'd been happily telling myself that it was because, as we got further through the progress, the house was being freed from all the clutter and could be seen properly. The high ceilings, large windows, beautiful cornicing were all there for me to see and fall in love with. But, what if the house wasn't the only thing I'd fallen for...I stood up so suddenly I had to grab the banister as the force of the action gave me a head rush.

No! That was absolutely ridiculous.

There was no way I could have possibly…except I'd got the same feeling when I'd woken at Janey's and seen Michael sitting there. Which was in a different house entirely. Which meant…what? I plopped down onto the stair again, my mind spinning. The key turned and Michael came through the front door, minus Pilot. He glanced up, stopping when he saw me sat there. In a few strides, he was up the stairs and crouched in front of me.

'Are you all right? I knew you were doing too much so soon after that bug knocking you out.' He put a hand on my forehead.

I pulled his hand down. 'I'm fine. And can you not sit like that. It's making me nervous. I've got visions of you bumping backwards down the stairs!'

He swung his body round and parked himself next to me on the stair.

'So, what's up?'

'Nothing. I was just thinking.'

'About what?'

I glanced round, met his eyes for a moment and then turned back. 'About…what you'll need, you know, for finishing off the rooms and stuff.'

He took a deep breath, letting it out slowly. 'You finished thinking about that now then?'

'Yes,' I said, looking back at him. 'I've got everything straight in my head now.'

He didn't reply for a moment, just watched me, his eyes seeming to search mine for something.

'That's good then,' he said, eventually, giving a brief smile. 'Better go hit those shops then, eh?'

'Is breakfast still on?'

'Breakfast is always on.'

We didn't talk much on the walk to the Tube. Partly because there was still some remnant of weird atmosphere lingering since the whole 'romantic gesture/ not a romantic gesture/horrified look' thing this morning. I also got the feeling that Michael knew I hadn't been thinking solely about the house when he'd found me on the stairs. The other thing that prevented us from talking was that we were both wrapped up like little Eskimos – well, one of us a lot more little than the other – with scarves tucked up under our noses as the wind blew glasslike shards of hail at any bit of exposed skin it could find. Combined with the fact that the temperature was now falling below freezing, judging by the snowflakes that were now drifting down intermittently, and the pavement had become an assault course of frozen puddles and patches of black ice, right now, the priority for both of us was just keeping upright and in one piece.

We entered the station and flashed our Oyster cards on the reader before heading down into the depths to catch a train into the centre. The crowds squashed and yanked us apart. I'd spent over four years in London now, honing my skills in this area, but unless you were built like a functional brick outbuilding, like my companion, there were still times when it was hard not to get scooped up and hustled along a few feet in the wrong direction. When this happened for the second time, Michael reached over and grabbed my hand, pulling me back in the right direction. I expected him to let go, but he didn't.

'If you get swept off again, it's possible it'll put a serious delay in me getting food. So, if you don't mind, I'll keep hold of you for a while.'

I didn't mind at all.

'I knew this was all about the food.'

He grinned, the sound of the train entering the station and the swell of people limiting the ability for further conversation. Tumbling out at Bond Street, Michael's hand still firmly wrapped around my own, I stopped at the side of the pavement, momentarily watching the snow as it floated gently down. A shove in the back brought me out of my reverie and I saw the look in Michael's eyes at the guy who'd done it. I tugged on his hand.

He looked down. 'Please tell me I was never that much of a dick,' he asked.

'I've no idea. I never saw you in this particular scenario.'

He gave me a patient look. 'You know that doesn't reassure me a whole lot.'

'OK. How about this? I'm sure you weren't. Is that better?'

'Funnily enough, not terribly convincing.'

'Oh well. I can't help you then.'

Michael slanted an amused look my way as we arrived at Selfridges. He held the door, and we headed up to the Aubaine Bistro.

***

'That was utterly delicious,' I said, putting my cutlery to the side of my plate. Michael had already finished. Big surprise.

'I can't believe you've never been here.'

'Just never got around to it, I guess. But I'm glad I have now. Although, it might have been a mistake.'

'Mistake?'

'Don't look so worried! I mean that in a good way. I didn't know what I was missing before. Now I do.'

He nodded, a soft smile on his face. 'I can understand that.'

I smiled back.

'Can I ask you something?'

'Of course,' I said, finishing off my apple and pear juice. Again, totally delicious.

'On the stairs, earlier…'

Uh oh.

'I…just wondered if you were OK. You looked pretty serious. And I'd gone and blabbed something stupid about romantic gestures and here you are, having just broken up with…him. I didn't mean to upset you. I sometimes have a habit of saying the wrong thing. As you witnessed with Lily and the whole divorce thing the other week.'

Automatically my hand reached for his. 'You weren't to know that she was super-sensitive about that sort of stuff right now. It was clear how horrible you felt about it. God knows everyone can see how much you adore those children and that the last thing you would do is upset them!'

'I don't want to upset you either.'

'You didn't. Don't worry.'

He turned his hand so that mine now lay in his. 'Well, I know you weren't just thinking about home décor. You have your little happy face on when you do that.'

Laughter bubbled out. 'Excuse me? My "little happy face"?'

'Yeah. Don't be defensive. It's cute.'

'I am not "cute".'

'What's wrong with cute?'

God, he had the most beautiful smile when he really let it happen. Like he was doing now.

The waiter brought over the bill and put it down. I moved to take it but Michael was quicker.

'Answer the question.' He slipped his hand away and rummaged in his jacket for his wallet. He pulled out some notes, put them with the bill and we got up to leave. I let my scarf hang down as I drew my coat around me. Michael picked up the ends of it and gently put one over each of my shoulders. 'Still waiting.'

'I just think it's a little inappropriate of you.'

His eyes bulged for a moment and then he caught the tease in mine. 'Inappropriate, huh?'

'Entirely.'

'Good. Add it to my list of faults.'

'Already done.'

'How wonderfully efficient of you.'

'I don't like to disappoint.'

He gave me a look that was hard to read but the twinkle in his eye gave me a clue. I threw him a mock snooty look back.

'As I said, entirely inappropriate. Now, get that wallet back out. You're going to need it.'

Chapter Twenty-One

Several hours later we returned to the house, each of us laden like a mountain mule with Christmas decorations and various items for the house itself, including a clutch of goodies to make the master bedroom into the retreat it should be. We also had a list of items being delivered tomorrow, including decorative cushions for nearly every room, another couple of throws, plus a few scented candles for the bathrooms which, although gorgeous, had weighed a bloody tonne so we'd opted to test the courier's muscles on those rather than ours.

'What about the tree?' Michael asked.

'Emmet promised he'd saved me a good one for you. When do you want to get it?'

Michael looked at the clock in the hall. 'Is now any good? Or do you have to be somewhere?'

'No, I booked out the whole day for you today.'

A smile spread on his face. 'Great.'

* * *

Emmet, my contact, had been true to his word, picking out a huge, gorgeously thick pine that let out its delicious scent as Michael manoeuvred it into the back of the pickup.

'This brings back memories.' I could hear the smile in his voice, even though he was mostly hidden by the tree.

'Good ones by the sounds of it.'

'Very good ones. I'd forgotten how much I enjoyed all the little things like this.' He came around the tree and gave it another shake to make sure it was secured.

'Despite your initial worries, I think you're looking forward to hosting Christmas now, aren't you?'

He stopped beside me. 'I really am. We try and get together pretty often but Christmas was the one time everyone ensured they were there…until I met Angeline, of course.'

I felt his mood change a little. 'But before? Tell me about your Christmases.'

He moved and I felt him relax again. 'They're full of noise, but in a good way. Lots of laughter, banter, catching up. We eat way too much, play board games, have crossword puzzle races with boys against girls, and there's probably the odd glass of booze or two.' I could see him grinning at the last part.

'Just the odd one.'

'Obviously.'

'It sounds wonderful, Michael. I'm so glad you'll all be getting that again this year.'

'Me too. Do you know, I even made some mince pies last night as a trial run, now that I can find everything in my kitchen. Even more amazingly, they're actually pretty edible.'

I wrapped my arm around his automatically and gave it a squeeze. 'That's great. And this,' I turned and pointed at the tree, 'is going to look beautiful in your living room. I'm so excited to see it when it's done. Will you send me a picture?'

He stopped tying the rope. 'You realise that leaving me alone with this and all the stuff we bought today is going to result in a tree looking like the decoration fairies went on a bender and threw up on it, don't you?'

'That's not exactly the image I was hoping for in my mind.'

'It's the one you'll be getting if you leave me unsupervised.'

'I think you probably have more skills than you think you do.'

I heard the low laugh in the darkness. 'Oh, I've got skills, just not in this department.'

I was playing with a branch that had fallen off another tree, and at his comment, gave him a tap on the side of the thigh with it. 'Behave.'

He gave the tree a last wiggle and turned to me, his face lit only by distant streetlights. He lifted my hand with the branch still in it, and turned his head to face it.

'Adding to your toolkit I see?'

'My tool – ' I flung the branch down as I realised what he was referring to. 'I told you none of that stuff was mine.'

I could see his teeth white in the half-light.

'Stop grinning. Perv,' I said, pulling open the door of the pickup as Michael's laughter followed me in.

'Did I just blow my chance at getting you to help me wrangle this thing into something presentable?' he asked, pulling his own door closed behind him.

I pulled the seat belt out and plugged it in. 'Possibly.'

'But the children will be so disappointed.' It was actually pretty impressive just how much feeling he forced into this statement.

'Oh wow,' I said, turning in my seat. 'You're actually sneaky enough to use your nieces and nephews?'

'I prefer the word resourceful.'

'I prefer a word I'm too ladylike to say.'

He laughed and turned over the engine. 'I'm pretty sure I could get you to say it.'

I gave a huff. 'If anyone could, it'd be you.'

'That's not a compliment, is it?'

'Not really.'

I peeked across at him as he concentrated on the traffic, waiting to pull out into the flow. His baseball cap kept the hair out of his eyes, although it was still curling down over his collar. However, the untidy not-quite-beard had been trimmed back to a length of stubble that now lent him the air of almost groomed, rather than hobo. And the smile that he wore beat the hell out of all of it.

We drove along for a few minutes, not talking but easy in the company of just the radio on low, the station's playlist full of festive favourites.

'So, what were your Christmases like?'

I looked away, not wanting to remember the fraught and brittle atmosphere that would begin the day and would inevitably dissolve into either silence or screaming at some point around the Queen's Speech.

'Nothing like yours, sadly. Although I always wished they could be. I had this image of a big family dinner with everyone laughing and smiling. It was ridiculous really as I was an only child, as my mum had been, and most of the remaining relatives either lived abroad or wanted nothing to do with us anyway. But it was a nice thought.' I smiled over at him but his face was serious. He dropped his hand from the steering wheel and took mine within it for a moment.

'I'm sorry you had such a rough time, Katie. I really am.'

My throat suddenly felt too tight to speak so I gave a little nod instead and squeezed his hand back, hoping the gestures conveyed at least some of what I wanted to say.

A few more minutes passed and Michael's hand had by now returned to the wheel as he manoeuvred the pickup around a junction. Eventually he spoke again. 'You aren't seriously going to abandon me with this tree, are you?' He glanced over momentarily before switching his eyes back to the road, wipers flicking away the snow and almost beating in time to the Christmas song playing in the background. The light from the dashboard showed hints of concern on his features. 'I know all this – today and everything else you've done in the house – I know it's all way over what you normally do. I really, really do appreciate it, even if I'm not that good at saying it very well. I'll never be able to thank you enough for bringing Pilot into my life either.'

'Well, that's definitely a two-way street. Knowing he now has a wonderful home with someone who's nuts about him is more reward than I could ever ask for.'

Michael pushed his bottom lip out momentarily. 'I wouldn't say I was nuts about him.'

'Oh really?' I crossed my arms.

He cleared his throat. 'All right, I'm completely nuts about him but don't go spreading that around. It hardly goes with my reputation.'

I blew a raspberry. 'That's what I think to your reputation.'

His eyebrows shot up as he laughed. A ringing over the sound system interrupted the radio. Michael peered at the GPS screen and pressed a button on the steering wheel.

'Hi, Gerry.'

'Hi, Mike. How are you?'

'Yeah, not bad, thanks. Yourself?'

'I'm good. You still getting that house in order for the big family Christmas?'

'Pretty much there, actually.' Michael smiled, including me in it momentarily, then quickly switched his eyes back to the road. 'Finishing touches now. Got a bloody great tree in the back of the truck as we speak.'

'Good to hear. It looked like a bomb had hit it last time I came round.'

Michael winced and I realised that he'd actually been far more bothered about the state of his house than his initial declarations had claimed. 'Yeah. Sorry about that. You'll have to come round and see it in its new incarnation. And meet Pilot, of course.'

'Sounds good to me. Who's Pilot?'

'I sort of got another dog.'

'About time! Puppy?'

'No, just over eighteen months. Rescue dog. A...friend found him for me.'

'Even better! Buy that friend a beer.'

I wrinkled my nose and Michael chuckled.

'So what can I do for you?'

'It's about this dinner dance thing that Solway are hosting...'

Michael groaned.

'I know. I know. But listen to me, Mike. I know you're not a big fan of stuff like this but this one you need to come to.' The man's voice was serious now and Michael picked up on it.

'Why? What's going on?'

'Nothing especially. But I do know for a fact that the other guy you're up against for this project is going and he's kind of a schmoozer. Solway really like you but if this guy shows up and starts sweet-talking everyone...'

'Yeah, I get it.'

'So, you'll come?'

'I'll think about it.'

'Mikey, lad, you need to do more than think about it. You need to do it. I'm going to be stuck working with this other clown if he gets the job and that is not a prospect I relish.'

'Enough said, I'll come. Although I don't think I ever replied one way or the other to the invitation. Won't it be a bit late to say yes now?'

'No. I got Wendy to put you down as a yes ages ago.'

'Did you now?'

'I did. And I put you down for a plus one. Old Ed Solway is a sucker for a pretty face and whilst Wendy seems to think you're the best thing since sliced bread, I know for a fact you'll do nothing for him. Why don't you bring that organiser lassie? She sounds great and you said she was hot.'

'OK, Gerry, I'll see you there. Got to go!' Michael hurriedly pressed another button on the steering wheel and the radio came back on.

I was looking out of the window, the snow now drifting at the sides of the road casting a glow, making the surroundings lighter than usual.

After a moment or two, Michael spoke. 'I didn't exactly say that you were hot.'

Can anyone say pin and balloon?

'Of course not.' I kept my voice neutral.

'I mean, not that you're not hot. You are. You're gorgeous. But what I meant...'

I looked away from the window, towards him. We were stopped at a four-way temporary traffic light. Michael pulled on the handbrake.

'I didn't want you to think I'd been talking about you.'

'But you have.'

'Well, yes. But in a good way. In a really good way, actually.'

'OK.'

He checked the traffic. There were still two more ways to go before our direction went back to green.

'Look, I know what you think of me and the fact I've not been averse to one-night stands.'

'Michael, I know you better now and I'm not judging you. You're single and enjoying it. Find a pretty girl to take to this thing and have a good night. It sounds like it could really be beneficial.'

'But I don't want to find a pretty girl to take. I'd like to take you.'

We both remained silent as that sentence filtered through our minds.

'That didn't come out right either.' The light changed and he pulled away. Hitting the indicator, Michael pulled into a layby, knocked the pickup into neutral and turned to me.

'I'd love it if you would come with me to this thing. It'd certainly make it a lot more fun.'

I smiled, preparing my answer but before I could say anything, Michael continued. 'I'm not asking for anything more than the pleasure of your company, as a friend,' he leant over and took my hand, 'which I hope is what we are now.'

I was running out of proverbial balloons to pop. Michael, however, seemed to misread the look on my face for the second time today. Typical that when I didn't want him to know what I was thinking he could read me like a book but now...

'Obviously I know you've just come out of a relationship, which isn't easy. I just wanted you to know that I wasn't suggesting...'

'Of course not.'

His face fell. 'Of course not, as in you're not interested?'

Boy, could he be more wrong?

'No, I meant that I understand what you're saying. You're right, we are friends and because of that there's no pressure on either side.' I fixed on a bright smile and hoped the low light would keep him from seeing the truth of it. 'Which means you can just concentrate on impressing this Mr Solway man and getting the contract.'

Michael straightened his cap unnecessarily. 'But you'll come?'

'I will. Thank you. Wait! When is it?'

He pulled a face. 'Umm, it's kind of tomorrow evening.'

'Kind of?'

'Actually tomorrow evening. I understand entirely if you can't come?'

'No. It's not a problem.' I whacked on that bright smile again and forced all thoughts of Michael as more than a friend out of my head. It was a ridiculous thing to consider anyway. I was pretty sure we had different ideas on what we'd like the future to hold. And what if we did try and something went wrong? How awkward would that make things for Janey? He was

301

right. We had got to a place where we could call each other a friend, which in itself was a real achievement. I trusted him. He said what he meant, even if it led to us disagreeing. But at least I knew where I stood with him, which was a trait I valued, especially after recent events. Yes. This was good. It was stupid to think anything else would be better – that heavenly face and body aside.

I knew exactly what had happened. I'd been so caught up in falling in love with his dopey dog, and his beautiful house, that I'd begun to think –

'You're awfully quiet over there.'

'I was just wondering what to wear for tomorrow.'

He nodded, not taking his eyes off the road. 'I see. Well, it's not black tie but it's pretty formal.'

'OK. Thanks. I'm sure I can find something.'

Michael dropped me back at my flat as the time was getting on and I had an early client.

'Don't forget Mary will be coming tomorrow at ten to deliver the new curtains for the living room. She'll help you put them up. She always likes to check everything is OK with them and that her client is happy before she leaves so she'll take care of you.'

'Great. Thanks for arranging all that.'

'My pleasure. Hopefully these will make you happier when you see them.'

'I'm pretty sure they will. So you're not round tomorrow?'

I laughed. 'Believe it or not, Mr O'Farrell, I do have other clients. I can't spend all my time with you.'

'Well, now that's a shame.'

I rolled my eyes at him. 'Don't worry, I won't leave you in the lurch with the tree. What time should I meet you tomorrow for this thing?'

He held up a finger as answer and jumped out of the cab, quick strides bringing him round to the passenger side where I had already opened the door.

'I'll pick you up at seven, if that fits in with you?'

'Sounds fine. Then I'll see you tomorrow.' I gave him a quick little hug and began walking towards the communal entrance. Michael fell in beside me. I stopped, a question in my eyes.

'Just walking you to your door.'

'You don't need to do that. It's just there.'

'Yeah, I know. But I can't see it from the truck and I want to make sure you get there safely.'

'Worried you might end up without a date for tomorrow? I hardly think that's a big concern for you.' I laughed, knowing that given the chance, I'd be mown down where I stood if word got out this particular man was free tomorrow night.

'I guess I did a pretty good job of convincing you I really was that shallow when we first met.' I couldn't see his expression in the low light but there was a tone to his voice that made me stop.

'Michael,' I put my hand on his arm, 'I don't think you're shallow. You're right, at first maybe I did. But that was what you seemed to want everyone to think. But people who know you know it isn't true. And you've proved to me that it isn't.' I squidged the puffy fabric of his jacket under my gloved hand.

He lifted his hand and took mine in it, the gesture saying everything that was needed.

'Thanks for today,' he said as we reached my door.

'You're welcome. I actually had a lot of fun. And breakfast was ah-maz-ing.'

He laughed. 'Good. Then maybe we should do it again.'

'That'd be fun. But I'm not sure your bank account would take it.'

'I just meant the breakfast part.'

'Oh. Right, of course! Absolutely. But I'm paying next time.'

'We'll see.'

He leant in to give me a kiss on the cheek and I leant back. The moon had pushed itself from behind a bank of clouds and the light, reflected by the snow piled around us, cast a strange, almost magical light. It highlighted the confusion on his face.

'I said I'm paying next time.'

Michael's hands lifted to my face, holding it gently, palms resting against my cheeks, his outer fingers spreading down onto my neck. He leant in again, his eyes focused intently on mine. Gently his lips placed a kiss on my forehead and then his mouth moved close to my ear.

'And I said "we'll see".'

The whispered voice, with its lilting accent and hint of gravelly roughness sent heat searing through my body. I half expected the nearby pile of snow to instantaneously melt into a puddle. Kind of like I felt like doing right now.

He stood upright and I took a pace backwards as casually as I could in an attempt to avoid Michael seeing just how well his charm and, let's face it, downright raw sexiness was still working. Unfortunately my studied nonchalance hadn't taken into account the step into the building and I tripped backward, landing with a damp thud in the muddy puddle of water that had accumulated in the slightly worn away dip of the step. I hastily pushed myself back up, as Michael put an arm out to help me.

'You all right?'

'Of course,' I replied, not looking up. 'And you can stop laughing.'

'I'm not.'

I looked up. His face was serious but I could see the little glint in his eyes as they caught the moonlight.

'But you're dying to.'

'I'm going to choose to refuse to answer that on the grounds that it may incriminate me.'

'Arse.'

He laughed and wrapped his arms around me.

'Are you really OK?'

My arms, despite strict instructions from my brain, wrapped themselves around his body – warm, solid...

It was perfectly acceptable to stay here for another hour, right?

'I am.' My voice was muffled as he squidged me close.

'I'd better let you go in and get some sleep.'

I nodded, my hair making a scratchy noise against the fabric of his coat. Reluctantly I pulled away, reached up on my tiptoes to kiss him on the cheek and then unlocked the door.

'I'll see you at seven.'

Agreeing, I waved and headed inside.

Chapter Twenty-Two

'Doing anything special tonight?' Janey asked when I gave her a call to say hi on the way to my first client. Her tone was so overly innocent that it was clear she knew exactly what I was up to this evening.

'I don't suppose there's any point in saying "not really", is there?'

'Absolutely none,' she giggled. 'You know, he usually hates these sort of things. He's not into the whole schmoozing side of business. You know our Mikey, he'd rather just call a spade a spade and be done with it.'

'The man on the phone seemed to think it was pretty important that he attended this one if he wanted the best shot at the job he's pitching for.'

'Mmmhmm.'

'Mmmhmm what?'

'I'm just wondering when one of you two is going to tell me something official.'

'There is nothing official. That is to say there isn't anything at all. I was there when the guy called and we got talking about it. Michael asked if I'd come. That's all. Why? What did he say?'

'About the same as you.'

'There you go then. He even made a point of stressing that it wasn't anything like you're suggesting. So, there really is nothing to get excited about. Sorry!' My voice was light so why my heart didn't feel the same way?

'I don't know what's wrong with that boy.'

From what I'd seen that day, there didn't seem to be anything wrong with him. He looked pretty damn perfect actually.

'There's nothing wrong with him, Janey. We're just not like that. I'm not his type anyway.'

'No, you've got depth to you. It might be an idea for him to try something different for a change!'

'Janey,' I laughed, 'much as I appreciate the sentiment of that statement – I think – I'm not really in the mood to be anyone's relationship guinea pig.'

'Aww, but they're so cute!'

'Ha ha. Right. I'm at my client's. Better go.'

'OK. Well have a great time tonight. In your non-guinea pig capacity.'

'I'm just looking forward to having a meal that doesn't start with it going *ping*.'

* * *

Bearing in mind this definitely wasn't a date, I was disproportionately nervous. It was ridiculous. Even though I'd only known him a little over a month, in that time I'd actually got to know him pretty well and, despite early indications, we were now relaxed in each other's company. So why the nerves?

'Come on, Kate. Pull yourself together,' I said to the reflection in the bathroom mirror.

It didn't reply but instead gave me a look that suggested it may take one or two stiff drinks before that happened on this particular evening. But at least my hair had gone right. OK, so it had actually taken six attempts for it to go right, but we'd got there.

I walked back into the bedroom and glanced at the bedside clock – ten to seven. I sat on the bed and put my shoes on, then checked on my dress. It was a simple Grecian-style halter sheath with a choker collar that joined to the main body of the dress with a delicate three-link chain. I'd bought it on a whim, which was most unlike me. And, having had no occasion to wear it, it had hung in my wardrobe for the last three years looking beautiful and a little sad.

I wasn't usually one for keeping things I didn't use – that was the ethos of my company after all – so tonight was this dress's now or never chance and I just hoped it was right for the occasion. This was obviously an important night for Michael and I didn't want to let him down. I'd never been to a big function like this and, frankly, the whole cool, calm, cope-with-anything persona was desperately making a dive for the window. I grabbed onto her proverbial ankles and yanked.

It's just a party. I can do a party.

The doorbell rang. I'd been expecting the intercom. The flats had an internal security system that was supposed to prevent people just turning up at a front door uninvited. In reality, people often just held the door for someone if they were close behind, whether they recognised them or not.

Michael was early and at my door. I pulled it open – except that it wasn't Michael.

'Calum. What are you doing here?'

'She left me.' His eyes skimmed me up and down. 'You look amazing, babe.'

'You didn't answer my question. What are you doing here?'

He held out his hands. 'I'm free now. There's no need for us to hide any more. We can be together properly.'

I stared at him, unable to see what I had once seen, the charming persona that had attracted me before. Because now I knew that's exactly what it was, just a persona.

'Calum. If you recall, you were the only one hiding something and that was a pretty big something. You lied and made a fool out of me. What on earth possessed you to think that I would ever want to see you again?'

He stepped forward and took my hand before I could move it. 'Kate. You know we were good together. And now there's nothing to stop us being together for real.'

'I'll have to disagree with you there.' Michael's soft lilt caused us both to turn. He smiled at me across my ex, whose face darkened.

'Well, that didn't take long.' Calum's mouth was almost a sneer as he looked back at me.

'I'm not one to waste the chance at something amazing.' Michael stepped closer, causing Calum to automatically back out of my personal space, allowing Michael to fill it instead.

'Sorry to just appear.' He smiled down at me. 'Someone left the front door on the catch. That's not exactly high security, you know.'

I shrugged in a what-can-you-do manner.

'You look stunning.' His eyes met mine after a detour of skimming me and my outfit. 'Are you ready?'

I nodded, still taking in what I was seeing after some eye-roving of my own. The unpleasant surprise of Calum turning up on my doorstep was obliterated by the incredibly pleasant surprise that stood before me now. I hadn't thought that Michael could possibly get any better looking, but he had proved me wrong. His hair was now short and cropped, his face clean-shaven and he was dressed in one of the beautifully cut suits I'd seen hanging unloved in the wardrobe. A pure white shirt stood out against the charcoal grey of the fabric, with a silk tie in a subtle version of the suit's colour to tone.

I grabbed my clutch and wrap from the table by the door and closed the door behind me, throwing the double lock before dropping the key in my bag. When I turned, Calum was still there.

'Calum, you should leave.'

'We have things to talk about.'

'She asked you to leave.' Michael spoke, his voice was calm but from the corner of my eye, I saw his jaw tense.

I reached down and took his hand, squeezing it gently to let him know I had this.

'I don't remember asking your – '

'Calum,' I cut him off before he ended up saying something that might result in him taking an unexpected nap in the corridor, and possibly being fitted for a new set of teeth. 'I'm not interested in getting back together with you, whatever the circumstances. Please don't come here again.'

'Shall we go?' I looked up.

Michael smiled back at me. 'Absolutely. Here.' He took the wrap and draped it around my shoulders, his fingertips brushing against my bare skin, causing a flash of heat to whoosh through my body. We turned, leaving Calum where he stood.

'Are you sure you're warm enough?' Michael asked as we got to the front door of the building. 'The cab's just out here but – '

'You have a cab waiting? Why didn't you say? Oh God, the meter is going to be sky high after faffing about with bloody Calum. You should have just rung – '

Michael placed his hands on my shoulders. 'You might want to take a breath.'

That was a good plan. Nerves about the party, Calum showing up out of the blue and then Michael walking in looking like the sexiest, most gorgeous man I'd ever seen was a lot to cope with in ten minutes.

'Good idea.' And I did as he instructed. 'But still. You could have just rung me and I'd have come down.'

'Katie, I'm happy to wait when it's something worth waiting for.'

I didn't really know what to say to that, so I opted for nothing. Or more to the point, my mind just stayed unhelpfully blank.

'Besides,' he said, opening the door of the waiting cab and holding out his hand to help me in whilst I held up my dress hem with my other one, 'it would have deprived me of the opportunity of meeting the clearly charming Calum.'

'Please don't start.'

'I wasn't planning to. I'm just saying it's nice to put a face to a name.'

Michael gave the driver directions and leant back. I slid a look to him. 'You had the look of wanting to put something else to his face.'

'And in my youth I might have done. Not, I hasten to add, something I'm necessarily proud of. But don't worry, I'm older and wiser now.'

'I'm glad to hear it.'

'Of course, that doesn't mean I don't meet people I'd quite happily deck. Tonight was a prime example.'

'You only met him for a few minutes.'

'Which was plenty.'

I turned in my seat to face him, the lights of the city flashing across the windows and his now clean-shaven face. 'Can we talk about something else?'

'Sure. Pick a topic.'

'OK,' I smiled back, 'let's start with this.' I waved my hand in his general direction.

'What?'

'You! The haircut, the shave, the wearing of a suit!'

He tilted his head at me momentarily. 'Wow.'

'What?'

Michael breathed in heavily. 'Despite your assurances that you didn't care what I wore, I apparently looked even worse than I thought I did.'

'Oh, don't be daft,' I said, swatting him gently with my clutch. 'If you looked that bad, you wouldn't have scored every night you felt like it at the pub.'

He gave a head tilt.

'That's the bit where you're supposed to show some humility,' I prompted.

'Ohhh! Right. Got you.' And then he grinned, which made my point completely invalid because when that smile hit you, it didn't matter what he was wearing.

'You're hopeless.'

'But at least tonight I look smart whilst being hopeless, right?'

'You look...very nice.' That wasn't exactly the description crashing around my head right now, but it was the only one that was acceptable for anyone other than me to hear.

We pulled up at the entrance to the hotel and a doorman stepped forward to open the taxi door. Michael handed over cash for the trip as I exited, then he followed.

I looked up at Michael. 'You also look like just the right person for this job.'

He gave me a slow smile that set off tingles in my stomach. Reaching across, he took my hand, pulling me ever so gently towards him and then tucked my hand over his arm.

'Now I do.'

'Good luck,' I whispered.

Michael's other hand lifted and momentarily twirled a loose tendril of my hair. Leaning down, he placed the softest of kisses on my cheek, just to the left of my mouth.

'Thank you. And thank you for coming. Even if I don't get the contract, I still got to spend an evening with the most beautiful woman in the room.'

Smiling, I looked up at him as we walked in, another doorman heaving the heavy glass door open for us. Michael's hand dropped to the small of my back as we stepped inside.

'Please don't think I don't appreciate the compliment, but I do feel I have to point out you haven't even set foot in the room yet to be able to make that judgement accurately.'

The green gaze settled on mine. 'I don't need to. I know what I know. I thought you were gorgeous when you were standing on my driveway freezing that cute little arse of yours off, and right now, Katie Stone, my statement still stands.'

My brain was processing as fast as it could. 'You thought I was...'

'Gorgeous. Yes.'

'But you were...'

'Unforgivably rude? Yes. Arrogant? Yes. Blind? No.'

'Well, you hid it well.'

He tipped his head towards me as we approached the door to where the main function was being held. 'There are lots of things I do well.'

'Such a shame being modest isn't one of them.'

'There's a time and a place for modesty.' His eyes flashed at me with mischief.

'Just get in there and win that contract.'

***

From the looks of things, Michael was doing exactly that. All evening, he'd been charming and funny – the Michael I now knew him to be. And they appeared to be loving him. Judging by the look on the face of the man I'd been informed was his main competition for the contract, David Heath, he obviously thought Michael was doing pretty well too. I'd actually be feeling bad for him if he'd been a little more polite during our own interaction. When he'd asked what I did for a living, he'd tossed a superior look around, making some comment about how he wish he'd known tidying his room as a child could have turned into something that people would actually pay good money for. Michael's arm had been resting on my waist, just lightly, his body close to me. At the jibe, I'd felt him tense, but he'd remained silent, taking on board our conversation of earlier.

As it was, Ed Solway, the man whom both men were trying to impress, gave me a smile. 'People will always pay good money for a service that they find useful, David.' Mr Solway then turned to me. 'Mrs Solway is so looking forward to her first appointment with you in the New Year.'

As Heath paled and made an attempt to laugh off his faux pas, Mr Solway gave me a conspiratorial wink and Michael gave me an almost imperceptible squeeze, his face betraying nothing.

It was true. I had indeed picked up the Solways as clients this evening, although I'd had no idea who the lady I'd been talking to was initially. She'd just introduced herself as Erin. I was already looking forward to having her as a client – straight-talking, funny, with that down to earth outlook Australians often seem to possess. We'd hit it off immediately. It wasn't until she'd called over her husband to fill him in and let him know that I was the woman who was, and I quote, 'going to organise the shit out of us', that I'd realised who she actually was.

'You know, I was dreading this.' Michael leant close to me, his fingers walking across the tablecloth on a mission to pinch my after dinner mint.

'And now?' I asked, swiping the mint from his reach, before unwrapping it and popping it in my mouth.

He grinned as I did so. 'It's been good. Apart from Heath being a dick to you.'

I laughed. 'Oh, don't worry. I don't think I'm the exclusive recipient of his rapier wit. And I think he rather skewered himself in that instant, anyway.'

'His face was quite the picture, that's for sure.' Michael moved his hand from where it was lying on the tablecloth and covered mine. 'I hated that he said that to you though. I can't lie.'

'I know. But believe me, growing up like I did was good training. I've heard a lot worse.' His face was serious and without thinking, I laid my hand on his cheek. 'Really. I'm tougher than I look.'

'I don't think you're that tough.'

I frowned and let my hand drop. He caught it quickly.

'Shit. Why is it I can chat up a random girl in the pub no problem, but every time I try to give you a compliment it comes out all wrong?'

'Probably because you've had a lot of practice at the former.'

He heard the tease in my voice and that heart-stopping smile slowly spread onto his face.

'Maybe I just need a bit more practice at the latter then?'

'Oh, you definitely need more practice at that, if your efforts so far are anything to go by. Although, in the interest of fairness, you did say I looked nice earlier, so you're not entirely failing.'

I looked up as he stood.

'Actually, I seem to remember I said you looked stunning and that you were the most beautiful woman in the room. Which you then questioned. Of course.' He pulled a face. 'But having entered said room, I was immediately proved right. Of course. And now, if she would agree to it, I'd love to dance with the most beautiful woman in the room too.'

He held out his hand. I hesitated a moment, wondering what line, if any, we were crossing here.

But the fact was, in front of me stood the most good-looking man I'd ever seen and he was asking me to dance. Maybe it wasn't the most logical thing, maybe it wasn't what sensible, risk-averse Kate would do, but right now, I didn't care. I didn't want to be her. I wanted to be the woman in Michael O'Farrell's arms.

'I'd love to.'

'I was really hoping you'd say that.' He grinned, a flash of insecurity momentarily showing on his face. I loved that. Not that I'd caused it, but that, contrary to what he'd initially shown me, he wasn't cocky enough to believe that no woman could say no to him.

Michael took my hand and held it firmly as we wound our way through the throngs of people and dinner tables onto the dance floor. Once there, he retained it, his other coming to rest at my waist, gentle enough to feel relaxed but firm enough for me to feel its warmth through the silk of my dress.

'Are you having a good time?' Michael asked, pulling me a little closer so that I could hear him over the music and general chatter.

'I am,' I replied. 'Thank you for inviting me.'

He laughed. 'Thank you for giving me a second chance.'

I shook my head. 'You need to forget about that. We're past it all now…aren't we?' I looked up at him, finding his eyes already on me.

'Way past.' He smiled that smile again and moved the hand at my waist, splaying his fingers, brushing my spine with the tips of them, sending sparks of heat up and down my entire body. 'Katie, I – '

'Mike?'

He shifted his gaze from mine to where the voice had come from and a look of surprise replaced whatever it was he'd been looking at me with. That part I hadn't quite figured out yet. I turned my head to see what had caused the change.

I recognised her immediately. Glamorous, elegant and stunningly, classically beautiful, Michael's ex-wife was even more striking in the flesh than she was in the photographs.

'Angeline.' His voice didn't hide the surprise, but none of us missed the cold edge of his tone. I glanced back at him. The softness had gone and in its place were the hard lines I'd been greeted with at our first meeting.

'How are you?' she asked him. Her eyes flicked to me and then focused fully back on him. 'You look great.'

'What are you doing here?' he asked. We'd stepped apart a little but his hand was still at my waist.

'I came with a friend. I...had no idea you'd be here.'

I studied her under my lashes in as surreptitious manner as I could employ, and I wasn't buying that last bit at all. My eyes shifted to Michael and it was obvious immediately – he completely believed her.

'I think I'm going to go and sit down,' I said, pulling away.

His fingers skimmed my back and dropped away as I moved. 'I'll come with you.'

'Mike.' Angeline caught his hand, stopping him. 'I know you have every reason to turn your back on me and I don't blame you. I know I hurt you.' Her fingers caressed his hand, whilst he looked back at her, not encouraging, but not moving away either. 'Please, can we have one dance? For old times' sake?'

Michael flicked his gaze to me. I could see he was caught. He wasn't the only one who'd seen the interested glances being thrown at the little vignette being played out here, and he wasn't about to make a scene.

'Go ahead. I'll see you in a bit.' I gave him a smile and walked away, back towards the table. A waiter passed me with a tray of champagne. I swiftly lifted one and took a sip, keeping my expression light. After all, I had no reason to be put out. The evening hadn't started out as a date. We were just two friends having a pleasant evening. Yes, he'd been charming and for a moment out there, there'd been the hint that maybe...

I lifted the glass to my lips as my gaze found the two of them on the dancefloor. They really did make the most beautiful pair. I watched as she whispered something, and he smiled, shaking his head slowly. She responded with her own widening smile, her hands moving up his shoulders until they rested at the back of his neck. She bent her forehead against his and...

Goodness, was that the time?

Of course there wasn't a taxi in sight as I left the hotel. The doorman and I waited, looking in vain for an available cab as he valiantly struggled against the wind and sleet with an umbrella until it finally gave up and flipped itself completely inside out, bending the spokes into something worthy of display in the Tate Modern.

'Sorry, Miss.' The doorman looked at me apologetically. Rain dripped from the brim of his top hat and I, dressed completely inappropriately for the weather, was now soaked completely.

'Not to worry. I'm sure I shan't dissolve.' I smiled at him, even though it was really the last thing I felt like doing right now.

A taxi came into sight, its light signalling its availability. The doorman let out a two-fingered, piercing whistle that cut through the whipping wind and, thankfully, caught the driver's attention. He began indicating and pulled up in front of the building, whereupon the doorman quickly opened the door for me.

'You go home and get warm now, Miss.'

I thanked him and promised that I would, then clambered into the cab as elegantly as I could with a dress that was now completely sodden and clinging to my skin. Using my wrap to casually disguise anything that might be a little X-rated in such a state, I gave the driver my address and sat back on the seat, watching as the water dripped off my skin and dress and collected on the floor around my feet.

As we made turns, rivulets scooted off, making little puddle tributaries. I watched as they did. Concentrating on them so that I didn't have to concentrate on anything else. But I knew I couldn't avoid those thoughts for ever. I pulled out my phone and noticed two missed calls from Michael, and a text that just said *Where are you*?!

Outside the cab, London still thronged with people. There were few things that stopped this city, and rain certainly wasn't one of them. As we sat waiting at a red light, I studied the reflections of the Christmas lights in the shiny wet pavements, the colours merging as the downpour increased in strength and droplets bounced up off the pavement. Pedestrians increased their pace, some dashing into doorways to take cover until the weather abated enough to move on.

Inside the cab, I drew my finger down the window glass, creating a line in the condensation that had begun to build as I steamed like dim sum in my favourite Chinatown restaurant. I looked back at my phone and opened Michael's text again. I pressed reply.

Hi. Really tired and have an early client so needed to leave. Sorry not to say bye but didn't like to interrupt. Hope the evening was successful for you and have my fingers crossed for you re the contract. As house is now finished, I just want to take this opportunity to say I wish you all success in the hosting of your first Christmas, and for the New Year. Merry Christmas!

I read the text through again. It didn't go anywhere near saying what I really wanted to, but that was probably a good thing. I'd spilled my heart out to Michael O'Farrell once before. It wasn't going to happen twice. And especially not now. Pressing send, I waited for it to show it had been delivered then switched off the phone and tucked it back in my bag just as the driver pulled in to the kerb in front of my building. About to hand over the fare, I pulled a face.

'Sorry. I left a bit of a puddle.'

His eyebrows shot up and he turned in his seat to look at the back of his cab.

'Oh! No, I mean it's just the rain! It dripped off me. That's all, nothing…else.'

Relief showing in his face, he took the cash, to which I'd now added an even more generous tip for giving him a fright that there'd been an accident on the floor of his taxi. He nodded, but I still wasn't entirely sure he believed me, which was about right for the way that this night had ended up.

For a moment, it had held so much promise. Promise I hadn't even known I wanted. But now I knew. I was more sure of it than of anything I'd ever known. I'd completely and utterly fallen for a client, something that went against all of my self-imposed rules. But Michael O'Farrell had been a rule-breaker from the start, whether intentionally or not. He was unlike any other man I'd ever met. And I wanted him more than any other man I'd ever met. And just as it began to look like that might actually become a possibility, that he might actually feel the same way, his past had walked back in, and from what I saw, she wasn't just in his past any more.

Chapter Twenty-Three

Bolting the door behind me, I hoiked up the wet hem of my dress, kicked off my shoes and squelched through to the bathroom. Whacking the shower on full, I stripped off and stepped under the water. Tipping my face to the stream of water, I let it pour down, enabling me to convince myself that it wasn't tears flowing down my face, just the shower water. Admittedly this charade became harder to keep up when I stepped out, wrapping myself in an oversized fluffy towel, and found that watery tracks continued to trickle down my cheeks. I sat down heavily on the side of the bath.

There was no denying it. After so many years of holding back, of seeing what sort of destruction loving the wrong person could wreak, promising that I would never be a part of anything like that again, never be part of such pain, here I was. My throat hurt, my chest hurt, my head hurt and in amongst it all, there was more pain in my heart than I'd thought possible to feel. I thought I'd protected myself against all this. And I had when I'd been paying attention. But falling for Michael had been gradual. Unplanned. Unexpected. And now unbearable.

I wiped my face with the back of my hand and padded into the bedroom. It was freezing. The outdated storage heater was having another of its moments. I stuffed my foot into a trainer, gave the thing a kick and made a mental note to give the landlord a call in the morning. Although, this close to Christmas I had a feeling it might not be the most successful call I'd ever make.

Shivering, I pulled out my fleeciest jammies and then shoved my arms into my cosy dressing gown, wrapping it around me tightly, making myself into a human fleece burrito. Pulling back the covers, I hopped in and quickly yanked them back up over me, leaving just my eyes peeking out. Closing them, I tried to push away all the thoughts of what might have been tonight. It wasn't like me to be fanciful and imagine what could be. I'd learned from my mother that that sort of thinking only brought heartbreak and disappointment.

Michael was someone else's. Maybe he always had been. And if he had a chance at making his marriage work again I should be happy for him, shouldn't I? But inside there was a voice that questioned this new turn of events. It was clear from his behaviour and the way he'd run his life since Angeline had left that he'd been totally in love with her, and that her infidelity, her leaving, had devastated him. But in the past six weeks he'd changed. He'd begun to get back to who he really was beneath all the hurt and anger that he'd been holding onto. Even Janey had said she couldn't believe the difference in him and that he seemed happier than she'd seen him in years.

I could understand why he would want to let Angeline back into his life – you only had to take one

324

look at her for the most obvious reason. But beyond that, he'd loved her with everything he'd had. And now she clearly wanted another chance. Her request for a dance for 'old times' sake' hadn't fooled me. The way she looked at him? That request wasn't anything to do with the past, it was all about the future. And I wanted to wish him well. But I couldn't help it. Something grabbed at me and just kept screaming that she was the one who broke his heart. She was the one who'd sent him spiralling down until he'd lost all sense of who he really was, and all that he could be, distancing him from the family he adored. And yet, I couldn't deny him happiness, if that was where he thought it lay. I cared about him too much for that. I loved him. And that was the real problem here. I loved him. And he loved her.

When I woke the next day I blearily realised that the room wasn't quite in the realms of ice hotel temperatures any more. Apparently the emotional impetus behind my trainer clad kick last night had had some impact. Unfortunately, the bathroom mirror confirmed that same emotional impetus had also had another effect and this one wasn't anywhere near as successful or welcome. My eyes were puffy and although the shower had got rid of some make-up, I hadn't bothered to finish my cleansing routine yesterday as I usually did. I imagined my pillow was going to need a bit of a soak in some Vanish if the state of my face was anything to go by. Cleaning my teeth, I made a point of not looking in the mirror again. Once done with that, I set about removing all traces of last night's make-up and starting again. In more ways than one.

***

I checked my watch as I waited for the train to appear through the tunnel, pushing the warm air out in front of it, thawing shivering tourists and commuters alike. The heavy rain of yesterday evening had, at some point during the night, turned to snow and I'd stepped out of the flats this morning to find my neighbourhood draped and muffled beneath a powdery white covering, inches thick. Instead of my heels, I wore a pair of fur-lined riding-style boots that served well as my stylish-but-still-practical option when the weather necessitated.

Two minutes: the display board indicated the arrival time of the next train as more people entered the platform. I shuffled further up and took my phone out of my bag as I waited. I'd switched it on earlier when I was getting ready but hadn't yet had a chance to check my messages. Again, not like me. Normally I was far more organised and efficient than this in the morning, even after two bottles of wine with Janey (pre-baby-bump, obviously). All I needed now was to have received a message from the client I was rushing out first thing to see to say that they'd changed their mind. But there wasn't one from my client. At least not that particular client.

There were now, in total, eight missed calls from Michael, as well as voicemail notifications. Of course, that wasn't necessarily him. But the fact that one of the six texts he'd sent said that he'd now left three voicemails and would I please call him gave me the idea that it probably was.

I closed the phone as the train pulled in, engine slowing, squeaky brakes protesting as it came to a full stop. Hearing his voice, that hint of gravel that made him sound slightly sleep-roughened, even when he wasn't, all wrapped up in that soft Irish accent, was exactly what I wanted. And exactly why I couldn't listen to them. His texts didn't say a lot, but they told me enough. Michael might have played the lothario in the last two years but he wasn't uncaring, as I'd first thought. He'd been hurting, and ashamed of the way his place looked and what he felt that said about him. It wasn't just the whole wham bam thing. It was detachment masking the pain. The pain caused by the woman he now wanted to try again with.

But he had asked me to that function and I'd left alone, something he apparently wanted to talk about. But what was there to say? It was my choice to leave. And he'd made it clear there was nothing romantic about the invitation anyway – at least initially. It was hard to deny that as we'd sat at the table and then taken to the dance floor together that maybe...

I grabbed for the pole to steady myself as I gathered my concentration in staying upright as the train swayed on the track. I leant my head against it momentarily, just as it shunted on a bend. Thanks to the laws of physics, this resulted in me swiftly head-butting the pole. Two people sitting on the seats across from me suddenly disappeared behind their copies of *Metro*, but not before I saw the hint of a snigger on their faces. In another mood, I'd have probably joined in their amusement. But today it just seemed par for the course. I gave my forehead a quick rub, not caring what anyone thought. As I'd hinted to Michael yesterday, I'd spent years hearing much worse things directed my way, thanks to the, let's say, unusual domestic arrangement of my childhood. At least something good had come from the mess of my younger years. I could nut a pole in a crowded Tube train and still walk out with my head held high – even if it did now sport a bit of egg.

***

The snow appeared to have no intention of relenting. Checking our diary, it looked like Bernice didn't have any clients this afternoon so I knew she would be getting back to the office soon. I gave her a call.

'Hi, Kate! I just got back and was about to call you. How did it go last night?'

'Fine. Everyone seemed to really like him.'

Including his ex-wife.

'Right,' Bernice said slowly, and I could practically see her frowning down the phone. 'That wasn't exactly what I was getting at.'

'Oh?'

'Come on, Kate! You, super hot ex-Grinch, twinkly Christmas lights, open bar, good food… You can't tell me nothing happened.'

'Nothing happened.'

'I just said you couldn't tell me that.'

'Sorry. Anyway, I just called to tell you to go home now. This weather's getting ridiculous and I don't want you stuck out somewhere.'

'Are you sure?'

'Yes. It's fine. There's nothing that can't wait.'

'I didn't mean about work. I meant are you sure nothing happened, between you and him?'

I let out a sigh. 'I think it's safe to say that any woman would remember if something happened between her and Michael O'Farrell.'

'You sure you didn't have a few too many glasses of champers?'

'Bernice. Really. Nothing happened. I actually left a little earlier than him in the end anyway.'

'Alone?'

'Yes, alone. Now please, can we just move on?'

'Of course. Are you seeing him again?'

So much for moving on.

'No. There's no need. The house is all done. I'd said something about helping him decorate the tree and stuff, but I'm pretty sure he's got that covered now, so he's all ready to go for Christmas.'

'Right,' she said again.

'Just before you go, there's a little something for you in my bottom drawer. You know where the keys are.'

'Oh, Kate. You shouldn't have.' It was one of those phrases that trips off the tongue, but in this case, I knew it was meant. It was one of the things I loved about my colleague and friend: her honesty. Even when it meant she enquired a little further than I might have liked, it was all done with the best intentions and came from a good place.

'You mustn't open them until Christmas Day though!'

I heard a squeak. 'That's ages!'

'It's a few days!' I replied, laughing at the level of excitement for the season Bernice still managed to achieve. When it came to Christmas, it was like she'd never got past aged five. In a good way. And I loved that.

She let out a sigh and I heard background noises as she found the key and opened my drawer. The deep file drawer held a bag full of goodies.

'Not all of these?'

'It's just a few bits.'

'Kate! It's too much!' Her voice was serious now.

'No, it's not. I'm not always the greatest at saying... stuff. And I just want you to know how much I value you and the huge contribution you've made towards the business and its success.'

'Thank you.' Bernice's voice was soft and I could tell she had tears in her eyes. Admittedly, that was pretty easy to make happen. She was soft as a brush. Another thing I loved her for.

'You're welcome. Now go home to that lovely fiancé of yours and have a wonderful Christmas.'

'Thank you, Kate. You're a very special person. I hope you know that.'

We said our goodbyes and I headed in the direction of the office, pulling my hat down further against the weather and making a couple of stops on the way for some food. I stood in the queue, glancing at the other shoppers with their trolleys piled high with festive fare. Placing my basket down on the self-service till, I scanned the few ready meals I'd chosen and prayed that today was the one time there wasn't an 'unexpected item in bagging area' because right now, I really wasn't in the mood.

When I finally got in, the office was quiet, most of our neighbouring businesses having closed for Christmas already or perhaps headed out for festive drinks. I switched on the little pre-lit tree by the door, its glow casting enough light for me to do the things I needed to – grab some paperwork to work on over Christmas, collect the exquisitely wrapped gift Bernice had left for me and update our client spreadsheet. Quickly, I fired up the computer, opened the programme and scanned down to find Michael's name. In the end column I put a tick:

Project Completed. I hit 'Save', made sure it updated and then closed everything down. As I left the office, I unplugged the tree, then shut and locked the door.

I wasn't ready to go home yet, so I wandered up and down Oxford Street and then made my way to Piccadilly and the huge bookshop in which I could quite happily spend an entire day. Or more, given the opportunity. Aimlessly wandering between the different genres, I ended up with an eclectic handful of reading matter. My phone beeped for the third time, notifying a missed call. Knowing Michael, he wouldn't give up until he'd said what he had to say. Except that nothing he could say mattered now. I didn't blame him for wanting to give things another go with his ex. They had history. Watching them last night, it was easy to see that familiarity, how well they fit together, how easily they remembered what they'd had. Yes, he'd flirted with me, but it was harmless. How was he to know what I felt for him? I hadn't even known it for sure until I'd seen his ex standing there and realised that I'd left it too late.

My phone cheeped a text alert.

Katie. Just answer the damn phone, will you? Please! I need to talk to you!

I didn't want to talk to him. I had no intention of embarrassing myself in front of him again and, if I actually spoke to him, I wasn't entirely sure that wouldn't happen but clearly I had to do something so I opted for another tactic. Settling into a bench seat in the basement café, I popped my books next to me. A sweet man brought my tray of tea and cake – needs must – out to me, laying it gently on the low table in front of me. I thanked him and pulled the phone from my bag. Opening my email account, I chose 'new message'.

Dear Michael,
I'm sorry not to have got back to you today. It's all been a bit of a rush with one thing and another.

This was sort of true. Besides, telling him that I didn't get back to him because I might end up saying something I couldn't take back, and cause myself mortifying embarrassment as a result, wasn't really the tone I wanted to go for.

Thanks for a lovely evening last night. As I said in the text, it seemed to be going well from what I saw, which was great! I know from your texts you feel bad that you didn't see me home, but it was no problem. It's not like we were on a date or anything so you have nothing to feel bad about. I had a lovely meal and met some very nice people – and I may have even got some work out of it, so I must thank you for that too.
I hope you are happy with how everything turned out at home and that you can now enjoy your beautiful house. I sincerely hope that your grandfather approves too when he visits you over the holidays. I'm sure he will. We were both a little (a lot!) sceptical at the beginning of this project – you as to how it all worked and me as to whether you would actually commit to it. But I think that we have both been pleasantly surprised – at least I know I have been. I'd like to say how much I enjoyed working on this project with you and helping you bring the house back to a place you love to be again.

I'd also like to thank you for giving Pilot a wonderful home. Please give him a hug from me.

And lastly, although this may not be my place to say, and perhaps I am overstepping the mark, but I saw the way your ex-wife looked at you last night and how you were together. I know she hurt you before but it's clear that she wants to try again. I wish you all the luck and happiness in the world with this and for a wonderful, family Christmas in your 'new' home – as well as for the New Year and beyond.

Take care of yourself Michael.

Of course the next question was how I signed off. 'Yours sincerely' seemed way too formal, but 'lots of love', although nearer to the truth, was a definite no-no. I settled on 'Best Wishes, Kate'.

My finger hovered over the send button. *Goodbye Michael.* The thought ran around in my head as I lowered my thumb onto the button and the message shot off into the ether.

Pouring my tea, I plopped in some milk, took a big forkful of lemon cake and picked up one of the books and started reading. Another pot and another slice of cake later and I thought I'd probably better start heading home. I took the books to the counter, paid and got my loyalty points, feeling slightly guilty but reasoning that they were Christmas gifts to myself. And if the festive TV schedule turned out to be a bit naff, I at least had these and Netflix to disappear into as others around the country contemplated the wisdom of having eaten that ninth sausage roll.

The snow was still falling as I plodded down the stairs of the nearby Underground entrance, entering the swarming flow of humanity down there. A woman next to me slipped on the wet floor and I automatically put out a hand out to steady her.

'Thank you,' she smiled. I returned it, unable to dismiss the flash of joy at the thought that the Christmas spirit was apparently even permeating the depths of the Victorian tunnels, and causing a break in that cardinal sin of strangers actually talking on the Tube.

After arriving at my station, I marched carefully up the pavement, enjoying the sound of my boots crunching and squeaking on the freshly fallen snow. But no matter how much I tried to push them away, thoughts of Michael kept barrelling back in – his voice, his laugh, the way he'd pulled me closer to his body as he'd bent to talk to me last night. Tears pricked at my eyes and I knew that this time it wasn't just from the cold weather.

Turning up the pathway of the flats, a gust of wind blew tiny shards of icicles and snowflakes across my face. Lowering my head against it, I shoved my hand into my bag to grab my keys. As I lifted my head back up, keys now gripped in one hand, I jumped. Sat on the front step of the building, looking decidedly damp, cold and serious – not to mention, wantonly gorgeous – was Michael. He stood as he saw me approach.

'What are you doing out here?' I asked. 'You'll catch your death!'

'Waiting for you.' He reached out and took the bags from me. 'You wouldn't answer my calls or texts so I came in person.'

Chapter Twenty-Four

I plugged the key into the lock and turned it, opening the door as another gust of wind practically blew us both through the door.

'I did answer them.'

Sort of.

Michael frowned as he closed the door against the wind, putting some effort behind it. 'Even when you were pissed off at me that first time I called, having sent Bernice back, you picked up the phone. You've never avoided me before, even when you hated me. But now you do?'

'I told you I was busy. I wasn't...specifically avoiding you.'

Nice one, Pinocchio.

'And I never hated you.'

'There was a rumour you wanted to hit me with a snow shovel.'

'Yes. Well. All right. There were moments that might have crossed my mind.'

A ghost of a smile played on his lips and I wanted to catch it with my own and trap it there. I looked away.

'And like I said, I did reply to you.' I cast a glance back out of the glass doors. 'That snow's not letting up. You should get –'

'This is the reply you're referring to?' He held up his phone, the email I had sent from the bookshop open on it.

I headed towards the stairs, avoiding the lift as I always did. And having just snarfed two pieces of cake, probably the best option anyway.

'Yes. See? Not ignoring you at all.' I turned on the stair and leant to take the bags back from him.

He inched them back out of my reach. 'I'll bring them. We're not done talking yet.'

I lifted my gaze to his and he met it evenly. The green eyes softened for a moment and he lifted his free hand to my cheek, his thumb brushing my skin.

'You've been crying. I thought it was just the wind blowing at you out there, making your eyes water.'

'It was. Is.' I turned, causing his hand to drop as I moved quickly up the flights of stairs and on towards my flat. Unlocking it, I thought about trying again to get rid of Michael. A quick glance revealed he was still studying me and I knew that look. He wasn't going anywhere until he was done. I let out a sigh, stood back to let him in and closed the door. Best just to get it over with. I pulled off my hat, shucked my coat and hung everything up.

'Jesus, what did you do?' Michael's hand caught my chin and he tilted my face to the light a little more.

'What?' And then I remembered. 'Oh, that,' I said, my fingers automatically going to the apparently noticeable bump on my forehead. I winced as I touched it. *Bloody hell*. I really hope it didn't look as big as it felt. 'I sort of head butted a pole on the Tube.' I met his eyes. 'Accidentally. Obviously.'

A flicker of a smile played around the corners of his luscious mouth at my clarification. 'Get some ice on it. It'll help take the swelling down.'

My eyes ran over him.

'Talking of ice, you look frozen.'

'I'm all right.'

'Do you want a hot drink? I can – '

'Katie. Stop. Please. Just talk to me.' His hand was encircling my wrist, just lightly, keeping me from turning my back again.

'What is it you want me to say that I haven't said?' I'd planned that to come out as strong and neutral. But my voice betrayed me, cracking on the last words.

He shook his head, the hint of smile back on his lips, but tinged this time with a sadness I couldn't explain. 'Oh, Katie, there's so much I want you to say.'

'I don't understand.'

Michael took a couple of steps backward, lowering himself so that he was resting on the arm of my couch. As he hadn't let go, I had no alternative but to follow. And now I was looking directly into those captivating eyes.

'You once accused me of not knowing anything about you and making a judgement anyway. I was wrong to do that and I promised myself I'd never do that again. But now you're doing the same thing.'

'No...I'm...'

He reached around and undid the clip that had been securing my hair. It tumbled down my back and gently, distractedly, he took a length and wrapped it around his fingers, letting it slide between them. Part of me wanted him to stop and part of me wanted him never to.

'I had no idea Angeline was going to be there last night.'

'I know. That was obvious from your face.'

'Apparently she didn't just "happen" to be there, like she said. She wangled a ticket from someone because she wanted to talk to me. If she'd have come to the house, the outcome was a foregone conclusion. So she wanted it to be on neutral ground, to catch me off guard. Which she did.'

I nodded, having forcibly unlocked my gaze from the tractor beam of his.

'You're right. She does want to get back together.'

I knew it. Of course I did. But having him confirm it, with his hand resting on my wrist, his fingers playing with my hair...

I pushed away. 'That's great, Michael. Like I said in the email, I'm really happy for you. But I do kind of have some stuff to do so...'

When I looked up, his face was tense, the chiselled features setting back into hard lines. He ran a hand over his now short hair.

'Katie, I got hurt before and I swore I'd never go through that again.'

'I'm sure she's realised that and – '

'Jesus, woman. Will you just let me say what I'm trying to say?' Exasperation broke in his voice, as, with two strides, he closed the space between us.

I opened my mouth to say something, then closed it again. Michael's hands cupped my face and he lowered his head, his lips brushing mine, soft at first, and then deepening into something more as he pulled me towards him, his arms wrapping around me, crushing me against him, as his lips moved from my mouth to my throat.

338

'Michael?' I forced out, using every bit of willpower I had to interrupt his touch.

He pulled away, his eyes searching mine. 'Katie, I don't want Angeline. For a moment last night I thought maybe there was a chance. But it literally only lasted a moment. It was like a flash of something from before. Something that's gone and can never be brought back.'

'Do you wish it could?' As painful as the answer might be, I had to know.

'No,' he answered. There was no hesitation. He tipped my chin up. 'No, I don't. Angeline is the same as she ever was. And once I thought that was what I wanted. That she was what I wanted. But she's not. She was never right for me. Everyone tried to tell me but I was young and stupid and I thought I knew better. Now I do know better. She's bored with her banker now. He makes a tonne of money, but he can't make her laugh. So now she's thinking maybe the grass wasn't so green over there after all. But it's too late, because, to keep up with the metaphor, I've moved onto pastures new.' He bent slowly and kissed my cheekbone. 'At least I'd like to.'

I frowned.

'What?' he asked, pulling away and standing up straighter.

'If I'm the new pasture, that gives a distinct whiff of me sounding like cattle.'

He rolled his eyes. 'I don't know what you did to me but until you came along, I had the gift of the gab with women. Then you ruined it all.'

I grinned. 'Good.'

He shook his head at me, the half-smile teasing his face. 'OK. Let's put this out there clearly. I am not referring to you as anything remotely bovine.'

'Good,' I repeated.

'I do, in fact, think you are the most beautiful, funny, intelligent, witty, talented and loving woman I have ever met. I've been in love with you since about five minutes into your first visit. A situation which frankly frightened the bloody life out of me and I had no idea what to do with that for a while. It scared me to feel what I did, what I do for you. But I couldn't bear not to see you again. And I'm forever grateful that you didn't just tell me to bugger off. And if you feel even a fraction for me of what I feel for you, I'd be happy until the end of my days. Katie, I don't want someone who's just a pretty face any more. I want someone who drives me crazy in all ways, good and bad, someone who knows the meaning of family, and values it as much as I do, and someone who can flat out tell me when I'm being an arse, which with your help, will hopefully get a lot less often.'

'Since the day we met?' My brain was fizzing and my jaw was somewhere near the floor, 'You...we...'

'Why do you think I really turned Bernice away?'

'I thought it was because you were private and just...'

He was shaking his head. 'I just wanted to see you again. In all your sensational haughtiness.'

'I am not haughty!'

He took his seat back on the arm of the chair and pulled me to him, my legs in between his splayed ones, his arms wrapped around my waist.

'Oh, but you are. And it's sexy as hell.' His voice roughened as he said it, causing a bolt of heat to sear through me, frazzling whatever was currently left of my thoughts. His day-old scruff grazed my face tantalisingly as he kissed along my jawline before finally, finally finding my mouth again. His arms tightened around me

340

and I pulled him closer, my hands at his neck, wanting him more than I had ever thought possible. His eyes glistened when, eventually he pulled away.

'Katie Stone, I love you. I know that you've had a hard time with things, that you've been hurt, and I know I'm a long way from perfect, but spending time with you has made me a happier man than I ever thought it possible to be again. You've made me a better man too and I want to continue to improve on that. But I can't do that without you.'

I didn't say anything. The words were there, in my head, but I couldn't get them out.

'Of course, if you refuse, I'm just going to have to go right home and mess up that house again. And keep messing it up until you realise that we're meant to be together. That we were always meant to be together.'

Those damn words in my head still wouldn't come out so I curled my fingers into his jacket, pulled him towards me and kissed him instead. He got the message.

* * *

Last night, on Christmas Eve, the whole family had descended on Michael's house and turned it into chaos, a wonderful, warm, loving chaos, which I was absorbed into immediately. It seemed that the rest of the family had been kept informed on the progress of The Christmas Project through Janey. Ostensibly, this was meant to refer to the transformation of the house where the festivities were planned to take place. But as Janey relayed this, there was a little twinkle in her eye. I saw Michael give her an amused, but suspicious, look before turning that gaze on me.

341

'I have a feeling we may have been set up.' His arm curled around me, pulling me in against his hard body.

'I have a feeling you may be right.' As I rested my head against his broad chest, watching children and adults smack the daylights out of imaginary sports balls on the television, I realised that sometimes not being in total control of everything wasn't such a bad thing.

Chapter Twenty-Five

Michael held my hand as we padded down the stairs. Outside the light had yet to show itself and despite splashing his face with water and cleaning his teeth, Michael still looked half asleep. And so damn beautiful that I was severely tempted to turn straight around and back upstairs. Except that was half the reason we were so tired already.

'What are you smiling at?'

He'd caught me.

'You.'

'Do I amuse you?'

'Yes.'

He cocked an eyebrow.

'In a good way.'

'I'm glad to hear it.' He snuggled his face down into the hollow of my neck and just held me for a moment, taking advantage of the fact that I was still a step or two behind him. And then I felt his fingers splay around my waist and his lips move slowly up my neck.

'Michael,' I whispered, not for a moment wanting him to stop.

He dropped his forehead onto my shoulder and made a low groan. Lifting his head, he gave it a brief shake, grinned and tugged me onwards down the stairs.

'Katie! Uncle Mikey!'

An assortment of nieces and nephews charged towards us as we entered the living room, and, at a glance, all of them far more awake than any one of the adults present. Pilot, already adorned with a collar of red tinsel, stood waiting patiently for his master's morning greeting. Michael and I both gave him a big cuddle and head rub before he went bouncing happily back to sit by the tree, and was soon further decorated by a giggling nephew popping a sticky bow on the top of his head. Merry Christmas hugs and kisses were then exchanged between everyone else and a corner of sofa freed up. Michael flopped down on it, pulling me onto his lap, cuddling me into him as fresh coffee was poured for us from the steaming pot on the sideboard.

I rested my head on Michael's shoulder, watching the children, listening to the banter between the adult siblings and the pretend remonstrations of them from their own parents and grandparents. The only light came from the delicate white fairy lights Michael and I had fixed all around the picture rail and those on the tree. The soft illumination, devoid of any other, lent it a perfect magical Christmas air.

As Michael gratefully took the mug from his brother, the clock on the mantelpiece gave out its gentle musical chime. Michael looked over at it, squinted, then groaned.

'It's 6 a.m. On a day off.'

Ripples of laughter washed through those around us.

'Welcome to our world!' they laughed.

And as I sat there, in the arms of the man I loved, in the midst of it all, I thought that it really was the most wonderful world to be a part of.

Loved *The Christmas Project*? Then turn the page to enjoy another Christmas treat from Maxine Morrey in her debut snowy novel **Winter's Fairytale**

Out now!

Chapter One

There were whole chapters dedicated to the throwing of the bouquet in the very many books I had pored over in the run up to this day, all instructing me on How To Have The Perfect Wedding. Oddly enough, there wasn't one sentence referring to the appropriate etiquette involved in throwing your first ever punch instead. In fact, there was also a conspicuously absent chapter on what to do if your spineless fiancé decides that the actual wedding day is the best time to tell you he doesn't want to get married. Not that it mattered. It turned out I didn't need tuition on how to punch – I was a natural, apparently. Unfortunately – or fortunately, depending on whose perspective you were looking at it from – my ex Groom To Be hadn't even had the guts to turn up to the church at all. Which is why Rob, the best man, a perfectly nice bloke, was sat on his backside on the vestry floor, holding a hastily acquired wodge of tissues to his now bleeding nose.

'I'm so sorry!' I held out my hand to help him up and he, understandably, looked at it warily before opting to push himself up. I let my hand fall back down to my side.

346

'I don't know what came over me. That obviously wasn't really meant for you. But honestly? It was either you or the vicar.'

We both glanced over at the vicar who had paled and was now the same colour as his crisp white robe.

Rob nodded. 'You probably made the right choice,' he pulled the tissues away and looked at them briefly before shoving them back on his nose, 'I think.'

An awkward silence settled on the three of us.

'I really had no idea.' Rob said, his voice muffled and thick through the barrier of tissues.

I looked up at him from where I'd been staring at the crystals on my dress. Each one painstakingly sewn on by hand. My own hand. Rob looked wretched. Almost as miserable as I did. Almost. If he was lying then he deserved an Oscar. I didn't think he was that good of an actor.

'No. Me neither.' I smiled, sadly.

Again there was silence. Eventually the vicar gave a polite cough. We both looked at him. He was looking at me.

'How would you like to proceed, my dear?'

He was a sweet man. Steven, my fiancé, and I had met with him several times, going over everything, confirming to him that we were serious about our intentions. We'd sworn (not literally) that this was what we wanted, and that both of us knew that it was not something to be undertaken lightly. And yet, here we were. Groom-less.

How did I want to proceed? I'm pretty sure that the vicar didn't really want an honest answer to that question as, right now, it involved a pair of nutcrackers, Steven and a soundproof room.

'I don't know. How do you, I mean, what happens normally if...' I couldn't bring myself to finish the question.

'Well, I can go out and make an announcement that there has been a change of plan, and request that everyone be kind enough to understand. Or if you wish, you can do it. But only if you want to.'

Oh God. What I wanted to do was throw up.

Rob answered before I could. 'I'll do it. It's supposed to be the best man's job to get the groom to the church. I seem to have failed spectacularly in that task, so it should be me that goes out there to explain.'

The vicar nodded sympathetically.

'What will you say?' I asked, quietly.

'I don't know yet,' Rob shrugged his shoulders, 'it's not exactly the speech I had prepared.'

I nodded, feeling numb. It all felt weirdly unreal.

'I'll think of something. Don't worry.' He gave me a half-smile, trying to lighten the moment. An almost impossible ask right now, but I appreciated the effort. The vicar moved towards the door and Rob followed. I touched Rob's arm.

'Thank you.'

His hand reached out to mine and took it, squeezing gently, 'I'm so sorry.'

That was a phrase I was going to have to get used to hearing a lot...

Chapter Two

'I'm so sorry. How awful for you!'

The friend of an acquaintance of an acquaintance was passing on her condolences on my failed wedding. Even though I had absolutely no idea who she was.

'And in front of all those people too!'

Yes. In front of pretty much everyone I know. Thanks for bringing that up. Again.

'Mmm.' I made a non-committal noise and tried to change the subject. 'So, are you looking for a dress for yourself or someone else?'

'A dress?'

'Yes, I mean, I assume you're looking for a dress. Is it for a wedding, a prom or another special occasion?' I tried again.

'Oh, I'm not looking for a dress, dear. I just popped in to tell you how sorry I was when I heard he'd just left you standing at the altar.'

Why is it when someone makes a comment you'd rather no one else heard, absolutely everyone in the vicinity hears it? The three other customers turned and peered at me.

'Oh right. Well, that was very kind of you. Now, I'd better see to my clients. Thank you for dropping in.'

I turned my back on her and did my best to find a confident stride and a happy smile with which to greet the other people in my studio, hoping that they had actually come to discuss occasionwear rather than my nuptials, or lack thereof.

＊

I glanced up at the old-fashioned station clock hanging on the wall. Nine p.m. My assistant had gone home hours ago but I'd declined the offer to walk to the station together tonight in favour of catching up on some paperwork and social media updates. I'd actually finished everything over half an hour ago but still I stayed. I loved my studio but even I knew it wasn't that healthy to be here quite as much as I was. Working had been my salvation after the whole wedding hoo-hah. It was the one thing I could rely on. Even with a ropey economy, there were still plenty of people in London with money, and weddings were still big business. Luckily.

My studio had been doing pretty well for a couple of years and I knew I wanted to do more, but with the planning of the wedding and having a relationship, I just hadn't really had the time to sit and think about exactly what and how. Now, thanks to Steven, I didn't have to commit time to either of those things – which is why, the day after everything had happened, or more precisely, not happened, I had lain on my studio floor surrounded by spreadsheets, brainstorm pictograms and a plethora of other paperwork. By the end of the day, I had created a five-year plan for my business. Amongst other things, I wanted to expand so that I could take on a couple more seamstresses – this would allow me not only to take on more commissions, but also to get those that I did take on, done quicker. Without the bother of a relationship to get in the way of things, I had spent the weeks following my non-nuptials burying myself in my work, and determined to follow my neatly planned out path.

'Hello?' a voice called out as the bells above my door tinkled. Damn. I thought I'd locked that after Tash had left. I got up and walked across the studio space, my one indulgent pair of Louboutins clicking hurriedly on the wooden floor.

'Hi!' I greeted Natayla as she turned back from closing the door against the wind that was once more howling down the street outside my cosy studio.

'I'm sorry to bother you. I wasn't sure you'd still be here at this time but we were passing.'

'Oh, I'm often here late,' I smiled, 'No bother at all. It's lovely to see you! How was the honeymoon?'

'Amazing!' Natayla gushed, 'Sunsets, sandy beaches, cocktails and relaxing by the pool. We didn't really do much else,' she said, then blushed and smiled shyly.

I smiled back at her and touched her arm gently. 'I'm glad it all went so well, Natayla.'

'Thank you again for making me look so beautiful.'

'It was my pleasure,' I answered, honestly.

'I brought you something,' she said, and handed me a large envelope.

Opening it, I pulled out a black and white eight-by-ten photograph of Natayla and her new husband. The photo not only screamed at me how much in love they were, but also showed her dress off perfectly.

'Oh Natayla! That's beautiful. Thank you so much. I shall put it up first thing tomorrow.'

My client smiled her shy little smile again and I wavered.

'Only if you're happy with that, of course.'

'Yes! Yes, I am happy. Very happy.'

'Wonderful. Thank you.'

We exchanged a hug and I walked her over to the door, pausing whilst she pulled on her gloves and hat before I opened it. She stepped out and waved again, before hurrying off to a waiting car and disappearing inside. I shut the door, this time throwing the bolt before turning back.

I looked at the clock once more, and once more thought that I really should be making a move to go home. That was the problem with living somewhere you didn't like. You never really wanted to go there. Instead I picked up my tea and wandered over to the wall covered in beautifully framed pictures. Sipping at my drink, I let my gaze drift over the happy smiles and gorgeous dresses. I lay the latest acquisition on Tash's desk. There was no need for a note. Tash would know what to do with it. She'd been a great find and she was excellent at all the admin side of the business, and with clients, but I still wanted to increase the number of staff. Part of my business plan was to accept an intern. I'd learned so much when I'd done the same thing after getting my degree – about all different aspects of the job, things you just can't learn in college – and I wanted to give someone else the chance to have that same experience. The thought of going to watch Final Collection shows with the view to employing someone, and then helping to nurture and develop that talent, gave me something to look forward to. My gaze went back to the photograph lying on the desk of the happy couple. The look of joy and love on their faces radiated out of the picture. I touched it briefly, almost as if by doing that I could experience that same joy, just for a moment.

Taking a deep breath, I took my mug and rinsed it out in the little kitchenette at the back of the studio. I slipped on my coat and belted it before grabbing the oversized leather tote bag I carried everywhere, and headed to the door.

* * *

'When's it going to stop?' I asked my best friend, Mags, as I relayed the surprise visit I'd had during the week. 'Honestly, I feel like the prime exhibit at a zoo! I have absolutely no idea who this woman was. I didn't even know any of the people she reeled off as having told her the "devastating news" of my being jilted at the altar.'

'Just ignore the old bag,' Mags said sagely as she refilled my empty wine glass.

'She even pointed out the irony of someone who makes wedding dresses for a living being left at the altar on her own wedding day. I mean, seriously! I felt like suggesting that she should join Mensa because, of course, that thought hasn't crossed my mind once!'

'Have you heard anything more from him?'

'What, since he left me that thoughtful note saying he was going to go on the honeymoon alone as it "seemed a shame to waste it" and it would be good to "have some space between us"?' I'd definitely had too much wine as I was doing finger quotes in the air. I never did finger quotes.

'Yes.'

'No.'

That was the good thing about living in London. It was big. You were much less likely to bump into people you knew than if you lived in a village. Of course Steven knew all our old haunts, and seemed to be having the good sense to stay out of them. I imagine he'd heard about my reaction in the church. I knew Rob wouldn't have said anything out of choice but announcing that the wedding was off whilst trying to stem a steady flow of blood from his nose, together with the obvious lack of a groom, had probably meant that there wasn't a whole lot of explanation required. Steven was many things, but he wasn't stupid. He'd likely worked out pretty quickly that going to the places we used to frequent together may lead to the possibility of the term 'regular haunt' becoming more literal than figurative for him.

'How are your parents doing?' Mags asked.

Mags and I had been friends forever. We were both army brats with our fathers serving in the same battalion, and I couldn't remember a time when Mags wasn't my best friend. When it had become clear that Steven wasn't going to make an appearance at the church, she'd automatically known that the last thing I wanted, or needed, was a crowd of people fussing around me. She'd gone over to my parents, tactfully explained the situation, then sat with them whilst my dad stared at the flower display – silently, likely imagining several different ways to kill Steven with a gerbera – and my mum repeatedly asked how Steven could do such a thing, intermittently dabbing at her eyes with an embroidered linen handkerchief. Of course, had Mags known I was about to deck the best man, she might have altered her strategy.

'They're okay. Devastated. Concerned. But okay,' I took a swig of the crisp, cool wine, 'I think so long as they know I'm all right, they'll be fine.'

'And are you?' Mags asked, looking at me directly, knowing I could never give her anything but an honest answer.

I drained my glass and thought about it. Was I okay?

'Yes. I think so. Now the shock's worn off. I still have days when I don't really want to get out of bed, but then my stubborn side kicks in and I think that I'm not going to give him the satisfaction of seeing what a bloody mess he's caused.'

Mags nodded. I knew there was another question coming.

'Okay. But what about how you *really* are? That's the "showing the world I'm okay" bit taken care of, but how are you inside. Really?'

I loved Mags to bits, but sometimes I wished she wasn't quite so insightful. I fiddled with the wine bottle cork as I let out a sigh.

'I'm not sure, to be honest. He hurt me. Totally humiliated me. But I am getting through it. And that sort of worries me in a way. I mean, shouldn't I be sobbing and wailing and declaring that my broken heart will never mend? It's made me question whether he was really The One after all. I mean, I thought he was, obviously. But now – I don't know! As much as I hate to admit it, I'm secretly wondering if he actually did me a bit of a favour. Would the marriage even have lasted, seeing as I'm not pining away for him?'

I took another swig. 'Of course, I'd rather he'd told me prior to the bloody wedding day!' I said, my voice getting louder as I finished the sentence.

It was the truth though. I was seriously wondering if I had very nearly made a big mistake. But the anger at Steven for humiliating me, and my parents, as well as his own, still boiled away. I didn't know how long that would take to go away. I hadn't seen Rob since the wedding day either, so it was likely he wasn't too sure about that aspect either, and, bearing in mind I'd punched him on the nose last time, he wasn't taking any chances. I could hardly blame him.

As if reading my mind, Mags looked over from where she was studying the label on the wine bottle.

'Have you seen Rob at all since then?'

I shook my head.

'You do know you actually broke his nose, don't you?'

I whipped my head around to face her. Thanks to the copious amount of alcohol now thinning my blood, it took the world a moment or two to catch up. I blinked, and waited a few seconds for it all to settle down. Mags pushed her own cute little nose to the side, as if to illustrate the point.

'I couldn't have! He's an ex-army, six-foot-three rugby player and I'm...' I paused to look down at my own far less statuesque frame, '...not. I didn't even hit him that hard!'

If I'm honest, I wasn't entirely sure about the last bit. In the days following the incident, my hand, with its perfectly manicured nails, had turned a variety of shades, none of which were particularly attractive, as the whole thing became one massive bruise. And he had ended up on his bum.

'Hard enough, it seems,' Mags confirmed, a small smirk catching her lips.

I saw it.

'Stop it! It's not funny.'

Her smirk turned into a grin.

'It's not!' I reiterated, 'Anyway, how do you know?'

'I saw him a few days ago. I was at Borough Market at lunchtime and he came into the pub with some colleagues.'

'Oh.'

'He was asking after you. He wanted to know if you were okay.'

'Oh,' I said again. 'What did you tell him?' I asked, after a couple more minutes.

'I just said that you were doing okay, under the circumstances, and that you would be fine because you're not about to let a lowlife piece of pond scum like Steven ruin your life.'

'Right. Good. Okay. So long as you were subtle about it.'

'Of course.'

And the funny thing was, that actually was subtle for Mags. It was lucky that it had been Rob and not Steven she'd run into. We'd been there for every good, and every awful, moment in each other's lives and her fury at seeing her best friend hurt was probably more than my own could ever be. If Steven appeared in her line of vision any time within the next few months, there was every chance a trip to the casualty department would be in his very immediate future. I was just entertaining that idea in my head when Mags broke into my thoughts.

'I think he'd like to see you.'

'Who?'

'Rob.'

'Me? Why?' My hand suddenly flew to my mouth, 'Oh my God! He's going to sue me for breaking his nose!'

Mags spurted out her wine over my kitchen table in laughter. 'He does not want to sue you for breaking his nose!'

'How do you know? Did he specifically say that? He is a lawyer! Why else would he want to see me?'

'Izz, he specialises in company law, not ambulance chasing! Like I said, he's just concerned as to how you are,' she said, mopping up with a paper towel, 'I think he feels some sort of odd sense of responsibility.'

'Well, he shouldn't.'

'No, I told him that too.'

'Good. Well, that's that then.'

'Excellent. Glad that's settled. Is there any more wine?'

ACKNOWLEDGEMENTS

I would like to thank the team at HQ, especially my amazing editor, Victoria Oundjian, without whose incredible support and continued belief in me the book may never have come to be.

I'd also like to say an enormous thank you to the wonderful Emma Dellow for her friendship, kindness and support. All of it has meant so very much to me, especially this year, and I can't even begin to tell you how much I value you. Big, big hugs.

Another huge thank you goes to the absolutely incredible book bloggers whom I met through their support of my debut. You are all such fabulous people and your support is valued so much. I was very much in at the deep end last year and you all were so kind and helpful and supportive, and I am incredibly thankful for that. You're all complete superstars.

And finally, I'd like to thank James – for everything.

HQ
One Place. Many Stories

The home of bold, innovative
and empowering publishing.

Follow us online

 @HQStories

 @HQStories

 HQStories

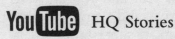 HQ Stories

 HQMusic2016